"Married!" Tristan _____ _____ _____ _____ erie. "Who said an _____ _____ _____ words seemed to freeze Marianna's chest, preventing her from breathing in or out. "Why the bloody blazes should I marry *you?*"

"If the fact that you have compromised my honor is not enough, Tristan De Costa, consider the fact that you pledged your love to me and asked for my hand. And if *that* is not enough," Marianna declared boldly, "then there is *this.*" She raised on tiptoe, clasping the front of his shirt with both hands.

Never in her life had she initiated a kiss with a man, and certainly not in the seductive way that she was doing now. Of course, Tristan began to kiss her back. Blood pounded through her veins, echoing in her ears until coherent thought was impossible to summon. Somehow, she managed to whisper the words that he must hear. "And if you are to get to Casa Valencia, this is what you must do."

He smiled then. "If I have to get married," he said, I intend to do more than this …"

Marianna swayed in the arms that held her imprisoned. Suddenly his answer registered through the warm fog that clouded her thoughts, and she swooned in his arms, a rush of scarlet fire stinging her face with heat. He crushed her lips once more in a searing kiss, then turned his face away for an instant.

"Send for the priest, *amigos!*" he shouted. Then he clasped her in his arms once more.

LINDA WINDSOR

MEXICAN CARESS

ZEBRA BOOKS
KENSINGTON PUBLISHING CORP.

"Between blue-silver mountains
And the Rio water's flow
Where dry, the cactus flourish
Grows a Mexicali Rose.

Tho' savage sun may scorch her
And winds blow harsh deceit
She braves misfortune's torture
Awaiting sweet release.

A kiss of tender moonlight
Her fevered blush reborn
With passion rising star-bright
To ride the wild *lovestorm*."

Prologue

Smoke filled the air, cloaking the heinous attack of the marauders in a gray-black fog of death and destruction. From the courtyard of the hacienda, screams of terror from all but one small throat mingled with the thunder of gunfire. Hidden under the latticed platform built around a century-old olive tree in the center of the beautiful garden her mother so diligently tended, ten-year-old Marianna Gallier watched the melee in frozen terror. Her mother had hidden her there, fearing the fierce revolutionaries would burn the hacienda to the ground. Then Eleanor had gone to join her husband, Louis, on the roof to defend their home against the attackers.

His stepsister Anita had warned him that this might happen. She'd implored him to change his name to avoid discrimination by the new *presidente*. Louis, however, had stubbornly refused, declaring that he would not give up his name or his pride. He had survived the expulsion of the French, becoming a Mexican citizen in every way. He paid his taxes to the new *presidente*'s regime and supported it as much as any other Mexican landowner. The public record was there for all to see.

But these animals had not looked at the records.

Eleanor Princeton Gallier, Mexican-American daughter of the late Colonel Matthew Princeton, who had been stationed in El Paso, knew their kind. Her father had led many a troop across the border to put an end to their plunder in the name of one political faction or another. Politics was just their excuse to rob and murder. They were no better than the Indians.

No, they were worse. The Indians, at least, had a nobler cause. They fought for the land that had once been theirs, their freedom. These vermin were motivated solely out of greed and lust . . . bloodlust. Eleanor would die before she would let the likes of this take her home, for like Louis, she too had her pride.

That pride faltered as she glanced back at the large olive tree where she'd hidden her little blue-eyed daughter. She'd warned Marianna not to scream or do anything to let the bandits know where she was. She'd even given the little girl a handkerchief to stuff in her mouth, in case she couldn't help herself. Then, preparing for the worst, she'd sent one of the servants to Casa Valencia, where her husband's widowed stepsister lived, to tell them what was happening. With luck, they could hold out until the men from Casa Valencia came to their aid. And if fate was not on their side, at least the others would know where to look for Marianna.

Marianna did not understand the politics that the men shouting the name of Díaz represented. All she knew was that they were destroying her home, and that her mother had instructed her to stay hidden. If something should happen to them, Eleanor had said, it was important that Marianna tell her aunt and uncle what happened so that the bad men could be brought to justice.

But Marianna didn't want to stay there. The bad men were riding all around her, their horses' hoofs clicking on the tiled courtyard. They were so close, she could smell them, a nauseating smell of unwashed bodies mingled with the sulfur scent of gunpowder. She wanted to be up on the roof with her family.

If they were still there. Blue eyes, almost wider than her face, moved up to the roofline, afraid of what they might see, and yet, having to know. It was hard to tell if the gunfire belonged to her father and his men or to the invaders. But her father and big brother were excellent shots, she told herself sternly. So was Mama. She would blow the bad men right out of their saddles, especially for riding over her flowerbeds.

If they had enough bullets. There were so many horsemen, as many as the army she had seen on parade in Mexico City when her family had visited there on her eighth birthday. Except that instead of the pretty red, white, and blue uniforms she had admired, these men were clad in clothing unfit for even the peasants who worked the mines near the hacienda. A frightened whimper escaped, in spite of her resolve to be brave as her mother had told her, and Marianna stuffed the handkerchief into her mouth as a precaution.

A woman's scream penetrated Marianna's consciousness, rising above the chaos with its familiarity. The child's own joined in, muffled by the handkerchief clasped tightly to her mouth by her small hand as her mother was tossed off the roof to a group of men gathered on the balcony below. Struggling frantically, the woman was carried down the mesquite steps to the courtyard and deposited roughly on the tiled floor. Marianna breathed hot through the cloth in relief when Eleanor Princeton Gallier climbed to her feet and stood defiantly before a small group of horsemen. For a terrible moment, she had thought her mother was hurt.

A man in the center dismounted from his horse and

walked, smiling, over to where her mother stood. He told her mother that she was beautiful. Marianna had to agree. She hoped to look just like her mother when she grew up—she had Eleanor's eyes, although her hair was dark like her father's, not that pretty golden brown that shimmered in the sunlight. To her astonishment, her mother spat at the man.

Bewildered, Marianna watched the man wipe the spittle off his face along with his smile. In a rattle of words too sharp and fast for her to understand at first, he jerked his finger over to where Marianna hid. Suddenly her mother was seized by the men who had delivered her to him and dragged over to the wide bench platform built around the olive tree. The man followed leisurely, unbuckling his gunbelt and trousers, his eyes glowing like those of a man burning with fever.

The tearing of her mother's good dress made Marianna flinch, staring up at Eleanor's dark form now covering the small cracks of the planking atop the latticed enclosure. Terrified by the scuffle taking place above her, Marianna peered upward, her hand clamped over her mouth in obedience to her mother's frantic screams.

"Don't move, Marianna! Don't make a sound!"

The men mocked her mother, laughing at her helpless struggles. They said terrible things about her. Marianna wondered where Father was, for surely he would not permit this. Glancing toward the balcony where more of the ruffians gathered to watch the show taking place beneath the olive tree, she saw the face of the man who had ordered her mother dragged to the bench. It bore handsome features, young like her brother, yet Marianna had never seen such ugliness.

She remembered her mother telling her how Satan had been the most beautiful of the angels before his downfall, but he was ugly in his soul. Certain that she

10

was looking at the devil personified, she stared through the lattice terrified. Surely his heart was as black as the eyes that watched while the last of her mother's clothing was stripped off. Perspiration beaded on his face and he breathed heavily, as if he'd been running, as he walked up to where his men held down Eleanor Gallier, mistaking her pleas as self-directed.

"Marianna, take your own advice and do not scream so!" His voice was cajoling, yet nothing had ever evoked such horror in the child's mind. "If you please me, I may let you live."

Her mother never stopped screaming her cautions, not even when the demon slapped her across the face. And then they became muffled, as though someone had stuffed a handkerchief in her mother's mouth too. Through the lattice Marianna could see the rumpled trousers that dropped around the man's knees, the gunbelt with them, and heard the pounding scuffle taking place above. She couldn't see what the man was doing, but he was hurting her mother. She could tell by the grunts and noises coming above her.

An unprecedented emotion filled Marianna's heart, hatred that went beyond her childish dislike of certain individuals. Her mother had told her not to make a sound, but Marianna could not let them continue to hurt her like that. Her gaze fixed on the man who was hurting her mother and a feral gleam lighted in once-innocent eyes. Reaching through the lattice ever so carefully with both hands, Marianna slipped a pistol from the leather holster.

She had watched her brother shoot bottles with his gun and imitated his motions, drawing the hammer back with both thumbs. Above her the demon growled and rammed the wooden structure around her, shaking it so that Marianna thought for a moment it was going

11

to collapse on her. When it became obvious that it would not, she pointed the barrel at the bare knee, only inches from her and lightly furred with dark hair, and, bracing for the noise she hated with closed eyes, squeezed the trigger.

The explosion rocked her backward, causing her to drop the gun as she pulled her hands back inside the enclosure. The thud of the bandit as he struck the ground, writhing in pain, drove her further in retreat until her back was pressed against the gnarled roots of the tree. The first thing that managed to penetrate the shock of what she had done was that not only his knee, but his face, was bleeding. A scarlet slash streaked from his jaw to the corner of his left eye.

"Your lust will be the end of you, Victor. You must have stepped on your gun," one of his companions suggested, picking up the gun from where Marianna had dropped it. The tattoo on his thick forearm—of a bleeding heart ensnared in the grasp of a fanged snake—fitted such evil men as these.

Victor, as the handsome demon was called, stared at the gunbelt suspiciously for a moment; his dark piercing eyes dared pain to enter them as they appeared to look right through the lattice to where two large blue ones stared back in unadulterated fury. Suddenly, he licked his lips, his tongue tasting the blood that had trickled down and drawing his attention to his face.

"Madre de Dios!" he cursed, glaring at the woman who now rose to her feet, mutual contempt seething in her gaze. *"Puta!"*

Marianna could see that her mother was naked, wearing little more than rags, yet she marched toward the down bandit like a queen in royal raiment. The other men stood speechless, confounded by all that had transpired and awed by her regal carriage, despite the degradation dealt her by their leader.

"You will die for this!" Victor sneered bitterly, fighting to ignore the agony in his knee and the beads of sweat that stung his narrowed eyes. He snatched the gun that had dealt him the curious blow and aimed it at Eleanor.

The explosion was deafening, and echoing in Marianna's mind along with the screamed and muffled "Mama!" that was never heard above it. As her world shifted into slow motion, she saw her mother collapse on the tiled courtyard floor. Twisting so that her face was toward the latticed skirt of the bench, Eleanor Gallier with her last breath mouthed the words, "Don't make a sound, Marianna," and continued to charge the hidden child with her command, with lifeless blue eyes that would haunt the little girl forever.

Chapter One

The wind from the storm that had followed Marianna Gallier across the narrow strait of muddy water nearby rattled the woven branches that made up the roof of the small shack. Outside, under a lean-to, the small burro from the convent near Valencia brayed nervously at the sound of approaching thunder. Taking a position as far as she could from the corner where the shelter had caved in, Marianna Gallier removed the headpiece of the nun's habit and shook out her raven tresses, as damp with perspiration as with the rain. Her hands shook as she dropped it guiltily in her lap, remorseful over the fact that she'd been forced to steal the clothing, as well as the burro.

She could wring her cousin's neck for getting her into this. She should never have left France, let alone ventured from her aunt's home in Mexico City. The last thing she wanted was to return to the province where the nightmare that had haunted her dreams for years had taken place. It wasn't until she and her cousin Elena had traveled to France to live with her paternal, and her cousin's maternal, grandmother to receive their formal education that the horrible memories were finally laid to rest . . . in the past where they belonged.

There Marianna became one of the favorites of Parisian society with her dark Hispanic features and contrasting cerulean eyes. Her fluent French, spoken with the slightest hint of a Spanish accent, intrigued the young Frenchmen as much as their speech and gallantry fascinated her. And her French and Spanish accents assaulted her English to the point that her English teacher was at his wit's end. Nevertheless, she could make herself understood in all three languages, and the unlikely combinations of accent and idiom were absolutely charming, regardless of which she used.

But Elena had had to return. Since her cousin's family had raised her after the death of her parents, Marianna felt compelled to heed her cousin's plea to return to Mexico City and help her out of the betrothal that had been made without the prospective bride's consent. It was a business merger that had nothing to do with happiness, Elena had ranted to her stepfather, who, until she became twenty-one, managed the estate and lands in Valencia that she'd inherited from her late father, Luis De Costa. When that had failed, her cousin came out with the real reason for her distress. She revealed her undying love for Emile Bienville, her riding instructor in Paris.

The outrage that followed managed to get both girls sequestered in their rooms, despite the fact that Marianna had not revealed her own interest in Emile's brother, a fencing instructor at a nearby gentlemen's academy. The brothers' aunt ran the school for wealthy young ladies, and Marianna could not see how that put them below the girls' station, as her aunt and uncle insisted. Besides, it was through the De Costa line that Elena was descended from Spanish royalty. Marianna had Mexican, French, and Texan blood flowing through her veins—not the slightest hint of noble blue, to her knowledge.

Although, after moving to Mexico City with her aunt after her parents' death, she was loath to admit to having any Texan blood. The gringos were animals, little more than white savages who raided and killed Mexicans at whim. They swaggered up and down the border carrying six-guns and wearing buckskins, faded denim and flannel, and large Stetson hats from which they drank straight from running brooks and streams. The fact that they hated Mexicans more than the reverse only made them more formidable in Marianna's young eyes.

That her mother had been the daughter of a Texas colonel and his Mexican wife was something she chose to forget. As far as she and anyone who knew her was concerned, she was Mexican and French. Her Texas heritage went unacknowledged, except when she resisted her stepfather's will. Then it was thrown in her face: that bad gringo blood that made her less a lady than her cousin.

Maybe it was bad gringo blood that had made her agree to Elena's desperate plan to avoid the marriage to Victor Romero, the *alcalde* of Valencia. All she had to do was go in Elena's place, while her cousin made haste to Matamoros where Emile Bienville was to meet her and marry her. Posing as Elena, Marianna would tell this Romero that she did not wish to marry him, that her heart belonged to another man, and break the betrothal, plain and simple.

Since Elena's mother, Anita, was too frail of health to accompany her, and her stepfather, Enrique Corazon, was too involved with his work for Presidente Díaz, Marianna was the perfect choice to attend the wedding as representative of the family. A healthy bribe paid to their servants who were to accompany them and falling on knees in tearful plea to their *dueña*, who insisted on accompanying Elena to the arms of her fiancé to be certain his intentions were honorable, made the plan easier to carry out than first anticipated.

It was fate, her cousin had declared at their tearful parting, leaving Marianna with two servants to accompany her to the awaiting wedding between the houses of Romero and De Costa. All would go well, they would wire when Elena was properly wedded, and Marianna could join them in Matamoros to meet Andre, who would be accompanying his brother, with the reply to the question she had left unanswered when she departed from Paris.

During the entire trip by train and coach across Mexico to the frontier province of Chihuahua, she dwelled on whether or not she would accept Andre's proposal of marriage. Unlike Elena, she was not so easily swept off her feet, although she found Andre's attentions delightful and ever so romantic. Of all the young swains who visited her grandmother's home on the Seine, he was certainly the most attractive to her. Those with blue-blooded ancestry were more impressed with their titles than she was and more impressed with Elena's wealth than with that of her orphaned cousin. Their interest in her was more of the primitive nature involving stolen kisses and familiarities which Marianna managed to stop instantly with a well-practiced slap of a fan, or palm, if she was so disposed.

Never in her wildest dreams was Marianna prepared for the man who met her upon arrival at Casa Valencia, Elena's father's ancestral home. That Victor Romero, reputable *alcalde* of Valencia, was the same Victor who had once ridden with the revolutionaries of Porfirio Díaz was beyond even Marianna's active imagination.

The sight of the ragged scar—cut by her mother's wedding ring across the man's face at the same time Marianna had fired the pistol at his knee, leaving him with a lifetime limp—nearly put her into an uncharacteristic swoon.

Once seated in the salon and fortified by a brandy to help assuage her indisposition from the long and harsh journey, she listened numbly as the voice that had cursed her mother showered her with compliments on her beauty. She answered his questions as to the welfare of her family in stilted sentences, unaware of the charming hint of French influence from her years in Paris that infiltrated her Spanish. How could this charismatic gentleman be the same animal? she wondered. Yet, even as she spoke, part of her began to burn with hatred, stirred by reviving memories.

It was only when the man rose to leave, promising to return on the morrow to discuss the wedding plans, that Marianna summoned enough reserve to carry out her intended purpose. She told him that she was in love with another man and could not go through with the betrothal. In the blink of an eye, the mask of pleasantries came off and on came the demonic image burned indelibly in Marianna's mind for years. She couldn't help but back away as he approached her and grasped her arms roughly.

"You will marry me, Señorita De Costa! Your stepfather and I made an agreement between gentlemen." A deriding gaze raked over her, stripping her as surely as her mother had been stripped by his men years before. "Unlike your parents, I will not let you get away with your childish tantrums!"

But for the intervention of Doña Inez, the ancient and well-respected governess of Elena's father and uncle, it was hard to tell just what the devil might have done with her. Threatening to report his unforgivable behavior to the governor, the gentle woman's nephew, she suggested that a milder persuasion than outright force might prevail. After all, surely the young lady was exhausted from her journey and needed time to realize the gravity of what she was saying. So Marianna was spirited off to a convent to confess her sins and contemplate the dishonor she was about to bring to her family while Doña Inez promised to contact Elena's father to plead his daughter's desperate circumstances.

Fearing that such a message might lead to the premature discovery of Elena's elopement, Marianna managed to convince the old woman—surely, based on Romero's nearly violent outburst—that her life was in danger and that to escape across the border until her father could come to her aid would be a safer move. Reluctantly, the old nurse gave in to Marianna's tearful appeal to permit her to stay with an invented schoolmate who had spent a year in Paris with Marianna's grandmother and sent her a servant to help her carry out her plan.

Thunder erupted again, closer this time, driving Marianna against the wall of the shack that creaked under her slight weight. Fearful of the shelter falling down around her shoulders, she moved away from it and huddled on the floor, a blanket drawn over her shoulders. She wasn't certain whether she had traded one danger for another, escaped from a man-made threat to a natural one.

Lightning flashed, causing her and the burro outside to scream at the same time. Maybe she should have remained at the convent, Marianna lamented fearfully. But she was afraid that not even the church could offer a safe harbor from the demon who had killed her mother. Thunder rolled, shaking the very ground under her, and she pulled the blanket over her head. Or just maybe he had already unwittingly driven her to hell.

The coming of the storm took the sun down early and blocked the light of the moon. Without prospective shelter, Tristan McCulloch kept moving north along the bank of the river with distant intermittent flashes of lightning to show the way. Hoping to find some semblance of shelter before the main body of the tempest caught up with him, he nudged Satanta at a faster pace to the top of another rise.

He'd seen the storm brewing over the border, but there was nothing he could do about it. They could use the rain, he supposed, but he'd hoped to get a few hours' ride in at night when it was cooler. The fact that there wasn't a town around for at least another day's ride didn't help, either. Hot as he had been earlier, baking in the afternoon sun, there was going to be a cold damp time ahead, from the way the wind was picking up. And night in the hills had a way of chilling a man to the bone, especially a wet one.

Plus, he was going to be late, he mused in chagrin, imagining Cólonel Manolo Benevides's displeasure. The man was still army, in spite of the fact that after the war the ex-army captain of the Confederacy hadn't been allowed to serve in the blue-uniformed ranks stationed along the frontier. Nevertheless, he had made it to the rank of colonel in the Texas Rangers, which commanded more respect from most men Tristan knew in these parts.

Too much of a maverick himself for the military, Tristan had signed up with the Texas Rangers and attained the rank of captain in less than two years at the age of twenty-six. Catching that gang of rustlers that had been giving the ranchers around Del Rio a hard time and tracking them into Mexican territory had not only gotten him a promotion, but made him a hero in his home county.

The attention didn't go to his head, although he didn't mind the way the ranchers' daughters found excuses to bring him fresh-baked delicacies or ask him if he'd mind riding the boundaries of their father's ranch to inspect the fences with them on his time off. At his age and being unattached, it was a downright pleasure. No, it wasn't the ordinary skills of shooting and being able to follow a trail as much as it was his father's unique training that set him apart. Many of the men in his outfit were just as capable with a gun and tracking, but Tristan, like his father, Ross McCulloch, was equally at home on either side of the Rio Grande and knew the ways and language of the Indians. He'd been trekking back and forth across the muddy river since he was old enough to accompany his father to the Hills or Lakes to hunt with the Honeyeaters, the Comanche tribe that had kidnapped and raised his father as a child.

No doubt, Benevides, his father's old friend and army buddy, had sent for him to scout into Mexico after some *bandoleros* or renegades, Tristan surmised as his sorrel stallion, a direct descendant of the wild mustang his father had captured in the same hills, snorted and came to an impatient stop. Large droplets of water began to splash over Tristan's plaid shirt, darkening its sunfaded coloring in spots. With an oath he'd never express in front of his mother, he hauled the slicker he'd readied over his shoulders and touched the sides of his big red stallion. The third-generation Satanta from the family ranch at Silverado burst into a short run, taking Tristan up to the top of a dusty knoll.

If he recalled correctly, somewhere along this stretch

21

was an abandoned *ranchería,* one of those farms that was once tended by nomads who came and stayed only long enough for the growing season. It had been in ruins the last time he rode by it, but it was better than his slicker, he supposed.

When he finally came upon the structure, it was exactly as he remembered it, nestled down near the banks of the winding river. Part of the roof had caved in, in one corner. Rags hung in the two windows, the remains of curtains long since dry-rotted. Nonetheless, it looked welcome to him as he gigged Satanta's sides and rode toward it, allowing the stallion full rein. Just as he drew up in front of the house, however, the red was startled by a smaller animal that bolted out of the lean-to next to it.

A burro ran straight for the river, braying in fear with its long ears laid back on an outstretched neck. More out of instinct than an urge to capture the beast, Tristan uncoiled the lariat hanging on the side of his saddle and started after it. With a practiced hand that accounted for the wind, he dropped the noose over the donkey's neck and brought it to an abrupt stop, yanking it back on its haunches. Tristan was off the stallion instantly and at the burro's side, soothing it with his voice. The animal still had a saddle on it, he noted in disapproval, glancing back at the dark shelter in the distance. Which meant, no doubt, the shelter already had an occupant, a foolish one, judging from the way the reins had been left over the burro's neck. If they'd tied it, it couldn't have gotten away. A scowl crossed Tristan's fair features as he pulled his hat down securely and tied the burro's lead to the pommel of his saddle. Hopefully, fool or no, they would be friendly.

"Hey, anybody home?" he shouted as he approached the cabin, certain the owner of the burro would be grateful to see that he had caught it and was returning it. After all, one friendly gesture deserved another.

When no answer came, Tristan became consciously wary. He'd already looked the place over in the distance, but saw no reason to draw a pistol. He still didn't, but his hand now rested on the carved ivory handle that his Indian cousin, Eagle Wing, had made for him. Now, what good would it do for a body to keep quiet, unless he was up to no good? He dismounted and shouted again, getting the same response.

Using the stallion as a shield, Tristan walked the animals to the lean-to and tried to peer through the holes left by fallen chunks of mud from the stick walls to see any sign of movement. When the lightning flashed again, he saw what he thought was a figure wrapped in a blanket waiting by the door. Not about to let himself be bashed on the head with the piece of wood he saw raised in the man's hand, Tristan pulled himself up on the wall quietly and took in the puny size of his prospective assailant before dropping through the hole in the roof behind him.

The victim twisted as Tristan landed, taking him down to the dirt floor and wrestling him over. From out of nowhere, a hand—no, a claw—lashed out at him. Thinking it a fist, he braced for the blow and shoved his elbow into the throat of the struggling opponent when the raw scrape of nails registered across his unshaven cheek. His own fist, already on its way to retaliation, halted as a strangled scream erupted from the terrified face highlighted by the flashing lightning.

"A girl!" he exclaimed in shock, more to himself than to the one who obviously knew what she was. A beautiful girl, he thought, taking in the delicately carved nose and eyes . . . Were they blue?

The claws came at him again, taking advantage of his

23

shock to go for blood this time. Tristan caught her wrists and wrestled the fighting fury back down until he could make some sense out of the situation.

"Let me go, you big bull!"

A blue-eyed *señorita!* "I'll be damned!" Tristan muttered in wonder at the curious accent that pronounced him a big "bool," becoming aware of the feminine curves crushed beneath his body. "What takes a pretty *señorita* out here in the middle of nowhere?" he asked, not so taken by her loveliness that he forgot caution. "Now I'm just going to check to see if you've got any hidden weapons on you. A man can't be too careful."

With an indignant snort, as if she didn't believe that was the real motive for the hands that roamed over the curves of her body, she struck a defiant pose which was just as distracting as the curves themselves. No doubt about it, the good Lord knew what he was doing when he put this young lady together. Tristan tried not to notice, but that was damned near impossible.

"You have a name?" he asked, rising to his feet with an extended hand to the lady.

"Mari— Maria Elena," the girl managed, backing away to the corner without taking her eyes off him. Something about the way she reached behind her pricked at Tristan's suspicion.

In a flash, he produced a drawn pistol, checking her movement. "Take it easy, lady. I'd hate to blow you away for nothing. Now show me what you have behind you, nice and easy."

To Tristan's astonishment, his companion produced a heavily starched white habit under which she hid the glorious cape of raven tresses that had all but covered her large white collar. Hell's bells, he'd just assulted a nun!

"*Sister* Maria Elena," Marianna asserted, sensing that

24

somehow she was gaining the upper hand. She had feared this man might be one of those who had no respect for the church, or worse, that he was one of Romero's men who had somehow managed to follow her. At any rate, she was prepared to deal with him accordingly with what little defense she had, a faggot of wet firewood.

Tristan snatched off his hat. "I'm sorry, ma'am. I had no idea . . . What were you afraid of?"

Her chin went up again, this time with a haughtier tilt. "That you were a villain. I am still not sure that you are not a bull."

That cute little way she pronounced her words . . . *vilaan, steel, sheur, bool* . . . it sounded French. Tristan chuckled. "You mean bully?"

"Oui, boolly!" she corrected in such a way as to bring a lopsided grin to his lips.

French. "What is a French nun doing out in the middle of nowhere. The closest mission I know of is across the border in Mexico."

Marianna gasped. "You mean to say that I am not in Mexico?"

Tristan pointed toward the river. "Across the river is Mexico. You're in Texas, *sen*— Sister," he corrected, chiding himself for the male thoughts that seemed to take off the moment he'd discovered a pretty woman under those robes instead of some renegade. A *nun!* For some reason he had difficulty adjusting to that . . . at least his body did.

Sinking to her knees in dismay, Marianna crossed her arms over her chest. She was in Texas! That explained the gringo, except that she had heard of gringos who crossed the border to loot and plunder Mexican ranches. In their own territory, they were known to hang Mexicans, just for being Mexican! They had even hung their own Mexican-Americans, or Texicans as many were called, without the proper identification.

And if ever there was a dangerous-looking gringo, this one was. He looked as big as a bear in that voluminous poncho and was so tall that he had to stoop over under the roof. No doubt the rain had washed away most of his smell, for it was well known that gringos did not bathe, but simply dabbed on more cologne to cover the stench of their unwashed bodies. But it was the gun he returned to its holster, the one that matched its mate on his opposite hip, that unnerved her. Marianna had no doubt that he would have pulled the trigger without blinking had she not shown him the headpiece she now wore like a shield.

"Sister, is there anything wrong? Anything I can help you with?" Tristan asked, noting her utter despair.

"Non, monsieur."

"Are you lost?"

With a confirming look that was intended to be one of dismissal, Marianna pulled the thin blanket up over her. She'd gotten wet standing under the opening in the roof to wait for the intruder to enter and now she was cold. At this rate, she would catch her death, for earlier her clothes had been soaked with perspiration in the relentless sun. Nonetheless, that was preferable to hanging. At least as long as people thought she was French, she would be safe.

The *people,* or person, she was primarily concerned with went back outside under the lean-to. She listened warily as he spoke reassurances to the animals in a velvet tone that somehow managed to ease her own trepidation as well. He had a way with horses, she mused, catching the grinding sounds of the sorrel and the burro as they ate from the grain bag.

And probably with women too. Even in her fear, she

had recognized the male power of the body that had held her down. It was devoid of excess flesh, all muscle, she noted as Tristan reentered the room and tossed his hat in the corner, uncovering damp golden hair that he combed back behind his ears with his fingers. He tossed the large saddle he carried in one hand down on the ground and held out her smaller one.

"Need a pillow?"

Marianna contemplated it skeptically. "But of course, *monsieur. Merci.*" She sat up to let him put it in place for her. This man was no threat, she realized, at least in the sense she'd feared. The smell of leather, horse, and ... man, was disconcerting in a way that Marianna had never noticed before with others. It was a masculine scent, undefiled by the cologne so many of her admirers used often to the excess of clashing with her own perfume.

"Hungry?"

"A little."

Tristan opened up the saddlebag he'd brought in and pulled out a chunk of jerky. After cutting a small piece away, he handed it to the girl.

Marianna delicately tried to bite it. It tasted like a salted piece of old shoe and smelled like charred firewood. "Did you burn it?"

Her face colored as the Texan burst out laughing. "You're not from around here, that's for sure. Just keep chewing until it softens with your ... saliva," he amended quickly, thinking *spit* too uncouth for the curious creature seated across from him. She had to be lost. From the look on her face when he'd told her she was in Texas, one would have thought he'd said hell. A nun! What a shameful waste of woman!

It was just as well, Tristan thought, easing back against his saddle. A man could make a fool of himself over a cute critter like that and he wasn't prone to be foolish, especially when it came to women. There were two kinds as far as he was concerned—ladies like his mother and sister and girls who liked to warm a man's bed for money. He glanced over at the girl drawing a blanket up around her shoulders. Three kinds, he corrected himself, closing his eyes before his imagination kicked up again.

The rain softened to a steady patter on the mud-packed thatching of the roof, lulling tired muscles and aching limbs into a relaxed state. Occasionally, the animals on the other side of the wall snickered, contented with the cessation of the thunder and full bellies. Tristan slept lightly, aware of every move of the girl a few feet from him. From time to time, he glanced over at her, a thousand questions coming to mind, before turning away to block out all thoughts of her.

When she first cried out, Tristan jerked up, gun in hand in anticipation of dealing with the source of her terror. But as he looked around the enclosure, littered with junk left by inhabitants throughout the years, he realized that she was dreaming . . . a bad one, from the contorted features on the face she swung from side to side.

"Maman! Maman!" she mumbled, a sob catching in her voice.

Tristan scrambled across the small space between them and grabbed the girl by the arms, shaking her gently. "Hey, Sister, wake up. Maria Elena! Easy, it's just a dream."

"Don't hurt her . . . please . . ."

"Maria Elena!" He shook her more roughly this time, snapping her head so that raven tresses fell like silken fibers across the back of his hand.

"He'll find me!"

"Maria Elena!"

Marianna gasped as the man holding her shouted the strange name at her again, penetrating the horrible nightmare that robbed her of breath and made her heart pound furiously against her chest. She screamed, certain that the black-eyed demon in her dream had come to life, imprisoning her in his iron embrace and calling her by that name.

Marianna stiffened against the hard chest, uncertain and confused.

"Easy, girl. I wouldn't harm one hair on your head," the man holding her went on in the same calming tone he'd used earlier, stroking her hair gently.

Like he was talking to a horse, she thought wryly, although she was far from insulted. Instead, Marianna sought the warmth of his body, letting the arms that had originally fought him relax about his neck. Timidly, she raised tear-filled eyes to his face, her fingers testing the golden hair that was further proof that he was not the man who had frightened her. He was the gringo . . . the gentleman gringo, if it could be said that there was such a thing.

Marianna knew that she should draw away, go back to the cold bed from which he had drawn her, but she could not. For the moment, strong arms were what she needed. And his shoulders were certainly more comfortable than the hard saddle that had bruised her derriere unmercifully that day. The burro had no gait but a trot. With a soft sigh, she closed her eyes again and waited, hoping that he would think she'd fallen asleep and continue to hold her.

At first, she thought she'd misjudged him, for she felt him moving toward the place where she had lain, as if to deposit her there. To her relief, however, it was only to snatch up the blanket she'd abandoned and tuck it around her. When he finally lay back against his saddle and relaxed the muscled body that served as a much warmer mattress than the bare earth, a tiny smile of satisfaction played on her lips. Perhaps not all gringos were cruel, but they certainly were susceptible to the wiles of a woman.

Chapter Two

The first crack of dawn was missed by the couple entwined in the run-down *ranchería*. Remnants of the storm the night before filtered the morning sun's light so that it failed to alert the Ranger as it usually did. As for Marianna, the warm body now harboring her from the cool damp earth was simply too inviting and comfortable to muscles aching from the jolting ride of the previous day. She enjoyed a rare contentment, which was visible on the placid features Tristan McCulloch studied upon opening his eyes from the rest that had claimed him.

A nun! He still could not accept what was obvious. She had fought him like a wildcat, gone into his arms like a frightened and innocent babe without reserve, and stirred all the manly instincts he usually kept under a tight rein, instincts that, even as he awoke, began to revive.

He'd have sworn the whole night had been a hallucination, if he couldn't feel her soft body breathing against his chest. He'd have thought the sight of those black lashes fanned out across cheeks a shade paler than those of most *señoritas* he'd known were a result of too much sun and not enough rest. They were like the Spanish lace the ladies coveted for their dresses and petticoats.

31

And her lips, generously gathered in what was the most kissable pout he'd ever chanced across, were more temptation than a Mexican moon.

Suddenly the lashes fluttered and lifted, revealing blue eyes that widened upon taking account of their rather-intimate embrace. A soft "Oh!" escaped the pout, and the body that had fitted so well against his own scrambled away. The flawless complexion with finely etched Hispanic features was flooded with color as the young lady struggled to gather her wits.

A nun! Once again Tristan found himself lamenting, watching her pull on the habit and tuck away the bounty of raven silk that had escaped it during the night. "Good morning, Sister."

Instead of an answer, he was afforded a darting look, a beguiling combination of mortification and reprimand that couldn't help but tug at the corners of his mouth. He supposed she was a bit taken aback to awaken in his arms. He knew he'd been. Unless he missed his guess, at that moment she was struggling with the womanly feelings she'd vowed to deny. What had happened between them was just as natural as it was innocent, but he didn't think she'd want to hear it. It was best just to act like the night had never happened.

"Which way are you headed today?" he asked, making conversation as she fussed with her wrinkled clothing.

"Where is the closest town?"

"That would be about a hundred miles north."

"A hundred miles! *Sacrebleu!*"

Tristan had studied enough French and heard enough spoken by his mother to catch the jist of the mumbled words that came out in a rush. What he had on his hands was one swearing and unhappy nun.

"It is in Texas, *non?*" The question was issued with

32

such despair that he nearly laughed. Someone had definitely biased her against Americans.

"Unless you want to go back into Mexico. The convent you came from is a good day's ride, but I get the feeling you were leaving there." Perhaps she had decided to give up her vows. He didn't know why, but the idea appealed to him.

"But this Texas town. What is it called?" Catching onto the man's rising curiosity, Marianna shrugged. "I am absent of mind a little," she admitted sheepishly, "and have forgotten the name Mother Maria gave me."

"Presidio."

"That is where you are going?"

There'd been a French girl whose father was an ambassador in Washington, not far from the school Tristan had attended back east. That funny little way she said *ees* for *is* and *leetle* for *little* had nearly set the young cowboy from Texas on his ear, just like it was doing now.

"That's right. You're welcome to ride along . . . if that is where you're headed."

The girl shook her head. "*Non,* it is another town. Are there any more?"

Tristan ignored the disappointment that rose to nag him, and thought. "Due east about a hundred and fifty miles is a little outpost called Perdido." She laughed at the name and he felt warm all over.

"Perdido? Lost? You are teasing me, *monsieur!*"

Uncertain of who was teasing whom, Tristan grinned. "Afraid not."

"Then perhaps I had best travel with you."

Too pleased to question his good fortune, Tristan set about starting a fire to make breakfast. Of course, it was her good fortune as well, for it was clear that the silly girl had no idea where she was going. She was probably depending solely on the direction of Providence, on some sort of mission ... one she didn't care to talk about.

"Why don't you grind some of that corn while I put the coffee on and I'll make up some hotcakes."

When Tristan returned from the river with fresh water, he was shocked to find most of the whole grain he'd carried in his saddlebag scattered on the ground while the French-speaking nun attacked a single kernel between two flat rocks with a vengeance. For a moment, he teetered between laughing and shouting, for she should have known better.

"Whoa, Frenchie, we'll starve at this rate. You're supposed to grind it, not beat it to death."

Taking over, he made quick work out of grinding the kernels into coarse meal while a piece of bacon fried in the pan he'd placed on the cookfire with the coffee. Mixing the resulting fat with a little water and meal, he soon had four patties, which he wrapped in some leaves from a nearby tree and tossed on the coals.

It wasn't a culinary delight, but it was filling and had sustained him many times. After a tentative bite, his companion found it more to her liking than the beef jerky and hungrily downed her portion. She tucked the second cake he'd made for her away in the small sack she hung on the burro's saddle while Tristan put out the fire. She wasn't very talkative, but she was a pleasure to watch, he mused as she walked back from the river where she'd taken a modest bath, affording him a glimpse of shapely ankles, no more.

"Those guns, *monsieur*, do you use them much?" she asked upon reaching him, pointing to the pistols he checked every morning and every night to be certain they were loaded and in perfect operating order. When a man needed a gun, he needed it that way and didn't have time to fool with it.

"I've had occasion to do so." He could tell from her expression that she didn't want to know just how many times they'd saved his skin.

"Might I see one? The handles are so pretty. That is a buffalo, *non?*"

Tristan handed a pistol over obligingly, telling her how his Indian brother had carved it for him.

"You know *Indians?*"

Damn, he'd frightened her again, just when she was beginning to accept him as civilized. "Not all Indians are as fierce as those you hear about. Do you think a man who was as artistically inclined as that is the type to lift a scalp?" Eagle Wing was capable of all the atrocities attributed to the Comanches, but he was not inclined toward them. He was a man of the times, interested in the progress of his people, not the stagnation of a passing generation. "You needn't worry about—"

Tristan broke off as the hammer of the polished pistol was pulled back, clicking the cylinder into place for firing. "Hey, be careful. You could hurt someone that way, Sister."

Apologetic blue eyes fixed on his face. "That I know, *monsieur.* Now take the other pistol out and toss it over here."

Doing as he was told, Tristan stared at the lethal gun in disbelief. He would venture she was a poor shot, but at this close range, even a blind man could hit him.

"And the knife in your boot," she prompted.

His face beginning to burn with anger and humiliation that he'd been so easily hoodwinked, he drove the knife that few had the opportunity to know about into the ground.

"Now, take off your clothes."

The way she made two syllables out of *clothes* no longer amusing, Tristan hesitated. "What if I refuse?"

"Then I will have to shoot you and wash out the blood."

The way slender fingers tensed on the trigger erased any doubt that the girl did not possess the guts to do exactly what she said. Nun, indeed!

"Just what do you intend to do, *Sister?*" he derided, taking off his shirt and tossing it atop his gunbelt.

The steady blue gaze faltered as his hands went to the buttons on his trousers. "I . . . I intend to borrow your horse."

"Hah! That's a new one." A horse thief! Pride stung beyond measure at having been outsmarted by a wisp of a girl and forced to strip down to his unionalls, Tristan all but growled as he tossed his pants aside. "Do you want these too?"

"*Non!*"

For one devious moment, her alarm tempted him to bare all, but since he had no idea what she was about, he preferred to keep some clothing on. "What do you want me to do?"

"Get your rope from the saddle and go over to the tree."

She was smart, he had to admit it. She was careful enough to stay out of his reach, but close enough to do considerable damage if he so much as excited her, the way her fingers were clenched to the trigger of his sensitive gun. Taking extra precaution not to do so, he followed her orders to the letter. "Do you want me to tie myself up?"

"Toss the rope over the limb, please, and make a loop in it . . . a slipping knot."

Tristan's blood chilled in his veins. God in heaven, was the saintly image of femininity standing before him going to hang him? "Isn't there something in your vows about thou shalt not kill?"

"I do not wish to kill you, sir," she confessed readily, as if she regretted her actions.

Tristan hoped she was as sincere as she appeared, but he no longer trusted her. He tied the other end of the rope to the tree securely, his suspicion that she would check the knot behind him confirmed as she made him step away so that she could do so. If she did intend to hang him, he would have to get on Satanta. Maybe he could run her down. She might shoot him, but he stood a better chance than the rope would afford him. Or he might be able to take her when she tied his hands behind his back.

To his chagrin, it was not Satanta on which he was instructed to mount, but the burro. "Now, I wish you to put your hands in the rope and tighten it ... the noose," she explained nervously, still too far away to reach and too close to alarm. "Then stand on the saddle, carefully, so as not to frighten Paquita."

She might not have strangling in mind for him, but it was foremost in Tristan's thoughts as he obeyed warily. Maybe if she came to lead the donkey out from under him ...

His plans to kick the gun from her hand vanished as she bent over and called to the burro in a voice that would make the devil come running. With a handful of corn as further enticement, the burro took off instantly, leaving Tristan swinging, bound wrists over his head and feet only inches from the ground.

"Now, I will leave Paquita for you and one of your guns."

"Muchas gracias, Sister."

Marianna ignored the cynical retort and started through the gringo's belongings. His shirt and trousers would be cooler than the heavy robes she wore, and his hat would easily fit over her hair. Finding a set of hidelike clothes fringed on the sleeves and yoke, she put them aside in distaste and hurriedly donned the more civilized of his clothing.

"You do not have to stare so!" she reprimanded, upon seeing the way the stranger eyed her as she dressed. She dared not step completely into cover. She feared somehow he might escape before she could get away.

"Pardon the hell out of me. It seems the sight of a little leg is the least you can provide, considering the circumstances."

Marianna stuffed the habit into the large saddlebag and tossed the buckskins into the river, eliciting a groan from her prisoner. "They needed washing anyway! They still smelled like the animal they came from," she declared smugly, pleased with the way things were going.

It was safer on the American side of the border, now that she had discovered her French would disguise her Mexican heritage. While she regretted taking the gringo's horse, it was preferable to another jolting day on the back of Paquita. And it would place more miles between her and Victor Romero. Perhaps Elena's message of her marriage would have arrived while she traveled to Presidio, as well as Doña Inez's vital one to her uncle. Tío Enrique would surely intervene on her behalf, even if she and her cousin had angered him. She might wire Mexico City for the money to return home safely, knowing Victor Romero was facing a prospective firing squad. Surely on the red stallion, she would make it to the town before the golden-haired stranger could catch up with her on Paquita, and there he could reclaim his magnificent steed. If her uncle sent her enough money, she might even leave him a reward for all the trouble she had caused him.

It was the least she could do, she thought in remorse as she climbed up on the stallion's back when she was ready to leave. "I regret to leave you so, but I am certain you will find a way down from there."

Tristan looked over at the girl seated in his oversized saddle, clad most becomingly in his clothes. Where his broad shoulders had filled out the plaid shirt, her ripe bosom swelled beneath the excess material. She had cut a small piece of his rawhide riata, or Mexican lariat, to hold up the trousers, accentuating a narrow span of waist that had been disguised beneath the bulky robes of the gray habit. "If I'm lucky," he drawled sourly, not wanting to give her second thoughts about leaving him alive, for, if he drew breath long enough, he would hunt the chaparral high and low until he found her and made her wish she had taken up a life in a convent.

"Au revoir, monsieur." With a playful puff of pursed lips, Marianna blew a kiss to the irate stranger and turned the head of the horse, exacting a slight pressure against its ribs with her heels.

The animal responded with a leap forward, anxious to be on its way, although it snorted nervously without its usual master on its back. Marianna adjusted the gait to a canter, moving north along the river, when a loud whistle pierced the air. The stallion came to an abrupt halt, nearly tossing her over its neck in the process.

"Come on, *mon ami,*" she cajoled gently, mentally cursing the man swinging in the shade of the tree behind her. Again, she nudged the stallion's ribs, but after traveling no more than a few yards, the whistle was repeated again and the horse came to a standstill.

Whipping the animal's head around, she galloped back to the *rancheria,* blue eyes blazing at the man staring innocently at her. "If you do not stop that whistling, I will have to shoot you! *Madre de Dios!*" she swore, breaking into a rattle of Spanish curses that lifted the golden brow of the source of her frustration. After searching through the saddlebag, once again, she eased the horse up beside Tristan. "Here!" she declared, forcing the bandanna she'd found into his mouth. "Whistle with that!" The icy stare that returned her heated one managed to chill her, in spite of the sun that was breaking through the hazy cover overhead. "I am sorry, *monsieur*. Truly, I am." She hesitated a moment. "I beg your pardon, but . . . is north along the river?"

Tristan was incredulous as he nodded toward the riverbank in confirmation of her guess. The river would eventually take her north, but only after it dipped deep into the south. Maybe by then, if she didn't kill herself first, he'd catch up with her.

From the top of the rise, Marianna glanced back once more, satisfied to see that the gringo was still hanging where she had left him. Surely he would eventually find a way down, although, from the parting glare he had given her, she hoped it would not be too soon. She shivered involuntarily. She couldn't blame him. He had been kind and she had repaid him horribly. But there was little choice in the matter. Besides, the gringo appeared adept at survival in this wilderness . . . more so than she, she thought, moving on toward the expanse of dry rolling brush country awaiting her with the bulk of his supplies.

She'd seen vast wastelands of cactus and desert as she'd traveled across Mexico, but that was from the window of a coach that took some of the shock of the terrain out of the trip. However, as the sun climbed to its midday peak, Marianna began to wonder if there was any end to it. The stallion's ride was smoother than Paquita's, but she felt as if her legs were being wrenched from their sockets as the day wore on. Although an accomplished rider around the parks and rolling estates of France, she was hardly accustomed to this.

By nightfall, the river wound its way through a small canyon and Marianna found herself camped near its edge, hungry and thirsty. Having watched Tristan make up passable cakes that morning, she tried her own hand at it after building a small fire with some dried brush and deadwood, which she lit with matches from the saddlebag. Tomorrow she would have to cross an arroyo she could see in the distance, a ragged ditch of land that had apparently filled with water from the storm of the previous night. That is, if she managed to weather the one brewing in the distance, she mused with a baleful look toward the darkening northeast . . .

Later, however, when the storm hit, Marianna found herself wishing for the warm embrace that had soothed her troubled sleep the night before. Wet from the water that ran down the bed of rock to where she tried to sleep, she wrapped the poncho around her like a tepee, pulling her head inside to avoid having to see the lightning that cracked and thundered in the distance.

Instead of sleeping, she pondered the situation concerning Victor Romero. She was innocent, but no fool. It was not irony that made the man who had led the bandits' attack against Mirabeau its current owner. He had taken the hacienda and mines by force under the pretense of driving out the *presidente*'s political enemies, no, murdering them. He had taken what was rightfully hers.

But what had possessed her uncle to betroth Elena to Romero? True, he was not around when Marianna's parents had been killed, but he was one of Díaz's most trusted men. Didn't he know what kind of man he dealt with?

Of course, Marianna had not been able to identify

the bandit who killed her parents to the authorities as anyone but a man called Victor who was young and sinisterly handsome. The villain could have been any number of men, she remembered her aunt telling her, trying to calm her down. Secretly, and childishly, Marianna had hoped the gunshot wound she had inflicted had somehow killed him. Although the nightmare haunted her dreams, the fact that he might be dead had somehow made it easier to bear.

And now he was alive, albeit with a marked limp, and worse, as the respected owner of her parents' estate and *alcalde* of the village. Once again, she prayed that Doña Inez's message had gotten through to Enrique Corazon, for that was her best hope. News of Elena's elopement would only put off the wedding. Perhaps, when Marianna identified Romero as the same man who had killed her aunt's stepbrother and family and left her an orphan, justice would be done.

When the sun came up over the eastern hills, showering the sweeping yellow and gray spectacle with its drying rays, Marianna climbed up in the saddle of the sorrel and nibbled on what was left of the hard corn cake she'd made the night before. Weary from the night without sleep, she couldn't appreciate the beauty of the wild scenery surrounding her. Her eyes were blurred and red, their lids growing heavy as the stallion plodded along slowly, confused by the lack of direction his rider offered. All night long, the most terrifying noises had kept her awake. When she had drifted off to sleep, after the storm subsided, the nightmare returned, startling her into a wakefulness from which she was afraid to retreat again.

Her shoulders ached from the penetrating rays of the sun that beat down on them as she finally approached the arroyo that had looked so close from the hilltop earlier. Marianna contemplated the idea of taking a swim in the muddy water—anything to get relief from the oppressive heat—but decided against it. If she kept going hard, she would be in Presidio by nightfall, according to the gringo's directions, although the rise of the mountains ahead of her did not look promising. Perhaps the town was at the bottom ... on this side, of course.

"Come along, *mon ami*," she said to the horse as he dipped his velvet nose into the water to drink thirstily. "It looks too deep to cross here, no?" Marianna leaned over, giving the stallion an affectionate pat on his neck, hot to the touch from the bright sun assaulting it.

In response, his head jerked up, ears laid back, as if he heard something. Glancing around nervously, Marianna felt her heart freeze in her chest. In the distance, two riders were bearing down on her, one wearing buckskins and a red bandanna tied in gypsy fashion over his blonde hair. A gunshot exploded, giving rise to a cry of dismay that strangled in her throat as Marianna kicked the stallion's sides in panic.

He would kill her, the gringo with the icy blue eyes that had pierced her with contempt when she had ridden off. Of that she had no doubt. But where had he gotten another horse? And where was Paquita?

Her startled thoughts vanished the instant the stallion plunged into the water. To Marianna's astonishment, the arroyo was not shallow like the river she had crossed, but deep ... deep enough for the stallion to sink in. But horses were supposed to be able to swim, she thought frantically, trying to pull the animal's head up with the reins.

"Let him go, you idiot!"

Marianna would not have complied, for she was trying to save the animal. However, in his powerful thrashing, she found herself flailing in the deep water and struggling for her own life. As her head bobbed above the surface, she felt a stab of relief to see the stallion regain his composure and stretch out for the opposite bank, snorting water from his nostrils furiously and whinnying loudly. All she had to do was swim after him.

Her shirt billowed behind her as she struck out for the shore, her strokes hastened by the telltale shouts and splashes of water behind her. Her heart pounded blood to her ears as she cut through the water, one stroke for each thundering beat. If she could just reach the stallion before he cleared the other side . . . At that moment, a hot wet breath burst against the side of her face and she screamed in sheer terror, uncertain of what monster nudged her under the water.

Suddenly a band of iron circled her waist and she was hauled back to the surface, coughing up the water she'd swallowed in her frenzy. "I ought to drown you, you little thief!"

"I'll get the red, *amigo!*"

Barely hearing his companion's shout over the threat she felt certain was to become her fate, Marianna twisted against the buckskinned gringo, reaching for his unshaven face with her nails. To her astonishment, the man was not on his horse, but swimming alongside, one arm about her and one about the pommel of his saddle. The bite of her nails against his cheek cost him his hold on the horse. Cursing, he went under as she climbed up his tall frame to reach for the animal, kicking as she went.

Her only hope was that he would drown, for surely there was murder in the face she had wealed with her nails before shoving it under the water. For a moment, she thought that was exactly what had happened and a contrary concern invaded her senses, slowing her long enough to search the water behind her for him. As she blinked and stared into the emptiness, an arm came up from behind her, drawing her against an ungiving chest by the neck and cutting off her air. Marianna kicked and swung her arms helplessly, making little choking noises that gradually faded along with her consciousness, so that she hardly noticed her feet had struck the ground on the opposite bank.

The darkness was short-lived. Dropped unceremoniously in the sand, she rolled on her back, her arms flung over her eyes, and gasped for air. Near her, she heard the man who had dragged her from the arroyo fighting to recover his own breath and soothe his anxious steed at the same time. She almost wished she had drowned during her faint. That would have been relatively painless. The heavens above only knew what fate awaited her now. He had been kind once. Surely the gringo wanted blood now . . . her blood.

Fighting the swoon that threatened her once again, Marianna tensed as a shadow fell across her. There was a thud at her side and a pair of hands seized her shoulders. "Frenchie, are you all right?"

It was a strange question, since he intended to kill her. Nevertheless, instinct prevailed and Marianna took advantage of the curious concern she detected and answered with a slight moan. Her fingers delved into the damp sand at her head as he leaned over her.

"Frenchie?"

She sensed, rather than saw, the gringo's position. Uncovering her face with one arm, she let the sand go with the other, her aim perfect. The startled man shouted in surprise, his shout ending in a grunt as equally well aimed feet struck him square in the abdomen, sending him sprawling backward. Marianna was up instantly, running for the horse that waited a few feet away. The stirrups too long, she had to pull herself up on the saddle and had barely assumed her seat when she was yanked off roughly.

She hit the ground hard, the breath she'd just regained knocked from her by the fall and the crush of the furious man who fell on top of her. Again she reached for dirt, but this time her wrists were pinned above her head as a fierce blue gaze bore into her.

"You little minx, you damned near drowned my horse, not to mention me! I ought to . . ." Tristan broke off, at a loss as to exactly what he wanted to do to the girl pinned beneath him. Strangle, drown . . . ravish, he thought, pondering the way his shirt clung to the wet breasts heaving beneath him. It was only the amused inquiry from his companion that brought him back to his senses.

"Necesita qué ayudarte, amigo?"

At the sound of Spanish and the sight of the well-dressed caballero seated on a saddle of Mexican tooled leather, Marianna came to life. With renewed strength, she brought her knee up abruptly between the legs of the cowboy climbing to his feet above her and scrambled out of his way as he dropped to his knee, bent over in agony. A viselike grip locked around her ankle, binding her to the man who rasped murderously, "I'm going to kill her!"

Marianna kicked at the unflinching grasp frantically, screaming in Spanish. *"Señor,* I beg you, it is I that needs the help! This gringo is a madman! *Por favor!"* At least if the other man were Mexican, they would have more in common between them than between him and the gringo.

"Cálmate, señorita!" The Hispanic caballero counseled her gently, taking her into his arms as she finally dislodged her ankle from Tristan McCulloch's vengeful

46

grip. "As an officer of the law for the province of Chihuahua, I will not permit this man to harm you."

The law! Marianna swayed unsteadily, overwhelmed by her good fortune. *"Gracias a Dios!"* she mumbled as the fog that had threatened her enveloped her completely this time.

Chapter Three

"Are you certain that this is necessary, *amigo?*" Mateo Salizar asked Tristan.

Tristan looked up from the rope with which he had just secured Marianna's hands to Satanta's saddle. The horse he'd purchased from a Mexican farmer had been turned loose, limping slightly from picking up a thorn in its hoof. Tristan had removed the offending burr, but didn't have the heart to put further load on it. The willow tail wasn't Satanta and, if the truth be known, the mustang stock of the area would be well served if he shot it, but it had done the job and caught up with the red. Of course, he'd counted on the girl following the river, certain the terrain would slow her down and confuse her. "*Amigo,* if you were as sore as I am right now, you'd hog-tie the minx too."

"For shame, *señorita,*" the man who introduced himself later as Mateo Salizar, captain of the Mexican border patrol, chided, bringing a scarlet flush to Marianna's cheeks.

Instead of answering, she looked away. She wouldn't speak to either of them. Instead of coming to her aid as a gentleman, the Mexican had betrayed his fellow countryman and sided with the gringo, who, of all things, turned out to be a Texas Ranger! She couldn't have taken the horse of a simple cowboy. No, she had to take that of a lawman! And now she going to hang for it. At least that was what this Captain Tristan McCulloch said was the penalty for stealing a horse.

"Don't try that wounded look on me, Frenchie. At least I didn't leave you hanging in a tree in your underwear."

At Mateo's snicker, Tristan shot him a warning look. That had been the height of his humiliation. Mateo had come up, just as Tristan had managed to swing his legs up around the tree branch from which he'd hung in order to loosen the bonds. Of all the places on the Rio Grande to cross, the Mexican official with whom Tristan had worked from time to time to catch bandits and rustlers on the Mexican side of the border had to pick that one. He was certain he would never hear the end of it. The man was itching to spread the story, so much so that he'd offered to ride ahead to let Colonel Benevides know that Tristan was on his way.

"I am not certain that I should leave you two, but I am sure that the colonel will appreciate knowing what happened to you . . . to cause your delay, of course. I can hardly wait to see his face when he sees this dangerous horse thief we have apprehended."

"Salizar, if you don't get moving, I might be tempted to forget our governments are friendly and knock the—"

"*Amigo,*" the Mexican tutted good-naturedly, "there is a lady present."

Tristan doubted that statement seriously, but ignored the comment intended to get a further rise out of him and swung up behind Marianna on the stallion. With friends like this Mexican whose wedding he had attended last spring, he wasn't sure he needed any enemies. "We'll see you tomorrow in Presidio."

49

Although Tristan knew that riding double would put too much demand on the stallion to keep up with Mateo's pinto, it still galled him to see his *compadre* ride off. He found himself wondering what the nature of the mission was that required Mateo's cooperation as well, for, during the tracking of the thieving nun, he had told Tristan that he too had received orders from his superiors to report to Presidio. Obviously it had to be that someone was causing trouble on both sides of the border, and he sure hoped they were easier to deal with than the girl sitting stiffly in front of him. He'd been taught how to treat ladies, and this was no lady. She had all the female wiles and knew how to use them. When they failed, she turned into a scratching, kicking she-devil. If he had his way, which he intended to have, she would regret the day their paths crossed.

"I did not mean to harm your horse," the girl said at length as they approached the river to cut across Mexico, the shorter route Tristan had neglected to tell her about. "I thought pulling his head up with the reins would get it out of the water."

Here we go again with that poor pitiful game. "You're no cowboy, that's certain," Tristan observed wryly. He'd exchanged his hat for the bandanna and marveled at the way the sun danced in the ebony lengths of silk cascading from the red cloth with which she tied up her hair. Wiles and beauty combined made her dangerous, his better sense cautioned against that more-primitive instinct that tended to weaken under such a beguiling assault. "Pulling on the bit will cause a horse to sink in deep water, Frenchie. You take him in over his head and wade in beside him, if you care much for him . . . or at least give him full rein."

"But I have seen the *vaqueros* cross rivers in the saddle."

50

"In the shallows, Maria Elena, or whoever the devil you are," Tristan pointed out tersely, sending her into another spell of silence.

Although she wanted to sit upright, the comfortable chest at her back became too much of a temptation to her weary spine, and the next time she became aware of where she was, Marianna was nestled against the yellow-haired Ranger, her head tucked under his chin. They stopped at a muddy strip of water where the man let Satanta take his fill while Marianna stretched her legs and splashed some of the cool liquid on her burning face. Her complexion not as dark as her cousin Elena's, the sun had reddened her cheeks to excess, drawing the skin tight across her nose.

"You better put some of this on your face."

Struggling to her feet, she stood still while her companion squeezed a clear liquid from the leaf of one of the plants growing nearby. It was cool and soothing, more so than the water.

"Are we in Mexico?"

Tristan had never seen a more disconsolate face than the one turned up at him, but once burned, he'd learned his lesson. "No," he lied smoothly. "We're traveling through the great state of Texas." There was no sense in putting any ideas in her head about trying to get away to where her fellow countrymen might help her—if she was Mexican, as she'd claimed to Salizar. There were Mexican-French *señoritas* from the reign of Maximilian, he supposed, although most of them were around the Mexico City area where the court had been. With that jumbled combination of accents, it was hard to tell just what she was other than trouble.

When they stopped for the night and Marianna dismounted once more from the wide back of the stallion, her knees nearly buckled beneath her. Wondering if she would ever walk normally again, she took a seat on a ledge of rock and watched as Tristan prepared a campfire. Idly she began to pick out the burrs and thorns that had caught in the material of her baggy and borrowed trousers. Would she ever see anything but this barren waste of cactus and shrub that seemed to reach out and prick at her as they passed by it? Without the protection of leather leggings or the buckskins the Ranger wore, her legs had taken a terrible abuse that tiny bloodstains here and there betrayed to the eye.

"Thanks to that little swim, we'll have to make do with this jerky tonight. Everything else was lost or ruined," the Ranger announced, leaving an accusing gaze at her that added to her misery.

Marianna wrinkled her nose and turned her face away from the dried piece of meat. Her shoe was surely as tasty!

"Suit yourself. If you want a Spanish supper, you're welcome to it."

Heartened by the suggestion, she rose to the bait guilelessly. "What is this Spanish supper?" It had to be better than the dried charred beef, if beef was what it was that the man offered her.

"Tighten your belt a notch and take a drink of water." Tristan laughed heartily.

Failing to share the humor the Ranger saw in his remark, Marianna stretched out on the rock dejectedly. She was tired, but her hunger gnawed at her insides. She wished she hadn't thrown away the other half of the fried corn cake she'd made. It hadn't been as tasty as that the Ranger had provided the previous night and she had thought to be in civilization by evening.

"You deserve every bit of it, lady," her companion averred, as if she were arguing with him. "Most horse thieves get a rope and no supper at all."

"Which is what you intend for me, *non?*" she rallied, driven to desperation at the thought of hanging. Her eyes glazed so that he became a blur before her. "I did not steal your horse, I *traded* it for the burro! It is *you* who are a thief to take it back and not give me my Paquita!" she accused indignantly. "Where is my Paquita?"

She did have a way of turning things around, Tristan had to admit. The tears almost made him confess that he had no intention of sending her to the gallows. But for that defiant tilt of her chin, he would have. She could get under a man's skin quick as a marsh mosquito and was twice as bothersome. "Paquita is living happily on a small farm about forty miles from here. I traded her for that willow-tail nag we cut loose earlier."

"And I would have left your horse for you at this Presidio!" Marianna went on indignantly. "I only needed to arrive there first. There are men who are after me."

Tristan squatted by the fire. "For what, stealing horses or their purses?"

"I am not a thief! I am——"

"Not a nun," her companion inserted dubiously.

"*Non,*" Marianna agreed. Did she dare take this man into her trust? Would he believe her if she did? He might have earlier, she reasoned in chagrin, but now it was doubtful. "I need to . . . to have some privacy into the bushes," she announced suddenly, eager to escape the reproachful gaze that leveled at her. If she was going to cry, it would not be in front of him . . . if she could help it.

Tristan straightened to his full height suspiciously. "Keep talking or I'll come after you," he warned somberly. "I might think the wolves made off with you."

Marianna halted in midstep. "Wolves?" Was that what she had heard last night? She had thought it was

53

perhaps dogs howling at the moon. She shuddered, unaware of the effort her companion made to keep a straight face.

"Or snakes, or wild hogs."

If she entertained any idea about making a run for it afoot, it died abruptly. Finding her voice, Marianna began to sing a French nursery rhyme her mother had taught her years ago as she made her way through the brush, too frightened to think about crying. As she carefully approached the edge of a steep incline thatched with brush, she spotted a silver streak of stream flowing below.

She stopped her song, her voice rising excitedly. "Tristan!"

In spite of all that she had done, the way she pronounced his name sort of skipped along his spine like running fingers. *Treestaan* . . . "What is it?"

"I see water there below."

"I know. I was going to take Satanta down and refill the canteens in the morning."

After riding most of the night, he was too tired to cut his way through the thorny chaparral that blocked them from the stream tonight. Besides, he thought he'd seen a hog wallow not too far back and didn't relish the idea of running into wild razorbacks this close to sundown. He'd just as soon tangle with a grizzly.

"Would you not like to go for a swim to cool off?"

"I'd have thought you'd have had enough water for one day."

Silence.

"Frenchie?"

"I do not think the hill is so deep that—"

A rumble of eroding rocks preceded the scream that brought Tristan to his feet at a run. His long strides carried him quickly toward the spot where he heard the familiar popping and cracking of the brush, combined with small gasps of pain and short sharp squeals. As he glanced down, he spotted the bedraggled figure of the girl come to stop at the bottom of the hill in an unnatural sprawl and his breath seized in his chest. "Maria Elena!"

The dirt and rocks rumbled beneath him as he dropped to his back and slid down the incline along the path she had inadvertently cleared. He winched as some of the longer spines of the thick growth pierced his buckskin and could well imagine the damage the first pass through it had done to the smooth skin he'd admired earlier. Suddenly, another scream pierced the air, followed by grunting sounds he could not mistake. Wild razorbacks!

Somehow he managed to get his pistols from the leather belt at his side and fired in the air, praying the noise would frighten the animals away. He could smell them now and heard the patter of their cloven feet plucking through the mud near the bank at a fast run. He fired again, shouting at the top of his voice, when high-pitched squealing drew his attention to where his remarkably recovered companion held on to the hind legs of a protesting piglet.

"Let it go!" he ordered, certain she had lost her mind. Sharp eyes searched the brush, expecting the others too rally to it at any moment. It had to be a small cluster, but one razorback, if it was a riled sow, was enough to tear him and the girl from limb to limb. Adrenaline pumping, he kicked at the arms that clung stubbornly to the squealing pig, costing them their hold, but it was too late. Charging from a magote of *huisache* came the mother hog, froth from her snorting nostrils and mouth flecking her breast as she charged directly at them.

Tristan unloaded both pistols at the animal, hoping

55

she was a young sow with a thin shield of side skin over her shoulder. The animal staggered, as if each bullet halted her for the blink of an eye, but continued on until, guns emptied, Tristan drew the knife from his boot and gauged his next move. However, just as he was about to leap upon the wild-eyed pig, she fell over, kicking in the throes of death. Bewildered, the piglet ran around to suckle the heavy teats of the sow, its squealing satisfied by the warm sustenance.

"Up!" Tristan ordered harshly, yanking the troublesome girl to her feet.

"But the pig, we can have something for supper!" Marianna protested, pulling away with more strength that he had given her credit for.

"And its family can dine on us—now get back up the hill! I need to reload my guns."

"But . . . the baby . . ." Marianna gasped as her arm was nearly jerked from its socket. "You are hurting me!"

"You troublemaking minx, I'm going to do worse than this to you if you don't shut up and do as I say!"

Marianna would have protested further, but the wind was knocked out of her by the muscled shoulder that rammed into her abdomen, lifting her off the ground. "You son of a beech!" she grunted, pounding on his back as he started up the hill. She hadn't intended to fall down the hill and had no idea the pigs were watering at the stream, but when the piglet ran across her, it seemed heaven-sent. "I catch your supper for you and you leave it to rot for the boozards! Damn your black soul!"

Great! Tristan groaned, ignoring the blows that grew weaker as he trudged upward. He wanted to get close to the fire and reload. Then he intended to tie his wayward charge to him and try to get some sleep. Of all the creatures for him to come across in these parts, there was no doubt in his mind that the wild ones were safer. And they couldn't curse him in three languages.

When the roofline of the town of Presidio appeared on the horizon the following day, the tall bell tower of its only church arching high above the tops of the other buildings, Tristan almost shouted for joy. A hot bath, a clean shave, and the prospect of getting rid of his trouble once and for all spurred him on with great anticipation. He could not wait to be rid of that accusing look that made him feel as if he had been the one who tossed her down in the ravine and then denied her of food. As far as he was concerned, the authorities could deal with Sister Maria Elena. He intended to wash away his guilt with the dirt of the trail, fill his belly, and wet his whistle in that order.

Not that she said anything to him to make him feel guilty. She'd hardly spoken to him since he'd hauled her back to the campsite. Instead, she'd wrapped up in his poncho, refusing to let him inspect her for the cuts and abrasions he was certain she had, and picked the thorns and briars out of her hair with bloodied fingers. Even after he'd made up a bed by the fire, she'd tried to maintain a distance between them, which suited him just as well. Although, as the night wore on and the coyotes and night creatures began their nocturnal lullabies, he noticed that she inched closer and closer to him. More than once, he stirred to see her sitting upright, wide blue eyes staring fearfully at the darkness beyond the glow of the campfire, but he resisted the urge to offer her comfort. Damn her ornery hide, she deserved to be scared. That little stunt by the ravine had taken more than a few years off his life.

Hell's bells, he was doing her a favor, putting her in

jail, Tristan justified to himself upon hearing a trembling sigh escape the throat of the girl as he pulled the red up in front of the jail. At least there she was safe and would stay out of trouble for a few days. Once he was on his way, Colonel Benevides could set her free. Hopefully, her experience in the brush country had taught her something.

"You are really going to send me to prison?"

The words were enough to tear out a man's heart, the way they were spoken. "That's where thieves go."

Marianna might have protested earlier, but now all she could think of was rest and escape from the Ranger who had kept her tied with a length of rope to his arm, even when she needed privacy to attend to nature's needs. He had turned his back, stepped around a rock, but it was the most humiliating experience she'd ever had. She'd have died before she admitted to the exhaustion overtaking her or the wounds from the painful thorns that had assaulted her body and made sitting in the saddle more than an ordeal.

She glanced up dully as Mateo Salizar emerged from the building with an older man who was well-dressed in a suit, as if he was about to attend a social, except for the guns hanging beneath his long tailored jacket. *"Madre de Dios!* What did you do to her, *amigo,* drag her here through the brush!"

"Yes, he did!" Marianna sniffed, holding out her hand to show the rope that bound her to the man dismounting behind her. "And now he wishes to put me in a jail because I *traded* horses with him! And you . . ." she accused Salizar as Tristan lifted her out of the saddle, "left me to this gringo's mercy. To think that I had thought you a gentleman!"

"Colonel Benevides, I'd like to present Sister Maria Elena—at least, that's what she calls herself," Tristan interrupted politely as he carried her past an astonished Manolo Benevides into the jail.

Marianna was forced to hold on to the man so anxious to be rid of her until she was certain her legs would support her. She had never been in a prison before and the sight of the steel bars was unnerving. There were two cells, one of them occupied by a man with a patch over his eye and graying hair. Her heart shuddered to a standstill.

"Must I go in there?" she whispered in a barely audible voice. She wondered how long it would be before the gringos decided to hang her.

"Oh, you can have your own cell," Tristan answered dispassionately, stepping toward the door and opening it for her.

The gaze that swung his way was nearly his undoing. It was glazed, although she obviously fought to hold her chin up high as she marched past and took a seat on the cot against the far wall. "Will I have to eat that jerky leather?"

"Do you not think that this has gone too far, *amigo?* She looks as if she needs a doctor," Mateo Salizar spoke up from the door.

Tristen laughed humorlessly. "You don't know the half of it, *amigo.* Stay out of this." He slammed the door and turned the key. "I'm on my way to the boardinghouse for a bath. Then to the saloon for a good steak and something to cut away the trail dust."

"Might I have some water to wash as well?" All eyes came to rest on the forlorn figure sitting erect on the edge of the cot, as if grossly wronged.

"Absolutely, *señorita,*" Manolo Benevides answered, taking charge of the office he had temporarily commandeered from the sheriff. He turned to the bristling buck-

59

skinned Ranger. "She may be a horse thief, but she is still a woman . . . a lovely young woman."

Tristan shrugged indifferently. "Be my guest, Colonel, but I warn you. The more you do for that little lady, the worse it will be for you."

"Nevertheless . . ." the older man acknowledged before turning to his orderly. "See to the young lady's needs, corporal. As for you, Captain McCulloch, I will expect you back here after you have finished that thick steak. I have waited long enough for you to arrive."

Tristan saluted in a friendly fashion before glancing back in the corner where his prisoner had curled up, resigned to her fate. He might even look up one of the girls at Rose's, a laughing obliging one who could take his mind off a French accent and blue eyes, he decided, stepping out into the street.

The bath was welcome, almost as welcome as the young lady who surprised him by climbing into the large wooden tub with him and shaving him right then and there in the suit nature had given her. Her eyes were blue, but not the shade of dark sapphire or that of a velvet star-studded night. They were a lighter shade, almost gray. While her hair was naturally dark, an application of henna had changed it to a bright red.

But she giggled and didn't make him feel the least bit guilty, even when he tumbled into her bed and satisfied the need that had been building to unbearable proportion the last three days. She even fed him his steak there, another unexpected pleasure that ended all too quickly with the ringing of the church bell that called the clergy to vespers at the other end of town. With all his hungers satiated, Tristan left a handful of coins on the pillow and headed toward the jail.

The first thing that struck him upon entering the room was the scent of perfume. His mouth slackened at the sight of the cell in which he'd left Maria Elena draped in sheets, hung like curtains to afford her privacy while Manolo Benevides and Mateo Salizar sat, heads bent over the only desk in the room, talking quietly. They stopped long enough to look up at the astonished young man, now freshly attired in the duds he'd sent Carlita to buy for him from the general store, his spares having been ruined by the lovely horse thief.

"What the hell is this?" he bellowed in astonishment.

"The lady could not be expected to bathe in front of her companion, could she?" Colonel Benevides inquired patiently, thinking that the fair-haired young man was more like his father than he had realized. At least, young Tristan seemed to have inherited his father's suave way with women.

"With the cell door open?"

"I don't think she is going anywhere, *amigo*," Mateo spoke up, pointing to a pile of familiar clothes tossed beyond the curtain. "And if she tries to escape, I am certain that between the three of us, we can stop her." Grinning widely, Mateo produced a gun and laid it on the desk. "But just in case . . ."

"Go to hell!"

"Gentlemen! We have business to discuss, if Captain McCulloch will take a seat," the colonel prompted, putting an end to the friendly ribbing that was not being received very well.

"Rustling?" Tristan asked, taking a chair and dragging it up to the desk backward in order to straddle it leisurely.

"Always rustling, Captain. But we are concerned with the robberies of the silver and other precious metals on its way out of Mexico to foreign investors, the United States among them," Benevides answered. "When they are not interfering in international commerce, they are crossing the border and stealing cattle as well as young men."

"They're not Indians," the Ranger stated certainly.

"No, they are *bandoleros . . . bandidos . . .*"

"And they are raiding on both sides of the border," Mateo interjected with a grim glance. "My guess is that the young men are taken to work in the mines."

"Ties in," Tristan agreed.

"Which poses problems diplomatically. Citizens on both sides of the border, as well as officials, claim the scoundrels are from the other side. The governor wants this resolved, and quickly. I have a letter here . . ."

As Colonel Benevides began to read the missive, Tristan's gaze was diverted to a movement, a shadowy form that rose against the background light of a small flickering candle. Even with the distortion of the folds, the figure was unmistakably female, from the ripe peaked breasts that stretched upward as she wrapped a towel around her hair to the decided curves of her buttocks. A faint humming sound made it impossible for him to keep his mind on the governor's concern over the raids, and in spite of his recent tumble at Rose's, he felt a warm stirring of manly desire that made his mouth go dry.

"And that is why I have selected you two. You've worked together before. If we can prove that Victor Romero is behind these raids, the Mexican officials will have to act upon it."

"Who?" Tristan shook himself and returned his blue gaze to the colonel.

"Victor Romero, Captain."

Aware of the impatience in his commander's tone, Tristan shifted his seat and focused on the table.

"He is well thought of by the local officials, *amigo*," Mateo informed him, struggling to keep the corners of his mouth from turning up. "They will not accept a simple accusation. It is proof that we need."

"And the governor's brother-in-law has invested in the mining operation Romero operates. He thinks Romero loses shipments to bandits too frequently to be coincidence."

"What makes you so sure it's Romero?" Tristan questioned, distracted in spite of his effort to ignore the brisk toweling that was going on behind the curtain.

"One of his men was captured and he talked."

He digested the colonel's reply. "Maybe we ought to start out by questioning this fellow."

Manolo Benevides crossed his arms and leaned forward on his desk. "The man is dead, murdered in his own cell."

A small frightened gasp prevented Tristen's own astonished comment. His gaze traveled with the others to where the silhouette stood motionless. Maybe one night was all she would need. A good dose of life in a border-town calaboose might change her ways, maybe even send her into the convent life she'd pretended to come from.

"He was shot through the window," the colonel went on to explain, turning back to the subject at hand.

Tristan dislodged his attention as well, but a glimpse of the man in the other cell straining to see through the curtain brought him to his feet. "What the hell do you thing you're looking at?"

The man moved away from the cover and settled on his cot. "Same as you, I reckon, Ranger."

At that moment, the girl inside the small blanketed enclosure inhaled sharply and grabbed frantically for something. In her haste, she backed into one of the curtains and down it came atop her. Her shriek brought the others to attention, scrambling to assist her as she hastily gathered the sheet round her.

Upon realizing that she had commandeered the fallen curtain, Manolo Benevides snatched a blanket off the cot and replaced it, apologizing profusely for the inconvenience while Mateo helped him secure the other end with a rope. Marianna clutched the sheet tighter around her and backed against the cot as Tristan stood, arms folded, in the doorway, a golden brow arched in disdain. Suddenly, it knitted with the other into a scowl and, with a muttered curse, he started for her.

Uncertain as to his intent, Marianna shrunk into the corner, eyes widening. "No! Get away, you puffy-chested toad!" Trying to hold the sheet around her with one hand, she pummeled him ineffectively with the other until the towel tumbled from her head, spilling her wet locks about her shoulders.

Ignoring her protest, Tristan seized her assaulting arm to hold her in place. "I ought to, but I don't want you to be so delirious with fever from an infection in one of these cuts to miss the hanging. Mateo, fetch me some kerosene."

"Madre de Dios!" the Mexican exhaled upon seeing the smooth white shoulders marred with ugly red nicks and cuts. "She needs a doctor!"

"Except that the doctor is not in town," Manolo Benevides observed somberly. "Perhaps one of the girls from Rose's can—"

"This is a horse thief, for God's sake, not some fine lady! If she were a lady, she wouldn't be in jail. Now get me the kerosene!"

At that moment, Marianna never hated anyone or anything more than the Ranger whose pale blue eyes dared her to protest further. Silently, she cursed him, her cousin, Victor Romero, and anyone else who had anything to do with her leaving her grandmother's comfortable estate on the Seine. She could be dancing on the arm of some handsome courtier or French soldier instead of exposing her back to the icy contempt of the heartless gringo who pried at her injuries with surprising gentleness.

She missed the challenging glower that sent Mateo Salizar out of the small enclosure to join Colonel Benevides at his desk. All she knew was that she was torn between wishing he had remained to protect her from the Texan and being glad that only one pair of male eyes were treated to the sight of her abused derriere. It was a torture, the way his fingers moved from one wound to the other with a maddening tenacity. Surely that was why her breath had become halting and her spine tingled with something not altogether unpleasant.

Not that she would recognize any pleasantry coming from the buffoon who had added a new dimension to her humiliation. Instead, she lay on her stomach and bit her lip to keep from giving him the satisfaction of crying out when he found the remnant of a thorn she'd missed and extracted it. Weak with hunger and exhaustion, her stomach reeled at the heavy smell of the kerosene with which he liberally dabbed each cut.

"That about takes care of the back. I think I've got them all."

As if to add insult to injury, roughened hands ran lingeringly over the curves of her buttocks one more time, causing her to gasp in indignation. It was, however, diluted by the mortification that followed his next order.

"Now, turn over."

Marianna crawled to her feet, struggling with the sheet to maintain what little integrity he'd left her. "That is good enough! I can see to the rest! Now get out of my room!" She'd have loved to scratch that cockeyed grin off the Ranger's face, but for the fact that she'd lose her cover completely.

"That's not very gracious, *señorita*. Some thorns are poisonous."

"Then I hope one is stuck in your finger! Now out of my room!"

Tristan made a sweeping bow and answered as if she had thanked him. *"De nada, señorita.* I'll leave the kerosene for you."

"I do not know what good my bath has been—now I smell like an old lamp!"

"I didn't go charging down an embankment of chaparral after a wild pig."

Marianna couldn't help bristling, in spite of the fact that she knew she was being baited. The gringo could set off her temper with just a quirk of his generous lips, let alone the prick of his goading words. "It was an accident! Do you think I mean to look like this?"

"Wild pigs?" she heard Mateo Salizar echo in astonishment.

"Let me tell you a story, *amigo.*"

Marianna sank onto her cot wearily, her skin hotter than the flickering flame of the candle on the shelf above her bunk. The man had no end to his ability to humiliate her. As she began to dab the rest of her abused body with the healing kerosene, she could hear the hilarious account of her escapade that had not been funny at all that the time.

The bank had given way—she hadn't charged, as the Ranger was telling his comrades. And she hadn't chased the piglet. The moment she landed, she saw it, just as frozen as she . . . and then, half-starved and remembering the succulent taste of roast pork, she grabbed it.

Even the prisoner in the adjoining cell was laughing at her.

Well, damn them. Damn them all! She would find a way out of this yet. She pulled on the nun's robe that she had taken from the convent and snatched up a roll from the plate that had been left on the shelf near the bars, where a slot had been neatly crafted through which to feed the prisoners without opening the door. As she nibbled at the bread, she caught sight of the window above her cot and shivered at the thought of the dead man who had informed on Victor Romero—the one who had been murdered right there in the jail.

Romero might have had her followed, but surely he would not have her killed, she reasoned, casting a dubious look at the window. He wanted to marry her. Casa Valencia would not be his without her. Then, no doubt, he would have her killed. Unless her uncle managed to intervene in time . . . or *unless she killed him first*.

Chapter Four

"If I did not know that you were immune to such things, I would swear that you have more than a casual interest in this prisoner of yours," Mateo Salizar teased Tristan as they stepped out into the street from the boardinghouse where they'd just finished breakfast. They paused long enough to let a burro pulling a cartload of vegetables pass them on the way to the market. "Carlita was disappointed that you did not join us as you promised."

"I haven't had a decent night's sleep since I ran across that little minx. Believe me, I'm not pining." A wicked grin lit upon Tristan's lips. "Besides, Carlita did such a good job with my bath and shave, I didn't need her later."

Salizar burst into laughter, clapping his companion on the back as they stepped onto the boardwalk in front of the jail. "Then my faith is restored in you, *amigo*. She said nothing of that."

"Like the boys say, it doesn't take long to catch up on such as that. Being a married man, you ought to know better than the rest of us." It didn't matter to Tristan, for he'd seen many married men act the same way. It was merely different from the example he'd had set for him by his father. To his knowledge, Ross McCulloch had never looked at another woman since he married Tristan's mother. To the young Ranger, that was the way marriage should be . . . if one ever found a woman like Laura Skylar McCulloch.

This time it was Mateo's turn to squirm. "Ah, *amigo,* you do not know the half of it. There is never enough money . . . and a woman can think of more reasons not to—"

"Excuse me."

Without thinking, both men moved aside to let the prim young lady wielding a broom with ferocity against the dirt that had been tracked into the jail past them. It wasn't until she stood at the edge of the boardwalk, returning it to its natural bed in the street, that they recognized the nun's robes of their prisoner.

"Hey, what do you think you're doing?"

Marianna turned and cast a scathing look at the hand that clutched her arm. "I am sweeping out the jail. It is absolutely filthy! Have you a problem with that, Monsieur Ranger?"

Raangair. She did have a way with words, Tristan admitted again. And spunk, he thought, glancing down to where she stood on tiptoe, as if defying him to do anything about it. As exhausted as he had been, it had taken him a while to block out the picture of her sleeping on the cot in the jail, a dark-haired angel in the pale gray robes of the church, soft and vulnerable. Before locking the door for the night, he'd peeked in on her and blown out the candle that had almost burned down in its holder.

"You're on my foot, Frenchie."

Marianna backed away, disconcerted. "If your feet were not so big as the rest of you, that would not happen. I would say that all your dancing partners are now crippled!"

"Nope, I just pick them up like this and carry them around." Grabbing her up, broom and all, in his arms, Tristan danced into the office and deposited her inside the jail cell, chuckling above her outraged protest.

"You big booll! I am sorry I did not shoot you through the heart . . . if you have one! You have pushed the breath out of my ribs!"

"Well, I'll be cussed, Mat, this is the first one ever complained."

Marianna glared at the amused Ranger, a devious glint touching her gaze before grinding her heel into the instep of his booted foot. *"That* for your complaints, you big booll!"

With a startled howl, Tristan lifted his injured foot, only to catch the full sweep of the broom that came swishing across his back, sending him sprawling forward on the plank floor. The slam of the metal door the girl shut between them was barely audible above the laughter of the other men in the room, including that of the other prisoner.

"Now ye asked for that, Ranger, and it does my heart good to see ye get your proper portion!"

"If you gentlemen are finished with your folly," Colonel Manolo Benevides spoke up sternly from the desk, "perhaps we might attend to some unfinished business."

"Is it a new Ranger practice to let prisoners wander about on their own cognizance?" Tristan grumbled irritably, picking himself up.

"No more than it is to dance with them."

"She's making a fool out of all of us."

"You seem to be doing that well enough alone, Captain." Benevides turned a reproving face from Tristan to the girl in the cell and smiled, disapproval melting away.

"Señorita, I believe the coffee is done, and those confections smell delicious."

Reassured that her benefactor had the gringo Ranger under control, Marianna ventured from the cell with a superior tilt of her chin and walked over the small woodstove in the corner of the room. It had two top burners and a small oven just wide enough to put in a single pan, but the honey-molasses buns she'd learned to make from her grandmother's cook had turned out perfectly. The Ranger colonel had been so considerate of her that she insisted he let her fix him a treat for breakfast. After all, there was nothing else for her to do in the cell except brood over her ill twist of fortune.

Aware that a frosty blue gaze did not miss her slightest movement, she assembled three of the four tin cups available on a wooden plank that served as a tray and poured the freshly brewed coffee. After handing out the cups, one to each of the Hispanic gentlemen and one to her fellow prisoner, she placed two sticky buns on each of the mismatched plates she found in the small cupboard next to the stove and served them as well. Then, with a pointed look that could not be missed any more than the fact that she'd purposefully avoided serving Tristan, she returned to the stove to clean up the mess.

Marianna could imagine Cook's horror to see her, granddaughter of the mistress, scrubbing the worktop of the tiny cupboard in the jail. Not even Marianna herself could have imagined such a thing a few days ago, but then, much had happened to her that she would never have imagined. She had never thought to be sleeping in the arms of a fair-haired gringo or stealing—no, borrowing his horse, she rationalized sternly. Nor had she thought that she'd have struck out across a wilderness alone or been subjected to the wrath of a Texas Ranger who was so despicable. She had never been touched by a man as she had been the night before, even though it was an impersonal examination and done to humiliate her. It had been distracting at the least.

"You're a fine cook, indeed you are," her fellow prisoner called out to her, his mouth still full of the hot sticky bun she'd given him.

His name was Liam Shay, she'd found out that morning over their breakfast of cold biscuits and ham. And he really wasn't as bad as she had at first thought. It appeared he'd been arrested for fixing a horse race, not a heinous murder. His trial was coming up when the judge arrived at the end of the month. Sad that it was, he had to remain in the prison until then, and him innocent at that! It hardly seemed fair to Marianna that either of them should be imprisoned. Their common dilemma made her feel not quite so alone.

"*Merci*, Monsieur Shay," Marianna responded with a short curtsy and playful smile. "Your manners are a credit to your mother."

"God rest her soul!" The man crossed his chest reverently.

Breaking away from the low conversation that had commanded their attention at the reminder, Colonel Benevides pinkened. "*Perdoname, señorita!* The buns were delicious . . . as was the coffee."

"Made by an angel," Mateo chimed him, affording the girl a flirtatious wink that clenched Tristan's teeth.

She was a consummate actress, the young Ranger thought acidly. She had them eating out of her hand, making total fools of themselves. Of course, the Hispanic blood did run hot and fickle over a pretty face. And who'd have thought she could cook? Although he'd just eaten, the smell of those sticky buns was enough to whet his appetite all over again . . . just like the strange scent of kerosene and wildflowers had worked its way with him the night before as he'd ministered to the flaw-less curves reluctantly revealed to him. He'd not joined Mateo and the girl for the same reason he wouldn't help himself to one of the sweet confections. He would not acknowledge that she had the ability to turn him inside out, if he'd let her.

"So how do you propose Mateo and I get close enough to Romero to set him up?" Tristan prompted, bringing his companions back to the conversation at hand. "Let alone find proof that he has been stealing his own silver shipments to the American investors."

"Perhaps if you went in as bandits looking for work . . ."

"That would take a long time," Tristan interrupted practically.

"Then what—"

A small shriek turned the men's attention once again to where the girl held her hand clasped to her chest, her face contorted in pain. "My finger! I burned my little finger!"

With a rattle of Spanish, Colonel Benevides sent Mateo off for some salve and rushed over to where the girl held up her hand for him to see. At a loss as to what to do, the genteel officer of the Rangers proceeded to blow on it. The sight of his superior and the girl puffing at the offended fingertip struck Tristan with disgust. He shoved his chair away and walked over to them.

"Let me see," he grumbled impatiently before taking her hand and examining the scorched skin. "Here."

Marianna froze as he popped her finger into his mouth and suckled it gently. For one startled second, she'd thought he was going to bite her instead of send-ing a warm charge of energy through her, generating a glow in her cheeks that she could not help and a weak-ness in the pit of her stomach that was nearly her undo-

73

ing. Nor was he totally unaffected, for amidst the frost that flecked the pale blue of his eyes she caught a glimpse of something else, a spark perhaps. But of what?

"That better, Frenchie?" he asked huskily, breaking the contact abruptly in shock at the bolt of invisible lightning that seemed to surge from the seemingly innocent contact, flashing hot in the most primitive of responses. The sooner he left her behind the better, an inner voice warned above the tumult in his mind.

"Colonel!"

Marianna tore her gaze from the one holding it captive to see Mateo Salizar entering the jail with a dusty cowpoke. Between them, they carried the limp body of an old man. Tristan and the colonel left her side immediately to clear the desk so that the burden might be laid out on it. Shaking herself into action, her finger forgotten, she took the basin of clean water she'd just poured to do the dishes over to where Tristan examined the figure, thinking to wash away the clotted blood that mingled with dirt on his wrinkled face.

"No need of that, Frenchie. He's dead."

Stunned by the cold brutality of the statement, Marianna's gaze fixed on the dead man's face, compassion darkening the blue of her eyes. He had been poor, judging from his tattered and crudely woven *jerga*, although it appeared that he'd been dragged through the same country she had just crossed with the Ranger. Cuts and bruises showed wherever there was skin visible. Suddenly the breath caught in Marianna's throat at the sight of a roughly carved cross made of rosewood like the one Doña Inez's servant had worn the night he helped her onto the burro and sent her off on this bizarre adventure into Texas.

It couldn't be! she thought wildly, stepping closer to get a better look. His face had been beaten badly, but the short flattened nose of the Mexican Indian and the wizened face, now fixed in death, undoubtedly belonged to old Marcos. A choking feeling constricted her throat, cutting off her breath. She didn't have to guess who had done this or why. Victor Romero had found her, and if she said anything, she would end up like Marcos and the man who had died in her cell days before.

Blood drained from her face, taking her strength with it. The basin clattered to the floor, spilling its contents on the boots of the man who caught her as she swayed unsteadily against him.

"You know him, Frenchie?"

Marianna shook her head fervently in denial and fought to keep the bile that rose to the back of her throat down. "I'm going to be sick. Please . . ."

Suddenly caught up in the strong embrace that had offered her comfort from her fears once before, Marianna clung to the broad shoulders of the Ranger carrying her back to her cell. When he deposited her on the cot, she was loath to give it up. But she did, taking her pillow and clutching it to her as a pitiful substitute as the man rejoined his companions and suggested the body be taken to the undertaker while they questioned the ranchhand as to how he had come across it.

The cowboy had been on his way into town for supplies and found the dead man lying on the side of the road just at the outskirts. As Tristan helped carry the body outside to hand him over to some of the other men, he confirmed what Marianna had guessed. The man had been dragged to death. There were rope marks on his wrists. But he had also been beaten badly beforehand. The reason eluded the lawmen. The victim was too poor to rob. Evidently, he'd been unfortunate enough to come across someone who either hated Mexicans or was simply cruel.

From her cot, Marianna listened to the conjecture, frozen in fear. If she told the lawmen anything, Victor would kill her. If she remained silent in the jail, he might *think* she'd told them and kill her. After all, they were going to try to prove him responsible for the kidnappings and robberies that plagued both sides of the border. Who was to say that she had not tipped them off? She bit her lower lip and squeezed her eyes shut. How could her aunt and uncle have betrothed her cousin to such a man!

Or was it fate? Her cousin was now safe in the arms of her true love and husband, and Marianna was almost within the grasp of the man who had killed her mother . . . the man whom she'd often vowed to seek out and exact vengeance upon. At one point, it had been such an obsession that their *dueña* had taken her to the priests to have her confess her sinful thoughts. Then time had worked its healing way with her. The dreams faded away and she'd found happiness in France with her grandmother and friends. Only now, the seedling of hate that had been nipped prematurely had begun to sprout again.

Even though she was awake, Marianna could see Victor Romero's handsome face saturated with lust as he'd unfastened his trousers and approached her mother. She hadn't known what it was then, but she knew now. She could hear his heavy panting and feel the jarring motions of the bench over her as he'd taken her mother roughly, without feeling. She could smell the sulfurlike aftermath of the gunshot that had dropped her mother to the ground, pleading with her final breath for Marianna to remain quiet.

Marianna shuddered violently. She would go back. She had to. A sob that escaped her throat was caught in the pillow, unheard by the men speaking in low tones and scraping their chairs on the floor, as if preparing to leave. Keeping her face buried, she heard the clang of the cell door being closed and the click of the key in the keeper locking her in with her living nightmare.

"Need anything, Frenchie?"

Marianna shook her head, refusing to look up.

"We'll be back shortly."

That was little comfort. In fact, Marianna doubted anything could offer her comfort at that moment, short of the embrace she would not think about. Although, he was good with a gun. All Texas Rangers were supposed to be, she mused philosophically.

"There now, lass, don't be takin' it so hard. Men die all the time out here."

Reminded that she was not completely alone, Marianna pushed up from the mattress. Liam Shay smiled at her sympathetically. It was a snaggletoothed one, but it managed to convey some consolation. Maybe if she could talk to someone . . .

She crawled to the edge of her cot where the man had tugged aside the curtain to see if she was all right. "The dead man was the one who helped me escape from the convent."

Once the first part of her confession was out, the rest came pouring forth, sometimes accompanied by tears. She told him about Elena and her parents, about her charade and the discovery of the man who had murdered her mother, and, lastly, she let on her plans to destroy him.

The Irish horse trader grimaced at the determination that had emerged from the despairing confession. "That's a might dangerous for the likes of you, lass. Why don't ye leave this Romero fellow to the Rangers?"

"You heard them!" Marianna averred strongly. "They intend to report him to the authorities with proof! He

77

probably owns half the authorities! He'll get away. His kind usually do."

"Now ye've a noble heart, there's no doubt as to that, but it's plain as that little nose on your pretty face that you're not familiar with the way things are here on the frontier. That Ranger and his Mexican *amigo* are . . . and what fiend in his right mind would send a man to help catch himself, I ask ye? It's sure, he don't pay off all the authorities." The prisoner snorted and, popping first one cheek and then the other, sent a brown-stained stream of spittle into the spittoon in the corner of his cell, ringing it clearly. "Now ye kin do as ye please and I'll not say a word, but I suggest ye tell these men who ye really are and let them send you back to your uncle, safe and sound."

Marianna digested the advice thoughtfully. "I don't know . . ."

"Just think on it," Liam counseled her, tapping his temple expressively. "You're a smart lass. Ye'll come to the right decision or I ain't Irish. 'Tis no wonder that young Ranger is stuck on ye."

This time it was Marianna who made an unladylike snort. "Now I know that you are loco! He hates me. He thinks I stole his horse and he is going to hang me . . ."

"If he does, he ain't got the brains I give him credit for." Again the Irishman tapped his temple. "I been watchin' 'im, and old Liam might be many things, but I'm no fool. 'Twouldn't surprise me a'tall if ye didn't have a soft spot for him in your heart yourself, not a'tall."

"If I've a soft spot for that boolly, it is in my head!" Marianna snapped back hotly. Her anger faltered at the grin on the Irishman's face and she realized he meant no harm. "But I will consider what you have said," she promised, pulling the blanket that afforded her privacy back into place properly.

The men didn't come back until later that afternoon, carrying with them a picnic basket with two platters in it for the prisoners. Marianna sat proudly on the edge of her bunk, ignoring the pale blue gaze that affixed itself on her, and concentrated on the colonel. After all, it was he who seemed to be in charge of the other two. Leaving the delicious-looking baked chicken and rice, mingled with corn and beans, she got up and walked to the door.

"May I come out, Colonel? I have something that I wish to discuss with you."

Manolo Benevides exhaled heavily. It had been a difficult day at best and, lovely as the lady was, she had not helped the situation overly much. They were no closer to solving their problem than they had been when they left. Nor did anyone know who the old man was. He was a stranger to the residents of Presidio. Still, he could not call himself a gentleman to leave her confined, even if she had outwitted one of his Rangers and relieved him of his horse temporarily. Besides, he believed that she had truly intended to leave it for Captain McCulloch.

"But of course, *señorita*. However, I must ask that you keep as quiet as possible. My *compadres* and I must attend to our work."

"That is exactly what I wish to speak to you about," Marianna announced, stepping through the door as the colonel swung it open for her gallantly. "I know how to get through to Victor Romero."

Colonel Benevides's face became a picture of astonishment. "Why did you not tell us before now?"

"Because I heard you say that Romero killed a man in this very jail for spilling his beans and telling on him." Taking the chair Mateo Salizar held for her, she sat down primly and waited for the colonel to resume his seat.

"This ought to be good," Tristan remarked dourly, straddling his chair and leaning forward for the performance.

Snapping her lashes at him in a raking gaze, Marianna cocked her head sideways. *"Non, monsieur,* it is not good at all. It is terrible what this man has done. I tried to tell you once that men were chasing me, but you laughed at me. The men are Victor Romero's men."

"Por Dios, what does Romero want with you?" Salizar exclaimed incredulously.

"Marriage."

"And just what do you have that any of his other women can't give him that would make him chase you into Texas?" Tristan challenged skeptically.

"I am not one of *his* women!" Marianna vowed vehemently. "I escaped the convent where he sent me to contemplate our marriage to keep from being one of *his* women! That poor old man, he ... he helped me and now he is dead for it." She lowered her chin to her chest to recoup the emotion that nearly came unraveled at the image of Marcos stretched out on the desk in front of her and shuddered.

"Why does he wish to marry you, *señorita,* aside from your obvious beauty of soul and countenance?" Mateo Salizar questioned, a compassionate hand resting on her white starched collar. "Who are you?"

Marianna's head came up proudly. "I am Elena Maria De Costa of Casa Valencia. Victor Romero seeks my land, not my hand. He wishes to acquire the old mines for some reason, although they have been closed for years." She glimpsed the exchange of sharp glances between Manolo Benevides and his captain. "I am telling the truth! I am Elena De Costa! My stepfather in Mexico City has betrothed me to this madman, not realizing what he is. I have had no say in the matter."

"Who was your father, Señorita De Costa?" the colonel asked gently.

"My real father?"

"*Sí.*"

"Don Luis De Costa of Casa Valencia. He married my mother in Mexico City and then abandoned her to return to Chihuahua upon his aunt's death. I, myself, never met him, for I was only just born when he left. My stepfather has kept my inheritance for me until my eighteenth birthday and foolishly betrothed me to this man."

"I think we've got our ace in the hole, Colonel," Tristan drawled, a smile toying at his lips.

"Would you mind telling me what it is?" Mateo spoke up, bewildered by his friend's immense satisfaction.

Tristan tipped his chair forward, balancing it on its hind legs. "I can go to Casa Valencia as the new heir. Being a foolish American, I will naturally seek the assistance of my neighbor in opening the mines . . . perhaps inquire as to where I might find cheap labor . . ."

"Victor Romero?" Mateo interjected dubiously.

"Of course!" Marianna assured him, hardly believing her success. She'd thought the Ranger would balk at her idea, instead of coming up with it himself. "With Tristan as my husband, I will be protected from the horrible man, and you men can get this proof that you need at the same time!"

"Your *what!*" Tristan choked, his chair settling back on the floor with a thunderous jolt. "Hell's bells, woman, you're crazier than I thought! I wouldn't step outside this jail with you if it was on fire, let alone marry you!"

Marianna felt the heat rising from her collar as she

tried to place a calming hand on the well-muscled arm exposed by his rolled-up shirt sleeve. "It is only for pretend . . . just to fool the scoundrel."

"That'd be like taking the pot to catch the kettle!"

Coming to her feet to stand up to the Ranger towering over her, she threw up her hands in frustration. "What has cooking pots to do with this? And don't look down your nose at me!" Angrily, Marianna climbed up on the chair so that she looked down at the thunderstruck Ranger. "I am half of the mind not to help you at all, you big booll!" she threatened, poking Tristan's chest with an accusing finger. "You have more muscles in those arms than brains in this head!" For emphasis, she knocked on the golden head sharply.

"What the captain means to say, Señorita De Costa," the colonel intervened, stepping between the two adversaries before the mounting anger erupted into further chaos, "is that your cooperation will not be necessary. While the captain would be honored to have you accompany him as his wife, your information has been reward enough to set you free."

Tristan coughed. "Honored my—"

"Captain, please stand aside so that I might help the lady down."

Reminded of the proper upbringing he'd had, in spite of his association with some of the rougher Rangers, Tristan swallowed the rest of his statement and backed away, fists clenched. If she was who she said she was, the best thing to do with her was keep her under custody until they had Romero behind bars. And thank God, he would be in Mexico with a cutthroat!

"But I do not understand, *Coronel*," Marianna objected as she was ushered back to her chair. "How can you hope to gain Victor's trust without me?"

"Because, my dear," Benevides explained patiently,

"there is another heir to Casa Valencia . . . two, actually."

"But I do not—"

"*Señorita,* may I present to you your cousin, Tristan De Costa McCulloch, the legally adopted son of Diego De Costa who was your father's older cousin."

Startled himself by the idea that this confounding creature was related, if only by adoption, Tristan took up her hand and, with a gallant sweep that was out of character, brushed it with his lips. "Delighted, *señorita.*"

Anger and confusion flooded Marianna's face as she snatched her hand away and jumped to her feet. "I do not believe this for a moment! I suppose you will tell me that Señor Salizar is the other heir?"

"No, *señorita,* Tristan's twin sister Catalina is, but that is of no consequence here."

Mateo Salizar interrupted hesitantly. "You mean to say that this is really true?"

"Then if this booll is her brother, she must look like a cow!"

Tristan flinched as the jail door slammed behind the girl who had stomped past him and rolled his eyes heavenward. "It's a long story, *amigo.* I'll tell you over drink at the saloon." He clapped his friend on the back and glanced at Benevides. "If we're going to get anything worked out, it's not going to be with *her* around. What do you say, Colonel?"

"I think that your suggestion has merit, Captain," Colonel Benevides concurred reluctantly.

Marianna watched with a sinking heart as her door was locked once again and the men left. Now what was she going to do?

"This is a fine fix, if ever there was one," Liam remarked, moving aside the curtain to peer at her curiously. "Got any more ideas?"

83

"Yes. Now that they know who I am, they surely will let me go ... I will ask them to send me back to my stepfather in Mexico City."

"But ye didn't tell 'em who ye really were, lass."

Marianna grimaced. "They wouldn't have taken me along, if I had." She shrugged in frustration. "Now they're not going to take me along after all. I can't believe that man is my ... Elena's cousin!"

"By the look on 'is face, neither could that Ranger."

Without commenting, Marianna dropped disconsolately onto the cot, her stung pride surfacing in the quandary of her mixed feelings. She'd been too shocked herself by Colonel Benevides's introduction to her cousin to notice his reaction, but she hadn't missed the adamant rejection of her earlier proposition. No one could have.

She had not liked the idea of having the Ranger pretend to be her husband, either, but the other man was married. She had expected him to object because it was dangerous. Never had she anticipated such abhorrence of the idea ... *she*, Marianna Gallier, who had had more proposals in Parisian society than any other eligible young woman her age. The man was a callous, witless buffoon, a product of this wilderness, she decided self-righteously, too coarse to appreciate someone refined and accustomed to the finer things in life like herself.

Chapter Five

"Some gratitude that you have!" Marianna declared contemptuously from behind the bars as Tristan and Mateo prepared to leave for Casa Valencia. "How can you leave your own cousin in such a place as this?"

It didn't matter that the Ranger had rid himself of the gringo clothes and now wore the tailored suit with the short jacket and tight-fitting trousers of the caballeros, that he was more handsome than she had even imagined in the finer trappings. He was leaving her to rot in a cell until he returned to hang her, *his own cousin*, for borrowing his horse. He didn't have the decency to send her to Mexico City, which was what she'd counted on. She should have known he was too callous to do the genteel thing.

"You do not know the first thing about being a gentleman! Without me to verify your story, Romero will see through your farce! He will brush you off his back like a fly! Look at me when I speak to you, you big booll!"

She was incredible, Tristan mused, purposely avoiding her demand to take the colonel's hand in a firm shake. He'd never seen such fire as that which flashed in her eyes. No, he took that back. Once, during the summer storm, he'd seen lighting flash blue like that, casting its glow on the mountainside.

"Oh, would you post this letter for me?" he asked, fishing the missive he'd written to Ross McCulloch the night before out of his jacket pocket.

Manolo Benevides scanned the address. "You are telling your father where you are going?"

"Thought he'd be interested."

His superior frowned. "Yes, but he will not like it. He hates the De Costas and all they stood for."

"You were going to keep it from him?"

The colonel shook his head. "No, I suppose not. We have been friends too long. I'll put this on the afternoon stage to Laredo."

Tristan smiled lazily, revealing even teeth, white against a rugged tan applied by hours of exposure to the sun and weather. Pale blue eyes taking on a hint of mischief, he excused himself to say good-bye to his prisoner and took the key off the wall. He probably needed his head examined, for it was clear that she was ready to scratch his eyes out at the first opportunity, but he just couldn't help himself. There was one thing he had to find out for himself instead of wondering about.

As the colonel and Mateo walked outside, he unlocked the cell door, the click of the bolt silencing the seemingly ceaseless chain of threats that had been coming at him in three languages since she'd discovered that he was not going to send her to Mexico City. His reason was logical, but he doubted logic carried much weight with Elena De Costa, at least in her current temper.

In Mexico, Romero could get his hands on her too easily. Even with a male heir to Casa Valencia, one who usurped her inheritance by being ahead of her in line, she was not safe. It would be too easy for Romero to kill him off and force the girl to marry him anyway. The colonel could keep her under protective custody until Romero was behind bars. Then she could go home to her stepfather.

"What do you think you are doing, coming into my room?" Marianna challenged, trying to muster the courage that vanished the moment the tall blonde gringo stepped inside her cell. "Even if you were to get on your knees and beg me, I would not help you now! Wait until my stepfather hears how you have treated me. He will put your ears in a box! If I were a man, I would do it myself!"

Tristan chuckled. "You mean box my ears." He wouldn't have thought it possible, but the sapphire eyes snapping at him took on a fiercer glow.

Marianna jerked her finger at his chest with false bravado, her back pressed to the cool mud wall of the enclosure with no place else to escape from the man closing in on her. "I would cut them off with my rapier and put them in a box!" With a sniff of indignation, she turned her back to him.

Hands came to rest warm on her shoulders while thumbs stroked the tight cords in the back of her neck with a disarming effect. "I just thought you might like to say good-bye, since you've just about covered everything else there is to say."

A shiver ran down Marianna's spine, in spite of the morning sun that baked the tiled roof of the jail. "Good-bye!"

Her voice faltered, and without actually seeing it, Tristan could picture the full pout formed on her lips. Perhaps her chin even quivered. He dropped his hands and sighed heavily. "*Adiós*, cousin. It's been an experience getting to know you."

Marianna heard the click of his heel as he moved away and was turning warily to watch him leave when her arm was caught in a firm grasp and she was yanked roughly against a powerful and unmoving chest. Her startled gasp was cut short by the lips that swept down and seized her own, taking their plunder with a mind-riddling effect that slowed the processes of protest forming there. Her fists remained clenched, but they did not receive the message to pound at the massive shoulders any more than did the teeth that might have bitten his forceful tongue in half. Instead, her limbs seemed to melt in the heat of the assault, conforming her soft curves to the hard planes of his body. When he lifted his head, Marianna leaned against the wall for support, breathless and speechless.

"I've been wanting to know what those lips tasted like since that first night during the storm when I watched you sleeping."

"And?" she managed in a timid voice.

That cockeyed grin that could make her heart trip and her blood boil spread over the mouth that had just taught her the meaning of the word *kiss*. "Now I know." He tweaked her nose and laughed as the dark fringe of black lace over her eyes fanned wide with incredulity. "Good-bye, Frenchie. Stay out of trouble."

Anger flared from the murky confusion swimming in Marianna's upturned gaze. "I hope he puts a boollit between your eyes!" She wiped her mouth emphatically with the back of her hand in belated distaste, trying to recover some semblance of dignity from the searing kiss that had rendered her all but senseless. "I will hate you forever!" she added as the door shut and the lock clicked into place. "Damn your soul, Tristan McCulloch!"

Tristan chuckled to himself as he joined the others. *Treestan Macoolack.* The girl sure had a way with words. But then, with lips that sweet and delectable, it didn't surprise him.

Liam Shay waited until the Ranger was gone before tiptoeing over the blanket curtain hanging just inside Marianna's cell. "Looks like we're both stuck here for a while," he commented in a sympathetic tone. "And both of us innocent as lambs."

Marianna stared at the floor, affording him no attention, and paced back and forth in the small space, her arms crossed over her chest. "I have tried being nice to them and this is what it gains me!" she fumed hotly. "Well, the colonel can sweep his own floor and cook his own coffee and cake!"

"Now don't go bitin' yer nose off to spite yer face, as it goes," Liam cautioned. "At least ye're allowed out and about."

At the sight of the one-eyed man peeking through the curtain, Marianna's ire faded slightly with compassion. "What ever happened to your other eye?" she asked curiously.

"Gouged out in a fight. I was tryin' to help me friend against some bullies, but there was more of 'em than there was of ourselves."

"That is how I feel now, even though I have both my eyes . . . surrounded by boollies. Why is it that justice always seems to work against the innocent?"

Liam sighed. "That's the way of it sometimes, lass."

"Victor Romero deserves to die for what he did to my mother, not have his hand slapped by the Mexican authorities!"

"To be sure. But that don't get us out o' here."

Marianna fell into silence, stricken with the emotions battling on her face: wounded pride, anger, hurt, confusion. But Liam was right. The first thing she had to do was get out of prison. Romero knew where she was, and heaven knew what he might do before Tristan arrived to claim Elena's inheritance. If justice was to be done, she would have to do it herself. To tell the authorities, even the right ones, what she had witnessed as a child would come to nothing. At the time, she recalled them saying in hushed tones that even if she could be more specific about the man who had murdered her parents, his was a political act. Many a bandit got away with murder under the thin guise of politics during those turbulent times when Díaz made his way to power.

"Monsieur Shay, I have a favor to ask," she began as a plan started to take shape in her mind.

Manolo Benevides dreaded to return to the jail where the disgruntled young lady who had been left in his custody resided against her will. Ordinarily, he'd be on his way back to headquarters by now, but for Tristan's request that he keep Elena De Costa under safekeeping until this thing with Romero was settled. But under safekeeping did not mean that the lady had to be kept in a jail. Hence, when he did go back, he'd made arrangements at the boardinghouse for a room on the second floor. His room adjoined it and a guard would be posted outside the door.

His step was rather light for a man his age as he entered the jail, eager to tell the young lady of her change in fortune. While she had been a trial to Tristan McCulloch, having Elena De Costa around had had its moments of delight. She put him to mind of another young lady who years before had turned the head of Tristan's father, not to mention Manolo's own. He'd thought Laura Skylar McCulloch the loveliest creature east of the Rio Grande. Had she not had eyes only for his best friend, Manolo might have given Ross some competition. Instead he settled for a career in the Texas Rangers in lieu of married life in some frontier settlement. Nevertheless, that was not to say that he did not enjoy a pretty *señorita*'s company.

"Buenas tardes, señorita, I—" Benevides broke off at the sight of the girl lying unconscious on the floor. *"Madre de Dios,* what happened?" he demanded of the other prisoner.

"Is somethin' wrong? I can't see, what with this blanket up." The horse trader pulled back the curtain curiously as the colonel fumbled with the key in the lock. "I thought she was mighty quiet! Is she dead?"

With a cutting glance at the man, Benevides swung the door open and rushed to where the girl lay. *"Señorita!"* he exclaimed, lifting her head and slapping her cheek gently. Before he realized what was happening, the girl came to life, shoving him against the divider of bars between the two cells. Liam Shay reached through them and yanked one of the pistols free of its holster, the loud click of the hammer going back freezing Manolo's attempt to reach for his other before the man warned him.

"Don't move, Colonel. Me 'n' the little lass here don't want to hurt nobody, but we will if we must. And don't even think of callin' for that corporal next door."

Marianna's eyes were wider than her face as she recouped her breath. She'd died a thousand deaths, lying on the floor waiting for the colonel to return. Then, when he had, her heart had started to pound so thunderously with apprehension that she feared it might give her away. But the plan had worked. At least, so far.

"Get 'is other gun, lass."

With an apologetic smile, she took the gun from the Ranger colonel's belt and backed away. "I can not stay here, *monsieur.* I have no wish to die in this cell like that other man."

"Señorita, we were keeping you here for your safety."

"Don't lissen to 'im, lass. Now come let me out."

Careful to stay out of the Ranger's reach, Marianna did as her partner ordered. Liam had promised to help her get to Carmelito, a day's ride into Mexico. From there she would take a train on the newly completed railroad back to Chihuahua. As the cell door swung open, Liam reached through the bars and brought the gun down across the back of the colonel's head.

"What are you doing?" Marianna gasped in a shrill whisper as the man slumped to the floor with a groan. "You said you would not hurt him!"

One gray eye shot up at her. "I'm just makin' sure he don't hurt us, lass. Now fetch me that rope, then stuff my blanket with my pillow like I'm sleepin' in it, in case someone should come in for a look later."

With a fretful glance at the colonel, Marianna rushed to get the rope. As Liam trussed him up, the Ranger began to groan and she breathed a sigh of relief that he was all right. The two of them managed to get their prisoner on her cot, where they covered him with a blanket to give the appearance that its occupant was also sleeping.

"Now, we'll be needin' guns and ammunition. I'll get that. You peek and see if the corporal is outside."

Thankfully, there was no sign of the junior Ranger. Since the sun had climbed to its fullest height, he no doubt had gone to get his lunch at the boardinghouse across the street. That meant they had but a short time to make their escape good. She turned to see Liam Shay opening a small strongbox in the lower desk drawer and helping himself to the money it contained.

"That is stealing!"

"Ye said ye was from a rich family, didn't ye? Well, we're borrowin' it, like you did the Ranger's horse."

"Then we must count it to see—"

"Later, when we've made it out of here," the older man said, tucking two pouches into his pocket. "Ready, lass?"

Marianna hesitated, her gaze traveling doubtfully back to the blanket-curtained cell where Manolo Benevides lay. Now she was an outlaw, of all things! Reluctantly, she nodded. After all, the Rangers had left her no choice.

The walk to the stables seemed to take an eternity. Chickens ran loose, pecking at the dry dirt behind a row of shacks, while a dog watched them warily from under a brush *ramada*, too lazy to give them chase. Pulling the headpiece of her habit forward to shade her face from the thousands of eyes that she imagined were watching, she followed Liam into the stables.

"I'll be takin' my horses now, sir," he announced, startling the livery hand with the gun he brandished.

Once again, Marianna was called upon to rustle up some rope with which to secure yet another victim. Her mother had once told her that once one told a lie, it continued to get bigger and bigger until it was out of control. She now could see the same thing happening in her embarkation on a life of crime. And she supposed, when she found Victor Romero, that it would end in murder. Hopefully, not sooner, she thought as Liam helped her up into the saddle of a chestnut mare.

"Are we stealing horses?"

"Now, lass," he chided, taking a prancing gelding that was as black as sin, save a white blaze on its forehead. "I'm a horse trader and these are my finest stock. The law sat fit to board 'em for me till me trial. I've two more in the back, but we can't take 'em with us, bein' on the run as we are."

Marianna nodded in relief and brought her mare's

head around to follow the black. At least this time, Liam knew where they were going. And his idea to take a train to Chihuahua would serve her better than trying the journey on horseback. She supposed they would need the money for that. She squinted as the sun assaulted her eyes and found herself holding her breath until the last of the buildings of Presidio were behind them. Thank goodness, someone was able to think for her. That blasted Ranger with the yellow hair had surely dulled her brain!

The river crossing was busy, but after waiting for a wagon loaded with the belongings of a Mexican farmer and his family, they were able to cross without incident. Marianna's lips thinned, recognizing the same place she had crossed on the red stallion only days before and knew that the Ranger had lied to her about their traveling in the great state of Texas when they had been in Mexico all along! The creek they'd crossed after he'd caught up with her had been the Rio Grande. Apparently the river widened and narrowed at the whim of nature.

Ruts from wagons and coaches marked the road moving northwest toward Carmelito where an offshoot of the railroad the miners were building toward the main line at Juárez cut across Chihuahua. To go south would take Marianna toward Mexico City. North would take her to Valencia. She was comfortable that Romero's men no doubt would expect her to try to get to Mexico City to her family and not expect her to return to Valencia. Surprise would be essential if she was to be successful.

"Now, lass, this looks like as good a place as any to lay in for the night."

"There is no town nearby?" Marianna questioned,

stretching in the saddle and admiring the fire-streaked sunset.

"Aye, but why draw attention to ourselves? Besides," Liam pointed out, "I have a feelin' if ye're set on shootin' this fella that someone had best show ye how to shoot a gun." He reached in his saddlebag and took out one of the boxes of bullets he'd taken from the jail. "I took extra for practice."

At his wink, Marianna laughed. "You think of everything, *monsieur*. You know, if you were to come with me, my chances of success would be greatly improved."

Liam dismounted and let his horse drink from the tiny stream of water that wound a crooked path down from chaparral-covered hills lying before them. "Now, that would make me a fool, and one fool is enough. As soon as I put you on the train, I'm headin' north to Juárez and back into New Mexico Territory. I ain't at home with these Mex's, no offense intended."

"None taken, *monsieur*." She let her horse drink, her countenance once again somber. "And I know that perhaps I am the fool. But I will have no peace until Victor Romero is dead." A surge of unadulterated hatred rose from the recesses of her memory, striking Marianna afresh, as if the horrible nightmare had happened only yesterday instead of years ago. "When will you show me how to shoot the gun?"

"After we get a fire goin' and eat some of these biscuits I took from the cookstove."

It amazed Marianna that the six-gun she had taken from the colonel's gunbelt continued to miss the cactus Liam had chosen for a target. She pointed the barrel at the spine-covered body from which four arms extended in distorted directions and pulled the trigger, but there was no sign that her bullet even came close. Liam patiently reloaded the pistol and showed her once again how to line up the sights.

"But the Ranger just pointed the gun at the pig and hit it every time!" she protested in confoundment.

"He's a might more practiced with a gun than you are, lass," Liam remarked wryly, handing the gun over once again with tongue in cheek. "Now look down the sights this time."

Marianna held the gun with both hands, arms stretched out, and squinted at the notch beyond the drawn hammer. When it lined up with the body of the cactus, she closed her eyes and pulled the trigger. Once again the plant went unscathed.

"*Sacrebleu!* I think this gun is broken!" Walking indignantly up to the plant, she fired at point-blank range, blasting a hole through its center. "I have to get this close to make it work!"

"That's the point, lass. Now will ye take the train to Mexico City and forget this crazy plan of yours? It would give me peace, if it wouldn't give the same to you."

Stepping back two paces she fired again, hitting her mark to the right of her previous strike. "That is what they would expect me to do. Do you not see, Monsieur Shay?" She moved back again and fired, skimming the spines protruding from the body. "This, they will not expect." She paced off the distance. "So I must not be further than this from him." She turned and smiled, eyes dancing with mischief. "I think that I might be able to get this close to Señor Romero . . . that is, with the right dress and his intentions to make me his wife, don't you think?"

"Bejesus, ye're a stubborn woman, Elena De Costa or . . ."

"Marianna," Marianna interjected obligingly.

"Marianna, then! Whoever ye are, ye're stubborn to

the bone! Like as not, ye'll end up like yer dear departed mother!"

Liam was furious. Furious at himself for encouraging the girl to help him break out of jail and furious at her for being so damned gullible. But that's what made her so easy to take care of. Still, he wasn't a wet nurse and he had himself to think of. There was ripe pickings in New Mexico, and if she wanted to get herself killed, that was her prerogative. So why did he feel the outraged father?

He watched as she marched indignantly toward the fire, dismissing him with a haughty tilt of her chin. But she had spirit, to be sure, and plenty of it. And she'd outwitted the Ranger, took his horse and, if Liam wasn't mistaken, a good chunk out of his heart to boot! He hadn't had to look on the other side of that blanket to know what was going on when the man said good-bye that morning. He scratched the beard that had grown since he'd been jailed for putting hot drops on the nose of his contender's mount in the race and setting it crazy so the black could win. Maybe she stood a chance after all. Either way, after tomorrow morning, he'd be done with her.

Done with her. That's what he was, Tristan mused, watching the dancing feet of the cantina girl through the whiskey in his glass as she entertained him and Mateo. And good riddance! Smoke drifted toward the lanterns hanging overhead from massive oak beams darkened with age, rising from the table next to them where a card game was going on. Yep, by the time he and Mat had the goods on Romero, Elena De Costa would be on her way to Mexico City with that bad temper of hers.

"I think she likes you, *amigo*."

Tristan banished the image of blue eyes and raven hair from his mind and finished the liquor in his glass before flashing a white smile at the *señorita* who swished her skirts playfully in front of him. *"Qué bonita!"*

The girl laughed at the compliment to her beauty and winked at him, giving him an extra show of the long shapely legs beneath her scarlet skirt. *"Qué guapo, gringo!"* she responded in kind.

"No one is going to believe that you are the heir to Casa Valencia with that yellow hair of yours," Mateo remarked under his breath. "You have gringo written all over you."

"Hopefully someone will remember me, my old nurse, perhaps."

"You *really* are the adopted son of Diego De Costa?"

Tristan grinned. "I *really* am," he affirmed once again to his incredulous companion. "De Costa married my mother and adopted my sister and I after ... his accident." It had been many years before Tristan and Catalina heard the ironic story of how the bandit leader and their mother came to be together after Laura McCulloch suffered amnesia from a terrible ordeal with the Indians who had left her for dead in the wilderness. Seeing no harm, he shared it with his companion, and when he finished, Mateo was more amazed than ever.

"Fate plays many tricks in the life of a man, does she not, *amigo?* For you, she plays the favorite. For me, she pokes at me with her fingers and laughs."

"I thought Carmen was a lovely girl," Tristan protested in defense of the bride he had kissed at the spring wedding.

"A lovely girl can become a demanding woman, *amigo*. Do not forget it. She thinks that I should be able to support her like her father who owns a large ranch in the valley . . . on *my* pay! To keep her happy, I would be better off to join the bandits!"

Tristan nodded sympathetically. "Upholders of the law do get shorted on that."

"But you, your father has a large rancho which is to be yours someday and now you have silver mines!"

"*I* don't have silver mines. *Elena De Costa does,*" the Ranger corrected.

Mateo raised his brow. "You can legitimately claim them and you would give them to her? I think she *has* affected your mind. What will you do, eh? Ride back to Presidio when this is done and ask her to marry you?"

Tristan rose to his feet and held out his hand to help the young lady who had finished her dance down from the table gallantly. "I couldn't do that, even if I was crazy enough to."

"And why is that?"

"Because I killed her father." Tristan slipped his arm around the waist of the *señorita* and pulled her away before Mateo could ask any more questions. The man had been lower than dirt and was assaulting his mother, but Luis De Costa was Elena's father. Tristan could never forget that.

"How about a fandango, *amigos,*" he shouted at the guitarists playing in the corner. He reached into his pocket and tossed a few coins on the table in front of them. "I'm going to be a rich hombre and tonight's my night to celebrate."

It was all part of the act he had concocted to present himself to the people of Valencia. He was a rough-mannered gringo aiming on reviving the mines at Casa Valencia, a belligerent Texan with more money than good sense. Someone who would appear easy prey for

99

the likes of Romero. Many of the guests in the cantina would be traveling on the train tomorrow to the same destination, and gossip about him could not hurt his scheme.

"Mateo, see that everyone has a drink on me!"

With Mateo as his servant, it was the perfect setup. It was only natural that he seek out the family home that his mother had finally told him about on her deathbed and check it out for investment. After all, Mexicans were hungry for American money to boost their economy. And while he asked his neighbor for advice, he'd find out if the mines were of any value, maybe start them in operation for Elena and her family. Tristan supposed that was the least he could do for his troublesome cousin.

As Mateo had said, Silverado would be his someday and he had no need for whatever the De Costa land had to offer. Wide open spaces, fine cattle and horses, and someday, a sweet Texas wildflower as hardy as she was pretty, was all he wanted out of life. Not some fragile rose, highbred and spoiled to a fault . . . like Mat's wife apparently turned out to be.

The dark-eyed *señorita* was practiced at her artful seduction, a tease who stayed just beyond Tristan's reach as they danced to the clapping hands of the onlookers who were only too eager to join in the celebration of his good fortune. But as the music began to climb to a crescendo, Tristan caught her by the waist and pulled her to him in a rough, yet wildly seductive kiss whose effects startled her.

He could almost get used to this, he thought has he dragged her, laughing and giggling, over to the table and resumed his seat with her in his lap. Yet, as she refilled his glass from the bottle on the table and he lifted it to toast her beauty, it was not the dark ebony eyes that dominated his mind, but a pair of blue ones the color of gemfire. Cursing silently, he downed the whiskey with a sharp tilt of his head. Like every night he'd spent since he'd met Elena De Costa, it was going to be a long one, the pretty distraction in his lap or no.

Chapter Six

The small stationhouse was no more than an office in a larger customs building. Wagons were pulled up to the train where goods were being unloaded to be taken across the border into Texas, where yet another accounting had to be taken. Some were heavily guarded, drawing attention to the fact that their cargo was most likely silver on the way to American investors who were developing the neighboring company through Díaz's new open-door policy to trade.

The black engine hissed impatiently at the head of the six-car train as Marianna waited around the corner of the building while Liam purchased her ticket. Near the edge of the tracks where some travelers were already boarding, she spotted two nuns in habits like her own and hoped that they would not approach her. As weary as she was from the trials of the last few days, not to mention emptying another box of bullets into the ill-fated cacti surrounding their campsite for the better part of the evening, she didn't think she could be very convincing as one of their peers.

"Here ye go, lass, a ticket to Mexico City, all bought and paid for. The train will leave tomorrow mornin' and ye can stay at the inn over there for the night."

102

Marianna stared at the ticket, confused. "Mexico City?" Then she spied the guilty flush creeping onto her companion's cheeks. *"Monsieur!"*

"Now I knew ye'd be mad, but I ain't got the heart to send ye off to yer death. I ain't so sure you can even get to your stepfather without findin' some trouble to stir up with that knack of yours."

"Damn you, Liam Shay!"

Liam lifted a warning finger at her. "Now ye kin fuss an' fume all ye want, I ain't leavin' ye with another cent, but for a bit of food along the way. Besides, ye're drawin' undue attention to yerself, raisin' yer voice like that at me."

Marianna lowered her tone, but the intensity of her ire was just as great. "Where is the rest of this money that we *borrowed?*"

The Irishman grinned, revealing a gap left by two front teeth that had also been lost during the fight in which he'd helped his friend. "Well, now, the way I see it, ye owe me for escortin' ye this far on a fine horse and them lessons in shootin', not that they amounted to much," he added with a pointed look. "Ye'd have never got this far without me, lass."

The man's last words were true, as much as Marianna hated to admit it. She had no sense of direction. The Ranger had proved that quite well with his trickery. And she was grateful that Liam had shown her her limitations with a gun. It was foolish of her to have thought it was as easy as the Ranger had made it look. But she was not going back to Mexico City.

She heaved a disappointed sigh. "I suppose that you are right, *monsieur*. But it was still a nasty trick you pulled me through!"

"Now ye're talkin' sense ... and that's *pulled on me*,"

he corrected wryly. "Why don't ye let me take ye over the inn and get ye settled in."

"You're not staying?"

Liam squinted into the sunlight as he looked back toward the post where the black and the mare were tethered. "I don't like the way them Mexes have been starin' at me horses. The sooner I take 'em out of temptation's way, the better."

"I see what you are saying," Marianna lied. The men looked to her as if they were asleep under their sombreros, too lazy to carry their own shadow in the heat of the day. She extended her hand. "Take your horses and go, *monsieur* . . . and I thank you from the bottom of my heart."

Impulsively, she stood on tiptoe to buss the man's cheek, only to be swept into the cover of the building and thrust against the wall. Her startled *"Monsieur!"* was smothered behind Liam's rough hand.

"Quiet, lass. We got trouble."

Her heart thawed from its sudden freeze enough for her to assemble a whisper. "What is it?"

"The Ranger and his Mex *amigo.*"

"Here?" Marianna gasped, before her chest stilled again. But how, why?

"They're gettin' on the train dressed like billy be damned."

"Who?"

"Fancified, lass," he explained with a snicker.

"Oh."

Liam was growing fond of his guileless partner, too fond for the good of an old gadabout like himself. He'd have never thought he'd enjoy being in jail so much, but watching her confound those lawmen had been a pure pleasure. "Ye see, I knew what I was doin' putting ye on tomorrow's train. It's all for the best." He reached into his pocket and took out a pouch containing a few coins. "Now, there's money in here enough for the inn and food."

Marianna took the pouch and opened it. "If I am thrifty," she responded with a skeptical arch of one eyebrow. She knew there had been more, but she did owe the Irishman a lot. "And what is this?" she asked, taking out a small tin box the size of a large coin.

"That's me hot drops. I don't know when ye might need 'em, but it's all I got to send with ye. A little dot o' that on a horse's nose'll set it crazy . . . got me out of more than one spot, it has."

Although she was traveling by train, not horse, Marianna had no wish to question the man further. There was much to do before she left and the sooner Liam Shay was on his way the better. "Thank you again, *monsieur*. I will take this back alley to the inn while you get your horses away from those *Mexes*," she mimicked playfully.

"Ye got your gun?"

Marianna held up the small satchel Liam had found for her, since a gunbelt on a nun did seem absurd. "Now put your money in there and get goin', lass. I don't like that Ranger here. Thought sure he would have taken his horse to Valencia."

"Maybe his backside is as sore as my own." Marianna grinned as she rubbed her derriere expressively.

Liam joined in her self-directed humor. "I guess ye ain't exactly used to such travel." He took a step back and pulled the hat he'd taken from the livery hand down over his eyes. "Take care of yerself, lass."

"And you too, *monsieur. Au revoir.*"

Marianna waited until Liam disappeared around the corner before rushing around the back of the building and emerging on the street from the opposite side of it.

There was little time and she needed to trade her ticket. The difference in the fare would enable her to travel more comfortably than the coach pass that Liam had purchased. Once she saw Liam riding his black toward the outskirts of town with the mare in tow, she stepped around the corner and into the small stationhouse. To her chagrin, the nuns she'd seen earlier were standing in line ahead of her, counting out their coins for a coach fare.

"It isn't the most comfortable accommodation, Sister Teresa," the older informed the other, "but the Lord provides our needs, not our luxuries. The difference is best spent on the poor." The woman smiled as she tucked the passes in her small purse and stepped aside so that Marianna might approach the counter where a thin dark-haired man in much need of a bath and shave raised an impatient brow at her.

So much for traveling in comfort, Marianna thought, putting her ticket up on the counter . . . at least, if she was going to maintain her charade as a nun. Besides, if the Ranger was dressed fancy, most likely he would be traveling first class. "My . . . colleague purchased the wrong ticket," she told him in fluent Spanish. "I need to exchange it for the train that is about to leave . . . coach, please."

That this was clearly an inconvenience showed on the clerk's face. He snatched up the ticket Liam had purchased, tore it in half, and shoved another at her, stamping it for authenticity before looking beyond her at the couple that was next in line.

"But I am due a refund, *señor*," Marianna reminded him politely, holding her ground.

"You should tell your friend that he should be more careful of losing the church's money. Now you'd best hurry if you wish to board the train."

106

"But—"

The loud whistle of the steam engine announcing the closing time of departure cut off Marianna's protest. Lips thinning at the outright robbery, she grabbed her ticket and rushed outside on the heels of the two sisters. As she handed her pass to the conductor, she glanced up to see the handsome Ranger leaning off the platform of one of the cars ahead flirting with a dark-haired *señorita*. Suddenly, the pale blue eyes shifted in her direction, driving her own gaze back to the ticket the conductor handed back to her, and she hurried up the metal steps behind the nuns.

"Are you traveling to the convent near Valencia?"

Marianna practically ran into the young novice who questioned her. "No, I . . . well, yes. I'm Sister Maria. Is that where you are going?"

"Sister Teresa is coming to join our order," the older woman told her, taking the odd seat on the aisle while Marianna and the other nun took the two seats opposite it. "She is my niece."

"How nice."

The train whistle blew again, and slowly the car began to move forward into the dissipating black smoke that filled the air from the stack, while passengers stowed their belongings above and below their seats. Her window already down, Marianna turned to watch the bustle of activity inch away until the all-too-familiar wilderness unfolded, hot and dusty, before them. Thankfully the nuns took her withdrawal as she intended and began to talk between themselves, too considerate to question her further.

Although it was possible to appreciate the scenery more easily from the window of the train than from the saddle of a horse, the ride was equally dusty. The preceding cars stirred up the bed of the tracks, so that those

107

riding coach and cargo caught the dust. Nevertheless, with the air rushing in over her face, Marianna relaxed on the hard seat, using her small satchel as a pillow, and surveyed the cactus flowers that added color to an otherwise bland stretch of chaparral. Conversation around her eventually faded into the distance as sleep claimed her.

A watering station marked by a small ranchero provided the noonday stop. Most of the people in her car had brought some sort of food with them and, after stretching their legs outside for a few minutes, resumed their seats to picnic on their fare. Not quite as prepared for travel, Marianna purchased a melon from one of the children, but the tortilla-wrapped concoctions provided by the lady of the ranchero were sold out by the time she got to where they were being sold, purchased by some rich gringo who traveled in the more spacious and comfortable car ahead. She did not have to guess who.

"Would you like some bread and cheese?" Sister Teresa offered as she settled on the hard seat that had numbed her spine.

Marianna's mouth watered. "I'll trade you some melon for it, if we can find a knife with which to cut it."

Sister Rosa apparently had put all that they would need in the little basket she carried in her lap, for she produced just the thing. In little time at all, Marianna was enjoying what was a feast compared to the stale cold biscuits she had had that morning for breakfast. The train whistle blew, warning the stragglers that they were leaving, and slowly the wheels began to squeal and turn.

The scene outside became a frantic rush for the cars that jerked into motion. A mother smacked the backside of a small child all the way to the train, fussing at it for running off too far. One man lost his hat and left it behind him in order to catch the rail of the car and swing up in time while the Mexican family that ran the ranchero waved good-bye, their pockets fat with coin from the travelers.

There was so much going on inside the jolting car that Marianna didn't hear the door burst open at the front to admit Tristan McCulloch and Mateo Salizar. It was his booming voice that nearly brought her out of her skin.

"Listen up, *amigos,* we got some fine grub here! Mat, pass 'em out to the folks, compliments of Tristan De Costa!"

Blood drained from Marianna's face as they approached, handing out the tortillas right and left. She clutched Sister Teresa's arm with an urgent "They mustn't see my face!" and turned away to the window, pretending to sleep.

It was all she could do to keep breathing regularly in her effort to feign slumber. Silently Marianna prayed that the good sister would not betray her and was astonished to hear her explain that her companion was not feeling well when Mateo Salizar leaned over to hand out the treat.

"We are on our way to the convent near Valencia," she heard the younger woman informing the generous men. "And, as you can see, we have plenty. Give your bounty to those more in need, *señores,* and God bless you for your generosity."

What on earth was that big buffoon up to, flaunting his money about so? Marianna wondered as the men took their leave to return to the less-crowded and more-comfortable coach ahead.

"He is gone, Sister Maria . . . *if* that is who you really are," Sister Rosa added in a tone that reminded Marianna of her stern teachers at the academy for young women. "You have caused my niece to lie by omission. I hope you have a good reason."

Marianna raised up, an apologetic smile trying to form on her lips. *"Gracias . . . I . . . he . . ."* She stopped, regrouping her composure. "There is a scoundrel who wishes to marry me when I am in love with someone else. He frightened me so that I ran away. Worse, I find that this man whom he sent to fetch me is my own cousin! Now he too seeks my hand! By marrying me, he will have the whole De Costa inheritance, instead of half—that is, if he doesn't simply kill me to get it all. Sisters, I am desperate to get away from him. He frightens me so."

"How did you come by the dress of our order?"

"The good sister at the convent near Valencia loaned it to me to help me escape into Texas, except that the gringo followed me. Now I realize that I will be safer at home with Doña Inez." Marianna's voice caught with genuine emotion. "The rogues even killed the servant who helped me . . . poor Marcos."

"Doña Inez's Marcos?" Sister Rosa exclaimed in dismay.

Marianna nodded. "You know him?"

"And Doña Inez! His sister is in our order." She looked at Marianna closely. "Then you must be Elena De Costa. I have not seen you since you were an infant." Her face suddenly grew incredulous. "That man, did he say *Tristan* De Costa? Why, he was one of the twins who was carried off by the Indians with their sainted mother, Doña Tessa."

"He acts like savages brought him up," Marianna averred with a shiver. "The man is horrible. I shudder to think of being married to such a greedy braggart. I escaped one dangerous man only to fall into the hands of another."

110

With an indignant sniff, the older woman reached over and patted Marianna's hand. "Don't worry, *Sister Maria*. You will be one of us until we get back to our order. I am certain that Doña Inez will be anxious to hear of *this!*"

"*Gracias*, Sister. I am indebted to you."

Marianna was able to doze off and on again the rest of the afternoon. As the sun started its westward decent behind the mountains, the train pulled into Chihuahua and she awakened to the stirring of the passengers grabbing their belongings up and chattering in excited anticipation. Lanterns were being lighted around the station, although it was still possible to see in the fading sunlight as she disembarked between Sister Teresa and Sister Rosa.

"You will stay with us at the inn tonight and tomorrow we'll return to the convent," Sister Rosa told her authoritatively, taking her under tow. "You must have been exhausted to be able to sleep as you have. Now you go along with Sister Teresa. I have an errand to run."

Marianna accepted the basket that contained the remains of their lunch with her free hand, grateful once again for her good fortune, and walked with the younger woman toward an inn near the station. Actually it was a cantina on the first floor where food and drink could be had. The second floor boasted balconied rooms that overlooked the dusty street lined with adobe buildings and shacks on both sides.

They were stepping up onto some planks that had been laid as a boardwalk of sorts in front of the inn when a hand dipped in front of her and took the basket from her. "Let me carry that for you, Sister, you feeling poorly and all."

Marianna's mouth flew open to protest, but upon

111

meeting Tristan McCulloch's chiding appraisal, fell shut in despair.

"How *did* you do it?" he asked with a wry snort of amusement. Tristan was not, however, prepared for the hand that suddenly shot out and slapped his face. "Help! Help us, please!"

Taking her cue, Sister Teresa began to shriek for aid as well from the two men accosting them.

Tristan grabbed Marianna as she started to bolt away and lifted her off the ground, kicking and screaming. Working one hand free, he tried to cover her mouth to stop the attention she was drawing while Mateo tried to calm the frightened nun.

He'd thought he'd imagined the blue-eyed nun boarding the car that morning, but as the day wore on and his hangover began to ease off, he could not get her off his mind. When the train stopped at noon, he'd concocted a scheme to walk through the coach compartment, just to put his mind at ease, and found her feigning sleep. He might have been fooled, but for the nervous flutter of black lashes trying to stay closed over a cheek that had been scratched by her tumble in the *huisache*—a cheek that still bore a faint red line as it healed. Without sufficient excuse to disturb her, he'd returned to his own car to figure out what to do with the girl that kept turning up like the proverbial bad penny.

"There! There he is, Carlos!"

Tristan turned at the high-pitched shout to see the older of the nuns charging down the street toward them like a mother hen ready to defend her chicks. At her side were two uniformed men carrying guns, bayonets flashing in the lantern light as they came to a halt and aimed them at him and Mateo.

"Put up your hands, *amigos,* and let the sisters go!"

A heavier-set man, no doubt their commanding officer, caught up with them, panting heavily. "For shame, *señores*, accosting the sisters of the church!"

"That is the one of which I told you, Carlos! He has threatened this poor child and driven her to seek our protection!"

The man's face became puzzled. "She is not a nun?"

"She is Doña Elena De Costa of Casa Valencia!"

Marianna seized the moment. "I want these men arrested! They abducted me and only by God's grace was I able to escape their clutches until now!" she charged, pointing an accusing finger at the still Ranger. Reinforced by the guns trained on him, she slapped him again. "I will never marry you! *Never!*"

Tristan's jaw clenched, his cold gaze driving her back a step. "Mat, you better do some talking," he grated out to the side where his partner stood with raised hands.

"Sergeant, I am certain that I can explain this, if we might go to your headquarters," Mateo Salizar spoke up. They didn't dare reveal their true purpose in being there, at least not in public. Never in his days had he seen such a troublesome creature as Elena De Costa!

"My aunt has already explained, *señor,* and I am shocked that a fellow Mexican would be involved with such a man as this. However," the man stipulated with an accommodating smile, "you and your friend are invited to spend the night in our jail and spare your purses."

Tristan flinched at the prick of the bayonet at his back and glared at Marianna. "You better think this over, Elena. I'm going to make your fiancé look like a saint if I ever get out of this one."

Marianna lifted her chin haughtily. "You already do, cousin."

"Do you wish to make charges against these men, *señorita?*"

113

"But of course! What must I do?"

"You have only but to verify the story my aunt told me. Perhaps we might step inside where it is cool and do so over something to nourish our thirst."

With one last parting glance at the two men being ushered at gunpoint down the street, Marianna took the offered arm of the junior officer of the guard and went into the tavern, followed by her guardian angels in gray. Once again she went through the story of how she had fled the ardent attentions of her fiancé, only to run into her cousin who also sought her hand.

"That is very understandable of him, considering your beauty, *señorita*, but unforgivable, nevertheless!"

"While I had been sent to a convent by the first, sir, the gringo had me placed in a jail until I changed my mind about marrying him! That is why I wish him to be jailed. Perhaps it will teach him a lesson!" Marianna sniffed self-righteously.

"Then you do not wish for him to stand trial for kidnapping?"

Marianna shook her head. "I only want *him* to think so. Once I am safe with my family, I will send a wire for you to release him." Upon seeing the official's skeptical frown, she added hastily. "With a generous reward for your trouble."

"*Señorita*, you are certain that you feel not the slightest bit of consideration for this man?" Sister Rosa questioned perceptively.

"Could you feel anything but contempt for one who locked you in a jail, dragged you through the wilderness, and threatened to have you hanged if you did not marry him?" She placed her hand over that of the sergeant. "A *very* generous reward, sergeant. Now, how might I go about getting a room for the night and a change of clothes. Thanks to your aunt and cousin, I have no need to travel as a nun any longer."

Once she returned to Casa Valencia as Elena De Costa, she would not run away in panic at the sight of the man who had haunted her dreams, terrifying her in the night, since she was a child. Dressed as the lady she had been raised to be, she would play his game of cat and mouse until she was close enough to end her nightmare once and for all. As for the Ranger, he too was due a taste of his own justice, and she intended to see that he got a *full* dose.

"But Salizar just told you, our mission is a secret!" Tristan ranted in frustration after the sergeant returned to question them. "We can't tell every red-white-and-blue-uniformed yahoo with a bayonet what we are about, except to say that both our governments are behind it."

The sergeant shrugged and turned away from the outraged Texan, preferring to deal with his more sedate companion. "Then, if all is as you said, you should have no problem with waiting for such confirmation from your superiors in the south to come. Until then, I will do all I can to make you as comfortable as possible."

"That could take days, sergeant!" Mateo exclaimed in equal exasperation upon seeing that the man did not believe any such confirmation would be forthcoming.

The officer sat down at his desk and helped himself to a liberal helping of some beans a girl had brought in from the tavern for his supper. "So you are not really this Tristan De Costa my aunt says was captured by the Indians years ago?"

Tristan came to his feet, his patience expended. "I am

De Costa and I'll have you skinned alive when you find out the mistake you've made.

The man was unimpressed. "Your cousin, she is very pretty."

"Not to mention conniving and an adept liar."

"Where is your *capitán?*" Mateo interrupted, thinking to move up a step in the line of command to someone not so easily duped by a hysterical female.

"He is away at a wedding. He will be back sometime next week."

Tristan pushed away from the bars with an irritated groan to stare at the mats lying over a bed of straw that was their accommodations for the night. He'd kill her! He'd choke her with his bare hands until those blue eyes popped out on her porcelain cheeks. How could Manolo have let her go? *Unless he didn't.*

"Are we to dine this night, or is starving the prisoners part of our punishment?" Mateo inquired wryly.

"Your supper is coming, thanks to the good heart of your friend's cousin. She said to tell you it's a special dish . . . a Spanish supper, she called it." The sergeant grinned. "I hear the food from Spain is very good."

Tristan slid down the mud wall to his haunches with a muttered curse that drew his companion's attention. "I hope she brings plenty of water. My mouth is so dry, I need scissors to spit!" The woman was a witch, he thought acidly, a walking, breathing, vengeful, little witch!

But when Marianna walked into the jail later, when the only light in the room was provided by a lantern hanging on the wall, she looked more like a breath of spring than a shriveled hag. Gone was her nun's habit, and in its place was a colorful embroidered skirt, dark blue with bright red, yellow, and green flowers bordering the fringed hem. A plain white blouse with a ruffled neckline held up by a tasseled draw string, tied in a bow where it dipped between her breasts, hung off white shoulders that were marred only by the fading scratches from her fall into the hog wallow.

She tossed back the heavy dark cloak of silken tresses that fell forward as she held out her hand to the sergeant. He took it to his lips with all the gallantry of the caballeros, bubbling with compliments over the change in her. She'd left the bath, provided as compliments of the house at the sergeant's request, for Sister Teresa to enjoy before taking her fill of the most delicious meal she had had in weeks. It was hardly the fine cuisine to which she was accustomed, but it was hearty, filling, and delicious, just the same. Two canteens swung from her other hand as she turned to face the prisoners.

"Where is their supper, *señorita?*" the sergeant asked as they clinked together with a dull metal ring.

Marianna pasted on a bright smile. "Why, right here, *monsieur*. It is the same that the gringo fed me while camped in the wilderness when there was fresh pork to be had only yards from us. I only think it fitting, don't you?"

If she intended to get a rise from the tight-lipped Ranger whose heated glower she could feel through the bars, Marianna was disappointed. Instead, he simmered, like a pot with a tight lid ready to boil over at any moment. Except that this time, it was he who was helpless, locked behind bars. Her smile widened, reassured, and she passed the canteens through to the silent men.

"Now you know how you made me feel, cousin."

Tristan ignored her taunt. "What did you do to Benevides?"

"The colonel?" Marianna asked with an innocent rise of brow. "He is well, but for a little headache and some

117

wounded pride," she told him lowly, not wanting the Mexican standing in the doorway to overhear.

"*Señorita, por favor!*" Mateo intervened over Tristan's hissing oath. "Do you not know the danger you put yourself in, not to mention us? Why did you not flee to Mexico City?"

"And save us all a lot of headache. Of course, if she gets herself killed, she wouldn't keep turning up on us," Tristan philosophized with a look that ran Marianna through. "Then, when we get out, we can do what we came to do and I'll get the mines all to myself. After all, they killed that man in the jail, not to mention that poor bastard that had been dragged. Now me, I can take care of myself, because I have enough sense to know the kind of man I'm dealing with."

Marianna's eyes flashed. They were trying to frighten her again. "You are little better than he is!" She swung away loftily and looked over her shoulder with a dip of lashes that curled hot in the lower part of Tristan's stomach, changing rage into something just as intense, making him feel more helpless than ever behind the bars. "Enjoy your Spanish supper, *monsieurs. Buenas noches.*"

Chapter Seven

As Marianna made her way back to the inn, she was quite pleased with herself. Not only was she now free and clear to go on to Casa Valencia without the interference of the Ranger, but his insufferable treatment of her had been avenged beyond her wildest dreams. The very sight of him simmering behind bars had almost made her laugh outright. Although, if by some chance he should get free before she planned, her situation would lose some of its humor, she realized with a shudder. She would have to move in on Victor Romero quickly . . . or, suffice it to say, permit him to move in on her *on her own terms.*

The inn was in an uproar when she entered. Most of the occupants were gathered around the stairwell that rose to the second floor, where two soldiers struggled to make their way through them. The men broke free of the curious crowd just as Marianna reached them.

"Is something wrong, *señores?*"

Her smile distracted them from their pressing duty long enough to receive an assuring answer that did little to assuage the tiny spark of alarm that flashed instinctively in Marianna's mind. "Nothing that Juan and I can not take care of, *señorita,*" the younger of the two announced boldly with a gallant bow. "Two men burst into an upstairs room and tried to abduct a nun from her bath. They can not be far."

"Did they harm her?"

The other soldier, who realized the reason his partner was detained, joined them. "She is only frightened. Apparently they were looking for someone else."

Noting the color that drained from sun-kissed cheeks, the first gallant took her hand. "If you would but tell us your name, *señorita,* Juan and I will be honored to watch outside your door after we are off duty to ensure the safety of such a lovely woman."

Marianna assembled her shaken composure and lifted her chin with resolve. She should have known better than to have felt so secure in her success. But how could Romero's men have known where she was? She was certain they would think she'd fled back to Mexico City. "That won't be necessary, *señor,* if you catch the scoundrels. I pray that you do."

"Lancers!"

"Señorita!"

Marianna glanced upward to see Sister Rosa at the banister rail as the soldiers, reminded of their duty not only by her, but by a corporal standing next to the woman, hastily retreated. Hand clutched to her chest, Marianna made her way through the curious onlookers to the second floor where Sister Rosa enveloped her in a smothering hug.

"I was so worried! *Gracias a Dios* that the soldiers were having their supper here when the men burst into our room."

"Sister Teresa?" Marianna managed tautly.

"Is dressing," Sister Rosa told her. "And to think that I too was going to take a bath! I shall not part with my clothing until I am safe within the walls of the convent.

It's blasphemous! I've sent for my nephew. He'll post a guard and send an escort with us tomorrow."

Marianna exhaled heavily, pinpricks of fear over the growing danger of her situation assaulting her spine. "I doubt that will stop Romero's men."

"Whose men?"

Realizing that she'd voiced her thoughts, Marianna stepped closer, whispering for the nun's ears only. "Let's go inside where we can talk. Besides, I want to apologize to Sister Teresa for involving her in this."

Her humor no longer smug at all, Marianna followed Sister Rosa into the small corner room she had secured for the night where Sister Teresa, now garbed in the plain and voluminous folds of her habit, struggled to untangle her short wet locks of hair with a comb. Dark eyes met Marianna's instantly.

"They were looking for the De Costa woman."

"I feared as much," Marianna responded candidly. She walked over to the window to peer out into the back alley. There was no sign of anyone, aside from one of the maids from downstairs who threw out scraps from the kitchen to two scrawny mongrels with wagging tails.

Maybe she should have taken the train toward Mexico City. But surely Romero's men would have found her on that route as well. The truth was, she wasn't safe anywhere. Not in Mexico or in Texas where she was wanted for stealing a horse. She clutched her shoulders as if taken with a chill and shivered. Now others were endangered by her plans. It was bad enough to risk her own life, but she would take no others with her.

"I'm sorry I involved you two in this. I had no idea those men would go so far. I would never forgive myself if either of you were hurt."

"My nephew will protect us," Sister Rosa announced assuredly.

"They have already killed two men who crossed their paths," Marianna objected. "I don't want anyone else hurt. Tomorrow *you* go with the escort. I'll find another away."

"And who will protect you?" Sister Teresa fretted softly.

Marianna continued to stare out into the darkness. She couldn't panic . . . not this time. If they carried her to Don Victor, they would take her gun. If she went of her own accord, he would never expect her to be armed, particularly if she invited his attentions. But how would she get close enough with his men lurking in every shadow?

"Perhaps she should have married this cousin of hers. At least *he* is family, and he certainly looks fierce enough to fight Satan himself." As if stricken with remorse for her slanderous comment, Sister Rosa crossed herself and added magnanimously, "And he was generous to the poor."

"And he is handsome." Upon seeing Marianna's skeptical reaction, Sister Teresa pointed out quickly. *"You* did not see the way he looked at you when you pretended to be asleep, like a father looking at his precocious child in angelic repose."

"That is why I asked you if there were not some personal feelings towards him," Sister Rosa inserted, watching Marianna's face carefully.

Marianna schooled her features in indifference. "Had you seen him this evening, Sisters, you would not even hint that there was a tender bone in his body where I am concerned. Besides," she wavered thoughtfully, "even if there was, what good would it do?"

"He appears to be the least distasteful of the two devils who seek your hand," Sister Rosa answered practically, "and I am certain that Doña Inez would be delighted to have two of the babes she reared marry. That boy and his sister were a delight to her, as I recall, just as you were when you came along to lighten her grief over losing them to the savages."

Perhaps the idea was not so absurd. Marianna considered it cautiously. The Ranger was used to risking his life. He was going to Casa Valencia to do just that. He needn't know her purpose, which would conclude his own mission in the end. If they went together . . .

"Or we could pretend to be married until—" Marianna broke off before confessing her murderous intentions, only to be reprimanded sharply.

"Holy wedlock is not to be taken lightly, child. The gringo has compromised your honor by your own admission. He is family and has offered marriage rather than attempted to have you killed as you feared he might. Frankly, I think there is more to this than is being revealed."

Marianna shifted under the sharp gaze of the nun. But if she agreed to let Tristan McCulloch out of jail, he would choke her to death with his bare hands, not marry her. Yet, there was some logic to the sister's line of thinking. Right now, the cards were in her hand. If she could figure out some way to keep them there . . .

Lowering her head, more to avoid giving herself away than to feign shame, Marianna admitted in a rueful tone, "There is, Sister. I should have known better than to try to fool someone as perceptive as yourself. I've been very foolish, I'm afraid."

The story that came out, interwoven with shreds of truth, was more fantastic than any of her previous creations. Even as Marianna walked with leaden feet toward the jail with the two sisters and the sergeant, who had been immediately summoned by his imperious aunt the moment Marianna finished telling of the lovers' squabble that had led her to this end, she could not conceive that it would work. Yet it had to. Even if she had to cling to the gringo's knees and kiss his dusty boots, it had to.

"Do not worry, *señorita*. I am certain that when the gringo sees how truly repentant you are, he will see the error of his ways as well," Sister Teresa consoled her, noting the way Marianna wrung her hands and hesitated outside the jail. "I think this is all so romantic!"

With a foreboding that smacked of walking to an execution, Marianna preceded the sergeant into the dimly lit jail. She had convinced everyone else that Tristan De Costa was not only her cousin, but the true love for whom she'd run away from Romero to marry. Then, after a silly quarrel, she said, she had left him, only to be pursued. All she needed to do now was convince him to go along with it.

"Wake up, *señores!* One of you is a lucky man that this angel has agreed to forgive you for the way you treated her and accept your proposal."

Marianna stood back timidly as the sergeant raked the bars with his keys, bringing the stirring men inside the cell to their feet, brushing away the straw of their bedding.

The Ranger was the first to appear at the bars, his expression revealing, even in the dim light, that his disposition had not improved. "What the hell are you talking about, *amigo?*"

"Your fiancé," the sergeant explained patiently, as much caught up in the romance of the situation as the two sisters. After all, the De Costas were a noble family. Who was to say when the couple was happily wedded and bedded that a reward might not be in the coming to one who helped them get that way?

"My *what?*" the Ranger exploded, his face taking on

a thunderous and accusing look that turned on Marianna. "What are you up to now?"

Why her knees did not buckle, Marianna didn't know. She could actually feel the force of his anger across the distance between them. Somehow she managed to approach the golden-haired thunder god with a calm demeanor she was far from feeling.

"It is all right, my love. I have told them about us. Sister Rosa has but to send for the priest to end this nightmare and set you free to go on to Casa Valencia. You have only to do the honorable thing, which was our intentions to begin with before this silly quarrel." Uncertain that she would come back with her hand still attached to her body, Marianna reached through the bars and stroked the taut bristled jaw of the Texan staring down at her as if she lost her mind. "You do wish to go on to Casa Valencia, do you not, Tristan?"

Treestan. The way she said his name rippled through him like nimble fingers plucking at the strings of harp and diffusing the rage that seethed within. The truth was, he'd not been able to sleep since he'd heard that someone had broken into his cousin's room at the inn in an attempt to abduct her. Of course, he'd told himself that he didn't want anyone to deny him the personal privilege of strangling her lovely neck for her trickery. Yet, even now, he wondered what her skin felt like, warm and smooth beneath his fingers.

"Of course he does, *señorita!* The sooner you two are married, the sooner we might all go about our business," Mateo Salizar spoke up, catching onto Marianna's ploy and attempting to underscore them for his annoyed companion.

"Married!" Tristan exclaimed, snapping out of his reverie. "Who said anything about marriage?" Blue eyes seemed to reach through the bars with icy claws and freeze Marianna's chest, preventing her from breathing in or out. "Why the bloody blazes should I marry *you!*"

The derision in Tristan's tone fired a spark of indignation in the equally blue eyes that snapped in response. "If the fact that you have comprised my honor is not enough, Tristan De Costa, consider the fact that you pledged your love to me and asked me for my hand! And if *that* is not enough," she declared boldly, clasping the front of his shirt and rising up on tiptoe, "then there is *this!*"

Never in her life had she initiated a kiss with a member of the opposite sex, at least in the seductive sense that she attempted now. Marianna was accustomed to being pursued and, for the most part, tolerating an ardent suitor's attentions. Yet, this time she exercised all her experience, gained both personally and vicariously through the romance novels she and Elena kept hidden under their mattresses. She even borrowed from the gringo's own parting kiss in Presidio that had left her warm and quivering inside with foreign emotions that were decidedly disconcerting.

That they came rushing back shocked her as much as the fact that, somehow in the timeless embrace that suddenly enveloped her, pressing her to the cold bars that could not diminish the inviting warmth of the male body straining against them from the other side, he began to kiss her back. Blood pounded through her veins, echoing in her ears until coherent thought was as impossible to summon as resistance to the offense that had been so masterfully turned on her.

"And if you are to get to Casa Valencia, this is what you must do." The warning had been preprogrammed to come out and did just that, on a sigh meant for the ears of the Ranger only, just as his reply was meant solely for her.

"If I have to get married, I intend to do more than this."

Marianna swayed in the arms that held her imprisoned against the bars and blinked blankly at the handsome face pressed between them. Suddenly his answer registered in the warm fog that clouded her thoughts and she reeled away, a rush of scarlet fire singeing her face until it stung with heat. She winced as the Ranger raised his voice, a devious smile tugging at one corner of his lips.

"Send for the priest, *amigos!*"

"Doña Inez will be so pleased!" Sister Rosa averred, her hands clasped in front of her in delight at her part in the affair. A grand wedding at Casa Valencia would have been more appropriate, but after witnessing that kiss, she was certain that a prompt ceremony was in order, if not a necessity. An heir delivered a month or so early would be scandalous and the couple had spent more than one night together alone.

Marianna suffered another smothering hug and smiled weakly. What had she done? Tristan De Costa McCulloch was far more dangerous than Victor Romero. Romero only aroused contempt and hatred in her. The Ranger, on the other hand, stirred emotions she found difficult to manage.

Animal emotions, she decided, taking the seat the sergeant offered her with a distracted glance toward the cell where Tristan and Mateo Salizar were talking in low tones, casting an occasional glance in her direction. She, on the other hand, was civilized. The way to deal with animals was to be firm with them, to let them know who was in charge. If the Ranger gave her a difficult time, she would expose him to Romero. That was her high card with him, once he was her husband. As for Romero, the advantage of a husband like Tristan

127

gave her protection and, at the same time, the freedom to entice the bandit leader to his death.

The priest was rustled out of bed and the sergeant's wife came in with an armload of hastily cut flowers from her garden. Sister Teresa carefully wove a wreath of them, taking care to break the thorns off the roses before placing it on Marianna's head. All the while, the groom, who had withdrawn to his cot where he took in the proceedings in a sullen silence, was kept locked in his cell, lest he change his mind. Even when the ceremony started, the presence of armed guards with rifles and bayonets ready reflected the sergeant's distrust of the giant gringo who stoically pledged his eternal love to her in a tone that belied his words.

Marianna felt sick, physically ill, as she repeated her vows numbly. One source of her malady stemmed from the sheer mockery of the ceremony taking place. Not only did the gringo's words ring false, they promised a terrible retribution, reinforced by a cold steel gaze that would not leave her face for a moment's reprieve. The other cause of her distress resulted from the only thing she could summon to give her the courage to go through with her hastily conjured plan.

Although she met Tristan's gaze equally, the replay of her mother's death flashed through her mind, superimposing itself on the proceedings with all the horror Marianna had felt as a child. A cold sweat filmed her forehead and her hands grew damp, folded within the rough ones of the man being pronounced her husband before God and the witnesses. As lips that possessed a strange power over her lowered to claim her as a lifetime partner, it was not them that she saw, but those of her mother, pleading with her to be silent . . .

A small trickle of life-draining blood seeped out the corner as they became still and Marianna screamed, ever so careful to do so silently, lest the bad men find her and her mother die in vain. Every fiber of her being cried out in protest of the nightmare that suddenly blocked out reality, in spite of the strong, somehow reassuring arms that caught her and held her tightly. She stared up unseeing, yet seeing too much. It was real, so real. What echoed in her mind like the screams of a thousand banshees emerged as a tiny strangled sound, muffled by lips that grew suddenly still. With a terror that would not leave her be, Marianna retreated, not physically, but emotionally, seeking the blackness that promised sanctuary from all thought, all emotion, all fear.

Tristan caught the full weight of the girl as she collapsed beneath the retaliatory kiss he'd dealt her, thinking she'd devised yet another game. One look at her ashen face and the fear-stricken eyes that rolled upward in unconsciousness, however, told him that this was not make-believe like the wedding that had just come to a conclusion, but very real. Bewildered by the increasingly complex and confusing creature whom he swept up like a babe in his arms, he glanced at the sergeant.

"Am I to take my wife into the cell for our wedding night?"

"But of course not! I will personally arrange for a room at the inn!" The sergeant's grin wavered as he took in Marianna's deathlike pallor. "She is all right?"

"I don't think she expected to catch me so easily," Tristan retorted dryly. "What we have here is a nervous bride." Who had a lot of explaining to do, he thought grimly, permitting the sisters to slap the girl's cheeks gently in an attempt to bring her around.

The inn was full with the arrival of the train, so the nuns offered to give up the room the sergeant had secured for them to the newlyweds and share another with some women travelers who could not secure private rooms with their spouses. Leaving his unconscious bride to the care of the sisters, Tristan joined Mateo downstairs for the first opportunity to speak to his partner alone.

"Congratulations, *amigo!* I am not so sure that I envy you tomorrow and the days after, but I do envy you tonight."

Irritated with the delight his friend had taken in the absurd affair, Tristan grumbled a short "Go to hell!" and ordered a strong whiskey.

He didn't like being maneuvered, which was exactly what Elena De Costa had done to him . . . nor did he cotton to the protective instincts she managed to arouse in him in spite of her calculating intervention in his life.

"So what are we going to do with her? She can only get in the way at Casa Valencia."

"I'm going to send her back to her family in Mexico City on the next train headed in that direction. Let *them* deal with her," Tristan answered tersely.

Mateo waited for elaboration and, when it didn't come, inquired tongue-in-cheek, "And just how do you intend to get your bride's cooperation?"

"It doesn't make sense, Mat," Tristan went on, ignoring his friend's humor at his expense. "She said she was running from Romero. Now she's doing everything within her power to walk right back into his clutches. Yet, she doesn't want to marry him . . . obviously." He downed the drink, his brow creased in confusion. "So what is she after?"

Mateo shook his head in sympathy. "She has gotten under your skin, no? Surely you can see that it is her inheritance that she is after! By marrying you, she will have it all."

"She'd have had it all anyway."

"But *she* did not know that."

Tristan digested this while his glass was refilled. Maybe Mat was right. The girl realized that she couldn't get rid of him, that she might even need him to protect her from Romero. What better way than to force him to marry her to keep the money in the family? She was resourceful, he had to give her that.

He swilled the liquor in the glass, eyes narrowing. It was just as clear as his whiskey! Maybe his conniving cousin had affected him more than he was willing to admit. Which made it all the more important to send her packing to Mexico City, out of harm's way and out of his hair. "We're going to need to contact someone we can trust to escort her back to her parents."

Mateo shrugged. "I will do what I can. This is not my territory. In the meanwhile, it appears to me that you are going to have to do some serious convincing to your bride."

A wicked smile tugged at the corners of Tristan's mouth. *"Amigo,* after tonight, she'll jump at the chance to go to hell rather than move on to Casa Valencia with me."

"Then I take it that you do not intend to honor the wedding."

"Take it anyway you want, *compadre,* but when I do get around to marrying, it won't be to some calculating, money-hungry little bitch." Tristan finished off his drink and shoved away from the table. *"I'll* do my own tracking, trapping, *and* asking. Meanwhile, treat the folks to a few rounds, compliments of the new bridegroom. If we're going to tug at Romero's britches, it might as well be noticeable."

Mateo chuckled. "I will give them a love story that will bring tears to their eyes."

"It damn near has mine," Tristan muttered grudgingly as he turned toward the steps leading to his wedding chamber with the just-opened whiskey bottle in hand. Not that he intended to drink it. He needed a clear head to deal with his new bride. She'd hoodwinked him one time too many. But he had an image to maintain as a heavy drinker with more brawn and coin than brains. *"Buenas noches, amigo!"* His bellowed good-night quieted the general chatter of the crowded room until only the music of a single guitarist who was accompanied by a *señorita* playing a gourd in the corner could be heard. "Here's to an heir for Casa Valencia!" Tristan raised the bottle to his lips and gulped down a significant swallow, judging from the unpolished sound he made. Actually only a trickle burned his throat. It was some of the worst rotgut he'd ever ingested. "Hell's bells, maybe we'll make two!" he added, as if struck by a better idea. "Twins run in the family. To twins!"

"Drinks for everyone, compliments of the bridegroom!" Mateo Salizar chimed in, earning more of a round of applause than Tristan's bold toast.

From the confines of her honeymoon suite, Marianna pretended not to notice the uproar, let alone the crudely announced anticipation of her new husband. Nonetheless, from the pink flush on Sister Teresa's cheeks as she turned back the bed and the indignant snort from Sister Rosa as she pivoted away abruptly from combing out Marianna's hair, it had definitely been heard. Her stomach churned upon hearing loud booted steps on the staircase that forewarned of her new husband's approach.

"Sister Teresa and I must leave," Sister Rosa sympathetically informed her as a knock sounded loudly on the door.

Marianna plucked the voluminous cotton nightdress that the sergeant's wife had found for her away from her damp breast and wished it were the dead of winter. Yet she doubted even that would stop the nervous perspiration from trekking down the small of her back. Thank heaven the nuns had been present when she'd fainted. Otherwise, she might have awakened at the mercy of her new husband, perhaps even been ravished while she was unconscious!

"You look like an angel," Sister Teresa told her, planting an affectionate peck on her cheek as the older nun opened the door in the midst of the second round of knocking.

"We heard you the first time, *señor,* and no doubt so did the rest of the town. If you can, I would suggest that you try to recall the genteel upbringing you had before the savages carried you off. It would serve you better this night, I suspect."

Marianna's eyes widened as the tall blonde giant grinned and lifted the nun's hand to his lips. "Thank you for the advice, Sister. Although, and I mean no disrespect," he inserted with that lazy drawl of his, "what the blazes would you know of such things?"

Marianna flinched at Sister Rosa's indignant gasp and groaned inwardly. He was uncouth, with no regard for the church! The last she saw of the elder nun was the flying tail of her robes as she fled past the man with her younger charge in tow, abandoning Marianna to her fate. Avoiding the amused gaze that swung her way, she instantly took up the brush and attacked her shimmering raven locks with a fervor that unwittingly betrayed her nervousness.

"Well, well, this does have possibilities." The brush froze in midstroke as two long strides closed the distance between them and the bottle was thrust down on the table in front of her. "Join me in a drink, *wife?*"

Taking a deep breath to steady her hand, Marianna

put the brush on the table next to the bottle. "You know, as well as I, that this is a farce for us both, undertaken only to accomplish our different goals."

"Goals?"

"You wished to be out of jail to proceed to Casa Valencia. I wish to protect my interests," she told him crisply. She pointed over to a small loveseat under the window. "You may sleep there."

The responding laugh to her declaration did little to settle her nerves. "I told you I expected more than a kiss out of this, Frenchie, and I always mean what I say." Tristan cupped his hands on her shoulders, feeling the tightness coil there as she stiffened. But she did not pull away as he expected.

"And so do I, *monsieur.*" How Marianna managed to smile, let alone find the strength to rise from her bench, she would never know. Yet, she did exactly that, turning to placidly face the man taunting her. "Should you choose to test me, I promise that I will put up such a fight that all of Chihuahua will know that you are not the happy groom you pretended to be down the stairs."

Tristan stepped back to let her past, admiring the shape that was outlined by the lamp on the bedside table as she approached the side that had been turned back and dropped to her knees. With hands folded in front of her, she looked the image of an angel. Intrigued, he watched her lips moving silently, remembering the sweet taste of them. Suddenly he shook himself. A few moments more and he'd be eating out of her hand. The fact was, she was no angel and it was time to give the devil his due—or hers, in this case.

Her eyelids fluttered when he stripped off his shirt and dropped it on the floor at his feet, revealing that she was aware of his every move in spite of her attempt to appear the praying saint. His boots came next, landing

134

with two consecutive thuds next to the shirt. She started with the first, peeking to see what he was about, and braced for the second. Tristan found himself smiling. He always was one for a challenge and his cousin certainly could be called that.

It was hard to think of her as having Luis De Costa's evil blood coursing through her veins, with her head bowed, madonna-like, in undoubtedly feigned prayer. It was just as difficult to recall that her father's blood stained his hands when he'd sensed the woman responding to his kiss in a way that sent his body reeling with an all-male reaction. That contrary combination of innocence and treachery made her more dangerous than a roused rattler.

"Now, why should I care whether or not the world knows that my bride is a tempestuous lover given to loud tantrums?" he asked, walking around behind her. He began to massage her shoulders gently. "Maybe I should simply smother you with kisses until you beg for more."

His hand slid down her arms as she climbed to her feet and turned within the closing circle of his arms. "You flatter yourself, *monsieur*," she responded laconically. "You must first get close enough to me, which I think is not wise with this between us."

The cold press of metal against his bare abdomen kept Tristan from locking his arms about the girl as he'd intended. He glanced down to see a six-gun of the sort Manolo Benevides wore, with mother-of-pearl handles inlaid with silver. A curse erupted in his brain, but he was not fool enough to voice it.

"Now put up your hands and back away so that I might get some rest."

"Do you always pack a pistol in the folds of your nightgown?"

"Only when there are wild animals about. *You* taught me that," she informed him with a satisfied tilt of her lips.

"It wouldn't help you any to shoot your husband, you know."

"Nor would it do you any good, *monsieur,* so please . . . take the loveseat and let us both get some sleep."

Marianna settled on the mattress, the gun poised in front of her as Tristan unbuckled his gunbelt slowly. "I would not object to you keeping that close-by, *monsieur.* Those men might try to come back."

A golden brow arched in surprise. "How do you know I won't shoot you in your sleep."

"You may be an animal in some ways, but you are a man of the law. You would not shoot a woman."

More bemused than ever, Tristan dropped onto the loveseat . . . . at least, part of him did. His legs hung off, threatening his delicate balance so that if he relaxed, he might find himself in a heap on the floor. Muttering under his breath, he got up and brought over a chair to prop up his feet. Aware that his bride had bolted upright again and waved her pistol at him he settled back down on the uncomfortable makeshift bed.

Through half-lidded eyes he fixed his gaze on her. After a few wary moments, the girl returned to rest against the pillows, unaware of the way her hair fanned out about her face and shoulders, a raven halo of silk, more enticing than he cared to admit. Her wide blue eyes stared at the ceiling, waiting for sleep to claim them— and when it did, he intended to be ready to teach her a richly deserved lesson.

Chapter Eight

Treated to the first real bed she'd slept in in days, Marianna still could not close her eyes. Each time she heard footsteps on the stairs, she sat up warily and watched the door, listening for them to draw nearer. When the two mongrels that had feasted behind the cantina earlier began to bark, she quietly slipped from the bed and tiptoed to the window so as not to disturb the hulk of a Ranger sleeping on the loveseat under it. As she suspected, there was an intruder in the alley, but it was of a canine variety, an equally mangy dog who challenged the others' territory.

Her gun hand fell to her side in relief and she leaned against the wall, waiting for her heart to resume a normal pace. How long could a night be? she wondered, swallowing the lump of fear that had lodged in her throat. Inadvertently her gaze moved to the Ranger sprawled awkwardly before her, his bare chest moving up and down rhythmically in repose. Some help he was! He'd consumed so much whiskey, the commotion outside hadn't even stirred him.

Her attention was drawn to his face where an arm lay carelessly thrown over his eyes to block out the moonlight shining in through the open window. The lips that played havoc with her senses were relaxed, generous and inviting, instead of thinned with disapproval or twisted in mockery as they usually were. Not quite a pout, she decided, unconsciously moistening her own with her tongue, as if to recall the manly possession with which he'd claimed them earlier.

He had a dimple in his chin. She hadn't noticed that before. But then, this was the first time she'd actually had the chance to study him without suffering some sort of retaliation that would lead to embarrassment, if not humiliation. Animal, she reflected with reluctant admiration, taking in the rugged plains of his chest, furred with a golden mass that caught the moonlight and bathed in its glow. His lean torso consisted of muscle engaging muscle, entwined in perfection with graceful lines that few sculptors managed to capture in stone.

Marianna tore her gaze from the narrowing line of fur that dipped below his waistline where the indentation of a navel peeked wickedly at her. Suddenly aware of an animal heat that, until meeting the yellow-haired gringo, had been foreign to her, she wiped away the film of perspiration that had formed on her brow. An angry shout from below—someone else had been awakened by the fighting mongrels—gave her a start, sending her hand to her mouth to stifle the small gasp that was generated there.

Irritably, she scowled at her companion. Some protection she'd chosen, she thought, infusing contempt into the warm quandary of her thoughts. Not only were his guns on the floor, out of easy reach, but he was practically deaf! She walked over to where the gunbelt lay and concentrated on moving it closer to the loveseat, just in case. To her dismay, one of the pistols worked its way loose, forcing her to bend over to return it to its place.

Lips thinning in disgust, Marianna squatted, her own gun resting on her hip, when suddenly it was snatched from her grasp with lighting speed. Before she could react, the relaxed body she'd but moments before admired rolled off the sofa and onto the floor, taking her with it. Although her hair spilled over her face, blinding her, she struck out at her assailant with both fists, trying to move his heavy weight off her as he scrambled to catch her wrists. When that did not work, she tried to gain sufficient leverage with her legs to throw him off, but, to her dismay, his body settled between them, driving home her vulnerability with devastating effect.

"What do you think you are doing?" she hissed, shaking the raven tresses free of her face to glare up at him.

"It's called getting even, Frenchie. The way I see it, I've got you just about where I want you. The bed would be nicer, but never let it be said I didn't meet you halfway."

Marianna gasped and turned her face away as he lowered his head, but, instead of claiming her lips as she anticipated, he nipped at the erect peak of a breast, thinly covered with cotton. A flash of white heat erupted deep within her, giving rise to yet another sound, one of surprise, mingled with pleasure and a less-intense protest. Just the anticipation that preceded the equal treatment of the other, the hot damp prelude of his breath penetrating her gown, made her shudder beneath him. As it too was seized between white even teeth, a hand tugged roughly at the ribbon that held her gown chastely in place, quickly shoving the material aside to cup the swollen mound of pliant flesh beneath.

Realizing through the murky fog that assaulted her brain that at least one hand was free, Marianna brought it down sharply on his back. "I'll scream!" she warned, her breath ragged and rendering her threat as ineffective as her assault. Her second blow glanced off his ear. In desperation to survive the melting process that threatened all resistance, she grabbed it and twisted it vengefully until the mind-boggling attack ceased.

"You little . . . !"

Her wrist was immediately recaptured, and the only satisfaction Marianna received was the pained curse that erupted as Tristan yanked her hand away to pin it over her head once again. The friction between their bodies as he slipped upward to punish her lips with his own strangled her objection, turning the resistance of the legs that kicked to dislodge him into an embrace of surrender.

Twisting her face away, so that the sensitive spot on her neck behind her ear took the brunt of his attack, she managed breathlessly, "If you do this, you will be forced to spend the rest of your life with me. Surely you do not wish that!"

The words had the effect of a bucket of creek water on the Ranger, who threw himself away from her and rolled to his feet almost in one single motion. Cooled more by the sudden abandonment, which somehow was as stinging as it was satisfying, Marianna hastily rearranged her bodice with her back to the man and struggled to regain her composure. When she turned back, her quickly assembled reproach froze on the tip of her tongue, for instead of showing the least sign of remorse or discomfiture, Tristan stood gun in hand, his ear pressed to the door.

"What . . . ?"

Marianna's startled question died in her throat as he raised his finger to his lips. Instinctively she started to feel around for the gun she'd lost in the tumble. As she crawled about, feeling blindly in the shadow cast by the loveseat on the floor, her knees caught on her gown, rip-

140

ping the gathered body from the ribboned yoke with an earsplitting effect that once again drew the Ranger's unwanted attention. Even in the dim light, she could feel the sharp reproval in the glance afforded her and froze with the gaping remnant gathered to her chest. This time, she heard it: the creak of a floorboard outside the door.

Her hand flew to her mouth as Tristan suddenly pulled open the door and thrust his gun through, catching a small-framed Mexican in the belly with the barrel. The startled man threw up his hands and stumbled back drunkenly.

"Por Dios!" he cried out fearfully. "I am sorry, *señor*. I forgot which is my room." Although the wall was behind him, he wavered unsteadily on his feet. Even at a distance, Marianna could smell the liquor on him, mingled with that of unwashed body odor and tobacco.

"Señora . . ." he pleaded, peering past the suspicious Ranger at the girl on the floor. "It was a mistake. I have too much tequila . . ."

"That why you were lifting the latch so lightly?" Tristan challenged skeptically.

"I am sharing the room with others, *señor*. I was trying not to awaken them. Please, I am but a poor man on my way to visit my sister in Valencia." He pointed to a small purse tied to his belt. "Take my money. It is not much, but, I beg you, spare my life."

Tristan motioned the peasant away in disgust with a wave of his gun. "Next time I'll listen with this," he warned, eyes narrowing to drive his point home.

"There will be no next time, *señor*, I promise. *Gracias . . ."* he stammered in relief. *"A—adios!"*

Tristan watched until the man disappeared into one of the rooms further along the single corridor before closing the door and bolting it. His mouth pursed into a silent "Whew!" as he holstered his gun and sauntered over to where Marianna sat motionless, her torn gown clutched in her hand.

"Do you think he was telling the truth?"

"He had been drinking," Tristan admitted in a less-than-reassuring tone. A pang of guilt struck him upon catching a glimpse of a single tear making its way from eyes overwide with sheer terror. "But he's sober now," he added, lending a little more credence to his statement. "He won't be back."

He watched, more than a little puzzled, as Marianna curled up in a ball on the end of the loveseat, embracing her knees to her chest. If she was that frightened, why in the devil was she so stuck on going back to Valencia? "Look, Elena, I don't want your silver or Casa Valencia. You know why I'm going." He might as well get it out in the open since it didn't look like they were going to get any sleep. "I don't want anything to do with you. I only want Romero in the authorities' hands, plain and simple. Why don't you go back to your parents in Mexico City until Mat and I put him away?"

The toes that peeked out from under the ruffled hem of the gown disappeared as he lifted up the corner of the loveseat cushion and retrieved the pistol he'd shoved there. "Why should I trust *you!*" she accused, eyeing her lost weapon in despair. She had gravely underestimated him. She wouldn't make that mistake again. "You are a stranger—worse, a gringo! If our positions were changed around, would you trust me?"

The petulant purse of her lips was as intriguing as the defiance that managed to surface amidst the genuine fear and dismay in her swimming eyes. For one crazy second, Tristan was almost tempted to take her into his arms and try to win her trust. But a try was most likely all it would amount to, after that little episode on the floor.

He'd started out just to take her gun from her, maybe scare her a bit. After all, it was clear to him by the way she'd been bolting upright at the slightest noise that he didn't have to do much to accomplish the latter. But the softness of her feminine body yielding to his, in spite of her attempts to restrain the woman eager to be released to desire's abandon, and the little gasps of pleasure that overrode her protests, had been like fuel added to an already-raging fire.

"Well?"

Her challenge shook Tristan from the stirring thoughts that rekindled in a hot and physical sense in his loins. "No further than I could toss you, I guess," he admitted in a candor spawned by an attack of guilty conscience—rare where women were concerned, especially with tricksters like the one in front of him.

"Where are you going?" Marianna asked as he turned and strode toward the bed.

"Since you don't seem inclined to use this, there's no sense in both of us losing sleep. Besides," he said, hanging his gunbelt on the headboard, "I doubt there'll be any more excitement tonight unless some yahoo decides to climb up the drainpipe next to your window. So long as you stay down, I can pick them off from right here."

Marianna hadn't seen a drainpipe, but the Ranger was right about one thing. The bed was a waste for her. She couldn't close her eyes, even if she had to, for fear of the men outside, not to mention the one within. She waited until he settled back on her pillows before rising on the loveseat enough to see out the window. Aside from some vines that grew up the side of the building, she could see nothing that would aid an intruder in gaining access to their room . . . unless the pipe was hidden by the wide leafy foliage. For one fleeting second, it occurred to her to go to the bed where the gringo was now stretched out comfortably, but she changed her mind instantly, chagrined that the safest place in the room, in one sense, was the most dangerous, in another.

The next morning Tristan awakened to the crowing of a rooster and opened one eye to check on the girl who had climbed on her knees to peer out the window so many times that he'd finally become adjusted to her fidgeting and ignored it. Instead of seeing her curled in the curve of the loveseat as she had been the last time he checked on her, she was missing altogether. Lifting his head, he scanned the room, his pulse quickening with a dread that he might have driven her into doing something reckless.

He shouted her name as his feet struck the floor, his alarmed "Elena!" mingling with the sudden shriek that made him leap away from the spot where he'd landed. Unable to do more than stare in amazement, he watched as the hand he'd inadvertently landed on disappeared under the bed.

"My feenger is broke, you big booll!"

"What . . ." In spite of his initial worry, Tristan had a hard time restraining the slaphappy amusement that erupted as a result of too-little sleep. "What the bloody blazes are you doing under there?"

"Daamn you, Treestan MacCoolack! I h-hate you!"

Marianna did hate him. At that point, she hated the entire world. Exhaustion and frayed nerves tore at her, and she was enraged by the pain of the finger that was turning an unsightly bluish red. Tears she'd been holding back most of the night finally found a good reason for release and spilled down her cheeks, betrayed by a miserable sob that shook her shoulders.

"Elena, stop acting like a baby and come out from under there."

Marianna withdrew from the hand that reached under to coax her out. "I am not a baby! Put your finger down and let me step on it and see if it does not make you weep!" She slapped his hand away irritably. "Leave me b-be!"

"I'm sorry, Elena. Look, at least let me see your finger," Tristan reasoned with forced patience. "I want to make certain it's not broken."

"Or make certain that it is!"

"All right, suit yourself."

With a determined grimace, Tristan changed his tack and walked around the foot of the bed to where clenched pink toes could be seen smothered in a ruffled bed of gathered cotton. Dropping to his haunches, he seized the shapely ankles hidden beneath the gown and purposefully yanked their owner out of her retreat. Giving up her fight in order to keep her nightdress at a decent level below her hips, Marianna glared at her protector.

"If I were but a man, I would punch your face!"

"If you were a man, I wouldn't be inclined to be so generous with you," Tristan shot back, pulling the hand she clenched to herself up to examine it.

"Generous!" Marianna sniffed with a genuine attempt at anger that was destroyed by pain as he straightened her injured finger and worked it back and forth. "You couldn't be generous if you—" She broke off as he brushed it with his lips and leveled a sincere gaze at her.

"I'm sorry, Frenchie. I sure as the devil don't want to be married to you, but I don't get any pleasure out of hurting women. Come here."

Marianna would have resisted had she had the chance to think before she was engulfed in the strong

145

arms that surrounded her with a warmth and comfort that she recalled from another time—a night of terror from which they'd rescued her. This gringo was a puzzle to her, so kind and warm one minute and so cold and furious the next. Her reactions to him were even more confusing.

She wriggled her nose against the golden crisps of hair that tickled it, her cheek pressed hot against his skin. With a shaky sigh, she leaned against him and shut her eyes, giving in to the encouragement of the arms closed about her. This was something she could wish would last forever, this safe haven of flesh and blood her husband offered. Except that he was not her husband, nor did he want to be.

"I am sorry too, Tristan. I am so frightened of this Romero that I do not think clearly. When he is behind bars and you do as you say and return to your home, we can annul this marriage. There is nothing to it, *non?*"

Tristan inhaled the scent of the perfumed soap with which she'd washed her hair and nuzzled the top of her head gently. *"Non,"* he echoed lowly, wondering why his heart wasn't completely in agreement. "But there's no reason we can't try to be friends. Frankly, this little war of vengeance is wearing us both out. We got off to a bad start . . ."

"I did not *steal* your horse!"

"You didn't break out of jail, either, did you?"

Marianna seized her bottom lip with her teeth. "That was different. I thought you were going to hang me." She raised her face to his. "Would you hang me, Treestan? I only meant to borrow your horse." If they were going to be friends, it was important that he believe that.

When she said his name like that and rolled those bedroom eyes up at him, he'd just about believe the

146

earth was flat and the moon was made of cheese. He bent down and touched his lips to hers, moistening them with his own. At first, they were still, but under the gentle prodding of his tongue, they parted to permit him further exploration. He'd heard Mom Tillie, the housekeeper at Silverado, remark on more than one occasion that a man thought with what was in his breeches more than with what was in his head. Until now, he'd considered that the most ridiculous philosophy he'd ever come across. But something was playing havoc with his body as well as his thinking, and the sooner that something—or someone—was on the way to Mexico City, the better off he'd be.

A loud knock boomed on the door, driving the girl closer to Tristan. Her arms locked about his waist as she stared up at him in panic, her lips still moist and swollen from the searing kiss. Feeling as if he'd been struck by a lightning bolt that welded both sources of thought and reaction into one, he managed to disengage himself from the frantic embrace and grabbed his gun.

"Yes?"

"I understand that you wish to sleep all day, but it is time to get going, *amigo.*"

Tristan lowered the weapon and gave Marianna an assuring wink. "Be right with you, Mat. Soon as I can get my bride out of bed and moving."

As Mateo Salizar's footsteps faded in the corridor, Marianna's pale cheeks flamed at Tristan's insinuation. "Must you slander me so?" she whispered in mortification.

"You're my wife . . . least as far as anyone else is concerned."

"But he will think—"

"Exactly. That was your plan, wasn't it?"

Marianna pulled up the torn gather of her gown

where it had fallen away to expose a creamy expanse of breast that commanded her companion's heated gaze. "I . . . yes," she admitted, too confused and weary to argue.

Was the Ranger safer, now that they had settled their differences? Somehow she didn't think so, from the way her stomach quivered with a longing to go back into his embrace and bask in the male closeness. It was as if there were someone else within her, someone who had awakened and would not let her rest.

She took up her blouse and glanced over her shoulder as the Ranger turned his shirt right side out to don it. Confident that he was preoccupied, she hurriedly slipped her gown off her shoulders and tugged the blouse over her head. A camisole would have been appropriate, but the material of the blouse was sufficiently thick to be decent, she supposed. Putting on her skirt was easier. After pulling it on over her nightdress and fastening it about her waist, she removed the cotton garment and stepped out of it.

"I'm going on downstairs. You can join me when you're ready to travel."

Marianna sat in front of the small dressing table. "I won't be long. I've but to braid my hair."

"I'll order you up some grub."

"Some what?"

Tristan grinned as he tossed his saddle pack over his shoulder. He'd never thought of taking up teaching, but educating his new wife in English could, at the least, be entertaining, although English wasn't the only thing he wanted to teach her.

"Food . . . breakfast . . . *desayuno*," he translated.

Marianna chuckled, her laughter bubbling from deep within her throat. "I thought you were getting worms for me! That would be wonderful. *Grub*," she repeated

148

thoughtfully, committing the word to her memory as Tristan closed the door behind him.

Although she was tired from having spent most of the night waiting for Romero's men to take another attempt to kidnap her, she found herself humming lightly as her fingers made quick work of her hair. Soon it was styled in a long single braid and tied with the ribbon that had come from her shift.

She would be glad to get back to Casa Valencia, where trunks containing her more-fashionable clothes from France awaited, she thought, examining her image in the mirror. Not that she intended to impress her new husband. It was simply that she enjoyed looking her best, and the peasant garb, without proper corsets and underclothing, was not the most becoming.

After a brief unproductive search for her gun, Marianna thrust her torn nightdress and the few belongings that had been scavenged up for her by the sergeant's kind wife into her satchel and went downstairs to join Tristan. After all, now that their differences were settled, she would hardly need it . . . and it did belong to Tristan's friend and commanding officer. When the time arrived that she would need a gun, she was certain she could find one at Casa Valencia.

Her step was as bright as her smile as she tripped down the stairs, drawing more than one pair of admiring eyes to her lissome figure, including those of the Ranger seated alone at a table set for two.

"Where is your friend?" she asked, surprised when her companion rose to hold her chair. Was there a gentleman hidden beneath that half-wild facade?

"He went to arrange for some horses to go on to Casa Valencia."

Marianna made a face. "Can't we take a coach? I'm still bruised from my last ride on horseback."

"You'll survive," Tristan assured her, passing her a basket of freshly baked corn muffins. "Speaking of horses, I'm hungry enough to eat one," he remarked as he helped himself to two after she'd broken her choice in half to butter.

Reminded of the supper she'd denied him, Marianna grimaced. "I am sorry, Tristan. But it was cruel of you to mock me when I was so hungry and frightened." She looked down at the table. "I admit that I am not used to this land, even though I was born here, but—"

"I thought you were born in Mexico City."

Marianna bit into the buttered muffin, using the time it took to chew and swallow the mouthful to recover from her slip. "I was, but I lived at Casa Valencia for a short while as a little girl . . . after my father's death at the hands of the savages that carried you off." She looked at him curiously. "Do you remember any of that? You were, what—five, six?"

"I vaguely recall it."

"Did you see Don— my father killed?"

"I've blocked most of that memory from my mind," Tristan lied, wishing he had never started the questioning. "Have some frijoles?"

Marianna shook her head. "I wish such a thing were so easy for me."

"Anything to do with your nightmares?" Upon seeing her startled look, Tristan explained. "You had one the night we met, remember?"

She recalled only too well. Marianna blushed a becoming pink. "You were very kind that night. I . . . I am so sorry for having to borrow your horse. You surely understand, now that you know what sort of a man was on my tail."

"Trail?"

Her cheeks darkened and a small giggle escaped from

150

behind her coffee cup. "Yes, that is it! My English teacher at the girls' school said that I was an exasperation."

"I wonder why."

Marianna ignored the wry comment and placed a grateful hand on his arm. "I am so glad that I have you, even with the way that things are. I do not think that you are so bad after all. Perhaps, with some help, you might even become a gentleman instead of a *yahoo!*" she mimicked playfully.

It shouldn't have bothered Tristan that she was going to hate him in less than an hour, but it did. It was all he could do to reply in a like manner. "You have a lot of nerve, making fun of my speech and accent, lady! But, then, what can one expect from a woman that hunts wild razorbacks barehanded."

"That was an accident!" Marianna shot back in mock indignation. "Do I look like the type of woman who would roll in the mud with a pig?"

She was teasing, but there was fiery spirit, nevertheless, in the eyes dancing across the table. A beauty, full of fire, with a quick wit to boot. It was pure temptation to hold her to this reckless marriage, Tristan thought as Mateo Salizar entered the room. It would have been even more desirable if he thought he could trust her, but he'd seen her kind before—spoiled, selfish, and bent on having her way. Charming as she was at the moment, very shortly she would revert to her less-endearing character when she discovered that two could play at her game of deceit.

"Well, it appears the night went well for the bride and groom. May I kiss the bride?"

"Be my guest," Tristan responded flatly, wishing his companion was not quite so enthusiastic.

"Señora McCulloch, I am honored," Mateo announced after placing a chaste peck on Marianna's scarlet cheek. "I have seen to all our traveling arrangements, *amigo*. I told the man at the stable that we would be there in a half an hour."

"Then, you'd better notify the sisters. We're going to escort them to the convent on the way to Casa Valencia," Tristan explained, answering the question on his new bride's face.

"A man came to our room last night, but Tristan made him go away," Marianna whispered. For the first time, she was beginning to think that she really stood a chance of getting to Casa Valencia, and consequently to Romero, on her terms.

"So he told me, *señora*. I think the sooner we are on our way, the better."

"Here come the sisters, anyway," Tristan announced, shoving away from the table to see to his wife's chair.

"Did you arrange for a wagon for the nuns, Señor Salizar?" Marianna questioned, unable to picture Sister Rosa astride a horse.

"A small cart with a burro."

Any reply Marianna might have made was preempted by the arrival of the sisters who embraced her each in turn. They too agreed with Mateo that she seemed to have survived quite well what began as a tenuous wedding night at best. As Mateo ushered them out into the street, the conversation became stilted, but Marianna didn't notice. Safely nestled between the Ranger and his companion, she enjoyed the morning walk to the stable.

The building was near the edge of the town, not far from the water tank where the morning train took its fill of water for the southeast trip. A new set of faces gathered near the tracks to board the cars behind the one bearing the stacks of neatly cut wood, while freight was loaded in the latter ones. Her arm linked with that of her husband, Marianna inhaled the scent of fresh produce at the market they passed on the way and stopped to purchase some fruit to take on the trip, which she dropped into her satchel.

It didn't occur to her that anything was amiss until they stepped inside the large barn. Neither a cart nor horses stood ready for them. Instead, two men straightened beside a box that was wide at one end and narrowed at the foot, reminding Marianna of a coffin. As she turned a questioning face to Tristan, his hand flew over her mouth while his free arm seized her by the waist.

"All right, gents, let's be quick about this."

Marianna tried to scream, her eyes darting about wildly as the men produced ropes and bound her hands and feet securely. In the corner of her vision, she caught sight of the two nuns watching in dismay as a clean handkerchief was stuffed into her mouth and she was placed inside the box. They knew about this? she wondered, unable to believe her friends had turned on her so quickly. And Tristan . . .

"We all agree that this is the best thing for you, Elena," he was saying, resting his hands on either side of her. "I meant it when I told the sisters that I couldn't bear it if anything happened to you, now we've become man and wife. I'm not taking any chances, love. Much as I'm going to miss you, I'm sending you back to your parents. Once I get the mines going and I'm sure that it's safe, I'll send for you."

Marianna threw herself forward, bumping her head against the chest that had held her fascination only hours earlier. How could she have been so gullible? She growled and kicked as best she could, nearly knocking the box off the trestle benches on which it rested.

The two men who had backed away to allow the couple to say good-bye leapt forward to steady it and wrestled her legs down while Tristan eased her gently but firmly back. "We better get this lid strapped on before she jumps out, *señores*," one of them suggested with an anxious look at the mottled face of their reluctant traveling companion.

"You sure you put enough holes in it?"

"All around the side here, just under the lid so they don't show. If she don't put up too much fuss, no one'll suspect she's aboard, leastwise, not in this."

Tristan felt along the perimeter of the plain casket until he was satisfied that his cousin would have no trouble breathing. "You only need to keep her in here to the first watering station. Then take her out. I don't want her to smother in this heat."

He reached into his pocket and pulled out a fat purse.

"Señor Salizar has already paid us."

"This is to take extra-good care of her. She's special. If she weren't so blasted headstrong, I wouldn't have to send her off like this."

He glanced back at the muffled scream of outrage that rose from the casket in response. "Well, you *are*, love. Even the sisters realize that, but like me, they love you just the same." He bent over and brushed her forehead tenderly. "Have a nice journey and give my love to your mother." He hesitated, a devious glint lighting in his gaze as he placed a hand over her abdomen. "And just in case, take care of the twins."

The clang of the lid as the men Mateo hired forced it into place smothered the answering shriek. Tristan winced as he heard a faint banging noise that would scare the daylights of some unsuspecting soul who happened to come too close to the dearly departed traveling in the baggage coach, and groaned.

"What you have done was for her own good, *señor*," Sister Rosa told him compassionately. "Few men would have been so unselfish as to give up their new bride for her safety. I told the *señorita* that there was more to you than what she suspected."

Tristan forced a grin. "Thank you, Sister . . . and thanks for helping me. I don't think I could have pulled this off without your help."

"But Sister Teresa and I did nothing!"

"You put my mind at ease that I was doing the right thing. The least Mateo and I can do is escort your wagon to the convent in return."

By including the nuns in his plan, Tristan had hoped to avoid questions as to his wife's whereabouts, although he'd had to take the sergeant into his confidence as well. So far, thanks to his troublesome cousin, his secret mission had barely been kept that. Now he was married to the heiress of Casa Valencia and a sure target for one Victor Romero. But at least Elena was safe. Not that she'd ever have a thing to do with him again. He'd accomplished his goal, he thought grimly, glancing back to see the freshly built coffin being loaded gently onto the baggage car. Yet, as he took the reins Mateo handed him and mounted his new steed, a fine white appaloosa with black markings on its hind quarters, he felt far from satisfied.

Chapter Nine

The freight wagons were gathered in a circle around an area illuminated by lanterns of various description that were hanging on them. Their canvases had been spread over the ground to form the makeshift dance floor on which townfolk and wagoneers alike took advantage of the music provided by the fiddler, who also served as the company's cook. With a degree of envy, some guards watched the merriment from their posts near the wagons that had been loaded with silver to transport down the Rio Grande to Matamoros, where foreign ships awaited to take it to the mine developers in Europe.

From the perch her appointed escorts to Mexico City had provided for her inside the rickety wagon, Marianna also watched, but not for the same reason. Instead of wanting to join the fun, she intended to escape it and make her way back to Valencia. Now she had twice the incentive she had had before. There were two men with which to even a score. One she intended to kill. The other, she considered death too good for.

To think that she had trusted Tristan McCulloch . . . that she had been lured by that enticing lazy smile of his and those blue eyes that could melt her insides with a glance! By the saints, she would make him suffer as she had, smothering inside a coffin that had rocked from side to side on the train until she feared she'd either be sick or faint. When they helped her out of the box at the first watering station, his henchmen had insisted that her *loving* husband wanted her comfort seen to, but Marianna found that sending her downriver with a freight company was hardly her idea of comfort, no matter how they protested that this was the safest and least-suspect way to get her safely back to her parents. Yet, she had to admit, it was doubtful Romero would look for her to travel from Matamoros to Mexico City. The concept would never have crossed *her* mind.

That deceiving gringo was crazy, she fumed as one of her guardians left the other to join in the fun. According to the wagonmaster who had sought to invite her to the dance earlier, this was one of the regular diversions sought whenever the freight company camped close to a town, and a diversion was exactly what she had hoped for. However, it appeared that only one of her companions was going to leave. Her heart sank. It looked like yet another miserable night in the wagon with no more privacy than one could expect in the middle of the canvas dance floor.

Not to mention a third wretched day, she grumbled silently, considering tomorrow's prospects to be no better as she settled down on the small bedroll she'd been given. The train had taken them to the border that first sweltering morning. From there, she'd been bounced and jolted around in the wagon for another day and a half on the hot sun-baked trail running parallel to the winding Rio. Just a glass of fresh water, clear of the grit that gathered in her mouth in spite of the bandanna she'd kept over it, would be a godsend. A bath to soothe her aching muscles would be sheer heaven itself.

Forcing her anger and hurt over Tristan's betrayal from her mind to concentrate on more-pleasant thoughts, Marianna was eventually able to close her eyes and relax. The fiddle music and its accompanying singing and laughter soon became a lullaby that gradually faded into the background as sleep began its anesthetic effect. Maybe tomorrow would be different, she reconsidered drowsily, drawing her bare feet up under her skirts and shifting to a more-comfortable position. Maybe then she could find a way to escape, when she was fresh and more alert.

Sometime in the middle of the night, after the last of the townfolk returned to their homes and the wagon drivers were making beds for themselves under the stars, Marianna was jolted from her slumber by the sharp rap of a head beneath the wagon, followed by an unrestrained curse. The fright that it gave her erasing her drowsiness effectively, she sat up abruptly and listened to the two men under the wagon snickering in low voices. From the scent of whiskey that drifted up through the cracks in the floorboards, it didn't take much deduction to guess they had both been drinking excessively.

As she listened to the lurid conversation that ensued, some of which involved her, her initial indignation began to turn to calculation. If they had had half as much liquor as she suspected, they would eventually fall off to sleep like the dead. Her pulse quickened at the consideration. It was her chance! There was a town close-by from which she could find transportation. All she had to do was get the money.

The next hour became intolerable. Marianna nervously twisted the hem of her skirt in her fingers until it was puckered in several places. When the noise beneath the wagon at last died down, replaced by loud snores and grunts, she crawled carefully to the back and

158

dropped down onto the tall grass, the satchel Tristan had graciously sent along in her hand. She had never picked a pocket before, but she was going to need the money.

Fortunately, the larger of the two who carried the purse tied to his belt was sprawled on his back, leaving it within easy reach. Holding her breath, Marianna began to work at the knot that held the small pouch in place, taking every precaution to keep her fingers from shaking and dedicate them solely to their task. Just as the first of the loops came undone, however, the man rolled over on his side. Clutching her hand to her heart, Marianna swallowed her startled gasp and waited until he settled once more, the purse all but hanging by a single loop over his hip. Resisting the urge to snatch it away and run, she eased her fingers about the pouch with one hand while gently tugging at the remaining strings with the other. If she ever survived, she would make the gringo pay for putting her through this!

Suddenly a mumbled exclamation erupted from the man's lips and he slapped at his hip, his hand stopping long enough to scratch the stretch of skin bulging over his belt where his shirt had slipped up. After another equally damning curse aimed at the insects, he tugged his shirt down and began to breathe rhythmically. When the snoring resumed, Marianna, afraid to even attempt to wipe away the nervous perspiration that filmed her brow, began to inch away until she was clear of the wagon and able to rise to her feet.

She'd done it! She hurriedly put the coins in her satchel and, drawing her sleeve across her forehead in relief, searched the quiet campsite for the guards of the silver wagon. Thankfully they were on the opposite side of the camp and not likely to see her. It would be her luck for them to mistake her as a robber, she mused dourly upon starting off in a brisk walk toward the brush that dotted the hill just above the nearby village.

Elation made her step lighter in the sandy land that cushioned her footfalls. She neither cared that the low-growing brush was snagging her dress any more than she objected to the sand that filled the shoes taken from her satchel when she'd gotten far enough away from the wagons to consider it safe to don them. By the time the men Tristan hired awakened, she'd be on her way back to Valencia, if she had to steal a horse to do it.

However, it was coach travel that she favored, now that she had the means to hire one. From the weight of the coin in the purse, it did seem that her *loving* spouse had given ample to insure her comfort. It was just that his barbaric judgment as to the definition of the word *comfort* hardly matched her more-civilized one.

But then, she could hardly expect more from a gringo, a big rugged Texas gringo—who had been raised by savages, at that. Unbidden, the virile image of his half-nude body stretched out in awkward slumber on the settee came to mind, bringing with it a strange, far-from-unpleasant warmth. There was something about him that she found exciting, almost enticing. She wondered if a genteel woman of culture could make a gentleman out such a man.

Shocked by the train of her thoughts, Marianna caught the wistful smile that formed on her lips before it set and thinned it into a line of disapproval. Curse the devil! Even now, he was seeking forgiveness—and she would not give it. Not after the way he had betrayed her. There were no excuses for him. None! she thought emphatically, driving out all inclinations to seek one. Why, she would—

Her vengeful state of mind was distracted by a loud snorting noise, that of a horse or burro, and Marianna dropped to the ground instinctively. Her attention now focused fully on her surroundings, she became aware that the sound was coming from the west. Peering over the shrub behind which she'd taken cover, she spied several horses and riders making their way quietly toward the camp. Some of the men were on foot, walking their steeds and quieting the animals with strokes of the hand and soft assurances, while others led second mounts behind them.

Before the question ever entered Marianna's mind as to the whereabouts of the missing riders, she caught a glimpse of a half-dozen or so men crouched low near the outer edge of the circle of wagons and making their way around it toward the unsuspecting guards on the opposite side. A shiver ran up her spine as she realized what was happening. The *bandidos* were about to relieve the wagoneers of their valuable cargo.

She wavered, trying to deal with the inclination to run back to the camp and sound an alarm. Perhaps alerted, the wagoneers stood a chance against what looked to her like a small army. But if she did, would she be able to continue on her way? What if the bandidos saw her and shot her first? Marianna clutched the small satchel to her, her eyes glued to where the men on foot had disappeared from sight. Something had to be done, and soon, or the guards were dead men, the inner voice of her conscience prodded urgently.

Without further thought, Marianna found herself crawling frantically on all fours, dragging her bag through the dirt. After taking a deep breath, she screamed as loudly as she could.

"Thieves!" The shout pierced the quiet of the night, bringing the horsemen to a startled halt. Keeping under cover, Marianna summoned her courage and screamed again. "Help! Thieves!"

161

She flinched and collapsed on the ground as a rifle report cracked near the silver wagons. There! The alarm had been sounded. She'd met her obligation. The wagoneers had the guns to defend themselves. She could go now.

Yet, even as she made to move back in the direction of the town, a burst of shouts and the thunderous echo of charging horses mingled with pistol and rifle shots froze her in her place. The ground literally trembled beneath her knees, and the scent of gunpowder began to fill her nostrils as the camp came alive with return fire. Wondering if she would ever see a civilized place again, Marianna staggered to her feet in a run, clinging to the bag pressed against her chest.

Her footsteps were muted by the explosions erupting behind her, but seemed to strike the ground with at least every other blast. Her breath grew more and more frantic until her lungs began to ache from the burst of relentless exertion, for she dared not remain nearby and risk being captured by either side. Her heart thumped against her throat, pounding and pounding until it seemed that that was all she could hear . . . except that something was off beat. It echoed louder and louder until it sounded as if it were threatening to burst *from* her body and *catch up with her* at the same time.

It wasn't until the snorting, flared nostrils of a horse appeared in the periphery of her vision that she realized the source of the second sound. An arm reached down, catching her about the waist as she sped up her pace. Gasping with what little breath she had, Marianna twisted frantically, shoving with her feet and free hand against the lathered coat of her abductor's steed. Her resistance worked. The rider lost his grasp and she sprawled facedown on the ground in the dusty wake of his mount.

Stumbling to her feet, Marianna stubbornly charged on toward the town, hoping the man would give up his chase and return to the fray taking place in the circle of wagons. Perhaps some of the townspeople would hear the battle and send help! Her mouth too dry to spit the grit and grime she had tasted when she fell, she held her bag even tighter and raced on.

Again her ears filled with pounding blood and she closed her eyes, as if that would afford her more energy to keep going, when a rough-biting loop encircled her arms. As it closed mercilessly about her, yanking her off her feet, her satchel dropped. Marianna hit the ground with a sense-robbing thud that left her dazed and unable to move or think. But she did hear her captor approaching her on his horse. Then his soft-booted footsteps blended in with the noise that rose from the circle of wagons so that when he grabbed her and hauled her to her feet, she screamed, startled.

To her horror, he was an Indian! One look at his scarred and hideously painted face strangled the remainder of the scream in her throat. She clawed at him and tried to push away from the wiry chest to which she was drawn, her legs tangling with his corded, braced ones, but the hands that held her wrists were as relentless as steel. Laughter filled her senses, a sinister sound of mingled greed and lust to match that of the black eyes boring into her own, filling her with panic.

Tales of a thousand tortures associated with women captives flashed through her mind in a matter of fleeting seconds, and she knew that she would never see Paris again. In one last desperate measure, she brought her knee up between his thighs, only to have them clamp shut like a vise, stopping her short of her intended goal. His amusement turned into a guttural snarl, but before Marianna had the luxury of fainting from sheer terror,

163

a fist exploded against her temple and the world went into a spinning pain-crazed frenzy that sapped her strength and consciousness, leaving her vulnerable and helpless in his arms.

"What do you mean his *wife* is not with him?"

The caballero seated opposite Don Victor Romero flinched as the *alcalde*'s fist struck the desk. "Doña Inez told my wife that he sent her back to Mexico City to her parents until he got the mines reopened and established."

Victor Romero forced his outrage under control. He had already heard from his sources that they had lost track of his fiancée, that she had married and disappeared, leaving a gringo to claim the mines at Casa Valencia. It would do no good to permit his neighbors to see it, he cautioned himself sternly. Yet it boiled in his blood like a poison that his fiancée had not only eluded them but managed to get herself married to Tristan De Costa. Was that the man she could not marry him for? he wondered, recalling her impudent announcement that she could not follow through with her father's wishes. She had been so nervous that he had thought he might intimidate her. It appeared now that he had underestimated her mettle. "That is the only reason?"

"It is all that she said, except to say how romantic their meeting on the other side of the border was."

His sources told him they met in a jail, that De Costa had accused her of stealing a horse. Yet, one would hardly marry a woman who stole his prized steed. Nothing made sense.

"So romantic that he could not keep her close-by?" the *alcalde* sneered skeptically.

The other man shrugged. "It is odd, but then, the ar-

164

rival of Don Diego De Costa's adopted son is no stranger. Perhaps he paid court to her in order to get her land. I have heard he is quite handsome and charming with the ladies in a crude sort of way. At least, my wife and daughter were taken with him.

"How did he explain his being lost for so long?" Romero challenged, his tone infused with a mingle of indignation and doubt. "Perhaps he is not who he says he is."

"Doña Inez swears that he is the young man she helped raise. He told her about his sister Catalina, I believe was the name, who is now a doctor in California. His mother is married to a Texas rancher."

That idea was absurd as everything else his neighbor had told him, Romero threw up his hands. He needed facts, not speculation. "Did he say how he came to escape the savages who abducted them?"

"Their real father found them and took them back to Texas. I do recall that the lovely Doña Tessa had no recollection of her past when Diego married her."

Romero's face brightened. "So the marriage was illegitimate if she was married to someone else," he mused aloud.

"Even if you challenged his inheritance, he has married your bride, my friend."

"Which is probably why he did marry her." The *alcalde* rose from his desk and paced over to the window before turning. "Still, I can not think that this is all per chance as that silly old nurse does."

"*Perdonamé*, Don Victor, but there is a man here with a message that he says is urgent that you read."

Frowning at the interruption by his servant, the *alcalde* sent a searing look across the room. "Do you know him?"

The elderly servant shook his head and approached

in spite of his employer's annoyance. "I have never seen him before. He said to give you this." He handed the stained note over and waited expectantly. "He was a suspicious-looking half-breed, so I had him go around to the back where he could be watched."

Victor Romero did not acknowledge the precaution one way or the other. Instead he quickly scanned the poorly penned note.

Alcalde, we have captured a young lady who claims that she is your betrothed. We leave the reward for her up to your generous nature.

The note was not signed. Carefully, Victor refolded it, his bewildered mind trying to make sense of the words.

"Tell him I will see him. Don Hernando, I regret that duty calls, even in my most distressed time." He held out his hand to the man who rushed forward to take it.

"I only thought that it was something that would be of interest to an old friend. You must come visit us in the near future."

"Yes, *adiós,*" Romero finished, turning abruptly to his desk, his mind already on the impending conversation. A new set of questions began to turn over and over in his mind as his neighbor exited without further ado. If the half-breed was the man he suspected, his *compadres* had just sealed their own fate by sending him to Mirabeau—whether they really had Elena De Costa or not. At this point, little else would surprise him.

"Here he is, Don Victor."

The *alcalde* looked up to see a lean, wiry man clad in dirty tattered clothing. He wore a vest with no shirt. A bandanna was tied around one bicep, perhaps covering a bullet nick. His dusty trousers were too short, no doubt stolen from some unfortunate soul who was now with his Maker, and soft-soled buffalo skin boots made his approach silent.

Romero met his narrow-eyed gaze squarely, taking note of a long ragged scar across a face still smudged with war paint that had been hastily wiped off. He was one of Pico's men, soon to be as dead as the man who had dared to send him. A wicked smile stretched the *alcalde*'s mustache in a deceptive greeting as he motioned for the half-breed to sit down.

"So tell me about this young lady you have abducted. If she is who she says, I can promise you a very special reward."

Chapter Ten

The bells at the convent on the outskirts of Valencia filled the small hillside village with their pure sweet tones, calling the sisters to evening vespers. The quiet countryside was a picturesque scene of tranquility, the first lighted lanterns of the town glowing softly in the early evening while stars struggled for prominence in the fading light of the sun. Yet Marianna felt anything but tranquil as the half-breed Indian behind her reined in his horse in front of an abandoned shack near the village's edge.

Her very life depended on one Victor Romero. If the *alcalde* did not recognize her as his former fiancée and agree to pay the ransom she'd managed to convince her captors that he would, they would surely kill her. But not before the gruesome fate she'd thus far avoided had been dealt over and over, no doubt by each and every one of the bloodthirsty *bandidos*.

She'd done everything to block out the carnage that she'd witnessed upon recovering from the harsh blow her captor had given her. Few men been left alive or with their scalp intact. Some of the vermin even cut off the ears and strung them on leather thongs from their belts, like trophies. Those few survivors, all young healthy men, were bound and placed on one of the wagons.

A French nursery rhyme her mother had taught her echoed from her lips as they rode away, in an effort to thwart the impact not only of what she had seen, but of the bloodstained hands taking their liberties with her body, pinching and fondling here and there. All the while, her mind raced in a desperate search for a way to survive this new and unprecedented terror.

The bandits had thought her loco until they'd gone far enough into the hills to make camp. She began to fight like a wildcat the moment the half-breed dragged her from his horse and started off toward a shelter of rocks to satisfy the animal lust that had been impossible to ignore, pressed hard against her lower back with promising thrusts of what was in store. She cursed them in Spanish and warned them of the consequences of harming the fiancée of the *alcalde* of Valencia.

It was a risk, but a calculated one. They most likely would never have heard of Tristan De Costa, not that the Ranger would be inclined to save her anyway. He had everything he wanted, but Romero did not. If Victor Romero was the man the Ranger colonel believed him to be, the bandits would not only know him, but she could count on his greed and avarice to pluck her from her unsavory situation. True, she would be jumping from one fire into another, but dying at the hands of Romero was preferable to the torture and abuse that lay in store for her by her captives. There was an outside chance that she might even take Romero to his death with her.

The ploy worked. At least, the bandit leader took her from the half-breed to question her further. Marianna swore that she had been abducted by the *alcalde*'s enemy and that a handsome reward would lie in store for the ones who returned her to her fiancé. Hopefully, Romero would pay the reward to get his hands on her. If he didn't . . .

Her captors spoke in low tones as the half-breed hauled her off his horse. Marianna turned her face away from the mouth that attempted to cover hers and suffered the familiarity of the tight grasp that allowed no room for imagination as to his intentions should Romero refuse their offer. Grateful for the sharp command from the leader to take her inside, Marianna was released and shoved ahead of her captor into the darkness of the enclosure.

She tripped over the satchel that Liam had procured for her, now empty of all coin, and fell to the earth floor. For one terrifying moment, she thought the half-breed was coming inside as well, but after a leering look at her exposed legs, he shut out the moonlight that had illuminated them with the creaking close of the door. Above the thunder of her heart, she heard the bandit leader order her personal captor to take a message to the *alcalde*, and she breathed a sigh of relief. She'd been fretful that at any moment the Indian would disregard his superior's orders and take her then and there. After all, when the leader had stopped him to listen to Marianna's frantic story, he had argued fiercely for his rights as her captor the night before, half in Spanish and half in a guttural language that was foreign to her.

Crawling hesitantly to the ill-fitted door, she pressed against the cool mud wall and listened as some of the men rode away. Safe for the moment, she was able to consider her next major problem. If Romero paid her ransom—and she would not permit herself to even think otherwise—she would have to explain running away and marrying Tristan. One lie always led to another, her mother had once cautioned her as a child. Mari-

170

anna closed her eyes, partly from exhaustion and partly to shut out the emotions that threatened the frayed state of her nerves, and tried to rest. She would need that to keep a clear head, and she would need a clear head to face Victor Romero.

Astonishingly, she slept. At least, she was asleep when the sound of approaching horses awakened her to a state of instant alertness. Voices could be heard, exchanging cautious greetings, none of which she could identify as the one that had haunted her dreams for nearly a lifetime. But what they were saying was of great interest.

Romero was willing to pay a reward! Marianna sank against the wall in relief. One of the *alcalde*'s men had accompanied the half-breed to bring her back. She brushed off the unseen dirt from her skirt in the darkness as she struggled to her feet in readiness. Whatever fate awaited was better than her alternative.

She was at the door when it opened, flooding her bedraggled figure with moonlight. A uniformed captain, clad in a crisp red, white, and blue, broadened his smile upon seeing her, but before she could step forward to freedom, he suddenly shoved her inside, throwing his body over hers. At the same moment, the air seemed to explode with gunfire. Stunned, Marianna found herself being dragged over to the cover of the mud wall and pressed into a corner. She rallied from the shock in time to see the bandit leader charge into the room, his body jerking with bullets as he sprawled lifelessly to the ground.

A scream hung in Marianna's throat. She backed away, as if the wall would open up and swallow her. "*Cálmate, señora.* The *alcalde* is only dealing with those who dare to cross him."

The words were far from comforting. Fighting the

171

dizziness that clouded her brain from sheer fright, Marianna drew into a ball and waited for the gunfire to stop. When it did, the silence was deafening. Not even the shouts of the soldiers who had surrounded the shack managed to challenge it. The captain helped her to her feet, supporting her as her knees buckled beneath her weight.

"You are not harmed, Señora De Costa?"

"Non." Marianna licked her dry lips and shuddered as she was led past the bodies of the small escort that had brought her to Valencia. The Indian, even in death, seemed to leer at her, his yellowed and snaggle-toothed smile fixed on his face. *"Madre de Dios!"* she managed, crossing her chest reverently.

"The *alcalde* has no mercy for the *bandidos*. Do not waste your prayers on them."

Her prayers hardly for the men lying scattered around, Marianna numbly allowed herself to be lifted onto a horse and braced while the captain of the guard mounted behind her. "There are many questions the *alcalde* will wish to ask you, as I am certain you must suspect."

"And I have much to tell him," Marianna averred with as much courage as she could muster. God in heaven, what a savage land! The men were bloodthirsty animals, both gentlemen and murderers. Some worked outside the law, while others hid within it. There was only one way to see justice done, and if she survived long enough, she would see to it herself. The devil take Tristan McCulloch.

"The devil take him!" Marianna swore loudly later, rallying to the question Victor Romero posed to her concerning her marriage to Tristan McCulloch De Costa. She'd been brought into his office in her tattered dusty clothing to tell the story of her abduction. "He tricked me into marrying him so that he could take my inheritance and then packed me off like a piece of baggage to return to my parents! If only I were a man, I would kill him with my bare hands! Even *you* are better than he! At least you are a gentleman! I can not tell you what humiliation I have suffered at that gringo's hands."

The corner of Romero's mouth curled as if slightly amused. "Am I to take that as a compliment, Señora De Costa?"

Marianna felt pinpricks of fear lift the hairs at the nape of her neck at his tone. He was toying with her, hearing what she had to say. His thin smile barely concealed his contempt for her. She forced an indifferent shrug. Her parents had once told her never to act afraid of a vicious animal and it would stay its attack. Heaven knew there was no one more vicious than the man watching her keenly.

"Take it as you wish, *monsieur*. I am not the foolish maid who ran away from you and my father's plans for me only a few days ago. Your . . . your stern insistence frightened me. I was not accustomed to such treatment." Marianna looked down at her feet. "But now I realize that you treated me gentle as a lamb compared to that ruffian husband of mine. You were rightfully outraged over my childish behavior, but you remained a gentleman, which is more than I can say for Tristan De Costa."

A sob caught in her throat, not out of remorse as she intended her companion to think, but, nonetheless, genuine and full of despair over her situation. She turned away, pretending to study the gun cabinet on the adjacent wall to the collection of books on bold display. The one man she had finally come to trust had betrayed her and sent her to a grisly fate at the hands of outlaws. Now she was in the clutches of her most dreaded enemy

. . . worse, on his terms! If she should survive all this, she would happily enter into matrimony with Andre Bienville. At least the fencing instructor was predictable. She could handle him.

"No, you are not the same *maiden, señora.*"

Marianna gasped as a hand cupped her chin and lifted her face into the light cascading down from the black iron chandelier hanging overhead. She hadn't heard him get up from the desk and approach her. Her startled look seemed to please him.

"I am certain that your husband has seen to that." He paused, contemplating her features with eyes narrowed in speculation. "Still, you are a lovely and spirited creature who has managed to keep her wits sufficiently to save her life. I admire that . . . and I am not adverse to used merchandise when packaged so becomingly."

Catching on to Romero's insinuation, Marianna inhaled sharply, puffing with outrage. "I am not *used* merchandise, *monsieur!* That ruffian would not know how to treat a lady! Surely you did not think that I would allow . . . that I—"

"I do not think, *señora,* that you could avoid such a thing."

"Then you do not know men such as my cousin. He thinks more of his horse than he does a woman . . . I think, even of other men!" She had heard of such things and she had to come up with some convincing explanation besides the truth.

Romero's passive mask cracked with incredulity. "Are you saying that you have not shared your husband's bed?"

Marianna drew to her full height and lifted her chin haughtily. "I am, *monsieur,* although it is none of your affair. Even if he was interested in me for reasons other

174

than my inheritance, how could I allow a man such privileges when I detest him so?"

"You are indeed resourceful, *señora*. It seems De Costa and I have both underestimated you."

Her success thus far going to her head, Marianna smiled prettily. "But I do not underestimate you, *monsieur*." She cut her eyes sideways, attaining the provocative slant known to set many a young Parisian swain aflutter. "Perhaps we might set things to right and start over, once we have my husband out of the way."

Interest kindled among the primitive embers that sparked in the dark ebony gaze fixed on her. "And how is that, *querida?*"

"We will embarrass him before the public and have the marriage annulled. After all, but for his trickery, I would be free to marry you."

"And what of your real fiancé, the man without whom you could not have lived only a few days ago?"

Marianna winced at the pain resulting from the bruised cheek the half-breed had dealt and attempted a smile. "I have grown up much, *monsieur*. How could I turn away a man who is so willing to forgive, who came to my rescue, even after I had run away from him?" She forced her gaze to his, her heart pounding to carry through with the lie that would buy her the time she needed and give Tristan De Costa the humiliation he deserved. "I have seen much these last days and learned to recognize character, something in which my husband is sorely lacking." She stepped closer to him and placed a hand on the brocade lapel of his jacket. "Are we to be partners, *monsieur?*"

Romero regarded the thick fanned lashes framing eyes the color of a summer sky for some time before his lips parted to show the teeth that reminded her of the night creatures in European folklore. "In revenge at least, *querida* . . . and perhaps in time, in love."

His mouth claimed Marianna's. As he embraced her, she swayed weakly against him and groaned, her head lolling back in a feigned faint. When her knees gave way, her ardent companion caught her up in his arms and called in alarm for a servant to help him to one of the guest rooms. Pretending to stir as she was carried up the carved oak stairwell to the second floor, Marianna raised her head.

"I . . . I am sorry, *monsieur,* but my head . . ." As if to illustrate, she put her fingers to her temples. "I have been through so much . . ."

"But of course, *señora.* It is a miracle that you have remained standing this long. I will have food and a bath sent up and expect you to go straight to bed afterward. Then tomorrow we will plan our revenge on your deceitful cousin."

The words should have been pleasing, but any plans made by Victor Romero were cause for concern. Not that Tristan didn't deserve the worst fate for what he'd done to her, she reasoned grudgingly, resting her head against her benefactor's chest.

Besides, Romero wasn't as smart as he thought he was. He believed her. As long as she kept her head, she would do just fine. With luck, plotting one against the other, she'd see that they both got their just deserts! She looked forward to that almost as much as she did to the hot bath and comfortable bed that was in store.

The following day, the hacienda was astir with plans for the dinner party the *alcalde* was giving that evening. Don Victor met Marianna, who had slept through breakfast, for a light lunch on the patio. Marianna, refreshed and clad in a buttercup day dress her host had procured for her, tried to ignore the olive tree that still

176

grew, gnarled at the trunk and spreading like an umbrella over the bench that had hidden her as a child. Instead she concentrated on the fresh melon and rolls smothered in butter and jam and listened to Don Victor's plot concerning Tristan De Costa.

It seemed the Ranger and his partner were invited to the party to speak to some of the other miners and those who worked in the mining industry. Where better to expose him as a kidnapper who took advantage of an innocent girl to secure her inheritance?

"He will be so humiliated, he will wish he might flee for the border like a whipped mongrel," Romero chuckled, admiring the way the sunlight danced on the blue-black tresses cascading down his companion's back from a pertly tied ribbon.

"How I would love to give him a swift kick to help him along his way!" Marianna averred heatedly. "He might have shared the inheritance, but no, he wanted it all. His greed will be his downfall."

"*Perdoname, señor . . . señora.*"

Don Victor afforded a sharp glance at the servant that interrupted their repast. "What is it?"

"Don Miguel is here to see you about the bulls for the *corrida de toros* tomorrow."

Nodding, Victor excused himself from the table. "I will be busy for a little while. Perhaps you would like to rest. Not that you need it, *señora*, but I have heard that young ladies require a beauty sleep, no?"

"Think nothing of it, Don Victor. I do not need to be entertained."

"Victor to you, *señora*. After all, all of this that you see about you," he said with a careless sweep of his arm, "will be yours as well very soon."

"Then, you must call me Elena."

"Elena it is," he whispered, brushing her cheek lightly

177

in spite of the presence of the servant. *"Hasta la vista, querida."*

Although the servant followed Romero to the door leading to the front salon, after the exchange of a few words, he returned to Marianna's side and offered to show her to her room.

"I would like to look around," she announced authoritatively to the man upon rising from her chair. "It's such a beautiful hacienda. Then I thought I might borrow a book from Don Victor's library to read in my room."

With a cool reserve that disguised a thousand tormenting emotions, she began her ambling tour of her childhood home. It was strange how much smaller the house seemed now compared to her recollection of it. Perhaps if she faced it, saw the scene of the nightmare that haunted her sleep, she reasoned, it might go away.

Her watchdog remained a few steps behind her, as if he suspected that she might steal something, and she wondered what Don Victor had told him. When Marianna turned to step into the room where she had been questioned so thoroughly the night before, however, he barred her way.

"I am sorry, *señora,* but no one is allowed in Don Victor's office without invitation."

"I am his guest, am I not?"

"Well, yes, but—"

"And did you not hear him say that all this would soon be mine?" she demanded imperiously.

"I did, *señora,* but—"

Marianna softened her tone. "All I want is to borrow a book." She pointed past the man to the walls lined with leather-bound volumes. "There are so many to choose from." As he reluctantly stepped aside, she slipped past him and walked over to the fireplace, where a display of grandly decorated swords of various size and description gleamed in the sunlight coming in through the patio doors. "My goodness, your master does like the swords, *non?*"

"He is proud of his abilities with the rapier, *señora*, but some of the swords were used in the *corrida de toros* to kill the bull."

"The *alcalde* is a matador?"

"*Sí, señora.* He personally tries each of the fighting bulls before they go to the arena."

"Alonso! Don Victor is asking for you," a young woman who appeared to be some of the household help intervened. "He says to bring his capote and sword."

"Don Miguel is one of his favorite *matadores*. Perhaps they will exchange secrets of the art." Alonso grinned, bowing to excuse himself from Marianna's company.

When he hesitated at the door, Marianna waved him on. "I'll be fine as soon as I find something interesting to read."

"*Muy bien, señora*, but Don Victor will not like it."

"Then he can come tell me himself."

The servant wavered uncertainly before, shoulders falling in resignation, he took his leave. Marianna listened to his retreating footsteps and turned to peruse the shelves of volumes that ran from the floor to the ceiling, aware that the female servant still lingered in the corridor. Gradually she made her way toward the corner to the rear of the large oak desk and dropped to where the books on astronomy that her father had brought over from France still rested.

A wave of nostalgia caught her by surprise as she removed one and thumbed through the pages until she could no longer focus on the illustrations he had used to teach her the constellations from the rooftop of

179

Mirabeau. In the background she barely heard the servant being recalled to her duties. Her father's library was such a waste on a man like Victor Romero! But the winds of fate had blown in the villain's favor long enough.

Regaining her composure and resolve, Marianna reached through the void left by the book, searching for the small release that had fascinated her as a child. Upon finding it, she pulled firmly and heard the pop of the panel in the adjoining wall. Upon opening the hidden entrance the rest of the way, she exposed the cobweb-filled passage that led to her parent's bedroom, now occupied by their murderer.

Good, she thought, it was not only still there, but undiscovered by the look of it. She rushed over to the gun cabinet she had seen the night before and selected a pistol similar to the one Tristan had taken from her out of one of the drawers so as not to call attention to its missing. With shaking fingers, she loaded it as Liam had shown her and hastily placed it behind the panel in the hidden passageway before shoving the panel gently back into place.

Satisfied that she now had the way and means to accomplish her objective, for the secret passage would make catching Victor Romero off guard easier, Marianna carefully returned the volume to its place and rose to browse idly through the rest of the library. As she did so, her eye was caught by a familiar name printed on the binder of a ledger—that of the freight company that had been relieved of its silver.

It was identical to the one the wagonmaster had carried in his saddlebag the day he asked her to attend the dance to take place later in the evening. He'd torn part of a page out of the back and written his name on it for her, in case she forgot it was he that had asked her and not some other rival for the company of the prettiest girl he'd ever laid eyes on. Marianna's heart clenched as she took out the volume and turned to the back where the corner was missing from the last page.

It shouldn't have surprised her, but it did. She knew the sort of man Romero was, but even she did not think he would ruthlessly cut down his own men after they had done his dirty work. Yet it certainly appeared that way. The *bandidos* had robbed the freight company for him, and in order to make it appear to her as if he were coming to her rescue and exacting justice, he had had his soldiers gun them down.

Her hand shook as she slid the volume between others that, no doubt, recorded the booty from equally sinister deeds. Upon seeing a dark stain she had missed before, the blood of the man who had asked her to the dance, she inadvertently recoiled. What nerve he possessed, keeping the records of his amassed ill-gotten wealth so openly in his library! If Tristan and Mateo had these, they could prove to the Mexican government that the *alcalde* was corrupt in the worst sense . . . the *late alcalde,* she corrected, her gaze returning to her father's dusty books.

The sudden click of the latch from the patio entrance to the study brought Marianna about abruptly to see Don Victor Romero and another, younger and decidedly dashing, companion at his heels. Praying the revulsion she felt would not show, she schooled her features into a bright look.

"Don Victor! How convenient!" she exclaimed, finding her legs and walking over to greet the men as if she were the hostess she had been born to be. She pursed her lips into a most alluring pout. "I can not find any poetry among your books, yet I know a man of your breeding must have something a lady might find interest in."

"What good is poetry on a dried ancient page when it walks and breathes right here in this room?" Marianna's pout stretched into a smile as the gallant at Romero's side took her hand and pressed it enthusiastically to his lips. *"Dios,* such eyes! They warm my very soul with their fire and beauty. Who is she, *mi amigo?"*

Marianna ventured an inquiring glance at her host. The prompt prodded him from his suspicious scrutiny of her to a proper introduction.

"May I present my . . . guest for the festivities," Victor began cautiously, "Señora Elena De Costa. Señora, this is Don Miguel Alvarado. He will fight in the *corrida de toros* tomorrow."

"If he is as smooth with the sword and cape as he is with the women, I have pity for the bull."

"But if your favor lies with the bull, *señora,* I shall be surely lost. That, you see, is the alternative," the matador informed her with a courtly nod of his head.

"Then you must forgive me, Don Miguel. I did not think of it that way. I have never seen a bullfight before."

"Never, *señora?"* Don Victor questioned curiously.

Marianna thought quickly. Had she made a slip? No, she and Elena were like sisters. Not once had Elena's parents taken them to the arena. The very sight of blood had made Marianna ill since her parents' death, and they had not done so out of consideration of her. "I was squeamish when it comes to the sight of blood as a child, and there are no bullfights in Paris."

"So that explains that charming accent. You are part French!"

"Oui, monsieur," Marianna answered coyly. "But my

Spanish is fluent and I am comfortable to speak in your native language, which is also mine."

"And your husband is Mexican?"

"The poetry books are on that shelf," Don Victor interrupted, bringing her back to her purpose for being there. "You must excuse Don Miguel and myself as we are—" He broke off as Alonso entered the room with a sword and scarlet capote in his hand. "Busy," he finished curtly. "Alonso, once Señora De Costa has made her selection, you will show her to her room."

"*Sí*, Don Victor."

Don Miguel clicked his boots together and bowed graciously as Victor Romero took the cape and sword and started for the door. "It has been my pleasure, Señora De Costa. Tomorrow, I shall fight for you."

"Rest well for the evening, *señora*. It promises to be entertaining."

Marianna resisted the shiver that ran up her spine as Don Victor took his leave, ushering her guest out ahead of him. "I look forward to it, *señor*," she called after them.

At least she thought she did. She couldn't wait to see the look on Tristan's face when she made her entrance. She wanted to see him squirm and turn scarlet with the humiliation of having his misdeeds made public and the initiation of the scandalous proceedings to have the marriage annulled. She owed at least that to him for the embarrassment he had caused her, not to mention his treachery.

As for Romero, perhaps even tonight she might slip into his room, when the festivities were over and his brain was wine-sodden, to avenge her parents' death. With Tristan dismissed, she would have to do something, and quickly, for Romero's dark gaze could not hide the lascivious interest that kindled upon hearing that her innocence had survived her marriage bed. It made her feel like the mouse in the playful clutches of the hungry cat, doomed and helpless . . . except that this mouse had a trick or two of its own.

Chapter Eleven

The spacious salon at Mirabeau was filled with the gentry of the mining community. Without speaking to even one of them, Tristan knew of their success. Their clothes, some threaded with silver and gold and expensively tailored, bespoke it as much as their manner. No doubt many of them were descended from the Spanish nobility that settled the area. They had that look—the long aristocratic nose and pointed chin of the earlier settlers from Spain. A ruffled collar, and the effect would have been complete.

Although the men's conversation naturally gravitated toward mining, the lifeblood of the area, their hearts were not fully devoted to the subject. In spite of their genteel upbringing, Tristan could not miss the speculative glances cast his way. Ordinarily, he would have taken it as due. After all, he was a newcomer—a man considered lost for many years come to claim an inheritance that was his not by blood, but by adoption. To ensure his fortune, he had managed to snatch his lovely cousin out of the local *alcalde*'s hands as well. Even if his bloodline was challenged, he was married to the undisputed heiress, making Casa Valencia's mines his own. Even though they had been closed for years, exploited

185

as far as man could go with a pick and shovel, with new mining techniques there was valuable silver left to be taken.

The ladies looked on with haughty consideration as well, but each melted the moment he flashed a smile and gallantly took their hand to his lips. Doña Inez's romantic version of his elopement with Elena De Costa had circulated in every parlor in and near the town, giving the ladies' speculation a far different perspective from that of the men.

They were more than willing to welcome the gringo who made such an obvious effort to join their ranks. His clothing was impeccably cut and Hispanic, accentuating the rugged build and lean waist that brought more than one sigh to lips hidden behind lace and silk fans. His fair hair and sunbronzed complexion made him stand out even more. In spite of the fact that the gringo was married, it could be said that, at last, Don Miguel Alvarado, Valencia's handsome matador extraordinaire, had some serious competition.

"If we don't eat something soon, this liquor is going to set me on my butt," Tristan confided to Mateo Salizar, his gaze searching out the host to the small dinner party. "Wonder what the holdup is?"

"You amaze me, *amigo*," Mateo whispered lowly as he scanned the crowd. "Are you not the least nervous, here in the nest of the snake?"

Tristan turned away to refuse a fresh drink from the servant going from guest to guest with a tray of crystal goblets, but before he could answer they were interrupted.

"You do not find the wine to your taste, Señor De Costa?" a young lady with dark hair which was drawn into a tight coil at her neck inquired with a coquettish tilt of her head that sent the scarlet and black roses adorning it quivering as if in anticipation of his reply.

"No, *señorita*, I find it too much to my taste. I guess Don Victor is trying to starve his guests so the food'll look twice as good."

The girl laughed at Tristan's wry humor and tapped his arm with her fan. "You are naughty, *señor*, to slander your host so."

In keeping with the garrulous character he'd managed to create, he feigned dismay. "It doesn't have a thing to do with my host, *señorita*. It's got to do with my stomach."

"My friend has an appetite as big as Texas," Mateo chimed in, slapping Tristan on the back good-naturedly.

"For such a big handsome man, I do not find that surprising. I admire a hearty appetite in a man."

Certain from the flirtatious slant of the eyes cut up at him that the lady was not speaking of food, Tristan was about to reply in kind when the host clapped his hands loudly.

"May I have your attention, *por favor!*" When the chatter in the room died down, Victor Romero, resplendent in a gold and black brocade jacket, went on. "I have a very special guest this evening whom I wish to introduce at this time."

Tristan straightened as several eyes, including those of the host, fixed on him. He'd wondered why no attempt had been made at introductions, aside from the initial announcement of the servant upon his arrival.

"May I present Doña Elena De Costa of Casa Valencia."

The room burst into whispers around Tristan as a familiar young woman emerged from behind the double doors leading to the central corridor. She was familiar— that is, in face only—for he had never seen the natural

187

beauty of his cousin encased in such finery. Elena was as breathtaking as her unexpected appearance in a white silk gown embossed with royal blue flowers. Her ebony hair, drawn to one side of her head where it fell in ringlets interspersed with silver and blue ribbons, contrasted the skin of her bared shoulders, skin that glowed in the flickering lights of the chandeliers overhead.

"Madre de Dios, what do we do now?" Tristan heard Mateo mutter under his breath, making him aware of the alarmed grip on his arm.

The reminder shook him from the hypnotic effect of the smiling beauty with dancing blue eyes approaching him on the arm of Victor Romero and set his staggered mind to work quickly. Hell's bells, what was she up to now?

He started forward to meet them halfway. "Elena, I have never seen you more lovely. I am indeed indebted to my host for such a delightful surprise."

Marianna tried to ignore the open admiration that had initially flashed in the gaze now centered on her alone. She had fallen victim to this man's smooth and polished seduction once and would not be taken in again by it. She lifted her chin disdainfully. "I am certain that you are, *monsieur."* She pulled her hand away as Tristan reached for it. "You had my inheritance and thought you were well rid of me, didn't you? I thank God for Don Victor. But for him, you would have succeeded in arranging for my murder at the hands of bandits."

"Murder?" Tristan exclaimed in complete astonishment. "What the . . . ?" His startled question was halted by a pair of immaculately white gloves that flashed across his face, slapping him expressively on the cheek and drawing his attention from his new *wife* to his host.

"Perhaps it is best if we left," Mateo Salizar interjected urgently, catching Tristan's arm as he looked incredulously at Victor Romero.

"I insist on avenging this young lady's honor, not to mention my own outrage for your uncouth and avaricious behavior."

"What honor?" Tristan blurted out irritably. "Hell, she's *my* wife! If anyone should be outraged, it should be *me."*

Marianna gasped in disbelief as he returned the gesture with a loud slap that echoed in the deadly silence of the room. "What are you doing?"

"What are *you* doing?" the Ranger challenged, adding in a sardonic tone, "Just how long have you been a cozy guest of the *alcalde?"*

Was there no end to his ability to insult her? Marianna rose on her tiptoes and tapped an angry finger against his chest. "Since Don Victor rescued me from the *bandidos* that kidnapped me and robbed the freight company of the silver! But for him, I shudder to think of my fate! I wish our marriage annulled! You tricked me into marrying you, kept me a prisoner, and then sent me off to be captured by outlaws!"

"Not to mention abducting my intended fiancée. You have dishonored me as well as my intended bride and I demand satisfaction!"

Marianna turned to Romero in confoundment. *"Oh, non, monsieur!* Bloodshed I can not allow. To annul the marriage is good enough. Let him live with his disgrace!" Nothing had been said about a duel. They'd agreed to dishonor him publicly, nothing more.

Romero drew her gently to the side, yet there was nothing gentle in the dark eyes consumed with an animal lust she had seen before, a lust just as satisfied with the drawing of blood as it was with passion. "To annul the marriage will take time, *querida.* To make you a

189

widow will only take a few moments . . . that is, unless this man is a coward."

The cold steel in Tristan's reply sent shivers up Marianna's spine. "Choose your weapon, *amigo.*"

This wasn't at all like she'd planned. "No! I forbid this!" she cried out, forcing herself between the men once again. "His embarrassment over this is enough! I am certain he will agree to the annulment."

Looking over her head, Romero patronized Tristan. "The weapon is *yours* to choose, gringo, since *I* made the challenge."

Giving up her plea to the man who had tricked her, Marianna spun around to face Tristan. "You must be reasonable!"

"Reason doesn't seem to work with the likes of you, Frenchie," he replied tersely, picking her up and putting her aside. "Now go sit down over there and keep out of the way. I'll deal with you later."

Ignoring the threat, Marianna balked. Surely the bull-headed fool realized he invited death. "I will not allow it!"

"Go!"

The explosion of anger in his voice drained the blood from her face. She stood frozen by the icy contempt glaring down at her. Didn't he understand she was trying to save his life?" *"Now,* woman!"

"Señora, please," Mateo coaxed at her elbow. "He needs no distraction."

Marianna flinched as a hand caressed her cheek, drawing her attention to Victor Romero's smiling face. "Fear not, *querida.* You need not suffer such a tyrant for much longer." Far from comforted, she allowed Mateo to pull her to the side, Victor's "Choose the weapon, gringo" slamming into her conscience like a iron sledgehammer. God in heaven, what had she done?

"I counterchallenged, *amigo*. *You* choose."

"This must not happen," she whispered, her voice no more than a croak as the nightmare continued to unravel at a unrelenting pace.

"You should have thought of that before you set my friend up for the slaughter, *señora*," Mateo chided sternly. "If he lives, he will never forgive you."

Marianna glanced up at the Mexican miserably, realizing not only that he was right, but that it mattered to her. It was wrong, all wrong, but it hadn't been done intentionally. Humiliation was all she sought, not Tristan's life.

"Very well, then," Romero conceded to the breach of etiquette he made certain was not missed by the onlookers, "I choose swords."

Mateo's unrestrained curse at her side only emphasized the fear that grew to unprecedented proportion within her chest. It felt as if her heart would burst. *He is proud of his ability with the rapier, señora.* Alfonso's words resounded in her mind above the raised whispers of the astounded guests. Surely the rough backwoods Ranger had never handled any blade longer than his hunting knife.

"Swords, it is, *amigo*," Tristan answered in passionless voice. "But this is the way it's going to go: If I win, I take what's mine, leave, and that's that. You've settled this honor nonsense and it's over. Agreed?"

"And if I win?"

The fair-haired man swished the rapier through the air a few times as he considered the option, and Marianna groaned. His wrist was entirely too stiff to stand a chance. He looked as if he were swatting flies.

"You won't, if I can help it," Tristan replied, self-assured. He cocked a challenging brow at his opponent, achieving the mottled shade of red on Don Victor's face that he sought. "Shall we go outside? It'd be a shame to cut somebody for lack of space."

"*Señora?*" Mateo prompted as members of the group followed the duelists into the open courtyard.

"I did not mean for this to happen," Marianna murmured faintly. She took Mateo's hand. "You must believe me!"

An unexpected flash of sympathy crossed the Mexican's face. "Unfortunately, *señora*, our most noble motives often lead to ignoble results. You have toyed with two very dangerous men in this mysterious game of yours and now you are costing me the life of a friend. Are you coming?"

Sickened by the truth of her companion's words, Marianna shook her head. "I can not watch. You go."

As Mateo blended into the crowd gathered at the entrance to the courtyard, Marianna rose abruptly and raced out of the room toward Don Victor's study. She had inadvertently brought about this duel and she would stop it. Thankfully, due to her earlier preparation, she had the means to do so and kill Victor Romero as well. Beyond that, nothing mattered.

In the tiled courtyard, Tristan circled warily beyond the lethal tip of his opponent's blade. Instinctively, he'd assessed Romero's weakness and intended to make use of it. The opposing blade flashed in front of him and he parried the lunge clumsily, bringing a smile to its owner's face.

Certain that he was the superior swordsman, Romero would toy with Tristan for a while, which is what the Ranger was counting on. When his opponent's guard was down and he was certain of the kill, he would be more vulnerable and susceptible to the amateur prowess with the sword that Tristan had acquired in his school years back in Washington.

A fellow schoolmate, the son of a diplomat from France and a master swordsman, offered to exchange lessons with the sword for horseback-riding lessons, Comanche style. Having developed the interest as a child at Casa Valencia, Tristan agreed, never dreaming his skill would be put to the test. But then there was a lot he'd never considered where his lovely and deceptive cousin was concerned.

He parried again and ventured an awkward lunge that was easily dismissed by a skillful turn of his opponent's wrist. Instantly, he felt a sting and glanced down to see blood staining the new shirt he'd donned for the occasion. "I guess this means I'm not invited to stay for dinner," he quipped as he danced, nonplussed, away from the following slice. In the corner of his vision he caught a glimpse of a grim-faced Mateo and wondered where Elena was. The fact that she was not there worried him more than the flashing blade he dodged effectively. Was it possible she felt remorse over this?"

"Your humor is as poor as your skill, *señor,*" Romero replied, recovering with a quick backslash that nicked Tristan's other arm before he could twist away.

Damnation, that girl had gotten under his skin quick as chiggers and was twice as worrisome! "Now that I've spotted you two points," he responded mockingly as he moved away, "I guess I can start getting even."

Continuing his graceful turn, Tristan brought his blade around to clash loudly against Romero's. The air still rang as he made a circular motion with his wrist to cast the other blow aside and quickly lunged forward, slashing a long thin line across the pleated front of his adversary's shirt. Taken by surprise, the other man drew away, his free hand going to the spot and coming away with the stain of his blood. His face contorted with disbelief.

"*Dios,* you will pay for this!"

Tristan braced for the onslaught, the smile on his face set in concentration as he executed an effective defense against the angry blade cutting the air in front of him. He danced backward and lunged forward in a game of cat and mouse, feigning to be the mouse while leading his prey into his trap. The guests watched in breathless wonder as the remarkably lucky Texan drew blood twice more, once from the leg and once from the shoulder, infusing their host with a white-faced fury.

Backed against the bench that surrounded a huge olive tree, Tristan blocked Romero's slashing assault, locking the blades hilt to hilt. At that moment, only the sounds of the crickets and locusts broke the strained silence as, face to face, enraged dark eyes met cool collected blue and saw no sign of emotion at all. An icy chill that Victor Romero had never known ran through his racing blood, for he had never fought a man with no feeling, no emotion. For the first time, he considered that he might indeed lose this fight to the clumsy buffoon.

"Have you had enough, *amigo?*"

"Not until your heart is skewered on my blade," the *alcalde* sneered, letting his outrage override the uncertainty planted in his soul by the unwavering gaze. He pushed abruptly away and lunged forward, only to have Tristan's blade force his to the ground to lock hilt to hilt once more.

"It seems I have underestimated you," he ground out, perspiration beading on his forehead.

Tristan's voice was strained as well. "Shall we call this tomfoolery off and get on with business, then? I can't see letting a handful of petticoats interfere with what could be a profitable enterprise for us both."

Romero afforded his opponent an incredulous look

through the sweat that stung one eye, nearly closing it. "You are mad!"

"You're the one's loco if you want to keep going. You see, my boot is on your blade and I'm about to snap it in half," Tristan threatened calmly. "That doesn't leave much for you to fight with."

"I can not simply forfeit!" Romero protested tersely, his low reply meant for his opponent only.

A frown knitted Tristan's brow as he considered his opponent's plight. "No problem, *amigo.*"

With lightning speed, the Ranger forced his weight down on Romero's rapier. The snap of the steel near the hilt blended with the sound of his free fist exploding against his host's jaw. That should take care of it, he thought. Yet before his satisfaction could register or his opponent react, the sharp report of a pistol split the air.

Although he instinctively crouched, the resulting *ping* of a ricocheting bullet erupted in a stinging sensation across his shoulder. Tristan dropped on top of his fallen foe and reached for his pistols, only to recall that they were hung over the horn of his saddle, protocol having forbidden his wearing them inside the house.

A second shot followed, narrowing down the location of the gunman. Gun*woman,* Tristan corrected mentally upon seeing Mateo Salizar wrestling a pistol from Elena De Costa's hand. The cool reserve he'd kept during his duel with Romero began to simmer as his pulses rebounded from the sudden alarm. Teeth clenched, he climbed to his feet and helped his host up.

"Don Victor, you are a gentleman and I hope you will accept my apologies for marrying your fiancée, but, as you can well see . . ." He motioned to where Elena crossed her arms angrily and glared at his partner, "You ought to be on your knees thanking me for the trouble I've spared you."

"There is some merit in your words, I must admit," Romero replied, ignoring Marianna's indignant gasp. "And I offer my apologies to you for treating you so rudely."

Tristan held up his hand to interrupt. "'No need, *amigo*. I can't say that I blame you. But now that we know where we stand, why don't we just leave her out of this and get down to business. I hear you've done well by other American investors and I want you to set up a modern mining facility at the Casa Valencia mines, for a share of the profits, of course."

The murmur of astonishment that rose from the onlookers at the outcome of the bizarre duel nearly obliterated the *alcalde*'s gracious acceptance. "We will talk about it, Don Tristan. *"Señores y señoras,"* he announced in a louder voice, silencing the crowd, "to the dining room, please. Dinner awaits us. My guest and I will join you shortly. I think that we had best see these scratches taken care of before joining the others," he explained to Tristan. "I will loan you a clean shirt."

"I'm kind of anxious to hear what my wife had to say to you anyway, if you don't mind. I know she was miffed when I sent her home to her parents, but I didn't think her temper was this bad."

"I would leave no guns about, if I were you."

Tristan glanced to where Marianna stood stiffly in Mateo's custody. "You got a place to lock her up till we're through with business?"

"That is all you know, gringo. *Lock her up!*" Marianna mimicked irritably, hands flying to shapely hips.

"Alonso!" Romero called to the servant standing at the door. "Take Señora De Costa to her room and keep her there until her husband is ready to leave."

Marianna opened her mouth to protest, but closed it in view of the cold blast of the gaze leveled at her by the

196

fair-haired Ranger. At this point there was no one to appeal to. Damn her horrible aim and damn men! Never in her experience with them had she known so much anger and confusion.

Shown back to the room which, combined with exhaustion, had afforded her a good night's rest the previous evening, Marianna flounced down on the elaborately designed iron bed in dismay. She had thought to embarrass Tristan, celebrate his humiliation with Romero, and kill the latter in his room after the guests left. She'd even planned the parting speech to let Victor Romero know that she was the daughter of the people he had murdered to acquire Mirabeau ... that she was the one who had shot him in the knee. Now she did not know where she stood with either of the men, except that it was surely not in favor.

Second thoughts began to flood her mind as the door closed and Alfonso took his position outside. She should have given up her vendetta and gone on to Matamoros, where Andre awaited her arrival with his brother and Elena. She would never know such inner turmoil with Andre as she knew with the Texas gringo. Perhaps she could have been happy and returned to France, leaving Tristan and Romero behind to deal with each other.

Except that fate, it seemed, did not intend that to be, any more than it deigned to permit her her revenge. The odds were all against her. And then, there were the dreams. They had gone away once, but would they do so again, reinforced by all the gruesome bloodshed she had witnessed since?

Marianna shivered. And why hadn't her friends missed her by now? The plan was for her to join them after telling Don Victor she would not wed him. Surely they should have sent word to Elena's parents of the elopement and it would be a matter of time before Don Victor received some reply from Elena's father.

Such a tangled web she had woven! Even if she tried to tell the Ranger the truth, she doubted that he would believe her. And she dared not tell Don Victor who she really was. She had seen what happened to men who crossed him. Recalling the frosty glare she'd received as Tristan had ordered her locked away, she wasn't sure that a more-favorable fate awaited her now.

Marianna walked over to the window and stared out at the central olive tree through blurred vision. This room had been a guest room when her family owned Mirabeau. Marianna used to watch their parties through this very window and dream of being old enough to take part in them some day. The scene was much the same, with the lanterns illuminating the grounds and fragrant flower beds. Laughter drifted up from the open doors of the dining room as it had years before.

Why couldn't she remember this? she cried silently as the view below became obscured by smoke rather than her tormented tears and the lanterns mocked the flash of gunfire. She tried futilely to block it out, but the merriment drifting upward from below changed to screams of terror in a tortured mind. A sob wedged in her throat as she dropped to the floor. Clutching her knees to her breast, she closed her eyes, but the nightmare continued to unfold, chilling her blood and seizing her heart with icy claws that raked and tore at her until she knew the same suffering as she had as a child, hidden in the confines of the lattice-skirted bench.

She hadn't succeeded because she was a coward, she chided herself severely. Even as she'd pulled the trigger that horrid morning and blown away part of Romero's knee, she hadn't looked. It had only been the factor of short distance that resulted in success. Tonight had been no different. She had aimed as Liam taught her, but she had not been able to pull the trigger without closing her eyes. Would it have been the same, had she been able to sneak into Romero's room later on? As much as she hated the man, could she look at him and send a bullet plunging into his chest?

The image of her mother's breasts, naked and scarlet-soaked from the wound placed squarely between them, gave rise to a wave of nausea. Marianna shuddered and swallowed hard. No, she could not have run away again. She would be haunted forever until the man that had done such a thing was dead.

"I promise," she whispered, rocking back and forth against the wall beneath the window. "I promise, Mama."

"*Señora*, your husband has sent for you."

Blanched, Marianna looked up from the stupor that had claimed her. How long had she been there? Was the noise outside that of wagons leaving? Her skin was clammy and her knees threatened to buckle as she pulled herself to her feet. Brushing the wrinkles of the gown that had been one of the wedding gifts Don Victor had purchased for his bride-to-be, she tried to prepare herself for whatever punishment Tristan had in mind, yet she could do no more than concentrate on walking numbly beside the servant as he escorted her into the courtyard where the Ranger and his friend bade their host good-bye.

Her pallor was almost sickly as she quietly took her place at Tristan's side. She swallowed the terror that rose in her throat as she glanced toward the large olive tree in the center of the courtyard. She was a coward, she condemned herself without mercy.

"I thank you again for your hospitality and advice,

Don Victor, as well as for rescuing my wife from the hands of those outlaws." Tristan slipped his arm about Marianna's waist possessively and she did not resist. In fact she moved closer, as if he could protect her from the horrible memories that tormented her. He had once, she thought dully as he ushered her toward the horses Mateo brought around. And at this moment, he was the lesser of the evils.

"You're going to have to ride double with me, Frenchie." Marianna nodded mutely and waited for Tristan to help her up into the saddle with a look that managed to override the simmering anger over the outrageous accusations she made to Victor Romero about him and touch a shred of sympathy. He hadn't missed the ashen color of her face or that sheer terror she had shaken from her perfect features. It was probably an act, he told himself, shaking the tender turn of his thoughts abruptly. She was a consummate actress. He glanced at Romero, one corner of his mouth tugging upward in a half smile.

"Maybe your advice on handling womenfolk is right. Looks like my little tigress has turned kitten." .

"Do not count your laurels yet, *señor*," Don Victor cautioned him with equal humor, patting his back as if they had been friends for years.

Tristan laughed as he moved aside a mountain of petticoats that filled his nostrils with the sweet feminine scent of her perfume, and climbed up behind Marianna. "I'm no fool, *amigo*."

"That you are not, *señor*. I look forward to taking a look at your mines." He handed Mateo the dusty satchel his men had taken from the *bandidos*. The latter fastened it to his saddle.

"After the festivities'll be fine. I'm looking forward to that bullfight," Tristan lied. He thought they were a bloodthirsty atrocity, but he couldn't afford to turn down a chance to socialize with the man. He had to make friends quick, and so far, it had been by the skin of his teeth that he done this well. *"Hasta mañana!"*

"Adiós, señora! I look forward to seeing you at the festivities tomorrow."

Marianna resisted the urge to wipe her hand after the kiss her host planted on it. Daring to look into the ebony gaze, she wondered what he had told Tristan. And what was he trying to tell her now? Was that assurance she saw?

"Ah, nonetheless, Señor De Costa, I find myself in envy of you," Don Victor told Tristan candidly. "Any woman might react so hysterically considering what she has been through and witnessed. I implore you to keep that in mind."

"She is a bit high-strung," Tristan admitted in such as way as to bring a flush of color to Marianna's cheeks. "These sleek thoroughbreds usually are."

He heard a small noise of protest strangling to escape and nudged the sides of his horse sharply. It lunged forward, throwing her against his chest. Instantly, she recoiled, sitting stiffly in the saddle so that the steed's gait bounced her unmercifully.

A satisfied tilt crept to Tristan's lips. For a moment, he'd thought she was sick, but this was more like the woman who had miraculously managed to outwit everyone, outlaws and Rangers alike, who came between her and her return to her home. As furious as he was after hearing the wild story she'd told Victor Romero, he had to admit to a grudging admiration. Elena De Costa was as resourceful as she was pretty, he mused, noting the pert springing curls assaulting the creamy white shoulders displayed in front of him. Still, she had a lot of explaining to do before the night was out.

201

Chapter Twelve

"I was not shooting at you, you fool! I was shooting at Don Victor!"

Tristan McCulloch touched his shoulder. "Could have had me fooled, lady."

"But I had to let Don Victor think that I was angry at you . . . and I was! Damn you, Tristan McCulloch, if you had let me come to Casa Valencia, none of this would have happened!"

"Frenchie, I have nearly had my head cut off tonight because of you and your lies. Don't try to blame this on—"

"Doña Elena!"

The bent figure of Doña Inez moved faster than Marianna thought her years would allow, her voluminous dark robe billowing about her blue-veined feet as she descended the steps. "I am so happy to see you, my child!" she exclaimed, rushing up to Marianna and taking her into her arms enthusiastically. "But Don Tristan said that you were on your way to Mexico City!" The old woman, turned to her fair-haired lad inquisitively.

"It seems some outlaws intercepted her train—"

"A *wagon* train hauling freight! *That* is what my husband thought of my comfort!" Marianna intervened indignantly, grateful for the timely intervention. The Ranger and his companion had been firing questions at her quicker than she could think, not that she expected them to believe her, whatever she told them.

Ignoring the interruption and his old nurse's puzzled expression, he went on. "And Elena was rescued by Don Victor Romero's men. She surprised me at the banquet tonight."

"Which I have not eaten!" Marianna stepped beside the older woman, linking arms with her. "It has been a dreadful experience."

"Don't roll those lying blue eyes at Doña Inez," Tristan warned, catching on to her ploy. "You damned near got me killed tonight."

"I did not mean it to happen that way!" Marianna answered plaintively, but upon hearing his skeptical snort, she changed her tone to an equally accusing one. "And you damned near got me killed, or worse, by those outlaws! It was horrible!" A sob of frustration lodged in her throat.

"*Blue* eyes?" Doña Inez echoed in bewilderment. "My Elena does not have *blue* eyes." Squinting, the old woman peered closely at Marianna's face. "*Madre de Dios,* your eyes *are* blue! My sight is so poor that I did not notice before!" she exclaimed with a gasp. "You can not be Elena De Costa."

"That damned well does it!"

Before Marianna could react, she was seized roughly and thrown up against the wall. Her feet dangled just above the floor as the Ranger glared at her, eye to eye. "Who the hell are you, Frenchie, and just what the devil are you up to?"

"You would not believe me if I told you!" Marianna managed breathlessly.

"She is Marianna!" Doña Inez announced in bright

203

discovery. She rushed over to the couple. "Put her down, Tristan. She is Marianna!"

"Who the devil is Marianna?"

"Elena's cousin," the nurse explained, prying on his arm with her frail hands. "Now put her down before you hurt her."

Uncertain as to whether to be relieved that the truth was out or not, Marianna began to cry. She didn't mean to. It was just that the monster of her deceit had grown to such proportion that she was no longer able to control it. Tears streamed down her cheeks as she left Tristan's vengeful grip for the arms of the nurse who had helped raise her as well as her cousin after her parents' death.

"There, there, child. You must calm down and tell us what this is about! Why were you posing as Elena?"

As the old nurse led Marianna from the foyer where Tristan had stopped her abruptly to demand the answers to his questions, Mateo Salizar entered the house from having seen to their horses. In reply to his confounded expression, Tristan threw up his hands.

"Don't ask, you won't believe it anyway. Just come on in and listen."

It was a few moments before Marianna could abandon the comfort of her nurse's embrace, let alone speak. When she looked up through red swollen eyes, she spied Tristan standing near the door with Mateo, both watching her expectantly, and fought another surge of tears. Upon taking the fresh and crisply ironed handkerchief that was always folded in Doña Inez's pocket, she blew her nose and tried to even her breathing.

"Take your time, *querida*," the old woman consoled her gently. She folded Marianna's trembling hand in her own.

"I did not tell whole lies," the girl began brokenly.

204

"Elena did not wish to marry Victor Romero. She wanted to marry Emile Bienville, the riding instructor at our school in France. They wished to elope, so I came as Elena to tell Don Victor that the marriage arrangement was canceled. But . . . but he was so adamant that he frightened me and that I convinced you to help me run away from the convent. You saw how he was!" she added, seeking support from the nurse.

"And where is Elena?" the woman inquired softly.

"She should be married by now and in Matamoros," Marianna answered dejectedly.

"So why didn't you just keep on going? Why come back to Casa Valencia at all?"

"Because I was afraid that you would take my cousin's inheritance. She will be needing it, since Emile is not as well off as her parents would wish her new husband to be."

"I told you I wanted no part of it!"

Marianna resisted shrinking under the glowering look directed at her. "That was after so much had already happened."

With a skeptical snort, the young man rolled his eyes at the ceiling and fought to restrain his growing anger. "Like marrying me and leading me down a rosy path that almost got me killed?"

"I told you, I was not trying to kill you. I was shooting at Romero to keep him from killing you."

"Why?"

Her nerves completely undone, Marianna rose from the settee and crossed her arms. "I don't know!" she shouted, her voice bordering on hysteria. "I have seen so much bloodshed . . . all I want to do is go back home to France! This is the most uncivilized place in the world. There are savages, both red and white, and animals that are human. I want to dance once again and laugh . . . I hate this place! It is hell coming alive to me and *you* are the devil!"

"Child!"

"He hates me too!" Marianna retorted shrilly, pointing an accusing finger at Tristan. One look at his impassive face, however, and she dropped it. "I will leave in the morning," she murmured brokenly.

She didn't know where she would go. She only knew that it was out of this room—out of the room and out of the range of those cerulean eyes that could tear at her very soul, exacting all sorts of emotions, most of which she did not understand.

"Elen— Marianna, wait!"

"I said I will go!" Marianna shouted from the door, her hand grasping the jamb as if without it she would collapse. It felt as if her heart were being shredded with each beat, flying apart like the composure she had already lost.

Tristan caught her arm and turned her roughly, trying to shake off the hysteria that filled her eyes. "No, you don't, young lady. You sold yourself as my wife and I'm stuck with you. I need Elena De Costa now and, by damned, you're going to see this through."

"Tristan, can you not see the child is distressed? She is your cousin, as well as your wife, and deserves to be treated as such, not as a criminal!" Doña Inez reprimanded sternly. "Let the child be!"

Reluctantly, Tristan complied. The moment she was freed, Marianna fled like a wild bird in a swirl of white silk and petticoats up the steps. Her footfall pounded down the hall, interrupted only by the tortured sob that came back to him before the slamming of a door.

Wife, he thought, running frustrated hands through his hair as he walked over to the settee where the only one who might shed more light on this bizarre mystery

206

awaited, a reproachful look on her aged face. "She can't be my wife, because I married Elena De Costa . . . or . . ."

"You have shared a marriage bed, my son. Surely you have the courage and gentlemanly conscience to see that she is not dishonored."

"Marry her *again?* You can't be serious!"

Doña Inez leaned over and patted his head. "She is to be pitied, Tristan. Her life has been a tragic one. You see, Mirabeau once belonged to her parents. Her father was a Frenchman who remained behind after Maximilian's reign ended to become a Mexican citizen. There were those, however, who did not accept that. Some of the revolutionaries attacked Mirabeau and killed her parents. Her mother was raped and murdered before Marianna's eyes while she watched, terrified, from under the bench around the olive tree in the courtyard that is there to this day."

So that was why she'd looked as if she'd be sick when she walked into the courtyard. Or could it have been guilt? Tristan reasoned warily. Or both?

"That might explain why she wanted to kill Romero. He had what was rightfully hers," Mateo speculated slowly, echoing Tristan's next thought. "She missed with the gun, and the bullet richocheted and struck you by accident as she said."

"*Madre de Dios,* she tried to kill the *alcalde?*" Doña Inez remarked in dismay. She shook her head. "I always feared that the bloody massacre Marianna witnessed left her a little . . . well, afflicted in the mind. She had the most horrible nightmares where she would awaken the household screaming for her mother." The nurse turned to Tristan in alarm. "You must keep her from doing another such thing! Perhaps a strong man like yourself could make Marianna forget the horrors of her past."

"Wait a minute," Tristan chuckled humorlessly.

"She is such a beautiful, spirited child. You must have found her attractive or you would not have wed her. I know that you did not marry her for the mines, for they were already yours by law . . . and you said that you needed her . . ."

"*Ay ay ay!*"

Ignoring Mateo's groan, Tristan held back his denial. He was caught up in a web of deceit from which there was no obvious way out—at least for the present. "For her sake, I will keep up this charade until . . ." He glanced at his friend. "Until we can be properly wed again."

Obviously pleased, Doña Inez rose. "Wait until Sister Rosa learns that Marianna—"

"Doña Inez!" Tristan interrupted, "Marianna has to continue to act the part of her cousin for a while." Seeing the old nurse's bewilderment, he put his hands on her bent shoulders. "I did not come back to Casa Valencia solely to claim my inheritance."

"What other reason could there be?"

"I can't tell you, for your own safety. You are going to have to trust me that everyone must believe Elena and I are married or it could cost us both our lives."

"*Madre de Dios!*" Casting a suspicious look at Mateo, as if he might have something to do with the danger, Doña Inez crossed herself. "I will pray for you both night and day."

Tristan smiled, grateful that he would have no more to explain. Too many people knew too much as it was. "Thanks. We're going to need it." Nothing could be closer to the truth, he mused as the woman took her leave and made her way up the wrought-iron staircase in the foyer beyond the fountain it encircled.

"I hate to keep repeating myself," Mateo interrupted his thought, "but what are we going to do now?"

"My dad always had a saying for times like this," the

golden-haired Ranger replied dryly. "He'd say, it's 'time to dance to the fiddler.' Take it as it comes," he explained, turning back to ponder the empty stairwell where he and Catalina had once played soldiers and Indians.

Marianna . . . the name was more suited to the girl who had led him on a merry chase across the river. No one with the serene name of Elena could have pulled some of the stunts she'd managed. They would have been too reserved or misnamed—one or the other. No, Marianna suited just fine.

In the large bed in the master suite on the second floor, Marianna stared at the frescoed ceiling with swollen red eyes long after she heard Tristan try the lock on the door and go away. Her tears had dried on her cheeks and her heart had resumed a normal beat as the threat vanished, at least for the time being. Even after the strain of the interrogation downstairs had passed and she'd had time to consider her reaction when he halted her at the door, preventing her premature escape, she could not make out the conflicting emotions that battled within her.

Part of her wanted to flee, but there was also an undeniable part of her that longed to move closer and feel the reassuring embrace of the arms that seemed to threaten and offer consolation at the same time. Of course, it was guilt that made her afraid of him. She had used him in whatever way possible to get close enough to Romero, only to foil her chances with her bad aim and cowardice. And for what? Romero was alive and Tristan McCulloch would never trust her again.

· Not that it mattered. She intended to go back to France anyway. That rough-mannered smooth-talking gringo would look the total fool there. She would return to where men knew how to treat ladies. All she had to do was endure his company until he got the evidence he needed to turn Romero over to the authorities.

Marianna's eyes widened as the image of the wagonmaster's journal, nestled boldly on his library shelf, came to mind. If Tristan had that, it would be over and they could go back to the lives that made them the happiest—as far away from each other as they could get. She could help him get them, and if she killed Victor Romero in the process, the journals would exonerate her, particularly if she told them how she had seen him murder her mother. Perhaps now, someone would believe her.

Her fragile state of mind assuaged by the idea, Marianna tried to relax. It would only take a short time, perhaps one more invitation to Mirabeau. Then it would all be over, and once again she'd be able to sleep without fear of that nightmare invading her slumber.

Although her body subconsciously fought her exhaustion, later, when a hound began to bay in the distant stableyard beyond the high walls enclosing the open patio, she did not hear it. The strain of the evening had finally taken its toll.

On the settee downstairs in the salon where he'd stretched out after finding the door to the master bedroom locked, Tristan had also fallen into a sound sleep, his last conscious thought of a pair of tear-filled blue eyes widened in terror. The continuing flow of the fountain trickling in the inner foyer was like a lullaby, gentle and reassuring, although his guns rested on a table nearby in case he'd misjudged Romero's intentions.

Yet it was no threat that came in from the outer walls that snatched him abruptly from his slumber, but one so real and shaking that he bolted upright on the sofa, Marianna's name hanging on his lips. He'd seen her fighting for her life, perspiration filming on her forehead

210

as she lay on a woolen blanket, one woven by his father's adopted tribe, the Honeyeaters. Blood soaked the material of her dress as she writhed in pain from the fingers—his fingers—probing her warm flesh to find the bullet buried there. She called out his name in a voice that ripped at his insides and filled him with a sense of helplessness the likes of which he'd never known.

Breathing deeply to restore order to the pulses running rampant through his veins, Tristan unbuttoned the shirt Don Victor had loaned him. He noted as he shrugged it off that the sleeve had teased out of the stitching at the shoulders, a result of Tristan's wider build, and made a mental note to ask one of the servants to repair it before returning it. The cooler air assaulted his clammy skin, but Tristan still yielded to the beckoning call of the fountain in the foyer. Perhaps the cold water would help him shake the aftermath of the horrible nightmare and convince him that it wasn't real.

Or was it? His hands froze as they dipped into the round fountain and in which he and Catalina had played as children whenever Doña Inez was preoccupied. No, he decided, splashing water on his face and dabbing it around his neck. Those dreams belonged strictly to Cat and his father. He'd never had one and it was not likely that he ever would. It was just a nightmare.

As he blotted off the excess water with a towel, he became aware of the soft sound of padded footsteps upstairs. He started belatedly to move into the shadows when he saw a slender figure garbed in thin silk appear at the top of the steps, clutching her abdomen as if in pain. Color drained from his face, in spite of his resolve to dismiss the dream.

"Marianna?"

"Tristan!"

The name was sobbed as she burst into a run that swept her down the steps toward him, her unbound hair flying wildly about her face and shoulders. Tristan met her at the bottom step, instinctively catching her up in his arms and drawing her to him. Her cheeks hot and wet against his bare skin, she folded in his embrace, clinging to him as if her very life depended upon it.

"What is it, Frenchie? Another nightmare?" he whispered, his hand going, unconvinced, to her back where the bloodied wound had appeared in his own dream. It had been so real. Yet, all he felt was the smooth silk of her nightgown, warmed by the soft trembling body beneath it. Relief flooded through him, swift and undeniably warm, as if the cool water he had just splashed on his face and chest had not helped at all.

"Hold me, Tristan. Don't let me g-go."

The heat began to curl within him as he complied, becoming increasingly aware of the feminine curves pressed against him. Although, just the way she pronounced his name was enough to send his pulse catapulting, especially whispered against his chest by lips he had but tasted.

It didn't take a lot of imagination for him to know what she had seen as a little girl—what had reduced her to that same frightened child now. He'd followed the likes of the ones that had murdered her family and witnessed the atrocities left in their wake. It was enough to give a grown man nightmares, let alone a child. Only after witnessing so much of it was Tristan able to sleep at night, force it out of his mind. If he couldn't do that, he'd have had to find another profession.

"Do you want me to take you back upstairs now?" he asked dryly, when her crying had subsided to ragged gasps that seemed to shake them both. Although she acted the frightened child, there was no question that she was decidedly a woman. It was all he could do to keep his hands from roaming over the silk-clad curves highlighted in the moonlight and control his body, which was starting to develop a mind of its own.

"Non!" Marianna backed away and looked up at him. The cooler air rushed between them, breaking the stirring contact, but as he looked down, there was no denying the arousing spectacle of her gown clinging to firm upthrust breasts, its laced neckline dipping between them and skimming over their roundness as if to tease. "I . . . we must talk."

He cleared his throat. "About what?"

As if somewhat embarrassed by what she had to say, the girl glanced awkwardly at her bare feet. "About the way I am feeling . . . that I am afraid of you and yet I want you to hold me and . . ."

"And what, Marianna?" Tristan encouraged, suddenly robbed of breath.

"And kiss me," she finished, raising a searching gaze to his. "Make it all go away, Tristan, at least for the night."

It was all Tristan could do to keep from seizing her to him then and there. Instead he lifted her chin and brushed her lips gently. "We might get stuck with each other for the rest of our lives," he reminded her. It was an absurd idea, but at that moment, it didn't seem nearly as bad as when Doña Inez had suggested it earlier.

Pressing against him, Marianna shook her head, her raven tresses pulling silkily through fingers entwined in them. "Just help me through the nights, Tristan. I can not face them alone . . . and when this is over, I promise that I will go back to my beloved Paris and you can return to your Texas. After all, you are married to Elena, not me." She placed a tentative kiss at the hollow of his neck, and fire seemed to spread through his veins coursing like molten lava down a mountainside. "And she is already married, which makes it nothing to us."

The road to paradise had been cleared for him, yet he could not bring himself to take it. To do so now, when she was so visibly shaken, was to take advantage of her fear. "Well, just to make sure you're certain about this . . ."

The cold water in the fountain shut off Marianna's startled exclamation as it swallowed her up. She struck the stone bottom where she used to search for coins, which she and Elena had tossed in from time to time, and started up, when something brushed against her. Grasping the trousers of what she discovered was a leg, she pulled herself to the surface, sputtering.

"What . . . Have you lost your mind?"

Standing thigh-deep in the water himself, Tristan thought the girl standing in front of him was more beautiful than any nude water nymph he'd ever seen tipping vase. "It's mighty hot, Frenchie. Thought we both could use a little cooling off before we went upstairs."

Uncertain exactly how to react, Marianna looked at him incredulously as he dropped to his knees so that the water approached the broadest span of his chest. He didn't seem to be laughing at her. What she saw in his eyes was not merriment. It was as warm as the water was cool. Glancing down self-consciously, she saw the taut peaks of her breasts, pronounced by the wet clinging silk, and, crossing her arms in belated modesty, dropped to her knees as well. The water grazed her chin as she gave her companion another curious appraisal.

He wasn't angry, but he wasn't acting himself. Somehow she couldn't picture the rough and ready Texas

214

Ranger splashing about in a fountain. Backstroking in a river, yes, but there was hardly enough room for his broad shoulders to submerge here. Her mouth twitched with the sudden ridiculousness of it.

"Cat and I used to sneak in here when Doña Inez was busy."

"Is your sister as wild as you?" Marianna had not thought of him as having a family, either. He appeared such a loner.

"No, I was the quiet one."

His answer was delivered so seriously that Marianna couldn't help the skeptical giggle that escaped. She slapped a hand over her mouth and looked up at the stairwell. Their poor nurse had suffered enough surprises for one day without catching them half-dressed in the foyer fountain.

"We used to play soldiers and Indians here and in the inner courtyard. Cat was the Indian. She would sting the devil out of me with those blasted arrows of hers before I could get close enough to give her a good whack with my sword. She's a doctor out in California now."

"A *lady* doctor?" Marianna had never heard of such a thing.

"And successful at it. She's founded a hospital near Los Angeles and still has had the time to raise her children." Tristan grinned broadly. "We McCullochs are a single-minded bunch."

Marianna chuckled softly, finding no room to disagree, and marveled at this intriguing side of the man to whom she felt irresistibly drawn, in spite of herself. "And what of you? Are you planning to chase outlaws all your life?"

"I imagine one day I'll take over my parents' ranch— none too soon, I hope. Of course, if I hang around you too long, I may not live to see it."

The beguiling tilt of her lips faded. "I told you I did not mean to hurt you. I only——"

"I know," Tristan cut her off. "Doña Inéz explained it all to us—about your folks, that is. But you know that Mat and I will put Romero behind bars and before a firing squad, if possible. All we need is to get some proof. He's in pretty thick with the Mexican government, but Díaz wants foreign investment. If he can't protect the silver being shipped out, he'll lose it."

"I know where there is proof!" Marianna provided eagerly, rising up on her knees. "He has the manifests of the companies his men have robbed in his office. Can you believe his nerve?"

"You've . . ." Tristan fought to concentrate on what his companion was saying rather than the water that streamed off the tips of her ripe breasts, inadvertently displayed in her excitement. "You've seen them?"

"Yes! There are even bloodstains on the one that came from the wagon train you sent me away on. And there were prisoners," she added, recalling the men who had been bound and placed on the wagons. "Did you not once say that they might be kidnapped to work in the . . . mines?" Marianna stumbled, suddenly aware of the gaze fixed on her lips, as if contemplating them. "I . . . I would be pleased to identify the men and . . ." She groped for what it was that she had been about to say, but the fire that kindled in her companion's eyes seemed to have consumed it, spreading into her veins.

"I didn't mean for you to be kidnapped, Marianna. I wanted to get you out of harm's way."

Marianna swayed under the light touch of the crooked finger that tilted her chin toward him, so that she could not escape the hypnotic attraction that drew them closer and closer. Her throat grew dry. "The fates are playing games with us, are they not?"

216

Her heart tripped as he gathered her hands in his and raised her to her feet. Instead of answering, he kissed them, each and every knuckle, before turning her palm to brush the inside of her wrist with his lips. She barely noticed that he had stepped out of the fountain, but went willingly into his arms as he opened them to lift her out.

The moment their bodies touched, Marianna shivered, not from the cold water that dripped freely on the tiled floor, but from the stirring contact of the manly muscle against her thinly veiled flesh. It was warm, no hot . . . and breath-robbing, so much so that she could not respond to his husky question.

"Do you still want that kiss?"

Yes! Her body screamed the answer in the silence, broken only by the trickling of the fountain, and moved closer to him to convey its frantic sentiment. She nodded, her hands finding their way around and up the back of his neck as his mouth swept down to claim her own.

She did not understand the mind-boggling effect of the searing kiss, yet instinctively, she knew how to respond. Her lips parted under the possessive assault of his tongue and desire knotted deep within her, forcing her hips even closer in a grinding, hungry pattern that was emphasized by the hand that closed over her buttocks. Suddenly there was a lean hard leg between her own to bear the brunt of the pressure. The result was a burst of pleasure that ran through her like wildfire. She dropped her head backward, exposing her neck and gasping Tristan's name in a frenzied plea.

"Maybe I'd better take you back to your room."

Shocked by the staggering implication, Marianna raised startled eyes to his. "You are going to leave me?"

Tristan scooped her up in his arms and looked down at her. "Wild horses couldn't drag me away, Frenchie."

Marianna felt as though she were floating, inside and out, as she curled in his strong embrace. Pressed against him, she could feel the fluid interplay of his torso as he climbed the steps, two at a time, and carried her down the corridor to the door she had left open in her earlier fright. Never had she dreamed when she left the room for comfort and reassurance that she could know such delight.

Yet it was only the beginning. Once inside the locked bedroom door, Tristan stood her gently in front of the bed and slowly pulled the lace straps of her gown off her shoulders. The silk peeled away from her breasts, hard with arousal, inviting the lips that circled each in turn, the tongue that flayed their tips until Marianna felt her loins flood with liquid heat. The soft mattress welcomed her arched body into its softness as Tristan proceeded to strip the rest of the nightdress off, then toss it heedlessly aside.

"Beautiful," he murmured under his breath as he lifted her up on the pillow.

His gaze worshipped her naked form as he backed away to unfasten his trousers. It touched her, like a thousand warm fingers that found their way unerringly to her most sensitive places. She clenched her knees together, as if to stop the lovetide washing over her, stirred by anticipation. She wanted no pleasure until he was in the bed to share it with her, flesh against flesh.

Instead of closing her eyes and letting this heady spell carry her away, she forced her attention to the unsheathed sword of his passion, waving proudly as he stepped free of the pants and kicked them into a pile with her discarded gown. The word *glorious* emerged from the murky turmoil in her heat-infested brain.

She'd never seen a naked man, aside from classical statues, and now she knew why such visions were discouraged to young ladies. She was on fire, filled with a craving she knew only he could satisfy.

"You are beautiful also, *Treestan.*" A tentative smile formed on her lips, becoming more decisive as he joined her on the sheets.

Whenever she and Elena had talked of intimacy with a man, Marianna was certain that her first time would fill her with anxiety, yet here she was molding her body to his like an experienced vixen. She knew that she should act more reserved, for did not Elena's mother tell them that it was not for the woman to enjoy, but to endure? Nevertheless, she could not wipe the smile from her face except to return the fevered kisses that infected her with equal desire.

How many hands could a man possess? How many places could he touch that drove her so mad with cravings surely not of the world she knew. The questions whirled amidst tiny bolts of pleasure, driving her to wrap her body around his as if her very existence depended on it. The hard evidence of his own arousal ground against her until she was all but pleading for him to end this aching, craving need that consumed her. When he finally moved to oblige her, instead of drawing away at the first gentle touch as she had often feared she would, Marianna moved upward to receive his sudden downward thrust.

A small cry caught in her throat as somewhere in the hot fog of her thoughts a stinging discomfort registered. Yet it was not sufficient to lessen the need that held her so firmly in its grasp. And the moment he began to move, having given her a chance to adjust to this new and heady possession, it completely vanished. Opening her eyes in wonder, she caught his face in her hands, watching, between tiny convulsive shivers, the passion that danced in his heated gaze until observation became impossible and only feeling was left.

The dizzying tide erased all but that of the fiery possession that shook her with each pounding thrust of his own rapidly escalating passion. Her breath staggered with his, equally eager and driven, as the two lovers moved in an erotic dance as one. Marianna was so caught up in the rapturous tumult that she barely heard Tristan's moan of pleasure. Instead, she felt it, shuddering and explosive within the very core of her being. She embraced it, rocking with her own riotous reaction, her legs locked around his waist until his exhausted weight forced them apart in the languorous aftermath that overtook them.

As they lay still and spent, Marianna could feel his heart pounding against her breast, its rhythm just as wild and erratic as her own. This time taking account of the new and decidedly pleasing sensation, she reveled in the masculine possession that still claimed her. In time she found enough energy to run her hands along the lines of his back, to explore the well-formed torso that had always held a fascination for her, moving her golden lover to raise up on his hands and meet her wonder-filled gaze with one equally intense.

He neither moved further nor spoke. There was no need for words. Hearts did not need them to communicate. Marianna somehow knew that he was feeling the same precious and wonderful feelings that now drugged her and invited sleep. The corner of his mouth tugged into a lazy smile as he lowered his lips to hers and kissed her tenderly.

"Marianna," he reflected softly. It was only her name, but the way he said it had the same effect as his warm caresses. Suddenly he slipped his hands beneath her buttocks and rolled over so that her hair spilled over his face as he looked up at her. He brushed it behind her ear and drew her head to his chest with a deep satisfied sigh. "I like that."

This time, it was Marianna who smiled.

Chapter Thirteen

In the eyes of society she had irreversibly shamed herself, Marianna reflected as she prepared for the festivities in the village that afternoon. But she didn't care. She gave the girl in the mirror a challenging look, daring her to bother her with a guilty conscience. What if she lost her life to avenge her parents' death? Was it fair for her die and never know the intimate delights she had but read about, which a man had to offer a woman?

Her hand slipped down to cup her gowned breast and a hot flush inflamed her cheeks. To her astonishment, they were still sensitive, as if they remembered the hot caresses and kisses that made them throb for attention. Quickly she dropped her hand and took to brushing out her tangled hair once again. Heavens, she'd never felt so . . . so alive. Even if Tristan now thought she was some wanton creature, for surely he would, it had been worth it—worth his mockery as well as all the defamation she might have to endure when she returned to Paris, even though many of her acquaintances had not been as pure as snow when they walked down the aisle at the cathedral.

Tristan. She shook the dreamy look from her face and prepared for battle. Lifting a defiant chin, Marianna hurriedly wove her hair into a long single braid, taking time to work in red ribbons to match her dress. She should have known better than to expect him to remain in bed. Somehow, some romantic part of her thought that he would have been holding her when she awakened. She'd wanted to hear tender words of endearment and reassurance. Instead, she found an empty pillow and a pile of soiled, wet clothes left for the servants to pick up.

Her aunt would say that she had been used, but Marianna preferred to think that it was the reverse. After all, it was *she* who had issued the invitation, who received the comfort and—her blood warmed her face and neck to a deeper flush—and pleasure.

Dark lashes fanned wider as the idea took root. Of course! She'd seize the offensive and head off the disdain that was sure to come. Why give him the satisfaction of knowing that she was such a novice? Let him think he had been summoned to her for her own purposes, not his. It was whispered about behind fluttering fans in the best of parlors that some of the highest born of noblewomen in Paris had the equivelent of a male mistress. Granted, the men were usually younger, but who was to say there were not exceptions?

Somewhat assuaged by her plan, Marianna finished pinning up the braid in a double loop and left the room to face the day with a brighter outlook than that which she had awakened to. She was a woman now, in every sense of the word, and would not take any man's criticism for what she did.

When she entered the dining hall, Tristan was seated alone at the table, nursing a cup of hot coffee and studying what appeared to be a roughly sketched blueprint. For just a second, Marianna's heart quivered, for the light shining in the arched windows seemed to cast a halo around his golden hair. Reminding herself that he was far from being an angel, she drew back her shoulders in the most proper of postures taught at the young ladies' school she'd attended and glided into the room gracefully. The soft rustle of her scarlet skirts drew his thoughtful gaze to her as she approached.

It was as clear as the summer sky, she thought, her purpose of remaining aloof faltering as it seemed to take on a certain glow. Of what, mockery? Appreciation? Disconcerted, she glanced down, resisting the inclination to flee back up the stairs, to examine the gown she'd carefully chosen.

"Morning."

Naturally, she hadn't chosen it for him. She was going before the gentry of Valencia today, and her latest Parisian design would make her the envy of every female there. Marianna shook herself sternly, but an inner fire flashed hot on her cheeks to betray her insecurity.

He was a man. Of course he was thinking about last night. It was the mockery every decent young woman had been warned about, should she give up her innocence carelessly. Marianna shored up her resolve.

"Buenos días, señor, I trust our rendezvous last night was as enjoyable for you as it was for me." Taking up the fine linen napkin at the place setting next to him, she waited for him to pull out her chair and dropped into it, primly spreading her skirts about her. "Of course, a woman always sleeps like a baby afterward," she went on in an authoritative tone, spreading her napkin in her lap. "I doubt that you are aware of this, but in Paris, some men are compensated for that sort of thing, although *I* myself have rarely had to put out coin."

She sensed, more than witnessed, the stiffening of the tall Ranger next to her. Schooling her features with innocence, she glanced up at her silent companion to find

224

MORE PASSION AND ADVENTURE AWAIT... YOUR TRIP TO A BIG ADVENTUROUS WORLD BEGINS WHEN YOU ACCEPT YOUR FIRST 4 NOVELS ABSOLUTELY *FREE*
(AN $18.00 VALUE)

Accept your Free gift and start to experience more of the passion and adventure you like in a historical romance novel. Each Zebra novel is filled with proud men, spirited women and tempetuous love that you'll remember long after you turn the last page.

Zebra Historical Romances are the finest novels of their kind. They are written by authors who really know how to weave tales of romance and adventure in the historical settings you love. You'll feel like you've actually gone back in time with the thrilling stories that each Zebra novel offers.

GET YOUR FREE GIFT WITH THE START OF YOUR HOME SUBSCRIPTION

Our readers tell us that these books sell out very fast in book stores and often they miss the newest titles. So Zebra has made arrangements for you to receive the four newest novels published each month.

You'll be guaranteed that you'll never miss a title, and home delivery is so convenient. And to show you just how easy it is to get Zebra Historical Romances, we'll send you your first 4 books absolutely FREE! Our gift to you just for trying our home subscription service.

BIG SAVINGS AND FREE HOME DELIVERY

Each month, you'll receive the four newest titles as soon as they are published. You'll probably receive them even before the bookstores do. What's more, you may preview these exciting novels free for 10 days. If you like them as much as we think you will, just pay the low preferred subscriber's price of just $3.75 each. *You'll save $3.00 each month off the publisher's price.* AND, your savings are even greater because there are never any shipping, handling or other hidden charges—FREE Home Delivery. Of course you can return any shipment within 10 days for full credit, no questions asked. There is no minimum number of books you must buy.

4

GET
FOUR
FREE
BOOKS

(AN $18.00 VALUE)

ZEBRA HOME SUBSCRIPTION
SERVICE, INC.
120 BRIGHTON ROAD
P.O. Box 5214
CLIFTON, NEW JERSEY 07015-5214

that a winter chill had settled over the cerulean gaze narrowed at her. It reminded her of early morning sunlight dancing on an icy landscape, frozen and warm all at the same time.

"I don't doubt that," he drawled in sardonic agreement. "You're as good in bed as a five-dollar whore." The charged silence was broken by the creaking of his chair as he leaned against the back, watching her closely, as if he'd just paid her a polite compliment and was waiting for it to register.

Register, it did, staggering her and spurring an instinctive reaction. She lashed out at his cheek angrily. "How dare—"

The Ranger caught her hand easily, holding it just short of its intended target. "But you do have twice a trollop's penchant for lying."

Their gazes clashed. Never had Marianna been so insulted! How ever could she have allowed such an insidious man into her bed? She tried to pry the steel fingers away from her wrist furiously with her free hand.

"And since my services were so greatly appreciated, you shouldn't mind if I collect on the debt. After all, Mat's gone out for a while and it's just you and me." His chair fell over backward and clattered on the floor as he suddenly jumped to his feet, dragging Marianna with him roughly.

"Now?" She stammered, taken aback by the suspicion of his intent. "But what of . . . of breakfast!"

"Frenchie, in that dress, you look good enough to eat!"

Eat? Marianna's bemused echoing thought was cut off abruptly by the shoulder that heaved into her abdomen, lifting her into the air. The massive dark furniture in the room became a blur as it flew past her—a giant carved sideboard of oak, a stiff-backed leather settee with

225

matching chairs, a walnut table with a mirror beneath to check one's petticoat ...

Blood pounded to her temples, sending her thoughts racing. She'd expected derision, but not this! The man was an animal, an insensitive beast with a limitless ability to insult her! *Eat?* By all the saints, she thought, panic filling her chest so that it became impossible to breathe. Whoever heard of such a thing? She felt her strength draining, slipping away as her vivid imagination took over. There was no telling what he meant to do, unless it was one of those strange English idioms for making love.

Of course! Marianna checked the fists that balled to strike his back and blurted out in renewed desperation. "That was the point, you big bool! This dress has saved me many a coin!" She held her breath, hoping to undermine his intentions by her claim. If she could but convince him that this was her idea, perhaps she might turn this unexpected outrage against itself. After all, no one made love in the broad daylight, but for the animals!

Before an answer came, however, Doña Inez rushed into the foyer and blinked at the commotion on the staircase.

"What in the name of the saints ... ?"

Marianna looked up, her looped braids bouncing around her head, as Tristan mounted the steps two at a time. The old woman's eyes grew wide in disbelief. She clutched her dark skirts in her hands, chest heaving from the run to see if the newlyweds had taken to breaking the furniture in the great room.

"It seems," Marianna called out breathlessly, grasping her abductor's belt to steady herself, "that your Tristan is so taken by my beauty that he can not control his *animal* appetites, *señ ... ora!*" Her voice rose to a startled pitch as a callused hand found its way under her skirt

226

and slid up her leg. *"Mon Dieu, monsieur,* can you not wait until we are in the bedroom with—" She broke off, unable to finish. Her stomach curled with a burst of flame from the hidden fingers that probed beneath the silken material of her drawers. It was one thing to engage in a verbal battle with this rough-mannered Ranger, but this was an entirely different and hopeless affair. Marianna closed her eyes, shutting out the appalled face of her old nurse as they rounded the corner.

She had to keep her head, she told herself, inhaling as deeply as she could with the strong shoulder cutting her in half at the waist. The bedroom door exploded open with a booted kick, and a small shriek formed in Marianna's throat. Not only had he humiliated her in front of Doña Inez, but in full view of the upstairs maid, who stood openmouthed at the end of the hall with a bundle of linens in her hand.

Marianna grunted as she was tossed unceremoniously on the bed. Fighting her way to a sitting position amidst the layers of petticoats that piled around her, she glared at Tristan with open hostility.

Speaking through a clenched smile, the Ranger stepped back and started to unbuckle his trousers. "Time to pay up for all the inconvenience you've caused, Frenchie. Take off your clothes."

"Inconvenience! Was that what last night was to you?" she choked, her face mottled with wounded outrage.

"No, you covered last night well enough in your little speech downstairs. I'm talking about all the trouble you've been since I had the misfortune to cross your trail at that broken-down *ranchería.*"

"I would think that your sending me off to my death would more than make up for that!" Marianna demeaned with as haughty an attitude as she could muster, considering the fingers working on the buckle of his belt. She had to gain the upper hand. Lifting the tip of her nose, Marianna propped herself up on the pile of pillows she'd tossed to the head of the bed earlier. "This is a bit rougher than I had planned, but considering your background, I suppose I can hardly expect more. However, I will not take off my clothes. *I* prefer my men to undress me." She waved her hand imperiously for him to proceed with the fastenings of his trousers. "After they undress themselves, of course." Perhaps if he was naked, she considered, rapidly losing faith in her original plan, she might run out on the balcony and down the steps into the courtyard. He'd not dare follow her!

She thought her plan had worked. The golden giant considered her thoughtfully, halting the removal of his shirt. Then, he began to chuckle, a laugh that bore no resemblance to amusement. Even muffled in the confines of the shirt he pulled over his head, it made her shiver involuntarily. She watched, trying to feign indifference as he sat on the edge of the bed and pulled off his boots.

The powerful interplay of the ridges rippling on his back held a fascination that distracted her momentarily from the nimble fingers working at the fastenings of his trousers. It wasn't until he stood up and dropped them that she realized the sparseness of the time left for her escape. *Mon Dieu,* but he was even more beautiful in the light of day! Still, the moment he bent over to step out of them, Marianna rolled away from him and threw herself from the bed.

"Whoa there!"

As she sprang toward the balcony doors, Marianna felt a sharp tug on her skirt and turned to see Tristan stretched naked across the bed, a firm grip on her dress. "Let it go, you fool! You will ruin it!" she babbled in inadvertent French as he began to wind the material around his fist, drawing her in like a fish on a line.

The pants, which had kept him from running after her, dropped off his feet, leaving him as unrestrained as nature had brought him into the world. Marianna pulled away with both hands in a frenzied attempt to free herself.

"This is a new dress and worth more than a dozen nights with you, Treestan MacCoolach!"

"But there's my borrowed horse that you nearly drowned . . ."

"That was a mistake!"

"And then you nearly got us eaten alive by pigs."

"I did not know they were there! All I wanted was a bath!"

Tristan drew up on his knees, like a golden wolf crouching for the kill. "Then you had me thrown in jail and forced me to marry you . . ."

"I was desperate!"

As she was at the moment. Marianna seized the advantage of his unbalance and yanked with all her strength.

Suddenly there was no resistance at all. Her astonished scream died with a winded grunt as she sprawled backward on the floor with a thud. Somewhere behind her, a vase of flowers overturned on the table at her head, spilling its contents.

As the water struck her forehead, she glanced up to see the vase rolling over the edge and reached up to catch it before it crashed to the floor. The intended weapon had no more grazed her fingers when it was snatched away. Staring up into angry blue fire, Marianna once again twisted away, only to be seized by the hips and dragged to her feet. Her ankle hit the corner of the table as she was tossed once more on the bed.

"Must you berate me to death before you—" Marianna choked off her indignation upon seeing the flash of a hunting knife sweep across her face. God in heaven, this was no idiom of which the gringo spoke. He was going to kill her, to cut her up in small pieces like the Indians who raised him, and eat her flesh. Poor Marcos had filled her head with the gruesome heathen tales as he'd guided her to the edge of the convent lands to help her escape. The Indians had actually cut away a living victim's flesh and forced them to watch while they cooked it over a fire and ate it.

"Please . . ." she managed in a terrified voice. "You are a white man, not a heathen cannibal! The others will surely hear . . ."

"Cannibal?" Tristan maintained the hold pinning her against the mattress and stared down in bewilderment.

Marianna pried at the steel muscle at her throat, relieving the pressure sufficiently to continue to speak. "If you eat my flesh, I swear to the heavens that I will make you sick!"

"Eat your . . ." The echo suddenly erupted in a loud belly laugh that shook, not only her, but the bed as well. His full weight fell upon her, all but crushing the last of her breath from her. Tears glittered at the corners of his eyes and made their way down his cheeks, only serving to heighten Marianna's apprehension. Was he mad as well?

"I'm not going to kill you, Frenchie," he told her in a voice straining unsuccessfully to rein in his amusement. "I'm going to undress you."

Unconvinced, for the man was as unpredictable as her feelings for him, Marianna shrank from the cold touch of the knife that slipped between her breasts, and she closed her eyes, waiting for the stinging cut of its blade. Yet all she heard was the renting of material. All she felt was the loosening of the corset she'd carefully laced beneath her breasts. Too frightened to move, she lay motionless as her petticoats were shredded layer by layer and parted until the jerking and tearing stopped.

Inanely, all she could muster was a pitiful wail. "My dress . . . you have ruined my dress!" Her chin trembled and somehow a tear escaped her closed eyelids to trek down her cheek. Then the cool air that enveloped her exposed body was offset by the warm naked one that covered it. A voice, low and masculine, rumbled against her cheek.

"I don't know whether you are loco or dangerously smart, but whatever you are, Marianna Gallier, you are definitely the contrariest creature I have ever met. Now would you like to tell me just what the devil that little speech was all about downstairs?"

Marianna ventured a timid peek, blinking to oust the glaze of misery that blurred her vision. "I am no naive child. I know what a man thinks."

"And just what is that?"

"That I shamed myself last night. I invited you to my bed." She inhaled shakily. "It is all right for a man to do such a thing, but not a woman! It is not fair. You were looking at me like a common harlot!"

Much as he had wanted to torment the girl lying beneath him, Tristan couldn't bring himself to continue to bully her or have fun at her expense. She was pale as the linens beneath her and broken by a vivid imagination and a bit of female nonsense that no doubt some nun who had never known a man had put in her head.

"You are no more a harlot than you are one of those desperate women who has to pay to get a man to warm her bed." He pecked at her nose with his lips. "I may be a backwoods Texas clod in your eyes, Marianna, but I don't make love for money any more than I need stained sheets to know I've slept with an innocent."

"But I am no longer innocent. I am shamed."

"Marianna," he chided, turning her face back to him. "We're married, remember?"

"Not truly."

He couldn't resist assuaging the trembling pout a breath from his lips. "By the law of my red brothers, we are."

"But we are not heathens."

"I beg to differ, Frenchie. There's a little savage in all of us, and God knows, we seem to bring it out in each other ... especially here, like this. As to the matter of *eating*, I only meant a taste here ..." His tongue found its way to an unveiled breast and circled its tip playfully, evoking a shiver of response in the soft body beneath him. "And a nibble there." Teeth seized the mate that strained of its own accord for equal treatment in such a way as to constrict the inner muscles of her loins, making them ache to know a more-physical possession.

"There is nothing shameful about that, Marianna. Nor this ..." He planted a trail of kisses up the center of her breasts to the hollow of her throat and along a sensitive path to her ear to whisper huskily, "It only means that you are a warm-blooded woman eager to fulfill all you were made by God to be—the precious mate of a man."

Marianna took his head between her hands and stared up at his face. His words were poetry to her ears and a balm to her wounded pride. Where had this rough Texan learned such a way with them? "And you think me precious, Tristan."

He answered with a kiss, a tender sweet caress that melted the last of her reticence and banished all trace of the doubt that had made such a fool of her. Marianna

232

surrendered completely to its teasing, coaxing play, until she could not help but return it, begging for more. The urgency that filled her transmitted itself to the man who instigated it and he obliged her, parting her legs with his own and settling between them, his passion hard against her yielding flesh.

Yet, as she prepared for his fierce entry, she was treated to a more graphic education of his odd use of words. He feasted upon her, tasting and nibbling, until she could not mimic the gestures for the tiny gasps of delight that rippled through her. Her body came alive, electrified with the sensations forging wildly through it, turning down the other senses so that touch was foremost. Her skin burned, her blood boiled, and her loins were inflamed with a craving to be possessed, not by the skilled fingers that somehow found their way there to assure her readiness, but by the rigid shaft of manly flesh that replaced them.

"Treestan!" she cried out, her eyes flying open at the swift invasion that seemed to shatter what little reason she had left into shimmering shards of delight. Reveling in the powerful thrusts that scattered them over and over again, she caught his face once more and gazed up at him from the sapphire depths of her very soul. *I love you! I need you! I want you!* The sentiments spilled from her being, unspoken until her desire was such that only an animal satiation would suffice, one that lifted the savage in her to the highest heights of rapture and rocked her with the thunder of the very clouds upon which she floated.

When she touched the bed and reality again, Marianna found herself curled in her lover's arms, listening to his beating heart struggling like a pagan drum to find a civilized beat. She drew from his warmth, his strength, and snuggled closer to him. At the touch of his lips on the top of her head, she looked up to see him smiling lazily and was amazed to feel the embers of their spent passion still alive deep within.

"I wanted to do that this morning, but you were sleeping so peacefully, I couldn't bring myself to wake you."

"It would have been worth the waking," she confessed, averting her gaze sheepishly to the padded swell of his lightly furred chest. He hadn't thought harshly of her at all, her heart sang joyfully. He'd wanted her again! And even when he had frightened her, she had to admit to the excitement that coursed through her veins at the feel of his naked flesh next to hers. "You must think me a silly fool."

He shook with a gentle chuckle. "At times, silly, but you've hoodwinked me too many times to be a fool."

"I *what?*" Marianna raised up on her elbow, mulling over this newest word. Surely the Texans spoke another English altogether from that which she had learned at the ladies' school.

"Tricked me," he explained, eyes dancing as he gently moved her hair away from her face. "You know, Frenchie, I could get used to teaching you some proper English."

"I think that this *hoodwinked* is improper English," Marianna rejoined with a skeptical arch of her brow before adding with a giggle, "You Texas *yaahhoo*."

"That's *yay*hoo."

She shrugged and moved closer to him with an indifferent "Whatever," before kissing the grin she'd come to adore.

Although she'd but once initiated a kiss, Marianna had read much about them and employed all she had learned, both vicariously and from her recent experience with the man in her arms, to please him. The mo-

234

ment their lips touched, however, and his arms tightened about her, drawing her atop his lean rugged body, she did not have to draw on that knowledge at all. It was instinctive, born of this new attraction and curiously to learn all there was to know about him.

Permitting her the freedom to experiment, Tristan resisted his longing to respond with equally stirring techniques. As she tentatively licked the dark circles that tightened on his chest, she glanced up at him in surprise. "Salty," she remarked, running her tongue thoughtfully over her lips. He managed a hint of a smile, but it felt as though someone were pumping hot iron into his bloodstream, stirring the currents that had just settled in the aftermath of their passionate lovemaking.

"Your navel is dusty," she chided, delving into his abdomen with her little finger.

The combination of that and her long hair dancing lightly across his loins sent a burst of life straight to them. Disconcerted by the astonishing recovery, Tristan hardly heard her laugh, "It is only lint from your towel," but he felt the curious tongue that dipped in. He shuddered involuntarily. He'd always been of the opinion that it didn't take but once for a man to catch up after a long period of abstinence out on a drive—the need for more was in his head. What he was feeling at that moment, however, was definitely not in his head.

He found himself holding his breath as his bewitching companion moved away to contemplate his obvious reaction. Her fingers traced lightly along the lines of his hip, the inner plane of his stomach, even to where the muscles of the thigh wove into his torso, but each time they moved toward the straining control to his coiling desire, they shied clear. He swallowed dryly, wondering if he could stand the time it could take for her to summon her nerve.

"Tristan?"

"What!" Realizing the sharpness of his tone, Tristan repeated his answer with forced patience. "What, Marianna?"

"Would you think badly if I . . ."

She hesitated, turning a face to his as bright as the scarlet dress that lay shredded in the tangle of covers beneath him. Their gazes met and the charge that flowed between them finished the question without the use of words. Tristan took her hand with his own, cursing the tremble that made him feel like some green youth with his first woman, and placed it over his lust-hardened flesh.

"Tristan!"

For what seemed an eternity to him, neither of them moved. But when his name was repeated again, echoing above the thundering pulse in his ears, Marianna turned toward the door from where the male voice hailed him, her passion-glazed eyes growing wide with alarm. With a startled cry, she rolled off the bed, her raven tresses flying about her glorious body, and began to tug fiercely at a sheet.

"Answer him!" she hissed, gathering the linen around her in belated modesty.

Tristan shook himself to clear his muddled thinking. "Be right down, Mat!" He leapt from the bed on the other side, looking around blankly for his clothes. She was a seductress, a wild innocent siren.

"Are you all right, *amigo?*"

The amusement in Mateo Salizar's voice darkened his face. "Just helping the lady dress, not that it's any of your damned business."

"Did you have to tell him *that!*" Marianna whispered, a small squeak above Mateo's parting *"Hasta luego."*

Relieved of the urgency to deal with Mat, Tristan's usual good humor returned. He walked over to the appalled young lady, oblivious to his nakedness, and folded her in his arms. "Would you rather I have told him what we were really doing?"

"But *non!*" She pulled out of his embrace, looking at him as if he'd lost his mind. Upon seeing his grin, however, she realized that he was teasing her and struck him playfully on the chest. "You are a horrible man!"

As she wrestled with a smile, Tristan thought she was the most beautiful creature he'd ever seen, in or out of a bed. "I believe we have some unfinished business," he reminded her, closing the distance between them again. "Now, where were we?" He reached for her hand, only to have it snatched away.

"I have to have another dress prepared, thanks to your crazy business!" She pointed to his evident arousal sternly, endeavoring to smother a giggle. "Now put *everything* away and let me get dressed . . . again!" she added emphatically.

Tristan watched as she swept the train of her sheet out of her way and marched regally toward the shallow closet where more gowns and dresses than his mother and sister ever owned had been hung. He was tempted to strip away that high and mighty air of hers, as well as the bedsheet, but for the fact that she was right. He snatched up the trousers that looked like he'd just stepped out of them. They did have to get moving if they were going to make it to Don Victor's box at the arena before the parade. As tempting as Marianna was, he had a job to do.

As he reached for his discarded shirt, the girl glanced over her bare shoulder with a provocative dip of her lashes that sent thunder straight to his breeches. "It's improper to stare, Tristan."

Treestan. The name bounced around in his mind, making him shiver to the bone with anticipation of a quick afternoon and an early night. Damnation, he reflected wryly. She was prettier than a speckled pup under a red wagon and he felt like a one-eyed dog in a meat house.

Chapter Fourteen

"What do you *mean*, you can get us the proof we need to incriminate De Costa?" Tristan stared at the picture of innocence portrayed on Marianna's face, his own clouded with suspicion. A tryst in the room with the girl was one thing. Interfering with his work was quite another.

"Just what I said," Marianna answered shortly, the sudden change in the Ranger's humor affecting the carefree manner with which she had dressed to join the men waiting for her by the readied coach. After listening to Tristan and his Mexican partner speaking of trying to get another invitation to De Costa's home, she reminded him of the journal she had seen and spoke up, certain that he would be pleased to hear that she could help.

"Perhaps," Mateo intervened smoothly, "the *señora* might explain."

Marianna gave Tristan a pointed look and turned deliberately to Mateo. "This scoundrel is so certain of himself that he keeps the journals of the companies his men rob right in his library. I saw the very one the wagonmaster carried in his saddlebag the night he asked me to the dance. It had the last page where he tore a piece of paper off to write his name down for me and . . ." she hesitated, gooseflesh rising on her arms, "and his blood."

Tristan exchanged a surprised look with the Mexican. "He let you wander freely through his house?"

"I was his guest, was I not?" It was injured pride that put equal sarcasm in her tone. Had what had happened between them still not convinced him that she was worthy of his trust?

"Why did you not tell us sooner, *señora?*"

"Because *he* has given me little time to *speak!*" Marianna expelled in frustration, jerking an accusing finger at the Ranger.

The instant the words were out, she realized her error. Gentleman that he was, Mateo had the good grace to look out the window, but not before she saw his lips struggling to contain a smile. She could feel the heat of her embarrassment racing up her neck to burn at the tip of her head. At a loss to retract her statement, she leaned stiffly against the seat and stared straight ahead when Tristan claimed her hand.

"I'm sorry, Marianna. If I had had the good sense to stop accusing you and listen to what you were trying to tell me, things might have turned out differently all around. Doña Inez is right. It's my loss, *querida.*"

Querida! Marianna had never heard the endearment spoken so sweetly, flavored with that slow accent of the Texas gringo. She caught her breath as Tristan went on to press her hand to his lips in gallant apology, his eyes taking on a glow to match that which kindled in her own and lifted her plummeting spirits. When Mateo, however, swung a questioning glance at them, it was met with a quickly veiled gaze meant to perplex him and rescue her from her earlier blunder.

Gratefully following Tristan's lead, she found her

240

voice to speak. "You have been such a gentleman after all the trouble I have caused that I want to help you, Tristan. I not only know where the book is, but I think that I can get Don Victor to invite us to his house . . . at least for the evening. Everyone will be there to celebrate the founding of the village by the De Costas. While the peasants celebrate in the square, the caballeros will return to Mirabeau as the guests of the *alcalde*. It was all the talk among the servants."

Her unlikely knight, wearing a richly embroidered suit of russet serge in lieu of traditional armor, was adamant. "You've been in enough danger. Mat and I can handle it from here."

"But it is certain that the *señora* could sway Don Victor to an invitation quicker than you or I, particularly after that cursed duel!"

"And there are hundreds of books! I know just where to look!" Marianna protested urgently. She had to go along! How else was she to get close enough to Romero to—

"No!" Tristan inhaled deeply at the startled look on her face and went on, breaking the strained silence his vehement objection imposed. "We'll go back tonight and break in. I don't want her placed in any more jeopardy." Grinning widely, he tugged Marianna roughly against him. "Who knows, Frenchie, I might decide to keep you when this is all over."

"You had better watch your words, *amigo*," Mateo fell in with a hearty slap on his knee. "The ladies will make you eat every one of them."

Marianna straightened, assuming her most haughty of poses. "And just what makes either of you think that I would want such a big bool as this for a husband! A *gringo* at that! *Madre de Dios!*" she vowed, crossing herself as if to ward off such a fate.

Yet, when the men broke into laughter, she could not help but join them. To argue further at this point was useless. There would be time. Besides, Tristan was so charming when he was pleased. Who'd have ever thought there was a suave caballero hidden beneath that rugged sun-bronzed exterior of his!

The arena was filling with people on the sunny side, but the shaded area was reserved for the gentry, who would arrive at their leisure to observe the *corrida de toros*. Because of the gathering crowds and street vendors, it took almost as long for their coach to make its way through the village as it did to reach it from Casa Valencia. With Mateo on one arm and Tristan on the other, Marianna was able to reach the seats set aside for the guests of the *alcalde* without damage to the second dress she had donned for the day.

Although its hem no doubt collected dust, the gathered skirts of peacock blue, drawn over a white pleated underskirt, remained unscathed as she spread them daintily on the seat next to the judge's box. Instead of putting her hair up again, she left it down, gathered at the crown of her head with an ivory comb from which spilled a white lace mantilla. As she tossed it over her shoulder, she caught a glimpse of Victor Romero leaning over from the judge's stand to greet Tristan and Mateo.

He raised his hand to greet her, but a stir near the *Puerta De Cuadrillas* where the performers of the day gathered for the starting parade distracted him, drawing his attention back in the ring. Mateo stepped past her to take a seat on the other side as Tristan nudged her elbow gently.

"Seems that we missed the drawing of the bulls earlier. The fight's about to begin." He pointed to the empty seating on the bench left next to the judge's box.

"The *alcalde* wants you to move next to his box, so that he might explain the fight. He says this is your first bull-fight."

Marianna nodded, blanching beneath sun-kissed cheeks, and rose without objection to trade places with her husband. In spite of Tristan's reassuring wink, her stomach constricted instinctively at the thought of being so close to her mother's murderer, but she willfully ignored it. If she but had a weapon, her torment might be over and done with.

"It is a beautiful day for a bullfight, Señora De Costa, but even the blue of the sky can not compare to the brightness of your lovely eyes."

Reluctantly Marianna gave up her hand to the *alcalde*. "You are most kind, sir."

At that moment, the crowd burst into cheers, and a small band that she had not seen earlier began to play at the entrance to announce the entry of the participants. Clad in colorful costumes, glittering with silver and gold adornment, in marched the *matadores*, followed by the less glamorous *banderilleros*, the men who placed the adorned barbed sticks into the bull, according to her self-appointed guide. After them, entered the *picadores*. They would *pic* the bull to slow him down and weaken the neck muscle so that the animal could not hold up his head, making the placing of the sword for the kill easier as well. Their padded horses pranced about in the excitement that filled the air in the arena, tails lifted like proud silken banners flying behind them.

Rising to his feet as the entourage came to a halt in front of the judge's stand to salute him, Victor Romero waited like a king presiding over his court to take the honor as his due. He would be a king, Marianna thought bitterly, diverting her attention to where the three *matadores* who were scheduled to fight bowed gallantly and flourished their *monteras*, or hats, in a low sweep.

"Miguel Alvarado is on the left, *señora*. You met him at my home yesterday morning."

As the man Romero pointed out rose, Marianna could see that he was looking directly at her. To her astonishment, he gave her a slight nod and tossed a kiss in her direction.

"Like myself, he too is enchanted with your beauty."

Aware that the flowery compliment offered by the young *matador* that morning meant no more than the tribute he now paid her, Marianna afforded the man an aloof smile she had mastered to deal with the careless flirtations so abundant in the ballrooms and parlors of France. After all, she was married, at least as far as the likes of him were concerned.

"Damnation," Tristan whispered at her elbow, "I may have to fight my way out of Mexico with you before this is over! The wagonmaster, Romero, and now Alvarado . . . Do you have to flirt with every tall, dark, and handsome yahoo you come across?"

"I am not flirting, I am but smiling!" Marianna objected under her breath, turning to see that teasing grin that always sent her heart tumbling in her chest. She slapped a well-formed thigh with her fan to ward him off. "And do not sit so close! We are not supposed to be happily married."

Tristan started to argue, except that the girl spoke the truth. Affording her a contrived glare, he turned his attention back to the arena, now clearing for the first fight. Maybe that was just what he needed to get her out of the way—a good argument, and he could send her home and go on to the festivities without her. Besides, the way Romero was looking down the front of her dress, like a hungry wolf drooling over a forbidden treat, just didn't sit well with him.

Or her, either, by the look of things. The handkerchief she'd wrapped about her hand to still its trembling wasn't quite successful. If she was so blasted frightened by Romero, why did she keep trying to get to him instead of letting Mateo and himself take care of the man? All she talked about was returning to Paris, so that ruled out Mateo's idea that she wanted Mirabeau . . . unless she wanted to sell it. For someone with such a transparent face, Marianna Gallier was a complex little thing.

Victor Romero stopped speaking to Marianna long enough to signal to the trumpeteers to announce the beginning of the first fight. The band broke out into a lively stanza that came to an abrupt halt with the entrance of the bull into the ring. In his emerald *traje de luces*, or suit of many lights, Don Miguel Alvarado stepped into the ring with a large cape and began to wave it to attract the bull's attention. In spite of her discomfiture, Marianna found herself becoming intrigued by the explanation of the actions taking place below them.

The animal was fierce and needed little encouragement to charge the cape. After a few passes, Alvarado stepped behind the plank partition with a careless toss of his cape to an assistant and watched as the *picadores* rode into the ring for the *pic-ing*. The moment the bull spotted the padded horse, it charged at it, horns lowered at a lethal level. Marianna gasped as the horse and rider deftly avoided the charge, letting loose a barbed stick trimmed with multicolored ribbons that buried in the tough neck of the bull.

The arena shook with the bellow of the powerful beast as it made a wide circle to avenge its pain. Her knuckles were clenched white on the rail of the judge's booth, as Don Miguel Alvarado stepped back into the ring to taunt the animal with the cape in an effort to divert it from its determined vengeance against the horseman. After a series of successful passes, he returned to the cover of the *burladero* and the game of cat and mouse between the mounted *picador* and the snorting beast repeated itself.

Marianna stared in awe as the horse and rider dodged the deadly horns once again, leaving another *pic* deep in the bed of living muscle.

"He is a good one, that one," Romero remarked at her side, his dark gaze afire as it followed the angry bull around the ring.

"Is he not in pain?"

Romero flashed a patronizing smile. "Such pain as will make him all the more fierce and courageous. I raised him from a small calf at Mirabeau. He is worthy of my friend Alvarado," he replied, nodding to where the *matador* once again tempted the bull away from the horse and rider.

More appalled by her companion than by the spectacle below, Marianna turned back to see the torturous act was repeated one more time, marking the end of the first *tercio,* or first third, of the three acts. The band began to play and the *picador* turned the second phase of the fight over to the footman of their team, the *banderillero.* Marianna watched the bull, now stunned by the *pics* buried deep in its neck muscles, walk slowly around the ring, robbed of some of its belligerence. The footman walked to the center of the dusty arena carrying a pair of bright pink, green, and yellow barbed sticks not quite as long as those of his predecessor. He made as if to run a circle around the dazed animal and then, like lightning, charged in just beyond the closest horn and thrust the *banderillas* into its withers.

Twice the *picador* enticed the increasingly incensed

bull into charging him, each time narrowly missing the dangerous pass of the lowered horns, but never missing the opportunity to place additional pairs of barbed sticks into the animal's tough hide. The bull tore around the arena, bucking wildly in an attempt to shake the brilliantly adorned barbs off. Blood spattered the whitewash of the *burladero,* behind which Don Miguel Alvarado exchanged his large cape for a smaller one and awaited the call of the trumpet to announce the final phase of the fight.

The crowd erupted in an uproar as the *matador* entered the ring and approached the judge's box. Trying to ignore the bloody trail left by the anguished animal that rubbed against the walls of the *barrera* separating it from the tumult, Marianna wondered that Alvarado dared turn his back. Yet, when he moved closer, she could see that he was ever alert to the bull's movements as he bowed and asked permission of the judge to kill the animal.

"For the lovely Señora De Costa," he finished, dedicating the kill to Marianna.

Marianna turned from the brilliant smile cast her way, her hand tightening on Don Victor's arm. *"Non, monsieur!* It is suffering."

"As it was bred to do, *señora,"* Romero informed her in a placating tone. He signaled the matador to proceed with the kill and the bloodthirsty crowd shouted with cruel delight.

Marianna dropped her hand and glanced over to see Tristan watching her. She nodded weakly to his questioning look, praying that her stomach would not betray her. Chin lifted valiantly, she stared into the arena, refusing to focus on the deadly game that ensued. A burst of approval from the crowd, accompanied by equally exuberant music, lured her into thinking the ordeal over.

She searched the arena to discover the bleeding bull coming around once again to charge what was sooner or later to be his death.

The animal rushed forward, bloodied pink foam flying from its flared nostrils to fall in the dusty wake behind it. Calmly Don Miguel awaited the pounding hooves, holding his small *capote* just to his side. As the fierce horns dropped lower, the *matador* arched back gracefully and stepped aside, drawing the beast after the cape in a bizarre dance of death. Marianna braced for the flash of the metal sword, but it did not come.

The crowd screamed a lusty *"Ole!"* eager for the dance to end and the *matador* to make the kill. To taunt his audience, as well as his intended victim, Don Miguel coaxed the beast into several more passes. Undeniably a showman, he dropped to his knees; he turned his back to his pain-crazed adversary; he allowed each encounter to bring him closer and closer to being gored by the bloodstained horns.

The bull began to tire, its attacks losing their ferocity until it no longer followed through with them. By now the onlookers chanted in a frenzy, *"Toro ... Toro ... Toro ..."*

Caught up in the hypnotic death play, Marianna found herself unable to escape the drama unfolding before her eyes. Her thoughts catapulted to another time, another nightmare, that mingled with the present. Her heart seemed to beat to the chant in revulsion, but, nonetheless, with equal fervor.

She prayed that it would be done, and quickly. They had broken this magnificent creature, degraded it with torture and set it up for the kill ... just as they had her mother. The feral gleam in Romero's eye was no different now than it had been the day he had had his way with Eleanor Gallier and then placed a bullet squarely between her breasts.

Don Miguel approached the panting animal, the sunlight dancing off the metal of the curved sword. Grabbing its attention with the cape, he drew its head to the ground. Then suddenly, he raised the sword over the right horn and drove it between the bull's shoulder blades.

Marianna swayed and caught herself as the dying beast staggered away, refusing to give up the fight. She swallowed the bile that rose to the back of her throat, unable to tear her eyes from the spectacle. Don Miguel was handed yet another sword, marked by a strange crosspiece near the end. It was almost over, she told herself desperately. It was daylight and Tristan was nearby. In spite of the shade afforded them, a clammy sweat clung to her skin, and although it was hot, she felt cold, very cold.

Everyone was on their feet, cheering madly. The *matador* reached over the bull's back and dropped the animal quickly with a swift and precise execution. Marianna's fingers locked about the rail separating her from Victor Romero. The scene became a blur and she fought to maintain her consciousness. She had to stop being such a coward! She had to be strong for her mother . . . for Tristan.

"*Señora,* for you."

Dropping her gaze to the *matador* who had come to stand before her, Marianna spied a bloody piece of the bull's hide staining the white silk handkerchief in which it had been wrapped. As she focused, her stomach lurched threateningly and her knees buckled beneath her. God in heaven, she thought, the sky spinning around her head dizzily, it was an ear!

Through the heavy fog that enveloped her, Marianna

could hear voices, mainly Tristan's, rumbling against her ear from the chest against which she was cradled. It was as reassuring as the arms that carried her. He was concerned. How very sweet, she mused, the sentiment becoming part of the whirlpool of feedback registering in her dazed consciousness.

And there was Victor Romero's voice, insisting that they take the *alcalde*'s coach to Mirabeau rather than travel five miles further to Casa Valencia. Tristan, however, would not hear of it.

"But our carriage is entrapped by all the others. There is no way we can get it free until the crowd disburses after the other two fights," Mateo pointed out practically. "Don Victor's coach is here at hand, *amigo. Madre de Dios,* but she is pale!"

"She needs to go home," Tristan insisted stubbornly. "Perhaps if it is not serious, Doña Inez can take care of her, and you and I can come back to Mirabeau."

Marianna stirred, a frown knitting her brow as she realized his intention. She couldn't let them go to Mirabeau without her. She had to be brave. She rested her hand against the ruffled front of his shirt to get his attention. "I . . . I'll be fine," she whispered, drawing attention to the fact that she was coming around. "I don't wish to miss the dancing."

"You're in no shape to dance, Frenchie. You're white as a ghost."

"It was the blood," she objected, her voice catching. "I promise, I will be fine. You have but to put me down." Cautiously, she moved her legs to see if they would obey her command. "Please, Tristan. I promise I shall rest. Besides," she added, changing her ineffective tact quickly, "it is important for us to convince our neighbors that that silly duel is a matter of the past."

"The *señora* is as practical as she is lovely," Don Victor complimented, returning his expectant gaze to Tristan. "Now, I insist that you and your wife accompany me to Mirabeau, if only for a little while to show our *compadres* that our initial ill will was but a misunderstanding and is no longer of issue. Señor Salizar can bring along your coach when it is freed from this mob."

"I do need to get out of the sun, *monsieur*," Marianna reminded the brawny Texan holding her protectively against him. "Although we have had our differences, surely you will not torture me and force me to go home?" Slender fingers tripped up the starched front of his shirt. She lifted rounded eyes to his, her lips pursing with an imploring and irresistable pout. "It is the least you can do after nearly sending me off to my death at the hands of brigands." Daring to test the diminishing humor that tightened the jaw muscles on her husband's face even further, she added a kittenish "Please?"

"Only for a short while."

It was more a warning than an answer, but Marianna accepted it in relief. Much as she hated to abandon Tristan's strong embrace, she was determined to show that she was indeed up to attending the festivities at Mirabeau. She struggled to get down, calling on sheer will to restore her footing.

"It's very kind of you to offer your coach, *monsieur*, as well as your hospitality," she addressed the *alcalde* as he snapped his fingers to signal the coachman to pull forward.

"It is the least I can do, after our misunderstanding. I regret that you did not find the bullfight to your liking."

"I warned you once that I did not fare well at the sight of blood." Marianna forced a laugh while allowing the *alcalde* to help her into the coach. "I have been that way since my childhood, I suppose."

251

"Some ladies are more fragile than others," Don Victor conceded, pulling himself inside to take the seat opposite her. "Your wife is like the rose, as delicate as she is beautiful."

Tristan squeezed his broad shoulders through the narrow door and dropped into the seat beside Marianna without comment. He was not only indisposed to answer his nemesis, but uncertain of what he actually believed. There was little doubt in his mind that the girl had actually fainted. Her pallor and rapid pulse had been real enough. She'd collapsed like a rag doll next to him. But for his quick reaction, she might have struck her head on the wooden bench.

Yet the same "fragile rose" had been outwitting him and surviving situations some of the toughest individuals he'd known would have had trouble getting out of. She'd come out of her faint to wrangle the invitation he and Mat had spoken of, convinced Romero that all was well between them, and firmly entrenched herself smack dab in the way to boot! She might not have had knowledge of men in an intimate sense, but damned if she didn't know how to dangle them from the tips of her fingers like a puppet master.

A lilting laugh interrupted his brooding thoughts. Tristan glanced up to see her open the matching fan to her dress with a practiced snap of her wrist and peer over it in a way that even had Romero sitting on the edge of his seat. By thunder, *he* certainly wasn't going to be one of her conquests, Tristan vowed silently, ignoring the green-tinged irritation that pricked at his neck like a bothersome heat rash. Marianna might be used to tugging on a man's strings, but when he yanked back, she'd learn those coy Frenchie ways of hers wouldn't do her one speck of good . . . at least with *this* gringo.

The coach was one of the first to arrive at the brightly

decorated hacienda. Garlands of red, white, and pink bougainvillea bordered the dark double doors leading to the interior of the two-story section of the house and continued to mark the way to the courtyard in the back through a cool tiled atrium. Servants scurried about with stacks of linens, platters of food of all description, and frantic faces upon seeing the *alcalde* and his guests enter prematurely.

"Alfredo!" Victor Romero snapped his fingers, halting the elderly servant in his progress up the winding staircase. "Have Maria prepare my room for the Señora De Costa so that she might rest until the dancing begins. Meanwhile, I shall entertain Don Tristan in my office. You understand," he said, returning his attention to his companion, "that our guest rooms are filled with visitors from neighboring towns and provinces."

Tristan found the situation growing less and less to his liking by the minute. "I'd just as soon take Marianna home."

"If you are serious about opening your mines, Don Tristan, I would suggest that you stay. Don Heraldo Cabal is coming with his wife and daughter. It is from him that I would purchase the new bracing for the mine."

"Well, *that* should settle it!" Marianna interjected emphatically. "The mine certainly must come ahead of me. *You* can talk of mines . . ." She tapped Tristan playfully on the chest, a hint of challenge dancing behind a batting fan of dark lashes. "While *I* shall enjoy dancing with men who are more comfortable on a ballroom floor than by a wilderness campfire." Extending her hand to her host, she dipped gracefully. "I am, once again, in your debt, *monsieur*. A short rest and I shall look forward to your party with great anticipation. *À bientôt*, Tristan!"

"You wife, she is a dangerous woman to displease,

señor," Victor Romero remarked as Marianna disappeared up the paneled stairwell behind Alfonso.

"Aren't they all?" Tristan retorted sardonically. He shifted his jacket and shrugged his shoulders back, as to rid himself of the sneaking suspicion that Marianna was not purely intent on resting and dancing. Damn her worrisome hide, if she tried to get that book on her own, he'd wring her neck —if Romero didn't do it first.

Chapter Fifteen

Lanterns, hanging at intervals around the festive site of the *alcalde*'s party, had not yet been lit, for the setting sun provided ample light over the western horizon. In the master suite, Marianna drank the warm sherry Alfonso provided her, propped up on an elbow on the large canopy bed in which she had been born. A flood of memories bombarded her in the familiar room. Her parents had created her out of love there, she thought, her heart twisting in anguish. She closed her eyes, aware of the servant's movements about the room as he opened the windows to afford the most draft.

Although she hadn't meant to nap at all, the time it took to convince Alfonso that she was truly asleep, combined with the long sensuous night in Tristan's arms, lured her into it. But for the sound of the guitars heralding the starting of the dancing, she still might have been sleeping, she thought in dismay, bolting upright with a bound. Recalling Alfonso taking a post outside the door, she listened for any noise in the hall to indicate that the sound of the creaking bed had alerted anyone to her awakening.

The effort was met with complete silence. Perhaps the servant had gone about his way, she mused. There was certainly enough going on to demand his services, aside from keeping an eye on her. Marianna slid off the bed quietly and padded in her bare feet to the panel in the back of what appeared at first to be solely a closet. Determined not to take the conventional route through the hall to Don Victor's office and risk discovery, she quickly stepped inside, past the expensive suits hanging on pegs, and to the far right to what was, at first glance, an end wall.

Deftly, she felt for the catch in the corner until she found the piece of molding engineered to pull out of place. One fingernail and more than one layer of paint broke when it finally came free, releasing the swinging wall to reveal the opposite end of the hidden passage her father had installed years before.

It was his escape from his office to his bedroom when he chose to avoid troublesome visitors who wanted to speak to the liaison between Maximillian and the local officials. He had warned the emperor that the support of neither the caballeros nor the peasants was behind him and disassociated himself with the French regime before its fall. Still, it had come to no good in the end. The unsettled country that had captured his heart claimed his life.

The dust in the narrow corridor, sandwiched between a small parlor and a large linen closet, was undisturbed except around the area where Marianna had stormed in to fetch the gun in order to save Tristan from the deadly duel. In the darkness, she could see a thin line of light around the perimeter of the office wall panel and felt instinctively for the inside release. From what she could hear, the room was empty. A sharp tug on the latch and the panel popped open easily.

Skirts gathered close about her, Marianna stepped through the narrow passage into the vacant room and looked out the open patio doors to where the *alcalde*'s guests danced and laughed gaily. Although the sun had set while she was sleeping, there was sufficient illumination for her to find the section of books she had examined the day before from the now-glowing lanterns hung on the balcony overlooking the courtyard. She hastily plucked the thin black ledger belonging to the freight company from the shelf and held it up to the light to be certain she had the correct one. Upon opening it, she discovered the identifying torn page.

Without bothering to read the backs of the others, she selected a few more before rearranging the remaining books so as not to call attention to the missing volumes. Just as she turned to pick up the incriminating journals from the corner of the desk where she had put them, the sound of laughing male voices drew nearer. Snatching the books to her chest in panic, Marianna slipped through the panel and pulled it to behind her, the click of the latch blending with that of the opening door to the office from the patio.

"You see, my friend, I have the ability to predict the future," Don Victor's voice resounded, filling the quickly vacated room as he stepped inside. "My lovely ex-fiancée will find herself a widow very shortly."

"And, of course, you will be there to console her," the other man remarked with a laconic chuckle. "Her stepfather would expect no less."

"It is my duty!" the *alcalde* protested in mock indignation.

"And such an enviable one," came a sighed response.

Marianna pressed closer to try to make out the second voice over the thumping sound of her heart beating against her chest. By all the saints, they were plotting to kill Tristan! This man who was so obviously taken with her might well be the prospective murderer.

257

"Just be careful to keep your interest in Elena De Costa to envy only," Romero warned his companion, all hint of his previous humor vanishing. The very nature of his changed tone sent a chill up Marianna's spine.

"*Alcalde*," his companion protested, "I think you have nothing to fear from me. I doubt that the lady will speak to me again after presenting her with the ear of my kill."

Marianna's lips thinned as laughter erupted once again at her expense. So the *matador* was also involved with Victor Romero's sinister sideline of robbery and murder.

"Back to this Texas Ranger. What do you know of the Mexican who is with him?"

"My sources say that he is a member of the government's border patrol. The two have worked together in the past to track *bandidos* on both sides of the river."

"And the girl, she is in this with them?"

Her color fading, Marianna held her breath.

"I do not think so. I think she tells the truth about being frightened by you into fleeing into Texas. I hear that she stole the Ranger's horse and that when he caught her, she revealed her identity."

"Then that was the first he knew that he had an inheritance, then," Romero speculated thoughtfully.

Alvarado must have nodded in agreement, for he picked up with the conjecture, adding more as to how the marriage may have come about. "I believe he thought to combine work with profit and collect the inheritance, but somehow the girl managed to escape the jail. Perhaps she realized her mistake in running from you, for she had the two lawmen arrested for kidnapping her."

The room erupted in a peel of laughter. "*Madre de Dios*, here is a woman after my own heart! How I look forward to taming that wild spirit of hers!"

"If you expect to do that, it had best be by gentleness, my friend, for your previous tactics have been unsuccessful. She might not have agreed to marry the Ranger, had you not tried to force her hand and have her kidnapped."

"While your success among the ladies is well known, *señor*, I am not without experience on that account. I expected an obedient little twit," the *alcalde* reminded him, "not a fiery independent beauty with a mind of her own. But winning her heart is not of consequence at the moment. We must first get Tristan De Costa and his friend out of the way. Considering the way he has treated her, she will be ripe, shall we say, for the picking. I shall be her hero in this."

"What do you propose?"

Marianna clutched the books to her chest and swallowed dryly. Naturally, Romero would never achieve his grand ambition, but the very idea left her weak with fear of his plan. She would warn Tristan and—

"There you are, you naughty man!" a woman's voice sounded from the other side of the room.

"Don Victor, for shame that you take away the *matador* of the ladies' hearts and deny us his presence at the dancing!" a second chimed in. "Can not whatever your business is wait until the morrow?"

Obviously unable to continue their conversation with their newly arrived guests, Don Victor assumed a light-hearted contrition. "A thousand pardons, *señoritas*. I was not thinking. Don Miguel, by all means, go to your adoring company. We shall discuss this later." As smooth and charming as it was intended, Marianna could not help but think that this was surely the tone the serpent used to entice Eve in the Garden of Eden.

"I thought the two of you were enchanted with the

259

gringo De Costa," Miguel Alvarado admonished play
fully.

He was answered with a feminine sniff of disdain tha
immediately grabbed the hidden girl's attention. "Alici:
Cabal will not share him with anyone! All they talk of i
horses and mining and *she* cares not the slightest for ei
ther. I prefer a man with an interest in women."

That ill-bred bastard! An irritated pout formed or
Marianna's lips at the picture of Tristan De Costa anc
some doe-eyed *señorita* hanging onto his every word. He
was so concerned about her that he hadn't even both
ered to check on her since she'd laid down, she fumec
silently. The voices moved away from the panel, making
it harder for her to overhear what they were saying.

"Are you not coming too, *alcalde?*" the second lady
asked coyishly, making it plain that the *matador* was no
the only eligible bachelor in demand.

"In a moment, *señorita*. I must see to a guest first anc
then I shall join the festivities."

The closing of the patio doors, shutting out the noise
of the celebration, spurred Marianna into action. For
getting her peeve where Tristan was concerned, she
hurried down the corridor and through the hidden en
trance in the back of the closet. As she had emerged, she
glanced down at the books in her arms in alarm. She
hoped to conceal at least one of them in her underskirts
but now there was no time. Romero mustn't see her
with them!

Hastily she put them in the hidden corridor and slid
the panel into place. A suit fell off the peg as she
brushed past it to get into the bedroom before Don Vic
tor looked in on her. Blood pounding in her ears, Mar
ianna scooped it up and shoved it back. Voices sounded
at the door, those of Alfonso and, undoubtedly, the *al
calde*. Holding her breath, as if it would give her away,

260

she closed the closet door and leapt lightly toward the bed. In a scramble, she tugged the coverlet over her and closed her eyes, fighting to resume a normal breathing pattern.

It was impossible. Her heart felt as if it would burst from her chest, starved for oxygen. Upon hearing the telltale creak of the opening door, she started to toss her head to the side and moaned.

"Non, please . . . please do not hurt me . . ."

The rush of booted footsteps to her side reassured her that her desperate ploy had worked. She was shaken gently.

"Señora?"

"Non!"

"Señora, wake up! You are having a bad dream."

Marianna blinked her eyes and widened them with a contrived start upon seeing Victor Romero leaning over her. "Señor Romero!"

Romero was instantly on the defensive. "I would not have come in but for hearing your cries, Señora. Alfonso and I thought that something was wrong."

Crossing her arms, Marianna shuddered. "I . . . I thought those horrible men were after me again . . . the ones my husband sent me to. It is ridiculous, I know, for they were killed . . ." She glanced toward the window where music drifted gaily. "The dancing has started?" she asked, skillfully changing from what she intended them to think a disconcerting subject.

"For some time, *señora,*" the *alcalde* informed her, his dark eyes inscrutable as he considered her thoughtfully.

Marianna tossed back the coverlet with a self-recriminating *"Madre de Dios,* I did not mean to sleep so long!"

"You were distraught over the bullfight." Following her lead a little too well, Victor Romero caught her by the waist and lifted her to her feet as she made to slide off the high mattress.

When his hands lingered there, she raised a troubled gaze to his face. "In truth, I do not make a good Mexican, *non?*"

"You are but a sensitive flower in a savage land." He caressed her cheek with the back of his hand, the same hand that had killed her mother after exploiting her nude and helpless body.

Like Eleanor Gallier? Marianna inhaled shakily, this time not having to act. Her stomach reeled with a sickening fear that weakened her knees, yet she tried not to collapse in his arms. That was the last place she wanted to be, but she had to find out his plans for Tristan. She steeled herself and straightened. God in heaven, she would kill him. Somehow, some way . . . for killing her family and before he killed Tristan.

"I fear for my very life here, *señor,*" she managed. "Last night I could not sleep. I was terrified that Tristan might seek revenge for my shooting him." She took another breath to steady herself and added in a wooden tone, "Would that my aim had been better. Even prison is better than living with that money-hungry ruffian. I so feared that if he survived that horrible duel he would kill me for telling you how he plotted to send me away."

"He did not *hurt* you?"

Marianna shook her head. *"Gracias a Dios,* he only locked me in my room and threatened me," she lied. If she could make Romero think that she wanted Tristan dead, perhaps he might take her into his confidence and reveal his plan. "If only I had not been so foolish. I should have married you as planned!" Forcing aside her repugnance for the man, she threw herself against him with a conjured sob and clung to him.

The tears that filled her eyes came naturally, for her

distress was genuine. This man had murdered her family and now he threatened to do the same to Tristan. Now it was up to her, a coward who trembled in fear of him, to stop him, she told herself, trying to overcome her shame for even breathing the same air as such a swine.

"Now, isn't this a fine flock of feathers?"

Such was her concentration on her task at hand that the voice coming from the open door didn't register at first. It was only when Victor Romero jerked his head toward the young man watching them curiously that she pushed away with a start. "Tristan!"

"*Wife.*"

His contemptuous address made her previous pallor flame with the blood that climbed rapidly to her face. How dare he insinuate . . . Marianna's indignation faltered with the realization of the way things must appear.

"The *señora* was having a bad dream and alarmed Alfonso with her cries, Don Tristan. He sent for me . . ."

"And you came to offer her your comfort," Tristan finished dourly. "Now, that's downright neighborly of you."

"Now that you are here," Victor Romero went on, ignoring the insulting tone in the Ranger's voice, "I shall leave you to your wife and join my guests."

Marianna stiffened under the icy blue gaze that refused to leave her as the *alcalde* walked out of the room. She would explain once the opportunity presented itself and he would see for himself what a fool he was acting. "If you give me time to freshen up, husband, I will join you for the dancing."

Tristan considered the servant still standing guard at the door. "I'll wait," he answered, folding his arms across his chest expectantly.

With battling emotions of relief and indignation, Marianna took a brush off the polished top of a gentleman's dresser and used the mirror to restore her coiffure. To her frustration, everything she did only served further to indicate a guilty conscience rather than a rightfully indignant one. Under the detached scrutiny of the man in the doorway, her fingers became thumbs, but eventually she managed to pin all the loose raven tendrils into place. Determined more than ever to set things right, she took the arm mockingly extended to her, and walked past Alfonso down the corridor to the patio entrance where the gaiety beckoned warmly from the open doors.

At least a dozen pairs of eyes sought out the handsome couple as they entered the courtyard and stiffly took their place among the dancers. It was apparent that the duel of the previous night had hardly been forgotten, and the fact that, until now, the mistress of Casa Valencia had been missing only heightened their curiosity.

Not only was the gringo and his French wife the most interesting of the *alcalde*'s guests, but they were the handsomest couple there, earning looks of admiration from both genders at the gathering. The lady's peacock-blue dress only served to heighten the color of her wide dark-fringed eyes. Her cheeks rivaled the rose of the abundant flowers that wove through the garden trellises, and her lips had surely been chewed to the point of bleeding to attain that color of perfection. They were poised in a gracious smile as she moved about gracefully to the steps of the country dance and bowed to the gentleman next to her husband.

At the promenade, however, she returned to her dashing fair-haired partner and seemed to float effortlessly on his arm. There the fairy-tale appearance of the scene ended, for it was evident from his brooding countenance that he was not at all pleased with her. Since the *alcalde*'s arrival had only preceded them by a short time, and the gringo had been the epitome of the gay cavalier until collecting his wife, the curiosity of the crowd reached an almost scandalous proportion that not even the unfurling of practiced fans failed to hide.

"You are drawing unnecessary attention, *monsieur.*" Marianna whispered through her smile upon returning one of the curious gazed pointedly and driving it into retreat behind a screen of pleated lace. "I have told you that I was merely trying to save your life."

Tristan stood in one spot and held out his hand for her to spin around. "Spare me, Marianna. I've already lost one patch of skin on your account. He slipped his arm around her waist, where gathers of tulle were drawn into a lace-edge bow, unaware that his fingers bit into her corseted flesh.

"Ouch! *Monsieur!*"

The effect of the provocative pout turned up to him was just as maddening as that of finding Marianna enclosed in Victor Romero's ardent embrace. Tristan didn't understand her, and he never trusted anyone he didn't understand. What game did she play with those nightmares of hers? Had he been just as gullible as the *alcalde* in wanting to soothe her fears? He loosened his hold. "We'll leave after this dance. Maybe I can get you home before you create another scene."

With a gasp, Marianna started to pull away, only to have the arm about her tighten. "Another scene! *Monsieur,* I am warning you . . ."

"I'm warning you, Frenchie. If you don't want to be hauled out of here over my shoulder, you'll do as I say."

A summer storm flashed up at him, lashing out of sapphire depths, and her wounded pout thinned, pressing out the inviting wine color of her lips. For a moment, the electricity ran through the charged air between them, disconcerting Tristan in the way that his body reacted in spite of his anger. Tarnation, she was as pretty as a July storm at midnight and twice as unpredictable. Something about that was as exciting as it was infuriating.

"Well?" he challenged, almost hoping she would balk. He wanted her to taste a hint of the humiliation that had swept over him when he walked up to the open door and found her swaying in Romero's arms. Of course, she would have a reason, one that would sound good to him. But dare he accept it?

A finely etched eyebrow arched imperiously over one eye. He watched the struggle of indecision on her face as she contemplated his threat. Delicate nostrils flared from a nose lifted in taunting haughtiness. Never had he known such an urge to resort to physical violence as he did at that moment, but it had nothing to do with striking her. It was a much more base humiliation that came to mind.

"Fine! But I will not offer to help you at all, ever again!" she threatened under her voice. "You are a stubborn bool!" With an emphatic stomp of her slippered foot, she marched away before Tristan realized what she was about.

Oblivious to the guests that stopped in midconversation to watch them, Tristan was on her heels in an instant, seizing her elbow. "Just where do you think you're going?"

"I am going home! That is what you wished, *non?*" Marianna glowered over her shoulder, dropping her searing gaze to his restraining hand and returning it to his with even more fiery intensity. As far as she was concerned, he could get himself killed! It would serve him right! How could he think that she could feel anything but contempt for Romero? "Mateo!" she called out, snapping her fingers over her head unnecessarily to gain Mateo Salizar's attention.

Mat hurried up to the couple that had commanded everyone's undivided interest. "You are feeling worse, *señora?*"

"I find my current company has given me an unprecedented ague of the head. Will you fetch the coach before I—"

"Don Tristan, you are leaving so soon?" Marianna's request trailed off at the interruption of a young woman no older than herself who rushed up to Tristan and placed a small manicured hand on his arm. "My father had so hoped to talk to your husband about borrowing some of his scaffolding until Señor Romero can order yours," she addressed Marianna sweetly.

"Then, by all means, *husband*," Marianna derided, "You must stay. Far be it from me to cause you to disappoint this young lady's father . . . or *her*," she added with a withering look that sent the young woman back a step.

"Tristan?" Mateo questioned, noting with alarm the purplish veins that rose to the surface of his partner's neck, a result of the barely restrained fury darkening his pale eyes. He felt as though he'd stepped between two fierce storm fronts and now waited in the falsely assuring silence that always preceded the resulting tumult.

"They teach some strange manners in Paris," Tristan remarked finally to no one in particular. "Yeah, go ahead and send her home. The coachman can come back for you and me later." The Cabal girl had been a nuisance all evening, but at the moment she served a spiteful purpose that suited him. "Me and the lady here have some *business* to discuss."

Marianna was well aware of the way the Ranger covered the delicate hand of his adoring companion, but refused to give him the satisfaction of the wounded rage it inflicted. A typical man, she fumed, spinning away to take Mateo's offered arm. She should have known him incapable of caring for her on a level above that of his belt buckle.

She took the reticule Alfonso fetched hurriedly for her as Don Victor approached them. "Don Victor, I regret that I must leave, but I am certain that my husband will be entertained in my absence." She extended her hand to his. "I thank you for your warm hospitality. It has been refreshing."

"It is my hope that you will enjoy it again soon, *señora,*" Romero replied, taking her hand to his lips. "In the meanwhile, we shall endeavor to take care of your husband." The wicked gleam that danced in the ebony gaze fixed upon her sent a chill up her spine, diminishing the heat of indignation Tristan had provoked with his base insinuations.

Marianna stammered a reply, hardly aware of what she said. What on earth was wrong with her? She, Marianna Gallier, who always kept the cool head, even on the rare occasion when her escort's attention was diverted, threatened by the charms of another female.

"Actually, Don Victor," Tristan spoke up, interrupting her reflection, only to provoke her further. "I invite you tomorrow, *señor.* Elena has just been itching to have company. Maybe we can walk through the mines and get an idea of what we need to do . . . and of course, you and your father are also welcome, Señorita Cabal.

The young woman beamed brightly, oblivious to the tiny choking noise Marianna tried to swallow. "Then you must extend the invitation personally, Don Tristan."

Then, remembering her upbringing, she turned to Marianna. "I am looking forward to it, Señora De Costa."

"I can see that, *señorita.*" Marianna turned away from the dainty hand extended to her toward where the coachman approached with the black Butterfield. As it slowed to a halt, she started for the door. Accepting Mateo's assistance with a cursory smile, she stepped inside the coach and took her seat, her reticule primly clutched in her lap.

"Hope your head feels better, Frenchie," Tristan called out, stubbornly refusing to budge from the spot next to Alicia Cabal. He wasn't certain what had set her off about Alicia, but at that particular moment, he didn't care. He needed all the help he could get against someone who could get mad at *him* for finding *them* in another man's arms.

"It does already, *monsieur,*" Marianna shot back crisply with a raking gaze that encompassed not only Tristan, but his smiling companion. *"Bon appétit!"*

Tristan's face burned with the scarlet flush that spread up from his neck to the top of his head.

"Bon appétit?" Mat repeated curiously.

"Yeah, she wants me to eat something so the liquor doesn't keep me out all night," he recovered awkwardly.

Although he took Alicia Cabal's arm gallantly to escort her back to the party, his thoughts were on the coach disappearing down the moonlit road. Marianna Gallier had a lot in common with the Indians she was so frightened of. Her tricks were not conventional in nature and left the enemy at a decided disadvantage. But if the young lady from Paris thought this battle was over, she was in for a surprise of her own, he mused angrily, determined to get away at the first opportunity to finish this one, gloves removed, once and for all.

His enthralled companion, however, had other plans,

plans that made it next to impossible to leave until the party was over and she was forced to retire to the room she shared with two other *señoritas* who were spending the night along with their parents at the *alcalde*'s hacienda. She was pretty enough, but her wiles were so obvious to Tristan that he found himself trying to find excuses to avoid her small talk and prattle and ply her father with pertinent questions about his mining operation.

The ore in the hills around Valencia was brittle and crumbled easily, necessitating a specially designed scaffolding to support the tunnels and keep them from collapsing on the miners. It was the same as that used in the Comstock Lode up Nevada way—square sets of short timbers joined in a boxlike frame that were stacked as the tunnels grew deeper and expanded laterally with the veins of the ore. Winzes, or long hollow pipes, ran down the center of the vertical vein to afford ventilation and communication from level to level.

Ordinarily, Tristan would have been fascinated, but the words Marianna had said to him came back to haunt him, something about helping him and saving his life. Was it possible she really *had* found something out? The more practical side of him pointed out that had he not been so muleheaded and fired up over discovering her in Romero's arms, he might have found out.

It was with great eagerness that he finally took his leave with the other guests at midnight after finishing a full plate of delectable dishes set out by the adept kitchen staff. The sangria he had consumed infected him with a lethargy that made planning his approach to Marianna an effort and almost caused him to nod off on the short run to Casa Valencia. Mat rode beside him silently, engrossed in his own thoughts until the carriage came to a halt in front of the hacienda.

"The night has not been a total waste," his companion spoke up as Tristan leaned forward to open the door of the coach and disembark. "It seems your jealous wife has left a light on for you."

Tristan looked to the second floor where the window of the master bedroom glowed softly, alone in the otherwise dark wall. "She may be waiting with a gun," he snorted facetiously. He wiped the grin off his face, suddenly sober. "You going to try again tonight?"

Mateo nodded in affirmation. "There were so many guests, I could not get close to the office. With luck, the sangria will have put everyone else to sleep like it almost did you."

"Maybe I should go along."

"I mean no offense, *amigo*, but you are likely to stand out suspiciously if you should be seen. I might pass as just another servant cleaning up after the festivities."

Reluctantly, Tristan agreed. It wasn't only his hair that set him apart, but his towering six-foot-plus height as well. He wasn't exactly built like his smaller, more-compact Mexican counterpart. "I'll wait up for you. *Buena suerte.*" He shook Mateo's hand in earnest.

"It is you that will need the luck, *amigo.*" Mat replied meaningfully, glancing once again at the lighted window. "*Adiós.*"

Tristan waited in the yard in front of the hacienda for the coach to be put away for the night. He waved to the coachman as the man made his way toward the building of apartments that housed the domestic servants and watched until the man disappeared in one of the doors on the second-floor balcony that ran the full length of the building. A few moments later, Mateo Salizar quietly led his horse from the barn and mounted it. He was but a small moving speck down the long dirt road that

271

wound toward the village when Tristan turned and walked into the tiled entrance of the main house.

The trickling waters of the fountain were the only sounds in the sleeping household when he made his way up the steps and down the hall to the room he had shared with Marianna the night before. Still wary, he pressed his back to the wall and quietly lifted the latch to open the bedroom door. A gentle light filtered into the dark hall as it widened noiselessly and he peeked inside.

Instead of a pistol-packing fury, a dark-haired angel awaited him, lying in sweet repose on the fluffed-up pillows of the bed. The book she had been reading had slipped off her lap and onto the coverlet that only rose to her silk-clad thighs. She hugged a spare pillow, nuzzling her cheek against it gently as he removed the book and placed it on the bedside table next to an empty decanter of sherry—one that had been half-full the night before, as he recalled. His disapproving grimace faded, however, as he looked back at the sleeping beauty. On the rose-hued cheek turned to him were telltale tracks of tears, one of which still glistened at the corner of the dark lashes resting there.

Determined not to let such a tempting sight disarm the engagement he'd planned, he shed his clothing silently so as not to disturb her. His hands, however, swift and sure with a gun or a knife, suddenly became clumsy and awkward with the stamped silver buttons. A curse hissed through his teeth as one popped, flying across the room to skitter under a large linen press.

What manner of temptation was this bewildering creature? Not even with his first woman, a golden-haired soiled dove in one of El Paso's finest houses, had the control on which he prided himself been so devastatingly undetermined. With each article that fell to the floor, his pulse rate increased until he could hear his beating heart above the breath that labored, as if he'd been involved in hard physical exertion. Forcing it still, he slipped into the bed and pulled the sleeping girl into his embrace, but the touch of her warm buttocks brushing his unencumbered loins released it in a warm rush against her neck. Tomorrow, he mused, shoving aside the confrontation he had originally intended. Tomorrow he'd find out what this charming little minx was about. But for tonight . . .

As she stirred, turning sleepily in his arms, he cupped the pliable flesh of her breast in his hand, catching its peak and teasing it into alertness. With a soft moan, half protest and half pleasure, she pursed her lips in a soft "Ohh!" and drew up her legs, betraying the instinctive female response curling within. Tristan leaned over her and claimed his straining reward with his teeth, soaking the silk that separated them from her naked flesh.

Marianna gasped and blinked in the dim light. Her blood was afire from the touch of her dream lover, a touch so real that even now the press of his virile flesh against her made her insides quiver with unfurling desire. He was sorry and he had come back to her to apologize, to beg her pardon for his accusing looks and insinuations.

Taunting fingers found their way under the hem of her gown, lifting it as they zeroed in on the most sensitive of all places. It flooded warm with welcome. "Tristan?" she breathed against his face as he found her earlobe and nipped seductively, drawing her from the sleepy lethargy that had claimed her. His lips tasted hers, his tongue tracing the outline of her lips as he parted her legs and settled between them. "A good sherry, Frenchie. Almost as delicious as you . . ." he rumbled against her mouth before claiming it as fiercely as he claimed her body.

Marianna's eyes flew open and remained so as her hips were seized roughly to receive the whole of his ardor. In a single moment, she knew an explosive sweetness that bade her embrace him with her legs and the startling realization that this was indeed no dream lover, but a very real one. From the fog of her sleep-ridden brain she struggled to summon the anguish and rage that had driven her to finish the remains of the open bottle of sherry from the downstairs liquor cabinet, but the passion so easily tapped when her guard was down flared to undeniable proportion, sweeping her feeble objections aside with a fiercely rising tide of ecstasy. Lost to all but him, she clung to her lover with all her being to simply survive the wild sweet tempest.

Chapter Sixteen

Marianna awakened to a movement in the dark room followed by whispers. Wondering if this was yet another dream or reality, she sat up on the bed and made out Tristan's tall figure in the doorway, a blanket wrapped about his waist. His low whisper drifted back to her.

"I'll be right down."

Bewildered and slow-witted from the sherry she had consumed earlier, she pushed up from the bed. "What is it? And what are *you* doing in here like *that?*"

"We are supposed to be married," the young man reminded her with a wicked grin as he pulled on his trousers over his lean and naked hips. "You'd tempt a saint, Frenchie."

Marianna glanced down to where his gaze dropped and gasped, aware for the first time that she was as naked as he. Her gown, she thought, scrambling for the covers in confusion. Surely she had put it on before . . . A slip of silk swinging from Tristan's extended hand brought her head up with a jolt that shook the vague memories of what had happened to the surface.

"Why, you . . ." she stammered, realizing the torrid session of lovemaking that had filled her with undreamed-of pleasure had been very real indeed. But then, she remembered with a resurgence of heat to her face, of course it had been real! She had tried to protest, but Tristan had been so insistent, so devastatingly convincing. "You sneaking bastard!" she cursed, recovering enough to sling the pillow she'd grabbed for cover at the amused Ranger. "You *knew* I was angry with you and yet you crawl into my bed and make the love to me like I am some of your saloon sluts!"

"Come on, Frenchie," Tristan chided, knocking the pillow aside. "You enjoyed it and you know it."

"Non! I thought it was . . ." Marianna broke off in the midst of her inadvertent admission. She hardly wanted him to know that she dreamed of such things concerning him. "A . . . a nightmare," she groped awkwardly. "You know of my bad dreams. They seem so real."

Her skin burned with humiliation, for she could hardly convince herself, let alone him, that what had happened was displeasing at all. How could she have allowed him such privileges after the accusations he had made against her?

With a justifiably skeptical look, Tristan buckled his belt and started for the door. "You go on back to sleep. I'll be downstairs."

"At this hour?" Marianna shriveled behind a blanket as the Ranger swung around and grinned.

"I'll be back as soon as I can, *I promise.*"

"The devil take you, you big bool!" As added emphasis, she let fly another pillow. It struck the closed door and fell uselessly to the floor.

Useless, Marianna reflected in frustration at her inability to resist the handsome Ranger's midnight seduction. She had been so hurt and angry when she went to bed. She'd almost hoped that Tristan would follow her, but after she had taken a long hot bath, she realized that he

276

was indeed taking her advice to remain at the party to entertain Alicia Cabal.

And why not? Alicia was pretty enough and obviously was taken by the fair-haired good looks of the newest caballero, she reasoned, sliding off the bed and tossing her gown aside. Unlike herself, she thought ruefully, who managed to find something over which to argue the moment they were together. She had been waiting to confront him earlier that night, fortified with a healthy portion of sherry. And then he had not come.

Damned dirty rotten gringo, Marianna swore to herself, dragging on a dressing gown to see just what the subject in question was about in the wee hours of the morning. Still, he had no right to look at her as if she had done something so horrible when she was only trying to find out more about his prospective murder. It was for his sake she had been in Victor Romero's arms. Her lip curled in distaste. How could Tristan even think . . . ?

Dismissing the repetitive argument that had occupied her thoughts before she succumbed to sleep, Marianna slipped out into the corridor and made her way down the steps to the dining hall, where a flickering light indicated the source of the low voices she heard on her approach. She peeked around the arched entrance to see Tristan standing over Mateo Salizar, applying wet cloths handed to him by Maria.

"Do you think they recognized you?"

Mateo shook his head to deny Tristan's question. "It was dark. Fortunately I was able to climb over the wall before the servant who discovered me could sound the alarm."

"How'd you get this nasty bruise, then?" Tristan glanced up from his task to see Marianna and motioned her in.

Mateo twisted as she entered the room silently. "I apologize for disturbing you and your husband, *señora.*"

"What happened, Señor Salizar?" Marianna exclaimed, leaning over the injured man to examine the bruise revealed by the removal of the cloth Tristan handed to Maria.

"I jumped from the wall of the *alcalde*'s courtyard into a pile of rocks. It was my head that took the worst of the beating," Mat added, twisting his lips into a halfhearted smile.

"The *alcalde*'s! But what were you doing there?"

"He was looking for those nonexistent books you told us about."

Marianna covered her mouth with her hand in dismay. "But you should not have!"

"*Señora,* I—"

"Wait, Mat. I want to hear why you shouldn't have tried to get the books. After all, earlier today, they were imperative to our mission."

"And they *still* are," Marianna insisted, adding in an admonishing tone, "I told you that *I* would get them."

Tristan's irritation broke with incredulity. "You mean *you* have them?"

"Of course! I took them while everyone was celebrating."

"Then why the bloody blue blazes didn't you tell us! Mat could have been killed tonight."

"Because *you,* Señor Big Pants Ranger, did not give me time to tell you anything! Instead, you insult me when I am trying to save your miserable skin! And while *I* am risking my life, *you,*" she averred, poking his bare chest with her finger irritably, "are flirting with the daughter of some big silver-mine owner. So do not blame me if I could not tell you about it."

"You could have told me when I got home."

Marianna turned away from the mocking gaze to face Mateo Salizar. "I will tell *him* nothing, Señor Salizar, but to you, I give my deepest apologies. I took the books from the office before I left."

"They are *here, señora?*" Mat ventured hopefully.

"Not exactly."

"So Romero still has them," Tristan intervened.

Marianna shifted her gaze uncomfortably from one man to the other. "Not exactly." Upon seeing Tristan roll his eyes heavenward, she explained hastily. "I hid them. I would have hidden them in my skirts to get them out of the hacienda, but the *alcalde* came into the room." Her crossed her arms defensively. "Then *you* came."

"So you pretended to have a bad dream to distract him," Tristan filled in derisively. "That's a handy little trick you have there, Frenchie. Convinced the hell out of me a few times."

The words hurt Marianna more than she cared to admit. *"Non,* you fool! I only tried to win his favor to save you! Why, I do not know, but I did!" She covered her trembling chin with her hand self-consciously.

"I wasn't aware that I was in any immediate danger. *You* looked like the little fish about to be swallowed by the big one," he pointed out.

She wondered why she bothered, but Marianna went on to explain. "While I was hiding, I heard the *alcalde* planning to have you killed—in a mine, I think. I heard him and the *matador* discussing it. They were laughing at making me a widow so that Don Victor might marry me. Tristan," Marianna pleaded fervently, "they know that you and Mateo are lawmen!"

"How?"

"Sources of the *matador* in Presidio. You and I have been watched since I left, except that they believe that

279

I was forced out of fear of Don Victor into your hands. They think that I hate you." She sighed shakily. "So, I thought that if the *alcalde* continued to believe that, he might tell me how he was going to kill you. It was for *that* that I was in his arms, and no other reason."

Tristan spun away from the table and ran his hand through his hair. "That does it," he exclaimed irritably. "I want her out of this!"

"But—"

He turned and seized Marianna's shoulders, forcing her to look up at him, her interrupted protest frozen on her lips. *"You* could have gotten yourself killed tonight with your careless shenanigans, Marianna. Romero is a dangerous man. Now I insist that you go to Silverado until this is over."

"It appears that it is over anyway, *amigo,*" Mat spoke up. He tossed a rag in the wash bowl and straightened in his chair. "Romero knows who we are. There is nothing more to do."

"We can still get the books," Tristan shot back. "Remember, he doesn't know that we know he's on to us." He cupped Marianna's chin and raised her gaze to him. "I'm sorry, Frenchie, I was a *beeg foolish bool,*" he mimicked gently. "It just rubs me the wrong way to see the likes of Romero with his arms around you."

Marianna felt as though her bones were turning to water as she looked into the depths of Tristan's earnest gaze. "And I am rubbed wrong when the likes of Alicia Cabal is hanging on your arm." She folded his hand in her own and brushed his knuckles with her lips. "I do not want you to die, Tristan. That is why you must let *me* get the books. Romero believes me to hate you."

"I think you are *both* crazy!" Mateo interrupted, reminding them of his presence. He got up from the chair and stalked over to the hearth to light a cheroot from the lamp on the mantle.

"Where did you put the books, Frenchie?" Tristan persisted, ignoring his companion's outburst.

"Where no one can find them but me." At his disgruntled expression, she giggled. "Surely, Tristan, you do not think that I am so foolish as to tell you, so that you can send me away again!" The touch of his bare flesh against the inside of her arms as she slipped them around his waist was inviting. To her astonishment, she found herself reacting warmly. "We must work together, *mon cher, non?*"

"Damn it, Marianna, I told you—" Tristan was silenced by a slender finger pressed against his lips.

"Have you not argued enough for one night, *gringo?*"

If she was charming when she wasn't trying to be, this girl was absolutely bewitching when she was. Tristan let the rest of his words trail off into a kiss. He knew not the nature of this obsessive attraction he felt for Marianna Gallier, he only knew he wanted her . . . *again*. She was like a strong narcotic and he was becoming addicted.

"Perhaps we had best sleep on this and discuss it again in the morning when our heads are clearer," Mateo suggested, as much to himself as to the couple entwined in each other's arms. He stubbed out the cheroot in a dish and paused at the door, but his companions neither answered nor showed evidence that they even knew he was there. With a whimsical smile, he trudged into the foyer and up the steps to the guest room, leaving Tristan and Marianna to settle their differences in their own way. Perhaps tomorrow, when moonlight and romance did not play havoc with their minds, he could talk some sense into them.

* * *

Marianna worked diligently with the fresh flowers she'd cut from the gardens in the courtyard at Casa Valencia. Humming softly to reflect her irrepressible good humor, she carefully arranged the blossoms in a vase Doña Inez had fetched for her. A bright gold day dress with a square neckline and square overskirt that lay flat across her abdomen and gathered to a puff in the back made her appear as sunny as her mood. Black piping about the edges of the skirt, neckline, and sleeves provided a stylish contrast to the gold.

Tristan had been angry the morning after she'd refused to tell him the whereabouts of the books. Since then, a most amenable standoff had ensued, broken by delightful rides over the hills of Valencia, picnics where he told her about his colorful family and their ranch, and rapturous nights in his arms where only she was the subject of his attention.

Tristan McCulloch was unlike the men Marianna was accustomed to. He did not chase her on his knees, seeking her favor, but he left no room for doubt that he did not desire her. His clothes were not the most fashionable, particularly those horrid buckskins he had put on that morning, but they never failed to draw attention to his well-defined masculine body. He was all male. It showed in his walk, his easygoing manner, even that boyish grin that made her toes curl. Sometimes he was bold, others teasing, but he always made her feel as though her body were alive for the first time in her life.

Of course, he was determined to wait her out, Marianna knew, just as she was prepared to do the same for him. Sooner or later, he would tire of this silly notion that he should single-handedly bring Victor Romero to justice and include her in his plans. Until then, there was little to do but to enjoy the charade of husband and wife that they maintained for the servants and visitors.

Before he and Mateo rode off that morning, he had informed her that he'd invited Victor Romero over for lunch to discuss the opening of the mine and take a look at the main shaft afterward. Although she was apprehensive, she knew he had done so in an effort to force her hand. Tristan knew that she was fearful for his life. What he did not expect was her plan to turn the tables on him and wrangle another invitation to Mirabeau for the two of them over the delicious meal Maria was preparing under Doña Inez's supervision. As for Tristan's safety, Marianna had overheard him and Mateo talking that morning about going through the mine to make sure all was as it should be before Romero arrived. If the *alcalde* had somehow set some sort of trap for them, they would find evidence of it ahead of time.

"Doña Elena, what a lovely centerpiece!" her former nurse exclaimed, coming into the courtyard from the inside corridor.

Having grown accustomed to the name Tristan insisted they all use whenever other ears might be close-by, Marianna rearranged the last of the flowers and stood back to admire it. "It did turn out well, didn't it?" She wiped her hands on the apron tied daintily at her waist. "If you will have Maria clean off the table, I shall go freshen up before the *alcalde* arrives." She glanced at the sun high overhead, grateful for the spreading ornamental trees that afforded shade over the tables in the hottest part of the day. "I wonder what is keeping Tristan and Mateo. Don Victor will be here any time."

"You have never been inside a mine, have you, Marianna?" Doña Inez asked her with a fond smile. She was thrilled beyond words to see the two young people she had helped raise so very much in love. Although there were no declarations to indicate their feelings, it was obvious to her, even with her failing eyesight. Naturally there were the problems of their independent wills that clashed periodically, but they were nothing that time would not take care of.

"*Non*, I have not." Marianna's dark hair, pinned up pertly on the top of her head in a tumble of curls, shimmered in the sunlight as she shook her head in denial.

"A shaft can be miles long, running deep into the earth, so I have heard said. No doubt the boy in the man has gotten the best of them and they have forgotten the time. I'll send one of the men up there to fetch them."

If Tristan McCulloch left her to entertain Victor Romero alone, she would give him a piece of her mind, Marianna thought peevishly. Worse, he will have worried her for nothing! It was true that she had never been in a mine shaft, but she had read about them, and the descriptions of the dark oxygen-starved tunnels sounded straight from the corridors of Hades itself. She certainly hoped that the irascible Ranger would give up this mining venture, once Romero was out of the way. If Elena wanted to reopen the mines, let her new husband do it for her.

After scrubbing her fingernails briskly with the small brush Maria fetched for her, Marianna checked her dress for specks of dirt that might have fallen from the table during her floral arrangements and returned downstairs to see the table set for five. The same napkins Elena's mother had used were set out, starched and folded stiffly on each of the patterned plates that also were reminders of Marianna's short stay at Casa Valencia. Her mother had had a matching set of the French china, but it had been destroyed during Victor Romero's rampage.

At least he had had to rebuild the place, she mused

flatly, distracted from her supervision by her wandering thoughts. She recalled how the floors had been ruined by the horses the men rode through the house, the walls stained with the blood of their victims and pitted with bullet holes. Why fire had not been set, Marianna could never quite guess. Perhaps even then, the bandit was considering to make the place his lair.

"*Señora*, the *alcalde* is here," Maria announced, bringing Marianna back to the present.

"Did you send someone for Don Tristan?"

"While you were freshening up, *señora*."

"Then show the *alcalde* into the courtyard and bring us some lemonade. We'll hold the meal until the men arrive."

Fortifying herself with a deep breath, Marianna pulled out a chair and sat in it, arranging her straight skirts primly. When Victor Romero appeared in the entrance from the foyer, she held out her hand to him, a queen inviting him into her parlor.

"*Señor*, I regret that my husband has not yet returned from his morning errands, but I am certain that he will be along shortly." She paused with a sniff of disdain. "But what can one expect from a Texas gringo?" She joined in Don Victor's amusement at her jibe. "Please sit and share a lemonade with me until he comes. Maria is bringing it."

"*Señora*, if I am to judge from your appearance, I would say that your marriage has improved of late. You have the glow of a woman in love."

"I have the glow of a woman who has spent too much time in the flower garden without a hat, *monsieur*," Marianna objected, "although, I have made an effort to appear happily married to the servants. Everyone knows how they will talk." She smiled under the inscrutable contemplation of her guest. "He is as boorish as ever, I

285

fear. I am surprised he has waited this long to inspect his precious mines. He is counting on you to make them profitable again."

"If there is profit to be gained from them, *señora*, rest assured that I have the means and resources to get it. I am a man who always gets what he wants."

Marianna smiled prettily in spite of the churning in her stomach. "That frightened me once, I am ashamed to say. The men in Paris . . ." The appearance of the maid with the lemonade interrupted her. "Ah, Maria, *muchas gracias*. It looks so cool and delightful."

"De nada, señora. It is nothing," the servant responded, beaming under her mistress's approval. "Shall I bring—"

A sudden rumble in the distance startled the maid into silence. The glassware on the table rattled with the tremor that seemed to run directly under them. Marianna caught her lemonade as it tipped over, sloshing the sweet nectar on the tablecloth.

"Sacrebleu! But what is that?"

Victor Romero shoved his chair away from the table and jumped to his feet. *"Señora*, where did your husband go this morning?"

The blood drained from Marianna's face as the meaning of the *alcalde's* words registered. "The mine," she managed in a strangled voice.

"Send for my horse!"

"And one for me," Marianna shouted after the running servant.

It couldn't be, she told herself sternly. Tristan and Mateo had gone to the mine to *avoid* an accident. It was probably a bad thunderstorm building in the distance. Yet, a glance in any direction revealed an endless stretch of blue sky, dotted only here and there with clouds.

When she emerged from the hacienda, Don Victor's

horse was already being brought from around the corner where the servant had tied it. At the barn a distance away, the bay she had been riding on her outings with Tristan was being hurriedly saddled along with more riding horses. Other steeds were being hitched to available wagons while men hastily tossed shovels and picks into the backs and piled aboard.

"Madre de Dios, where is my Tristan?" Marianna turned to see Doña Inez rushing out into the yard. Their eyes met and a terrible dread plucked at the girl's chest. "I have not heard that horrible sound in years, but I can never mistake it. There has been a cave-in."

Fighting sheer panic, Marianna started running toward the barn, no longer content to wait for her mount to be brought to her. The stirrup had no more than been dropped over the girth when she sprang onto the saddle, throwing her leg over the hook without regard for the show her rumpled skirt provided. Although her horse was no match in speed for that of the *alcalde,* she was able to follow him at a distance over the rolling hills that grew steeper and steeper as they progressed away from the hacienda.

The pounding of her horse's hoofs was the only thing that registered in her fear-strickened mind. She didn't dare think beyond getting to Tristan. The pins with which she'd carefully tucked up her curls fell with the jarring gallop over the rough terrain and her hair came tumbling down in disarray about her shoulders. Once, under her frantic urging, her horse stumbled and she was nearly pitched over its head, but for her deathlike grip on the back of the saddle.

Señora, por favor," one of the servants struggling on an old mule to keep up with her pleaded in desperation. "You will be no good to your husband with a broken neck."

Her husband. The words echoed above the mad scrambling of the racing horses and the bouncing creaks and squeals of the wagons. *My place is beside my husband,* Marianna recalled her mother arguing after hiding her small daughter under the bench around the olive tree. If Tristan had not become her husband in every sense in the last few days, what was he?

A group of men were already gathered around a small opening in the wall of a hill. At first, Marianna thought it was on fire, but upon riding closer, she realized that it was dust that had not yet settled from the disturbance. Victor Romero stood at the entrance to the mine shaft and peered into the gaping darkness intently, conversing to the side with the others in a low voice.

A nearby whinny drew Marianna's attention over to what was left of a rundown building where two horses were tied, the ones Tristan and Mateo had taken out that morning. "Tristan!" The name tore out of her throat as she threw herself off her horse and fell to the ground. Her legs buckled, pitching her forward on her hands and knees. The rough terrain scraped her palms without mercy as she pushed herself up with the help of one of the servants.

"*Señora,* you will hurt yourself!"

Marianna pulled out of the concerned man's hold and raced toward the opening. She pushed the spectators with picks and shovels aside and wove through them until she was able to reach the spot where the leaders discussed the nature of the problem inside.

"Tristan!" she shouted, stumbling past Victor Romero and into the dark void.

As her voice echoed hauntingly in the shaft, an arm caught her by the waist and dragged her back out into the sunlight. Blinded by the sudden change from light to dark and back to light again, Marianna blinked furiously. "Let me go! My husband is in there!"

"*Señora,* it is not safe. Even now there are further cave-ins! Believe me, I tried to get back to him and—"

Marianna focused on the dust-covered young man with a bloodied bandage tied around his head. "Mateo!" The impact of his words struck her like a mighty blow from a sledgehammer and she fell against Victor Romero.

"I was cut off from Don Tristan by the cave-in."

Swinging her frightened gaze back to the entrance, she whispered hoarsely, "Then we must try to get him out."

"*Señora,* we must wait until the repercussions have stopped. To send anyone in would be suicide until then."

"But *I* will go! Give me a lantern and I will go in," Marianna objected hysterically. "There may only be a few rocks between Tristan and the way that Mateo escaped! If more fall, we may lose the advantage!"

"*Señora,* the timbers are old, some are rotten. We must reinforce them before it is safe to move into the tunnel."

Marianna was moved out of the way as the first group of men from one of the wagons started into the entrance with boards they'd pulled from the outbuilding. "There is nothing to do but to let the men who know how to handle these things deal with this."

She grabbed the dazed Mateo's arm. "He was alive when you last saw him, *non?*" The quick exchange of glances over her head caused her insides to turn over.

"He *could* have been, *señora.* He had fallen beneath a timber and then there was so much dust that I could see nothing. The lantern had been knocked out of my hand and I had to feel my way out as it was."

289

"You are fortunate that you did not take a wrong turn. There are so many offshoots."

Marianna sank to the ground, her legs no longer capable of holding her up. *He could have been.* Mat's answer refused to settle with her stubborn perception of the possibilities. She crossed her arms and closed her eyes in prayer, oblivious to the arm Mateo placed over her shoulder. Tristan had to be alive, she thought fervently. *He had to be.*

Chapter Seventeen

The lanterns around the mine entrance cast an eerie glow under the nearby tree where Marianna waited with Doña Inez for news, any news, of Tristan. The seasoned miners had cleared away one blockade of debris and shored up the tunnel in order to keep on going. Carts had been coming out periodically loaded with broken timbers, rocks, and dirt.

"You must eat something, child. You will need your strength," the old nurse encouraged gently.

Marianna shook her head. She couldn't eat. There was this blade wedged in her throat that would not move up or down. She wiped away a single tear that trekked down her dusty cheek, streaking it. Just as she was about to speak, she spied a moving light near the tunnel entrance and stumbled to her feet.

"They're coming out!" Her words were hoarse. She rushed over to the opening to meet Mateo Salizar and Victor Romero. Behind them was the cart that had been emptied a short while ago, filled halfway with rubble. She looked from the cart to Mat's face, bewildered that they would come up before it was filled, unless . . .

"It is no use, *señora*. We have been digging through

solid debris now for the last hour. The entire roof of the tunnel must have caved in."

"But what about the other entrances?" she asked, recalling the map of the mine that Doña Inez had brought out for them. "Tristan might be in one of those."

"Your men have been checking them all afternoon," Victor Romero reminded her sympathetically, "at least those that are not completely blocked. It is best if we stop for the night."

"Non!" Marianna averred vehemently. "I will not stop, if I have to dig out the tunnel myself, piece by piece with my bare hands!"

"Señora, the chances of Don Tristan surviving are non-existent."

Marianna swung around to Mateo Salizar. "Then I want his body! You said you saw him fall. How far in the mine were you?"

Mateo shrugged helplessly. "It was dark, *señora.* I do not even know how I got out."

"His escape route is now carved in, *señora,"* Romero argued gently. "Will you risk more lives to find a dead man?"

A sob rose in Marianna's throat. She choked it back and wiped her tears away with her sleeve. *"Non,* I will only risk my own life." She marched over to the entrance and took a lantern from the men who had come out of the tunnel.

"Señora, be reasonable," Mateo pleaded, catching up with her. "Look at them! Do you think that they will allow their mistress to go into the mine alone to find her husband? No, they will not. If you go in, you will take them with you, regardless of what you wish."

"In the morning, I will bring some men and equipment over from Señor Cabal's mines," Victor Romero suggested, trying to find a way to placate the hysterical woman. "We will do all we can to find your husband's body." He took the lantern away from Marianna and handed it to a servant. "There is nothing to do but go home tonight."

Marianna searched the tired dirty faces of the men watching her, torn between what she wanted to do and what she had to do. Her shoulders sagged in defeat as she fixed her gaze on the arm placed over her own, Gradually a peculiar tattoo, a red and blue bleeding rose at the crux of two crossed daggers, came into focus, revealed by the *alcalde*'s rolled-up sleeves. "Very well, *monsieur.*" She was too numb to pay particular attention or pull away when the *alcalde* took her under his arm and walked her over to her horse. All she could think of was Tristan. If she had told him where the journals were, he wouldn't be dead. She had killed him.

"I did not expect to see you so distressed over the death of your gringo husband, Doña Elena."

Marianna looked up at the *alcalde*, bemused. "What? Oh!" she went on, his words finally taking hold. She had forgotten the charade, her reason for being there—everything but the loss that was tearing her apart inside. Pulling her wits together, she glanced around to see Mateo speaking to the men around the mine entrance.

"It would not do well to act joyous, would it, *señor?* You just find me the body so I will know that I am truly a widow. Then I may find cause to thank Providence for this unforeseen accident." Her voice was flat, devoid of emotion. She prayed she was convincing enough. "Or should I thank you, *señor*, for my good fortune?"

"There will be time later, Señora De Costa," Romero evaded smoothly, "after the funeral services. Then we will talk."

Marianna was saved comment by the wagon carrying Doña Inez that pulled alongside them. The older

293

woman was crying quietly into a lace-edge handkerchief. Tristan had been the light of her life since his arrival at Casa Valencia. She had plied Marianna with stories of his childhood escapades, her eyes glowing with pride over the little golden-haired caballero. It had meant so much to their former nurse that two of her charges had wed. Distracted by the other woman's grief, Marianna handed the reins of her mount over to her companion.

"If you will, Don Victor, please tie my horse to the wagon. I believe Doña Inez has need of me."

Without waiting for his agreement, Marianna walked to the front of the wagon and climbed up on the seat beside the older woman. Victor Romero was right, she supposed, slipping her arm around the bent shoulders of her former nurse. Life could not go on until the dead were honored properly. The *dead*. Her face contorted with the pain wrenching in her chest. All evidence pointed to the fact that Tristan had been killed, but somehow, she could not bring herself to accept it. Even when her parents had been murdered, she had been able to face the horrible truth. Perhaps it was that she had seen their bodies.

"We must send word to his mother," Doña Inez sniffed shakily.

Marianna looked into the pained gaze lifted up to hers and nodded solemnly. Of course, Doña Tessa—or Laura McCulloch, as Tristan referred to his mother—would have to be notified. And Mat would have to get word to Colonel Benevides. Would Salizar ever forgive her? she wondered, glancing back to where he rounded up the men to return to Casa Valencia. Would he tell Tristan's family how she had brought about his death? Her chin began to quiver uncontrollably. Not since she was an orphaned child had she felt so alone and frightened.

"It's all right, child," Doña Inez whispered broken-ly, feeling Marianna's pain. Assuming the role of com-forter, she drew the girl into her arms and hugged her tightly. "It may seem as though you will not live through this horrible grief, but you will." She clucked her tongue affectionately as the sobs Marianna had fought so val-iantly to hold back broke free. "So much pain for some-one so young," she sympathized brokenly, as the wagon lurched forward, taking them down the winding narrow road that stretched ahead of them like ribbon in the moonlight.

It was only after Doña Inez insisted that she take a mild dose of laudanum that Marianna was able to sleep. Even then it was not a restful sleep, but one fraught with disjointed nightmares that caused her to toss and turn fitfully until the morning sun found its way into the room through the open French doors and bathed the bed in its cheerful light. The uplifting sound of birds singing in the courtyard was so contrary to the desola-tion of her dreams that Marianna reached for Tristan upon stirring, anticipating his strong arms to close about her in response. All she found was a cold and empty pil-low, which brought home the reality of the nightmare she was living.

Don Victor had kept his promise to bring over addi-tional men and equipment and was already at the site when she rode out to join them. Clad in a pair of Tris-tan's trousers and a shirt, Marianna insisted on going into the mine and working along with the men, overrid-ing the *alcalde*'s indignant objections. At first, her success with the pick was awkward and teeth-jolting, but her de-termination made up for her inexperience in a short time and soon she was holding her own.

When the men quit at noon, she was forced to go up with them. Her nails were broken, and her hands were so badly blistered from the hard work that they stung unmercifully when she washed them for the bit of lunch Maria had sent out to the workers. Too tired to join in the conversation among the miners, she sat under a shade tree and nibbled on some cornbread with little appetite.

As she climbed to her feet to return to work, Heraldo Cabal and Victor Romero approached her. Marianna knew from their expressions, before they even spoke, that they were going to call off the search. She wanted to argue with them, to keep on going, but she had personally chipped away at the solid wall of debris that showed no sign of ending. According to the map of the mines, it could conceivably go on for hundreds of yards.

Covered with filth and broken in spirit after the men informed her of their decision, Marianna mounted her horse and turned it toward Casa Valencia. Yet, as she approached the sprawling hacienda, she circled around it, not ready to face the guests who, judging from the strange carriages in the front, were already arriving to offer their condolences. Instead she sought out the little grove where she and Tristan had picnicked a few days before and sat down under the trees to think. Until now, there had been no time for that.

It was there that Mateo Salizar found her crying, curled up at the base of the tree. He held her and absorbed her soul-wrenching sobs until they were spent.

"It's all my fault! T-Tristan wouldn't be dead if it weren't for m-me!"

"Nonsense, *amiga*. Perhaps if I had not panicked and tried to escape, I might have helped him to safety. Would to God that I could change places with him now, but I can not. All that we can do now is not to let his death be in vain."

Marianna lifted her head from Mateo's chest. "W-what are you suggesting?"

"We must bring Romero to justice. You must tell me where the journals are."

Inhaling shakily, Marianna stepped away. "Yes," she agreed, "Romero must be brought to justice. We will kill him, you and I."

"No, *señora*, we must entrust this to the authorities ..."

"The authorities!" she derided in contempt. "They never listened to me, an eyewitness to what that murderer has done! I saw him kill my mother! He ... he raped her and then shot her without conscience." She shuddered, but refused to acknowledge the sympathetic hand placed on her shoulder. "No one would listen to a child. *I ... want ... him ... dead!*" she sobbed bitterly.

"A firing squad ..."

Marianna shook her head hysterically. "*Non*, I will not tell you! You must work with me or not at all!"

"But—"

"I will not listen!" she averred, placing her hands over her ears and turning away.

After a spell of silence, she felt hands come to rest on her shoulders. "*Muy bien.* Very well, *señora,* but I can not promise your safety."

"You have a young wife to worry about. I have no one," she replied, her voice flattened by spent motion. "You see, Señor Salizar, I do not expect to come out of this alive." She turned to see the astonishment on the young man's face. "That is why you must go get the authorities while Don Victor pays me court. I intend to kill him, but should the opportunity not present itself, when you arrive with Colonel Benevides, I will show them the books."

"And if he kills you first?"

Marianna's jaw set stubbornly. "Then I will leave in structions as to where to find them."

"Where?"

"Where you will be certain to discover them."

"This is *madness!*" the Mexican muttered, pacing a few feet away to vent his frustration.

"We must fight madness with madness, *señor.*"

Faced with no other option, Mateo gave in. "Very well," he sighed in defeat. "I will go for the colonel after the funeral services, but I will not like it."

Marianna grimaced in an attempt to smile. Like her plan for vengeance, it was as much as she could muster.

The afternoon sun shone bright, highlighting the spots Laura Skylar McCulloch had missed dusting on the rich mahogany top of the sideboard in the large room that served both as dining room and living room to Silverado's main house. In the back kitchen, now attached under a shed roof instead of being in the separate cabin it had occupied when she first came to the ranch, she could hear her husband pouring a cup of coffee. A muffled curse betrayed the fact that he'd scalded a finger or his tongue, causing her lips to twitch wryly.

Ross had been like a cooped-up wildcat since he'd awakened earlier that week in the middle of the night and paced the remainder of it trying to remember the dream that made his head ache so. Since then, he'd stuck close to the ranch, as if expecting some news. As much as she loved Ross McCulloch, Laura found his uncharacteristic presence unnerving. She knew it meant something. The future-telling dreams were never wrong. The problem was, she wasn't sure if this one was good or bad. Worse, he wouldn't talk about it, leaving her to think that he was either protecting her or that he, too, was confused.

"Laura, are you and Tillie fixing to wash today?"

And the last thing Ross McCulloch was interested in was laundry! This was the third day in a row he'd asked her that question. "No, Ross. You know we always wash the first of the week."

"Not always," her husband pointed out, his face coloring as he dropped into a chair at the oak table and concentrated on cooling the hot coffee. "I mean, there are some weeks in the month you wash every day."

Laura stared at him blankly.

"For the love of God, Laura, you know, women's things," he exclaimed in exasperation. "Do you have something you want to tell me?"

Her mouth dropped open upon realizing what the tough ex-Ranger was trying to say. "At *my* age, Ross McCulloch?" She walked over to him and wrapped her arms around his neck from behind, giving him a hug. She couldn't believe he took notice of such things. "That's very flattering, my dear husband, but it's normal at my age to skip that bother from time to time." A giggle slipped out. To think that that was behind this strange behavior of the last few days! "I think we'd best leave the little ones to Catalina and Alex!" She sobered suddenly. "Is *that* it? Do you think the reason Cat and Alex are coming to visit is to announce our third grandchild?"

"I've heard of women your age having babies," Ross replied stubbornly. "We're not so old."

"You saw something in that dream, didn't you, Ross McCulloch? What was it?" Excitedly, Laura sat down in front of him and waited. She'd traveled to Los Angeles for the birth of her first two grandchildren, and the prospect of another visit was easy to adjust to.

Ross scowled thoughtfully and then sighed in resignation. "I might as well tell you, because damned if I can make it out."

"All right," she answered brightly. "Let's hear it."

"I heard a baby crying."

Laura's brow knitted. "That's all?"

"No, it was coming from Tristan's room . . ."

"Tristan's?"

"And when I went in there, the room was empty. I mean, nobody was in it. There was just a cradle by the bed."

"Well . . . the children do stay in Tristan's room when Cat and Alex visit, although 'Trina is old enough to sleep in a regular bed now," she remarked, recalling the tidbit about her youngest grandchild in Catalina's letter. She laughed lightly and squeezed Ross's hand. "What's the matter, Grandpa? Aren't you up to a night pacing with the grandkids?"

A hint of a smile came to Ross's lips, inviting the impulsive kiss Laura placed there. "I'm certain it's nothing we can't handle, especially with Cat being a doctor."

That was one of the things he loved about the woman he married, Ross thought, turning away from the table to draw her into his lap. She had a way of seeing the bright side of everything, especially when it came to Catalina's children.

As much as he wanted to believe Laura was right, there was something about that dream that left him unsettled . . . something wrong. Considering the note Tristan had sent him the week before, it was possible that his son was in trouble. The De Costas were dead, but killing one snake didn't mean they were all gone. Agreeing with his son's suggestion, Ross hadn't told Laura about Tristan returning to Casa Valencia. He saw no point in both of them worrying.

"When did Cat's letter say she and Alex were coming?"

"This Friday," Laura chided, poking him playfully in the chest. "As if you've forgotten! Do you really think we're going to be grandparents again?"

"Could be, Mother—I mean, *Grandma.*" It was odd how one's perspective of age changed as they grew older. He didn't mind being called Grandpa at all, considering the lovely woman he was holding was a grandmother. Once she claimed to have found a gray hair, but he'd yet to see it. She fretted over a wrinkle here and there, but they weren't permanent. As far as he could tell, they only showed when she smiled or squinted at the sun. Even then, they served to highlight her sparkling eyes and china-perfect features. As for her figure . . .

"I wish Catalina and Alex would move back to Silverado," she sighed, caught up in a whimsical fancy. "Wouldn't it be wonderful to have grandchildren close-by?"

Ross's fingers almost touched as he spanned her waist and he smiled in satisfaction. "So you can spoil them?"

Laura twisted in mock indignation. "*I* didn't sent them matching ponies on their first and third birthdays like some people I know."

"Indian babies are put on horses as soon as they're old enough to sit up on their own," Ross countered defensively. "Besides, the colts can grow up with the kids." Like Tristan and Catalina grew up with theirs, he mused, caught up in a nostalgia of his own. As much as he complained about the fuss and lack of privacy, he had to admit that he thoroughly enjoyed Catalina's family's visits. It took him back to when the twins and Alex turned the house upside down with war whoops and chaos.

"Mr. Ross, we got comp'ny!"

At their housekeeper's bellowing announcement, Ross's mind returned abruptly to the present. He came out of his chair so quickly that Laura had to catch herself on the edge of the table to keep from being dumped in the floor.

"For heaven's sake, Ross McCulloch! What has gotten into you?" she demanded irritably as he stalked over to the door and unhooked the gun belt hanging behind it. The color drained from her face, taking with it her spontaneous ire. She hadn't noticed that he'd taken his guns out. "Something *is* wrong!" she whispered to no one in particular, for her husband was already out on the porch.

Laura stepped outside in time to see Ross walking out to meet Manolo Benevides. One look at their old friend's face and her heart stilled in her chest. Ordinarily, the two clapped each other on the back until they were winded in their delight to see one another. Today, they stood in silence, carrying on a strange communication that, although it eluded her, managed to alarm her as well. It was Manolo who finally broke the strained silence.

"I can see that you have been expecting me."

"I've been expecting something," Ross answered candidly.

Laura came off the porch, unable to stand the suspense any longer. "What is it, Mano?" She had to force the words out, her throat constricting even as she asked, "Is Tristan all right?"

Manolo Benevides climbed down from his horse and straightened stiffly. "There is no good way to say this, Laura. Tristan was killed in a mining accident."

A cold numbness swept through her, mingled with disbelief. "A *mining* accident?"

"Where's the body," Ross asked tersely, his face a

stone mask of solemnity as he slipped a supporting arm about the waist he'd only moments ago measured in speculation.

"He was buried in a cave-in," Mano went on, reaching into his pocket to retrieve the note addressed to Tristan's parents that had accompanied the notification of the young man's demise. "They have not found the body yet. I . . . I have a letter from his wife."

"His wife?" Laura echoed, shaken from one shock by yet another. "Ross?" Swimming whiskey-brown eyes turned up at the tall ex-Ranger, seeking some assurance that this was all a bad dream.

Ross took the note stoically and unfolded it. It was written in English, the formal version of one who did not speak it as their native language. "Dear Mr. and Mrs. McCulloch," he began after temporarily clearing his throat of the restrained emotion lodged there. "I am sorry to tell you of your son's death. I am trying in every possible way to find his remains, but am told that it is impossible. I will not cease my hope, however, until the men have tried every means of getting to him." Ross felt the biting grip of slender fingers on his arm and read on. "I did not know your son very long. Our wedding was one of convenience. Yet in that short time, I came to care for him very much. You should be proud of him as I was. As soon as matters are settled here, I shall return to my family in France."

"She's French?" Laura murmured in confusion.

"Her mother, I believe, is French."

"Who was her father?" Ross inquired with a curious rise of a golden brow.

Manolo dreaded voicing the answer. "Luis De Costa."

"Ross!"

303

Ross caught Laura as her knees gave way and scooped her up in his arms. "We'll finish this inside."

"That dreadful animal!" the woman in his arms cried, venting her grief upon his shoulder. "How could that have happened? What was Tristan doing in Mexico anyway?"

Ross deposited Laura in a chair and sent Tillie Reyes, who had stepped out on the porch in curiosity upon seeing an old family friend ride up, after some tea. Himself he helped to a straight shot of liquor while Manolo Benevides started the story from the beginning.

He told them how Tristan had met Elena De Costa, although he was at a loss to explain the marriage, considering the animosity between the two. "She is a delightful girl, as pretty and resourceful as someone else I know," he added, looking pointedly at Laura, before elaborating on how the young lady had stolen Tristan's horse and broken out of jail.

Ross leaned forward. "Seems to me she's in a bad way. Someone had best fetch her before this Romero gets his hands on her."

"Bring her *here* to Silverado!" Laura exclaimed, astonished at the idea. This woman had hoodwinked her son into a marriage of convenience, possibly contributed to his death, and Ross wanted to bring her home. "But she forced Tristan to marry her."

Ross tapped the letter. "Sounds like they were making the best of it, from the way she writes. I remember I wasn't particularly thrilled when I had to marry you, but I found reason enough not to complain," he reminded her dryly.

Instead of responding, Laura grabbed the letter and finished reading it. "I feel as though my heart is buried under that rubble with him. I shall be only an empty . . ." Her voice broke. "An empty shell returning to Paris, but return I must. I can not bear to remain in this savage land where everything reminds me of your son, nor can I bring myself to visit your Silverado. Tristan told me much about the ranch and you, his wonderful family. I do not think that I could stand to meet you without him."

Laura's hand trembled as she put down the note, unable to read the signature through her tears. Resolutely, she shoved up from the chair and stared toward the staircase.

"Laura?" Ross sprang after her, catching her at the base of the wide oak steps.

"If you think that you and Mano are going to Casa Valencia without me, you are mistaken."

"Now wait a minute. We're going in after Tristan's murderer and to rescue his bride."

"It will not be safe for you, Laura," Manolo chimed in.

"Besides, you need to be here when Cat and Alex arrive," her husband reminded her. "Someone has to tell her and, if Cat is expecting, I'd think her mother should be with her."

Laura bit her bottom lip to hold back the sob that rose in her throat. It was a day she had lived in dread of since Tristan had joined the Texas Rangers, following in his father's footsteps. Yet, now that it was here, she still was not prepared for it. She looked at her husband, his somber face blurred by the tears that spilled down her face unashamed.

"It was Tristan crying, wasn't it, Ross?" she anguished brokenly. "My beautiful baby boy!"

Chapter Eighteen

Marianna thought the days following Tristan's fatal accident would never come to an end. Services were held at the village chapel. It was a mockery of a memorial. The priest who eulogized the male De Costa heir had not known him and lamented over the tale of the young man's kidnapping by the Indians and his eventual return to his rightful home with his bride. The mourners were many, however. Some showed up out of curiosity and others to comfort Doña Inez, a pillar of the local community known for her charity.

Aside from the offer of a few polite condolences, most of them ignored Marianna. If not for Mateo, she would have felt completely isolated, for the elderly nurse was kept busy overseeing the care of the guests. The De Costa family home was overwhelming in its loneliness. It was empty, not of bodies, but of soul, of love.

And now it was almost over, she mused resolutely, checking out the gun Liam had given her. She'd found it in Tristan's saddlebags. The rest of his belongings she'd sent on to Manolo Benevides with Mateo, who had left at sunup the morning after the funeral, as planned, to fetch the colonel and his own superiors to Mirabeau. To cover the very real possibility that she might be killed as Mat warned, she had posted a letter to Silverado disclosing the whereabouts of the secret passage and the contents hidden there. Since Tristan's father had been an ex-Ranger, he would know what to do.

She placed the loaded gun in her old satchel, her reticule being too small to hide it adequately, and caught a glimpse of herself as she marched toward the bedroom door. The black mourning dress had belonged to Tristan's mother, but fit her perfectly. Doña Inez had kept it in an old trunk all those years. Although out of fashion with its full bell-shaped skirts and sleeves, it had been well preserved. A good airing, brushing, and pressing and the black velvet and silk had come out like new.

His death had, of course, stirred some talk, but then talk had been circulating about her and Tristan since the night of the duel at Mirabeau. She had even heard ripples of gossip in the kitchen earlier that morning after she'd ordered her horse saddled to ride over to the *alcalde*'s the week after her husband's funeral. The servants surely thought her a wanton tramp.

But enough was enough. Her plans had been too long delayed. She steeled herself before the girl in the mirror, determined as she had never been before. This time she would not fail. She would look Romero squarely in the eye and pull the trigger. She might even feel a sense of satisfaction. At least, she hoped so. She craved some relief, some consolation from this terrible ache that would not subside except under the effects of Doña Inez's laudanum.

Time and random thought seemed suspended on the ride to Mirabeau. Marianna allowed only one purpose to dominate her consciousness. She knew exactly what she was going to do and how. She'd sent a servant over earlier to let the alcalde know that she intended to visit that afternoon to discuss the carrying out of her husband's wishes to reopen the mines. Unless she misjudged him, he would not be surprised, but pleased that she was walking so promptly and innocently into his grasp.

Victor Romero came out of the house to meet her as she tied the reins of her bay to the hitching post outside the fortresslike front of Mirabeau. His black mustache, stretched over ample and uneven teeth, reminded Marianna of the brush she and Dona Inez used to restore her dress.

"Buenos días, Señora De Costa. This is indeed a delightful surprise considering your recent loss. I would have thought you needed more time to mourn," he added lowly, a hint of reprimand in his voice.

Marianna gave him her free hand, the old satchel clutched tightly in the other. "I only wish to see my husband's wishes carried out. Besides, now that I am a wealthy widow, I don't really care what people think. I may return to Paris and leave them to their gossip."

The *alcalde's* smile froze on his lips. "Then, I shall have to think of a way to dissuade you."

"Charm never hurt a *business* relationship," she inferred with a coyish slant of her gaze. "And it could make it more lasting. Shall we retire to your office?"

"I had thought to entertain you in the salon . . ."

Marianna put her hand on his arm, certain that she was the source of the amusement painted on the faces of the shabbily clad men lounging in the shade of a building nearby. "Let us start with business, *monsieur.* I doubt that you would discuss mining with my husband so."

Romero laughed as he stood back to permit her to enter the hacienda ahead of him. "My office it is, *señora."*

Marianna managed a smile at Alfonso, who stood dutifully by the door to take her bag. "No thank you, *mon-*

sieur. I have the maps of the mines in here, along with other business papers which I will need." She let out a sigh of relief when the old man nodded without question and moved aside to let them progress down the hall.

The office doors to the courtyard were open and the fragrant scent of the flowers growing in the neatly trimmed beds her mother had had built up with brick wafted in on the slight breeze. Marianna started for the chair next to the desk, leaving the *alcalde* to close the door, but was startled to have the satchel snatched from her grip and tossed recklessly on the desktop.

"Monsieur, what are you doing?" she demanded, disconcerted by the sudden removal of her weapon.

"What I have wanted to do since I first looked into those magnificent blue eyes of yours, *señora.*"

"But the servants . . ."

"Will not disturb us," Romero assured her, his hot coffee-scented breath assaulting her nostrils as he seized her lips with his own.

Marianna struggled in the tightening grasp, trying to move away from the body that forced her back against the edge of the desk. She wanted to retch from the tongue that pried at her clenched teeth. Her blood boiled to her face on a tide of outrage. Realizing that she was physically unable to repel the unsolicited assault, she stiffened coldly and waited for the man to recognize her lack of response. When he finally backed away, she was literally seething.

"I should slap you for that!" she grated out under her breath, eyes glowering to match the anger that flushed her cheeks.

"And I should kill you, *Señorita Gallier,* but I won't—at least, not for the time being."

Marianna grasped the edge of the desktop for support as the impact of his words doused the fire of her indignation with shock. Her mouth slackened, as if to deny the accusation, but she was too numb to say anything. How could he have known? How long had he known? The questions bounced around, echoing hollow in her stunned mind.

"No doubt from the thud your bag made when it struck the desktop, there is more than a few papers in it. A gun, perhaps?"

Shaken from her stupor by the reminder, Marianna turned and lunged for the satchel, only to have it snatched away by her nemesis. She watched in helpless frustration as he opened the bag and took out the gun.

"To think that I believed it was the Ranger whom you sought to kill the night of our duel," Romero tutted, as if he chided a small child.

Marianna lifted her chin haughtily. If she was going to die, it was not going to be like her mother. She would force Romero to kill her before he could follow through with the thoughts surfacing in his lascivious perusal.

"If you are going to kill me, *monsieur*, then be done with it!"

He smiled, and her blood turned to ice. She had seen that smile before, years ago. It was the most frightening thing she had ever witnessed, the smile of a maniacal murderer. "Eventually," he conceded, moving around to take the chair behind the desk." He waved the gun at her. "Take off that dress, *señora*. Black does not become you."

Marianna backed as far away as she could, pressing her back to the paneled wall of the fireplace. *"Non."*

He heaved a heavy sigh, as if his patience were being tested to its limit. "Very well, then. I shall have my men come in and remove it for you. They would be most delighted, I am certain.

"Get him over here!"

Marianna started at the hushed whisper that reached her ears, seemingly out of thin air. Her hand flew to her throat as she fell against the false panel. That voice! No, it couldn't be, she told herself sternly. It was the result of the cowardly fear turning her blood yellow and filling her with hysterical thoughts. She swallowed hard as Victor Romero shrugged and spun his chair toward the open French doors.

"Miguel, Hugo, Pepe!"

"Damn it, Frenchie, get him over here!"

"Non!" Marianna gasped, her eyes wide with a combination of terror and disbelief.

Romero turned expectantly.

"I . . . you . . ." she stammered, "I would prefer that you undress me yourself. *Please,* no strangers."

A slow smile spread on the *alcalde*'s thin lips. Her heart pounded so loudly in her ears that she was beginning to doubt that she had heard anything . . . that the voice was not just a figment of her imagination after all.

The men the *alcalde* summoned appeared at the door, the ones she'd seen lingering around the front of the hacienda like mangy hound dogs waiting for a handout as she rode up. "See that I am not disturbed for any reason," Romero snapped briskly, his hand on the latch of the French door to close it. "The lady and I have some *private* business to settle. Again leering grins broke out on the unshaven and unwashed faces as they glanced over at Marianna in speculation before taking their leave.

"Get his back to the panel."

Marianna started again at the hissing order, but the *alcalde* mistook her action as a reaction to him.

"I have been told that I am a good lover, *señora,"* he assured her, leaving the pistol next to her satchel to cross the room. He removed his jacket as he approached her, limping slightly from his stiff knee, and tossed it on

311

the floor. "I have become more polished since the day I ... enjoyed your mother's favors." He stopped in front of her. "Now I know why your face has haunted me so. You are the image of her. Of course, I might spare you the humiliation by my men as well if you tell me where you hid the journals you took from my library."

Marianna withdrew instinctively against the panel from the hand that moved from her cheek over the swell of her bosom, in spite of the whispered order to maneuver the *alcalde's* back to the wall. As his second hand moved to cup her other breast, a wave of nausea washed over her, infecting with bitterness the hatred that filled her voice.

"I have noticed that your knee has improved much since the day my bullet shattered it. At least I shall carry to my grave that satisfaction ... and damn your journals!" she swore defiantly.

Marianna gasped as the grip tightened painfully. "You?" Victor Romero exclaimed incredulously. "You were but a child!" he sneered, pinning her against the wall as if to force the truth from her.

"Yes," she ground out through clenched teeth. "Small enough to hide beneath the very bench you raped my mother on. Small enough to reach through the lattice and fire your own gun into your knee. And even now a letter telling the location of the journals is on its way to the authorities. Dead or alive, I will have my revenge."

Marianna saw the fist draw back to strike her and twisted away, raising her arm to block the harsh blow that still sent her reeling to the floor. As she struck the carpet, the room seemed to explode. She stared as the hidden panel shattered with the angry charge of a tall golden-haired warrior clad in filthy buckskins. The crack of bone against bone as his fist rammed into a startled Victor Romero's jaw made her flinch. She scrambled aside just as the *alcalde* struck the floor dazed.

"You *are* real!" she cried out, as reluctant to believe her eyes as she was her hearing. Tristan, alive! A mixture of joy and disbelief battled for dominance in her staggered consciousness. "But——"

"Later, Frenchie. Put those journals in your satchel and let's get the hell out of here." Tristan pulled a gun on Romero as the *alcalde* recovered. "If you have half the sense I give you credit for, Romero, you won't move or breathe."

Marianna rushed through the shattered entrance and gathered up the books she'd left there on their last visit. "How did you know about the secret passage?" she asked, stepping around Romero to stuff them into the carpetbag.

"I figured there had to be a connection between Romero's bedroom and office for you to move about so freely without getting caught and you would know it. I was hiding in Romero's closet after searching his room for those damned books when I accidently discovered it. You hadn't closed it completely the last time you used it. Hold it, *amigo*," Tristan snapped, noting the hand Victor Romero moved slowly down his leg toward his boot. "Now take it out, slowly."

Freezing in the midst of shoving the books into the carpeting, Marianna watched as the *alcalde* inched a long-bladed knife out of its hiding place.

"I will cut your heart out, Ranger and feed it to the dogs."

"Is that before or after the firing squad?" Tristan remarked cryptically.

"There will be no firing squad." Both men turned to see Marianna holding the pistol she had smuggled in

313

held at arm's length and pointed at the man on the floor.

"Frenchie, drop it!"

Marianna shook her head. "I can not, Tristan. I want him to die, to see the bullet coming like my mother did." Her voice faltered and she concentrated to steady her shaking hands.

"But can you watch this bullet smash into my chest, *señora?*" Romero inquired skeptically. "You, who swoon at the sight of blood? Will you be able to stand the tearing flesh and the scarlet soaking the front of my shirt as my heart pumps out my life's blood in gushing spurts? And the smell of gunpowder? Are you ready to smell it, mingled with the stench of death?"

He was trying to frighten her, Marianna told herself. She shook her head to destroy the gruesome image he so descriptively placed there. But it wasn't his chest that she saw, but that of her mother. It was not his shirt soaked scarlet, but porcelain-white globes streaked with the life that pumped furiously from within. And her lips, the small trickle that seeped out the corner as she kept on whispering over and over, "Don't move, Marianna! Don't make a sound."

But this time she had a gun. She knew how to use it. "I'll stop him, Mama!"

"Marianna!"

The thunder of the pistol shook the chimneys on the mantel lamps and rang in Marianna's ears, shattering her nightmare with reality again. Victor Romero cried out in agony, grasping his abdomen with bloodied fingers. Suddenly the gun was knocked from her hand and her arm was seized roughly.

"Damn you, Frenchie, you'll get me killed yet! Get the bag!"

Marianna grabbed the handle of the bag and followed Tristan to the closed door. The entire courtyard seemed to break out in confused shouts. He turned away and jumped over Victor Romero, snatching the discarded pistol up before the *alcalde* could reach it. He tucked it in his belt and kicked the knife the man had dropped across the room. "Come on, we'll go out through the house. That courtyard's a death trap."

Alfonso jumped into a doorway with a startled shout as Tristan and Marianna barreled through the corridor. The Ranger gave him no more than a cursory glance, intent on getting out of the house to the horse he'd seen Marianna ride up on before it was too late. A gunshot rang from the back of the house, the bullet pinging against the frame of the double oak doors above their heads. Marianna screamed, tucked under the Ranger's arm as he returned the fire, driving the gunman into cover and sending the maid screaming into the open courtyard for help.

The moment the front door opened, a round of gunfire erupted outside, assaulting the thick oak wood and splintering it. "I never saw a woman who could cause so much trouble! I wish to hell you'd stayed in France!"

Stung by his angry words, Marianna rallied. "So do I! If we live, that is exactly where I am going so that you do not have to worry about me again!"

"Fine!"

"Good!"

Tristan fired over her shoulder at the gunman who stepped out of the kitchen doorway, this time striking him full in the chest. Marianna shrieked, covering her ears belatedly as the man reeled backward into a hall table, breaking the imported emerald-cut glassware displayed on it.

"I'm going to break for the horse and swing back by to get you." Tristan handed her the gun he'd knocked

315

from her hand and tucked in his belt. "I want you to reach around the door and fire like I'm going to show you—don't worry about hitting anyone—and be ready to jump up behind me when I ride by." Noting the paling color on her face as she took the pistol, Tristan leaned over and bussed her forehead impulsively, which was as startling to him as it was to her, for at that moment, he wanted to shake her. "We're going to make it, Frenchie."

Before she could answer, he reached around the door and fired twice in each direction. Marianna followed him with her gaze as he raced toward the whinnying bay, now tugging at its reins. The dirt near his feet exploded, his zigzag pattern evading the paths of the lethal bullets. Reminded of her job, she did as the Ranger instructed and fired the gun through the crack in the door. In the corner of her eye, she spied the young man crouch low and vault with seemingly no effort up onto the balking horse.

At that moment, the reins tore loose from the post and the animal bolted toward the gate at the far end of the dusty yard in front of the hacienda. Marianna's heart stopped beating as the horse ran away from her, rather than toward her.

"Tristan!" she shouted, leaving her cover in panic to go after him.

"Señora!" A heavy weight struck her from behind, throwing her to the ground in the cover of a low stone fountain. "Stay close to this."

Stunned, Marianna rolled over to see Mateo Salizar firing at the gunmen on the roof. "Mat!" Relief flooded through her. Perhaps there was a chance after all. The sound of thundering hoofbeats drew her attention to where her bay approached, black mane and tail streaming behind it. Tristan, however, was hanging off the animal, but for a portion of a leg circled around the hook of her sidesaddle.

"He is falling!" she cried out, starting up in alarm.

"He is riding like the Indians so that they can not hit him!" Mateo grabbed her skirt and pulled her back, shielding her with his body. "Now get ready! He is coming this way."

"Can we all ride one horse?" Marianna asked, her brow knitting in concern for her companion.

"I apologize with all my soul, *señora*, that it has come to this. They caught me that night I tried to find the journals. It was only for the safety of my wife that I agreed to help . . ."

Puzzled, Marianna turned to look over her shoulder when a burst of thunder smacked loudly against Mateo's forehead, drilling a tiny hole that began to spurt scarlet. The arm that held her in cover fell away as his lifeless body collapsed on top of her.

"You are not the only one who pays their debts of revenge, *señora*."

Shuddering violently beneath the fountain of warm blood that began to cover her, Marianna tore out of the limp grip of the Mexican and backed away. She raised a shocked gaze to where Romero leaned heavily against the doorjamb, a smoking rifle aimed at her.

"Let's go, Frenchie!" Tristan emphasized.

Sixguns spoke loudly above the pounding of a horse's hoofs behind her. Romero jerked convulsively and fell to the tiled floor where a pair of arms dragged him inside. Marianna spun on her heels and reached for the arm suddenly extended to her. Yanked off her feet, she struggled to right herself behind the Ranger as the bay galloped off. "Mat—" she shouted breathlessly.

"I know! You all right?" Tristan glanced around in concern at the blood on her face.

Marianna nodded. "It's Mat's blood," she grunted in assurance, pulling herself upright with Tristan's shirt.

"Hang on, we got to jump!"

Wrapping her arms about the lean hard waist, she straightened in time for the bay to sail clearly over the rail fence. The horse struck the dry hard ground on the opposite side, jarring Marianna's teeth. At the same time, fire from the depths of hell ripped through her back, pushing her against the wiry one of her rescuer. She tightened her hold and closed her eyes, as if to squeeze out the pain.

The move was a bad one. On top of the jolting ride, her head began to spin dizzily, threatening to draw her into unconsciousness. She blinked furiously and forced herself to stare at the ground rolling in a cloud of dust beneath them. "Mat was working for them!" she shouted, the sound of her voice helping her to continue to grasp reality. "He said he was caught breaking in to get the journals and they made him do it or . . ." Marianna swallowed, her mouth completely devoid of any moisture. "Or they would hurt his wife."

"I kind of figured it was something like that after he knocked me over the head and set off that charge!" Tristan shouted over his shoulder.

Distracted from her pain, Marianna tried to digest Tristan's shocking revelation. His friend had not only betrayed her, but attempted to kill Tristan! Such a deed was beyond her ability to comprehend, yet Mat had admitted it with his own words.

"I lost a good partner, thanks to your bullheaded ways."

Her breath caught at the harshness of Tristan's accusation. But it was Mat who betrayed them, she thought, too winded to continue the conversation. How could he blame her for that? How he must hate her! Marianna braved the danger of the darkness veiled behind her eyelids, forcing tears from her eyes that not even the awful agony in her back could unleash. It was an entirely different anguish that made her cry, one buried deep within. These tears were the blood of her soul.

How long they rode, Marianna had no idea. She merely clung to the now-silent Ranger out of sheer instinct for survival. In actual thought, she didn't care if she died. It was over now. While she had not killed Victor Romero, Tristan had. Justice had been done.

Her lips moved silently in prayer, asking forgiveness for her inadvertent part in Mateo's death. She'd had no idea that by hiding the journals so much trouble would result. But then, she had no idea when she agreed to masquerade as Elena De Costa that her entire life would be turned upside down. She thought of her grandmother's saying about one lie begetting another until the liar lost control of the situation. *Granmaman* was right. That sage advice certainly applied to her series of blunders and mistakes.

"We better hole up in one of these mine shafts. The place will be crawling with Romero's men. We'll travel at night."

"Is it safe?" It was an inane question, but then Marianna's thinking was becoming less and less coherent.

"Yeah," her companion assured her, drawing the lathered bay up in front of what appeared to be a thicket of *huisache*. "I happened to put away some supplies in here over the last few days in case you're hungry." Tristan swung his leg over the hook of the saddle, catching it hard against his inner thigh in the process, and swore vehemently. "I don't know how in the world you women manage to stay on a horse with those things!"

Over the last few days! Marianna looked down at him in-

319

credulously. "You mean ... you mean to say that you have been alive all this time and you let me think that you were dead! Damn you, Treestan MacCoolach!" she sniffed, her emotions and the pain in her back catching up with her. "One tear shed for you is more than you deserve!"

Tristan held up his arms to help her down. "You don't have any room to talk, Frenchie, when it comes to lying and holding back the truth!"

Ignoring his outstretched arms, Marianna glared down at him. "But I did not let you think that I was dead! If you only knew!"

"Marianna ..."

She slapped at his hands. "Don't touch me!" Her head grew light as she reached forward to grab the reins.

"You hotheaded mule stubborn—"

Angered beyond words, Tristan grabbed Marianna by the skirts and yanked her off the horse. A bloodcurdling scream ripped through the air as she fell into his arms, kicking at first. But as he struggled to hold her waist with one arm and silence her at the same time, she suddenly went limp.

"Frenchie, you—" Tristan broke off as his fingers registered a warm sticky wetness soaking the back of her dress. He jerked his hand away to see blood covering it. The withers of the horse was lathered pink from it. "Marianna?" he echoed in alarm, holding her away. Her head rolled back listlessly, the black shining tresses that had come undone during the narrow escape spilling down her back.

Growing weak with apprehension, he scooped her up in his arms and kicked the cuttings of *huisache* aside that he had used to hide the mine entrance. The Indian blanket he'd borrowed from the Mexican farmer who found him wandering about dazed from a severe concussion was rolled out on the hard dirt floor. Recognizing a pattern of the Honeyeaters, his father's adopted tribe, Tristan had sent the man with his belt to the Hills of Lakes. His Indian cousin would surely know it as the one he'd given Tristan and come, for, with Mateo Salizar's betrayal, his only hope of getting Marianna out of Mexico was to seek Eagle Wing's help.

Hopefully soon, he thought grimly, laying the girl gently on the makeshift bed. She whimpered, her face contorted in pain. A frustrating sense of helplessness washed over him as he leaned down and brushed her hair gently out of her face. She hadn't even cried out when she was hit! She'd argued with him and made him so damned mad, he would have dismounted and flailed the daylights out of her if he weren't concerned about Romero's men following them.

Her features relaxed again, indicating that she'd sunk back into the realm of anesthetic darkness. Tristan wrapped the blanket about her snugly, aware of the sudden pallor and coldness of her skin. He'd get the horse in, he thought, pushing himself to his feet reluctantly. Then he'd try to take the bullet out before she regained consciousness. He wiped his hands on his trousers as he started toward the mine entrance and stared at the scarlet-smeared leather. She'd lost a lot of blood.

Chapter Nineteen

"Am I . . . going to die?"

Tristan forced a reassuring smile as he set the lantern down beside the bedroll where Marianna stared up at him. Her eyes were wide with fright and glazed with pain. "I've had worse scratches," he quipped, uncapping his canteen to offer her a drink.

"It feels like more than a scratch." She tried to rise up on her elbows. Tristan slipped an assisting hand under her back, but before she could drink, she winced, crying out at the cost, and collapsed against him.

"Easy, Frenchie," he consoled, easing her down to the blanket again. She was starting to tremble. No, she was crying. A telltale tear squeezed out the corner of one eye. Wondering if *he* could stand much more, let alone if she could, Tristan fought the urge to take her up in his arms and hold her. She wasn't meant for this kind of life. She was a Parisian orchid, not a Texas rose. He steeled himself for what he had to do. The wound had to be examined, and this twisting feeling in his gut, part sympathetic and part a real apprehension that it was more serious than he count treat, wasn't going to go away by letting his emotions run away with him.

"I'm going to turn you over on your side, so that I can take a look at that wound."

Marianna shook her head. "I feel sick."

She was a deathly shade of white. "You're going to feel worse if there's a bullet in there and I don't get it out."

Blue eyes turned toward him beseechingly. "I am a coward, Tristan! I am afraid it will hurt more than it does now and I do not think I can stand that."

Tristan would have given anything he owned at that moment for a bottle of strong whiskey, both for soothing Marianna's nerves and for cleansing the wound. "I'll be as gentle as I can."

The complete trust that entered her gaze as she nodded only added to his anxiety. What if he couldn't help her? Lord, he'd never seen so much blood. Shaking off the quandary before it consumed him, he rolled her over on her side so that the dark gory hole that still seeped away life was facing him. Marianna coiled into a ball, her jaws bravely clenched to keep from crying out. "Here," he offered, upon noticing the way she was biting her lip. He tore a piece of hem from her petticoat and rolled it into a small cylinder. "Put this between your teeth."

Satisfied that he'd done all he could to protect her, he unsheathed his hunting knife and cut away the material of her dress to expose the flesh. As he probed the wound with his fingers, a strangled cry emerged from the girl's throat. She started to shake more violently than ever, recoiling with each touch. He drew back the sharp blade of the knife, nicking her flesh in spite of his attempt to avoid it.

"Marianna, I can't find the bullet with you jerking like that!" he expelled tersely. "You have to lie still."

"I will try, Tristan."

Aware of the deep forced breaths the girl attempted, Tristan started to probe the broken flesh again with the tip of his knife. Judging from the angle of entry, it had to have been a ricocheting shot. Either that or the gunman was on the ground—like Romero had been. An inner rage filled him, and suddenly it didn't matter that he'd shot the man he was supposed to have left alive. If he'd done it sooner, Marianna would not be suffering.

"Bastard!" he muttered under his breath as his blade met with something metallic, not of the flesh. It wasn't deep. A bone of the rib cage had stopped it. "Marianna, I'm going to have a cut a little to get this out."

The weak grunt of acknowledgment made him glance up to see a film of perspiration formed on her furrowed brow. "I am sorry for all the trouble I have caused you," she slurred, her fingers opening and clenching as if trying to grasp the consciousness that was rapidly slipping away. "If I live, I will go home to Paris and never . . . cross your path again."

"You'll be the belle of every ballroom on the Seine," Tristan agreed, encouraging her dream to return home in spite of the troublesome way in which it disagreed with him. "I'm going to have to squeeze this. It may hurt, Frenchie. *Frenchie?*"

Alarmed at the way her body suddenly ceased to react, he leaned over Marianna and grasped her face in his hand, twisting it toward him. Her eyes were closed and the grimace of pain that had contorted her flawless features was gone, replaced by a cold waxy pallor. Quickly Tristan put his fingers to her throat, and the breath that had lodged in his chest gave way to relief. Her pulse was faint and rapid.

He picked up the knife again and wiped it on his pant leg for lack of a better means to clean it. He dared not build a fire. The smoke would give their hiding place away, not to mention, most likely asphyxiate them. The fumes from the old lantern were bad enough. His horse snickered and stepped back nervously as he put the knife to the wound again, this time more firmly. Now he could afford to be quick and precise without hurting her.

When the bullet fell to the hard cold floor of the mine shaft, Tristan grabbed his canteen and poured water over the bleeding wound, flushing it out thoroughly. That done, he shoved his bandanna against it and looked around at the aged rough-hewn timbers draped with cobwebs that bespoke the passage's abandonment. He started gathering them in his hands until he had a ball sufficient to cover the bullet opening. With the ball pressed over the open hole with his handkerchief, he used strips cut from the hem of her skirt to secure it in place.

If it didn't get infected, she'd be fine, he told himself as he looked for evidence that the bleeding had not stopped. The outer strips of the bandage, however, remained clean. After a while, he wrapped the Indian blanket around the unconscious girl tenderly and put the rolled remainder of his shirt under her head. There were other matters that needed his attention. Her recovery wouldn't do a bit of good if Romero's men found them. In fact, she'd be better off dead.

Tristan fetched the Mexican *morral* from the supplies he'd gotten from the farmer and filled it with a ration of grain. After slipping it over the horse's nose, he sat down on his haunches, a large square support timber as a backrest, and reloaded his guns, as well as the rifle he'd taken from the sling. That done, he took one of the ledgers out of the sack that had cost so many lives and thumbed through it.

In the dim light, he made out the list of the cargo. It

was as he'd suspected from the heavily armed guards accompanying the ore on the train. There had been $350,000 in silver and $40,000 in copper bound for European freighters waiting in Matamoros. Why the bloody devil didn't the wagonmaster ask for a military escort?

Unless he was in on it, Tristan mused, turning to the front to get the man's name. Ricardo Nueces. The name didn't mean anything to him, although it could have been an alias. The back page was partially torn out and stained with blood that had spilled over the binder. It appeared that working *for* Victor Romero was just as dangerous as being against him.

Although, hopefully, Romero was dead, he needed to get these to the authorities, the Ranger thought sourly . . . and Marianna was in no shape to go with him. He ran frustrated fingers through the unruly locks of his straight golden hair. She'd lost so much blood, he was afraid to move her.

What he wouldn't give to have his sister Catalina here right now! But Eagle Wing would do, he conceded, his brow furrowing in calculation. Indians were geniuses with gunshot wounds. His Indian cousin could stay with the girl while he rode for help.

Tossing the book back in the bag, Tristan climbed to his feet and made his way to the entrance, now covered with the *huisache* that had pricked his skin as he pulled it into place to hide their whereabouts. He patted the nervous horse on the withers as he passed it, making a soothing comment to perk up the ears laid back on its head. The animal didn't like being cooped up in the mine shaft any more than he did, but he dared not risk taking it out, at least not until it was dark.

His buckskins protecting him from the biting thorns, Tristan slipped by the brush and, keeping to the cover of the rocks, scrambled toward the top of the knoll. If Eagle Wing was not there by nightfall, he was going to the farmer's house to get some food for Marianna, something soft like meal mush . . . maybe some milk to get it down with. The cold biscuits in his saddlebags were hard and likely to choke her, and she was going to need nourishment. There might even be some wine or liquor of some sort. At the time he'd laid in supplies, he hadn't counted on nursing an invalid.

There was a thicket of mesquite crowning the hilltop, sufficient for Tristan to conceal himself. As he looked down toward the small farm nestled along a winding creekbed, his rambling thoughts froze. There were a dozen mounted soldiers, resplendent in red, white, and blue, in front of the meager adobe house speaking to the plump mistress. With four children clinging to her skirts, she was waving her arms and pointing northwest, no doubt explaining her husband's whereabouts, for that was the direction of the Hills of Lakes.

Tristan watched silently, praying that the soldiers would not harass the woman. She was part Comanche, part Mexican, and, he had been quick to discover, had no love for the *alcalde* or his men. They had killed her first husband and taken his land for their own use as a main thoroughfare between two of the largest mines Romero ran. She and her children had been turned out, homeless and penniless. Still, he was grateful he had not let on where he was hiding. A mother whose children were threatened could be convinced to talk, no matter how much she hated her inquisitors.

The beat of horses' hoofs from the south direction drew Tristan's attention to a second group of men riding up from the other side of the knoll. They were not uniformed, but when they approached the small farmhouse, it was clear that they were all looking for the same people—him and Marianna. He hoped the farmer's wife had been convincing—otherwise, it was biscuits soaked in water for his patient.

Making himself comfortable in the crook of a tree limb, he continued to observe the scene below as the two groups conferred, apparently forgetting the woman and her children watching from under the stick ramada in front of the house. Eventually, the men split up again, going in opposite directions. From his vantage point on the top of the knoll, he was able to watch them for a good while before they disappeared in the rolling contours of the land. To the best of his judgment, they had left no watches behind. His lips pursed in a whistle of relief, he abandoned his lookout to check on his patient.

At first, he thought she was still unconscious, but when his boot struck a rock and sent it skittering across the floor, she started visibly and her eyes flew open in alarm.

"It's all right, Frenchie," Tristan assured her, coming into her line of vision in the dim light cast from the lantern. "It's only me."

Marianna closed her eyes in momentary relief before returning her gaze to him. "I thought that I was in hell, but that it is too cold." She shivered involuntarily and winced at the pain it cost. "Can we go home? I wish for Doña Inez and our bed."

Our bed. The phrase mentally tripped Tristan for a second, but he recovered quickly. It had only been a charade, no more. "Me too," Tristan agreed, squatting down beside her to touch her forehead. Still cool. That was a good sign. "But right now, we can't." At the confusion swimming in her eyes, he explained. "We're being hunted like outlaws, Marianna. I think I killed

Romero, and his men are swarming through these hills. I can't even risk a fire to warm you."

The lost look she turned to him stabbed viciously, hurting more than any of the injuries marked by his career as a Ranger. "All I wish is that you hold me then, *Treestan MacCoolach.*" She tried to force a smile, a courageous attempt to make the best of things. It quivered on her lips. "If you can not warm me, I can not be warmed."

It took a few moments for them to settle. Taking care not to jar her wound any more than necessary, Tristan positioned himself between Marianna and the mine-shaft floor, using his saddle as a pillow. Although it was cold and ungiving, he hardly felt the discomfort. Marianna's words had filled him with a strange contented warmth that went beyond his understanding. All he knew was that he would hold her as long as she wanted; he would protect her from the cold as long as he could.

Her breathing was labored from the stress of moving, but once she laid her head against his chest, the girl began to relax again. The strain that had distorted her pale features faded as Tristan stroked the silken lengths of her hair away from her face. Suddenly, she tensed again and lashes fanned open as her gaze found his.

"You were not hurt, were you?"

Tristan chuckled and tightened his arms as much as he dared. "No, Frenchie, I'm hale and hearty—although a little while ago, that seemed to annoy you."

Her tension abated with a heartrending sob. "You do not know how I felt when I thought you were dead!"

"Hush, love," he cajoled, brushing the top of her head gently with his lips and swearing silently at his stupidity for bringing the argument up. With Marianna, words didn't always come out the way he intended.

"I d-dug with my hands with the m-men to find you!"
As if he needed proof, she shoved an unsteady hand in
front of his face. "I—I felt like part of me was buried
under those r-rocks!"

Fop the first time, Tristan noticed the calluses and
blisters barely healed, and again he was overcome with
that odd warmth that made him feel as though he
would burst with it. He took the hand and kissed her
palm until he'd covered every inch of it.

Marianna sobbed again, giving into tears spawned
by pain, past and present. They were wet and warm
against the bare skin revealed by the loose laces of his
buckskin shirt. Tristan cupped her quivering chin and
raised it so that he might take each crystalline drop
away with his lips . . . tenderly, sweetly, until he found
her trembling ones. As if to draw away her pain, to absorb her suffering and replace it with sweet affection,
he sealed them, a strong protective instinct welling inside him. He would do anything for her, *anything*, he
realized.

"I love you, Marianna." The words came out softly
against her cheek as her head rolled away limply. A
blade of icy alarm sliced through his chest. "Marianna?"
he repeated hoarsely, fumbling once again for the pulse
he found beating faint and rapid in her throat.

He was not a devout man. Other than attending a
few weddings, funerals, and holiday services shared with
his family, he'd avoided church. Yet he did not lack
faith. He'd seen too many incidences, too miraculous to
be a coincidence, in his lifetime to question it. So he
prayed, not as Laura Skylar McCulloch had taught him,
on bended knee with lowered head, but clutching Marianna's face to his chest and staring boldly up at the
braced ceiling. Silent vows, as well as pleas, echoed in

his mind, rising from the torture of his soul until his emotion was spent.

Hollow noises that betrayed the presence of rats and other creatures of darkness were the only sounds that broke the stillness of the mine shaft, aside from an occasional movement of the horse near the entrance. Tristan held Marianna, now curled around him comfortably. Eagle Wing should be along soon, he thought, his brain clouding with exhaustion and the residual trauma of the blow on the head Mat had given him, not to mention his bruising and narrow escape from the cave-in his friend had caused. A little shut-eye couldn't hurt, for, whether his Indian cousin came or not, it was going to be a long night.

Miguel Alvarado made himself comfortable in the *alcalde*'s office in the village, leaning back in the leather chair to observe the entrance of the Ranger colonel and the tall blonde Texan who had to duck under the low doorframe. Victor Romero had been expecting them before his untimely demise. It was only natural for the family to want to know what happened to Tristan De Costa. Even more so, it was inevitable that the worrisome Texas Rangers would want an investigation.

"Am I to understand that *you* are in charge here?" Colonel Manolo Benevides charged, taking in the *matador*'s glittering suit of lights with unconcealed incredulity.

Alvarado smiled widely and leaned forward. "No, Colonel Benevides. I am here, but to pass along a message that is both good news and bad, I am afraid. The captain of the guard is out with his men in search of an outlaw." He extended his hand to the lanky Texan. "And you must be Tristan De Costa's father! He is your image, *señor*."

Ross McCulloch's sky-blue eyes narrowed suspiciously. He dared not get his hopes up. "You mean *was*, don't you?" He had to force the words out, for he no more believed Tristan was dead than he believed all was as it should be in Valencia. He and Manolo Benevides had been stopped a few miles outside of town by a band of ruffians claiming to be searching for an outlaw named De Costa. But for Manolo's intervention, they would have taken him under custody, swearing that he was the yellow-haired bandit who had murdered two Mexican officials.

Alvarado glanced uneasily at the leader of the group who escorted them into the village. "I can see why you are confused, *señor*. The men should have told you more."

"I don't know as I like Tristan's being accused of murder any more than I liked the news that he was killed in a cave-in," Ross ground out impatiently. "Now what the hell's going on here?"

"Ross, let me handle this . . . *por favor, amigo,*" Manolo intervened, well aware of Ross's lack of respect for the establishment. "Are you saying that Tristan De Costa is wanted for the murder of Victor Romero?"

The *matador* shrugged. "I am afraid so . . . as well as the murder of one of our border patrol, a Capitán Mateo Salizar. As for his wife, it appears that she was a part of his plot to kill Romero."

"Elena De Costa?" Manolo questioned, confounded by all that he had seen and heard so far. Washington would have his head as well as young McCulloch's. As for the girl . . . "I think it is best if we sat down and you tell us all you know. This could cause serious problems with the relationship of our countries."

"You might start by how Tristan got hitched to this De Costa woman."

332

"Married," the colonel interpreted hastily on Ross's behalf.

The *matador* motioned for them to take the two chairs they had neglected upon coming in and helped himself to the tequila sitting on the edge of the desk in a leather-bound decanter. The two other glasses he filled, then shoved toward his guests.

"I will tell you what I know," he offered at length, sitting his portion untouched on the desk in front of him.

Ross Mcculloch crossed his legs, oblivious to the disdainful look afforded his boots and equally dusty and worn buckskins. He sipped the tequila sparingly. Every sense was alert, finely hewn from a lifetime on the frontier, and he had no intention of dulling them with cactus alcohol. He was here for one purpose—to find his son and take him home. Relying on instincts that had yet to fail him, he'd promised Laura to do just that. But he'd also promised Manolo Benevides that he'd try the proper channels first.

"First, your son's wife is not Elena De Costa. She is Marianna Gallier, the daughter of the previous owner of the *alcalde*'s estate at Mirabeau, a French traitor by the name of Gallier. We suspect that she seduced your son into marriage to gain, not only his silver wealth, but to engage him in a plot to kill Victor Romero and take back the land her parents lost during the revolution. It is known that she forced him to marry her in order that he might get out of jail."

The fair-haired Texan would have protested in Tristan's defense then and there, but for the shock that settled over him as he listened to the incredible tale of how his son had challenged the *alcalde* to a duel over the woman. The *alcalde*, thinking she was his fiancée, Elena De Costa, obliged the young man, only to be disgraced by his unethical conduct.

333

"Where is Elena De Costa, then?" Manolo Benevides interrupted.

The man at the desk shrugged. "Who knows, unless it is this Gallier woman, who, according to Doña Inez, the old nurse, is Elena's cousin." He glanced at Ross. "I can see by your face that this is hard for you to believe, *señor*, but this woman is a beauty and knows how to use it. I, myself, am left breathless by her charms."

"I won't say Tristan will ignore a pretty face and a swinging skirt, but he's not the type to lose his head over a woman."

"But this is no ordinary woman, *señor*. The *alcalde* himself was enamored with her. Even at your son's alleged funeral, she managed to get an invitation to Mirabeau. It was there that your son met her and helped her kill the *alcalde*."

"And Mateo Salizar, how did he die?"

"The Ranger shot him squarely between the eyes, Colonel—for trying to keep the woman from escaping after the *alcalde* had been murdered," he added in barely concealed contempt.

Ross clamped down on his jaw until the muscles twitched from the strain to hold back his denial. Tristan and Mat had been friends. But then, nothing this flashy *matador* was telling them made a lot of sense. Toying with the clear liquor in his glass, he bided his time until the man was finished and Manolo had all the information he needed.

"I do not suppose there is anything for us to do, but to take a room at the inn and wait," Manolo sighed reluctantly when the story was over. "If there is more to this, Tristan will explain."

"If he allows himself to be taken alive," the other man reminded them. "He has struck terror in the men who tried to stop his escape with his well-aimed pistols. But

I will send someone to the inn as soon as we hear anything."

It was with an odd mixture of pride and concern that Ross pondered the *matador*'s compliment to his son. He'd personally taught the boy to ride and shoot. Chances are, Tristan was holed up somewhere, and Ross intended to find him before the officials did. Once in the privacy of the room Manolo secured for them in the small inn, he revealed his intentions to his companion.

"Somehow, I suspected that was on your mind when you came along so obligingly," Mano replied with a fond grin for his longtime friend.

Ross peered out the window and then closed the shutters partially as the armed citizen who had followed them from the office took a seat on a bench across the street and pulled down his hat as if to nap. "And that's as I suspected," he grumbled grudgingly. "We're being watched."

"You do know this is very serious trouble your son is in. He broke the rules. True, Romero is dead, but that does not lead us to the ones who are in this, how do you say, *hornets' nest* with him. There had to be someone over him ... someone privy to the names of the foreign investors interested in Mexican silver."

"That lets out our spangled *matador*," Ross quipped. He checked his guns and tossed an extra belt of ammunition over his shoulder, although undaunted by the guard outside.

Manolo grimaced. "*Ay ay ay,* you never change, do you? Years ago, it was all I could do to keep you from causing upheaval in the army, and now you and that headstrong son of yours are ready to start a war with Mexico."

"Look at the bright side, Mano. Tristan's still alive

335

and he might be able to explain this mess better than our *amigo* across the street." Lips that had almost formed a smile thinned. "At least, he's going to have to do a passel of explaining to me and his mother." Ross leaned against the wall and looked out the window at the setting sun. "It'll be dark soon and I'll be on my way."

"Give me two days," the Ranger colonel spoke up, knowing it was futile to try to stop the man.

He had no doubt that if Tristan could be found, Ross could flush him out. He didn't hesitate to accept the fact that Ross could slip away from the inn unnoticed by the guard. But an international incident had to be avoided. That was *his* responsibility.

"I'll go to the governor and get help," he went on. "The man was aware of this joint effort. Perhaps Tristan was able to find some proof of Romero's involvement in robberies and fraudulent supervision of foreign investments." Sensing Ross's reluctance, he added practically, "Papers from the governor could make it easier to get back across the border, especially if you are taking a young lady with you."

"I am not so certain you could go as far as to call her a *lady,*" he remarked cryptically, reflecting on the truth of his companion's statement. He hated working with his hands tied! He was a man of action, not words. Things hadn't improved in this part of the country since the last time he and Mano had come into the town on a mission for the U.S. government, right after the end of the war.

Then, he had been out to save a Union colonel's son and discovered the wife he'd thought had been killed by savages years before. Now it was his own son he was after . . . and possibly the girl who had written the sympathetic letter informing him and Laura of their son's alleged death.

Ross's train of thought was jarred by a movement in the window of the *alcalde*'s office across the street where a figure peered back at him. The man was heavier set than the *matador*—an older man, the ex-Ranger judged, mainly from the portly silhouette that suggested a long life of wealth and ease. Romero? he wondered, urgently waving Manolo over to take a look.

"I do not trust them!" the man at the window swore, stepping back quickly to keep from being seen by the fair-haired ex-Ranger in the upstairs room across the street. "There is more to this than the girl's quest for revenge and that young man's inheritance."

He walked across the room and jerked his thumb for Miguel Alvarado to get up, before taking the seat Alvarado vacated behind the deceased *alcalde*'s desk. The only sign of nervousness that invaded his air of concentration was the way he repeatedly smoothed a neatly trimmed silver lock of once-black hair behind his ear.

At length he spoke again. "I do not think it a coincidence that the De Costa man was a Texas Ranger and that his companion was a member of the border patrol."

"We are having them watched, *señor*. What more can you ask?" Alvarado inquired, his jacket sticking to him with perspiration in spite of the cooler night air. Dealing with Victor Romero was a pleasant task compared to this. But if he served the cause well, it was not unheard of for someone such as himself to be given his own town. In time, the grim man at the desk would have the power to offer such a reward.

"I want those missing ledgers found and destroyed—as well as the Ranger and the girl! That fool Romero left too many loose ends. He's nearly ruined it for us all with his bold vanity! He has not changed since the last days we rode together." The older gentleman rose from the desk abruptly and irritably brushed the dust from the long journey he'd made off his coat. "And if either one of those men across the street try to leave town, *kill them.*"

"But, *señor,* a Ranger colonel . . ." Silenced by a drilling gaze that dared challenge, Miguel Alvarado broke off and nodded timidly. "Of course, *señor.*"

Chapter Twenty

Tristan held Marianna in his lap like a father would hold a child and coaxed her to nibble on the biscuit he put to her lips. Half delirious, she bit tentatively and rested her head against his chest.

"Wash it down with this, love." He tipped the canteen, groaning silently as part of the water dribbled down her neck. If he didn't get out soon, they would be out of water and food.

He had tried three times already to sneak down to the small farm since the sun had set, but the continuing traffic of the soldiers and their accomplices combing the hills made it impossible. It also, most likely, explained why Eagle Wing had not appeared. No doubt the Indian was crouched behind some crag, waiting, as Tristan was, for the right opportunity.

At least Marianna was a little improved. She was weak and didn't make a whole lot of sense at times, but the bleeding had stopped and she was able to sit up against him. He wished she'd sleep, but she seemed to be fighting it.

A limp hand brushed away the canteen and the girl turned away. "No . . . no more," she murmured under her breath.

Tristan contemplated the half-eaten biscuit and put it down in resignation. "Why don't you lie down and get some rest, Frenchie?"

The head beneath his chin moved from side to side in refusal. "I am not tired." Her words were not supported by her actions. It was all she could do to keep her eyes open while he'd fed her.

Lifting her chin, Tristan looked tolerantly into the drooping blue gaze that was forced wider, as if she were trying to prove herself. "Then just close your eyes and rest a minute."

"I can not." The sapphire surface clouded suddenly and she pulled out of his gentle grasp with surprising strength to sit upright. Her body swayed unsteadily, as if it were about to keel over at any moment, but she stubbornly resisted. "If I . . . if I go to sleep, you might leave me," she accused, her syllables running together like those of a town drunk on Saturday night.

Uncertain as to whether he should be aggravated at her stubbornness or relieved that she was as strong as she was, Tristan screwed the cap back on the canteen. Instead, he felt guilty that, sooner or later, he was going to have to do just that. "I'm not leaving you, Marianna, though I may have to slip out and get us some supplies until you're well enough to travel."

"And if they kill you?" she challenged anxiously, her shoulders already beginning to slump with weakness.

"I think I can get past—" Seeing her teeter precariously, Tristan reached out to catch her as she fell toward him. He felt her arms latch onto his waist, as if that hold were all that kept her from losing consciousness.

"Don't leave me, Tristan," she whispered in a small voice.

"I promise I won't, if you just try to get some rest."

"I can not rest!" Her sobbed reply was smothered against his shirt. She inhaled shakily.

Again Tristan lifted her pale face so that he could see it. "Why, Marianna?"

"Because I will——" Her voice caught and tears spilled gently over her cheeks. "Because I might not wake up."

Gathering her to him, Tristan eased back on the blanket, taking her along with him. "That's nonsense, Frenchie," he chided softly. "I got the bullet. It's a flesh wound only. Now stop being a hysterical ninny and——"

Fingers pressed against his lips, silencing them. "I would have you love me, Tristan McCulloch."

"You know I do."

She shook her head, her eyes taking on a wild glow in the flickering lantern light. She forced them wider yet. "I mean that I wish you to make love to me while . . . while I am still awake."

"Now?"

Marianna responded with a nod to his incredulous exclamation. He thought her mad. She could see it in his eyes, just as she sensed that he was not telling her everything. She had seen the bloodied rags and felt, still felt, the burning pain that ached as if her rib had been torn out through the flesh of her back.

"You're in no shape to be having those kinds of thoughts, young lady," he recovered in a mildly admonishing tone.

"It can not hurt more . . ." She managed a hint of a smile. "And it may take my mind off the pain."

"Marianna . . ."

"And it will make me sleep," she went on, ignoring his objection. Death had separated her from Tristan once, at least she thought it had. It was ironic how it once again reared its ugly head to separate them. But this time, she wouldn't let it . . . not before her Tristan

341

loved her once more. If she had but one breath left, let it leave her in his arms.

She reached forward and caressed the side of his face with her hand. It was rough and prickly with unshaven stubble, like the wild and dry land in which he had been born. Yet there was a certain attraction she felt that went beyond the obvious. That untamed fascination had begun to work its way with her.

"Love me, Tristan McCulloch. Make me forget everything but you."

Tristan studied her for a moment, his reluctance gradually fading under the assault of the frightened and beseeching gaze turned up at him. If she would sleep . . . He wavered . . . If he wouldn't hurt her, if . . .

Carefully, as though she might break, he coaxed her onto her back and tugged at the fastening of her dress, a long row of buttons that dipped below her waist to a vee over her abdomen. One by one, they came undone, exposing the creamy white flesh of her neck and chest and the pink-posied cotton camisole beneath.

Ignoring the darkening scarlet stains that nearly wrapped around her waist, he ran his hands up the gauntlet of buttons he had just opened and skimmed warm fingers over her breasts, locating their most sensitive spots and drawing them into hardened peaks. Marianna shivered and closed her eyes, but, upon realizing what she'd done, forced them open again.

"You're going to get well, you know," he whispered, lowering his mouth to cover hers. His kiss refused to let her deny him, as fervent in its effort to convince her as his hands were to riddle her mind with pleasurable sensations, enough to force the pain out, if only for a little while. The camisole slid down easily, permitting him a complete domination that promised more fevered delight.

He could feel her breath now, coming stronger with an urgency as he moved from her lips to cover her face with little reassuring kisses. "You come through this for me, Frenchie, and I'll personally carry you piggyback off the boat to France."

The picture his suggestion presented elicited a faint giggle that was cut off sharply as he dipped his hand into the low vee of the dress and found the soft haven of her femininity. But she smiled and he knew he had not hurt her.

Tristan didn't think he'd ever seen a more beautiful one. Her lips parted and the pink tip of her tongue could be seen moistening them as masterful fingers began to tease and stroke through the thin silken material of her drawers. She moved her hips tentatively against them, but winced upon the painful reminder of her wound.

"Relax, love. Let me do the work."

"Is that what this is?" she rallied, turning a reproachful gaze to him before giving herself up to his erotic ministrations.

"Allow me the *pleasure*, madame," he corrected wryly before seizing the tip of her breast with his teeth and flaying it with his tongue. With dancing fingers, he felt her moist response increasing and intensified the loveplay until she was literally quivering at his touch.

"Tristan!"

Her breathless gasp told him that she was suffering, but the way she pulled his hand against her revealed it was of a more pleasant and different nature than before. Her eyes were closed and her lips parted just enough to breathe his name once more in a plea to hold her.

Abandoning his sweet torment, Tristan followed the lead of the arms that reached for him and allowed her to pull him to her. Taking care to keep her from bearing his weight, he gently kissed the top of her head. "Sweet, sweet Marianna," he murmured lowly. Although it was not what he'd intended, his own arousal ached with the deprivation of release, but he ignored the primeval stirrings and concentrated on Marianna's needs.

"I had no idea how wonderful such things could be," she sighed in contentment, the slender arms encircling him falling away as if being drawn into slumber.

Tristan was almost afraid to move, afraid that he might disturb her if she had finally succumbed to sleep, and fearful that she'd once again lost consciousness. But she was breathing normally now and he could hear her heartbeat slowing down.

Inching a cautious hand around her waist, he probed the bandages he'd applied to the wound. A self-recriminating curse resonated in his mind as the damp sticky feel of blood registered. He'd let her talk him into hurting her! Abandoning his earlier precaution, he pulled away abruptly to examine the damage.

Instantly, dark eyelashes batted up at him. "You're still in your trousers," she mumbled in groggy reproach. Her brow furrowed in renewed concern as he rolled her on her good side, instead of remedying her observation. "What is it?"

Tristan wanted to shout at her that she was bleeding again because of her empty-headed idea, but held back. He was angry at himself, not her. It was just that he was so afraid for her, afraid with a fear that was as intense as it was foreign to him.

"Just checking your bandages to see."

His voice trailed off as he spotted the discarded remnant of one of the strips of her skirt that he'd used to soak up the blood earlier when cleaning the wound and threw off his premature guilt, slinging it into the darkness. Weak with relief, he sank back on his knees.

"Tristan?"

It was back again, that heart-twisting fright, knitting her brow and widening her eyes. He conjured a teasing grin. "Your bandage looks fine." He raised a warning finger at her. "Now don't get used to that without me."

For a moment, her ashen face was blank, but as his meaning took hold, a pastel shade of pink crept to her cheeks. "But how . . . you didn't . . ." Her gaze dropped below his belt and darted back to his face, disconcerted. "Are *you* all right?"

This time his grin was real. He couldn't believe she was worried about him. But then, there were a lot of things about Marianna he found hard to comprehend. She'd been one surprise after another since the first time he'd laid eyes on her. "I'm fine, Frenchie." He kissed his finger and planted it on the tip of her nose . . . one of the cutest upturned noses he'd ever seen.

"Then, hold me again?"

The way her voice trailed upward, making a question out of a statement was as difficult to ignore. She definitely had a way of making it hard for a man to keep his mind on his work. "Tell you what," he said, refastening her dress primly instead of taking her up on her invitation. "You wait here while I take another look outside, and I'll hold you when I get back."

"You won't leave?"

Tugging up the blanket, Tristan brushed her forehead gently and tucked it around her arms. "I'll be right back," he promised. Good, her eyelids were starting to droop with fatigue. Now maybe she'd sleep.

"Are you going to get Granmaman?"

His premature satisfaction plummeted, destroying what brief lift of spirit he had felt. She was talking crazy again. "If she's at home." It wasn't fever. Her skin was like ice. Blood loss, he guessed, recalling a fellow Ranger who had gone out of his head before he bled to death from a gut shot. Grim-faced, Tristan turned and made his way to the mouth of the shaft, channeling his thoughts toward dealing with the search parties outside.

This time when he crawled to the hilltop, he saw no evidence of them. The moonlight bathed the valley in a peaceful glow that hinted of no danger. Clearly etched out, dark against the lighter plowed fields and dirt yard, was the small farmhouse with the stable under the extended roofline in the back. The fowl that had pecked fastidiously in the dirt yard was now closed up for the night in a roughly constructed stick henhouse nearby.

Tristan scanned the surrounding area for any sign of movement, to no avail. It appeared the search had been abandoned, at least for the remainder of the night. Shaking the image of the pale girl he'd left behind following him out with eyes that could evoke all manner of emotion within him, Tristan started down the hill toward the house for the food and bandages he hoped to get. Much as he wanted to stay with Marianna and calm her fears, he couldn't. They needed food and water . . . and perhaps the Indian woman had heard from her husband and could explain the delay in their arrival, for he and Eagle Wing should have been back by now.

The dog that had found him the day he staggered out of the mind shaft, stunned and dizzy, barked once at him and ran out from under the ramada to greet him. Tristan roughed its head and walked up to the blanket stretched over the door, calling for the mistress of the house. A few seconds later, the woman stuck her head out and eyed him suspiciously.

"So it is you, gringo," she said, catching a glimpse of Tristan's pale blonde hair in the dark shadows. "They look everywhere for you and the girl." She looked beyond him curiously. "Where is she?"

346

"She's hurt. I need bandages, liquor of any kind, and some food—mush, if you have it."

The squaw nodded solemnly and stepped back from the door, holding the blanket aside for him to enter. "Come."

In the rear of the single-room dwelling, one much like that in which he had first met Marianna, except that it was in better repair, four children slept. They were arranged from oldest to youngest, graduating down in size as they neared the wall. The smallest was sprawled sideways, his head on his sister's abdomen, which explained why the wall had been chosen for him. There was no sense in making two children miserable.

As the woman gathered the things Tristan asked for, she told him that she too was worried about her husband. The soldiers and vigilantes were not above making sport with a poor dirt farmer. Life meant nothing to them. Her black eyes glittered with hatred in the dim candlelight and Tristan was certain that she would have helped him even if he didn't give her the few coins he placed in her palm.

"You want me come see your woman?" she asked as he ducked under the low stoop to go outside.

"*Gracias*, but no. If you don't—" A movement near the chicken coop made him step back, shoving his companion into the shelter behind him. He hadn't heard any horses, he reasoned, leaning around to peer through the crack in the curtain. Perhaps he'd made a mistake. Maybe his eyes were playing tricks . . .

His hand flew to his gun instinctively as the dog who had settled down at the foot of the children's mat suddenly bolted out under the curtain, barking excitedly. It ran straight for the chicken coop and circled around it, dashing in and then retreating.

Tristan pointed outside. "Ask who it is," he whispered.

"Quién es?"

It was then that Tristan noticed the dog was not acting the least bit ferocious. Its tail was wagging, even though it charged and fell back excitedly. A figure rose from behind the coop, a man clad in a serape and hat.

"It is Pepito!" the woman cried, shoving past the young man before he could stop her to run out to greet her husband.

Gun drawn, Tristan waited, in case she'd made a mistake, but when they hugged each other in affection, he lowered his guard and stepped outside. Suddenly a hatchetlike pain struck his wrist, knocking the gun to the dirt at his feet, and a powerful band of muscle hooked around his neck, drawing him back over a wiry chest. Expecting to feel the stabbing blade of a knife slipping into his back at any moment, Tristan grabbed the arm and threw himself forward, taking his assailant with him.

As he struck the ground, his opponent landing beyond him, he rolled away and came to his feet in a crouched position, his other gun drawn and cocked. The guttural roll of Comanche issued from the man waving a knife in front of him was the sweetest voice Tristan had heard in some time. He lowered his gun and holstered it in relief as the half-naked savage followed his lead and sheathed the deadly blade.

Tristan's teeth flashed white in greeting. "Eagle Wing!"

The first rays of dawn had yet to peek over the eastern horizon when Tristan led his horse out of the mine shaft. The ground was damp with the night mist, and a slight chill made him grateful for the loose brown *jerga* suit and serape he'd borrowed from the farmer. The peasant's clothing and the flat-brimmed Córdova hat would hopefully disguise him from curious eyes. Within a few hours, however, the cooler air would be gone, banished by the warming rays of the sun, and he could well imagine sweltering under the woolen cloak. Maybe before it got too bad, he'd be far enough away to abandon the serape, at least.

He took the incriminating books from Eagle Wing and tucked them in his saddlebags before mounting, his face a mirror of consternation. He was worried about Marianna. She'd been sound asleep when he and his Indian cousin returned and had not stirred since. He waited as long as he could before trying to awaken her to introduce her to Eagle Wing and, even then, he wasn't certain that she registered what he was saying. She kept talking about her grandmother in France and how the woman would not approve of her lessons with someone named Andre.

He'd even thought about remaining with Marianna and sending Eagle Wing to the governor, but doubted that the authorities would let an Indian in to see him. This was the only way, he told himself again sternly. He had a job to do. The governor could then order Alvarado and his men arrested and it would be possible to get Marianna to safety and competent medical care.

He responded with a wave to Eagle Wing's stoic lift of his hand and tugged the horse around toward the south. Marianna was going to be all right. She was in good hands, evidenced by the way his Indian companion had cleaned and rebandaged the wound, refusing to pour the tequila over it, but covering it with a poultice of herbs and dark powder that smelled as bad as it looked. Tristan hadn't objected, though. He'd seen the same work wonders on gunshot wounds among the Honey-eaters.

The stretch of hills rolling below him decreased as he made his way south. Instead of taking the narrow roads carved into the dry grass by cart wheels and plodding livestock, Tristan kept to the higher plains, where he might see fellow travelers before they saw him, and made a wide circle around the town of Valencia. The sound of the church bell awakening the village to another day echoed behind him as he left it in his wake.

By noon, he had seen three groups of soldiers riding through the countryside and assumed the hunt had been renewed. One group in particular seemed to run parallel with him for a while, as if anticipating that he would try to head south to the governor. Although the sun beat down on him, he kept the serape on, hoping that if he was spotted, the soldiers would not question a peasant riding such a fine horse. He'd even thought of taking a burro and cart from the farmer, but needed to make good time and took the risk.

With a hill between him and the well-traveled route toward Chihuahua where the unwary soldiers split away from him, Tristan had no more than registered satisfaction at his progress when he noticed his horse beginning to limp. Dismounting, he led the animal under a wide-spreading mesquite and checked its feet to discover the hard flesh surrounded by hoof bleeding. With his knife, he cleaned away the debris to get a closer look and swore under his breath—devil's thorn.

Although he knew it was futile, he tried to pick out the vignaga spine with the tip of his knife. Like a fish hook, it usually only went in one way. The animal commenced to pull away from him as he probed easily, and reared in panic. Tristan grabbed the reins and tried to soothe it, stroking its neck and speaking softly. On the

350

ranch, he might be able to draw it out with a poultice, but there was no time here. The bay was lame. Yet, he dared not risk firing a shot to put it out of its misery. He supposed he'd have to cut it loose and hope someone better prepared might help it along.

Jaw clenched, he worked at the straps on the saddle and pulled it off, leaving a dark wet square where it had been. Sympathetically, Tristan smoothed the course roughened hair down and pondered his plight before giving the bay a smack on the hindquarters and sending it trotting off toward the town. There wasn't anything to do now, but wait by the road and try to get a horse—one way or the other.

Resigned to his fate, he picked up the saddle and trudged off in the same direction as his horse. The land dropped toward the road in gentle layers, each landscaped with scattered maguey and occasional crags of rock. Aware that he presented a curious sight, Tristan moved as quickly as he could from one thicket of cover to another and made his way to a cluster of gray-blue rock, protruding like large broken teeth from the earthy sand and shrub. Settling in to wait for his victim, hopefully a lone rider who would take his word that he'd return the horse later, he checked his guns and pulled his hat low over his eyes to protect them from the sun.

It was gunshots that brought him upright to stare at a cloud of dust down the road that seemed to be moving in his direction at a fast speed. Emerging in the front was a single rider, bent low over the saddle. Tristan crawled out to the ledge of the rock to get a better view. There were a group of riders following a distance behind, shooting wildly. As they drew closer, he recognized the red, white, and blue colors flashing through the earthy cloud and his blood chilled. Soldiers!

Without much deduction, Tristan knew instantly that

351

the lone rider, if he made it this far, would take cover in the same rocks that hid him. Wondering what more could go wrong, he hurriedly untied his saddlebag and hid it in a small hollow, which he quickly covered with brush and stone. He would know sooner or later whether they were Romero's men or those of the governor, and he wasn't taking any chances.

Eight, he counted, recognizing the number of the group that had been heeling him most of the morning, since he'd left Valencia behind. *Romero's men.* Tristan pulled back the hammer and waited for them to get close enough to fire. Perhaps he'd not only help some poor soul who had crossed them, but get himself a horse in the process.

Exactly as Tristan thought, the lone rider pulled up the galloping horse so abruptly that the animal reared in protest. In an instant, the man was on his feet and pulling the spooked horse behind the cover of the rocks. His fringed buckskin jacket looking oddly familiar, the man scrambled up into the pile of rock and threw himself forward, guns drawn.

Disbelief rang in Tristan's astonished, "Colonel!"

The man swung around abruptly, poised to fire when Tristan tugged off his hat, producing a head of rakish blonde hair to identify himself.

"Madre de Dios, what . . ."

A bullet struck the rock near Manolo Benevides's head and the startled man dropped back.

"I'll take the ones on the right!" Tristan shouted, aiming at the dual columns approaching at a full gallop.

"Bueno!"

The pistol in the young Ranger's hand went off. The smell of gunpowder had no more reached his nostrils when the lead man in the column pitched off his horse to fall into the path of the others. Immediately the column split to circle the rocks. "Hell's bells, that's not army!" he swore, climbing to the cover behind him to shoot again.

"Do not let those uniforms fool you, *amigo*. These are not regular *soldados!*"

Tristan ducked as a piece of rock fell on his shoulder, cut free by a gunshot. Rising quickly, he spied a big man, his face and neck covered with an unkept black beard, and fired, before dropping back into cover without seeing if he'd hit his mark or not. Bullets pingponged dangerously among the rocks, spurring him to become more daring. Rolling to his feet, he drew his second revolver and began to shoot at the moving targets, shouting and firing wildly around him. Another man fell, and a third's horse reared and bolted as a bullet grazed its neck, dragging its screaming rider away.

Suddenly a searing pain bit into Tristan's shoulder, spinning him around. Losing his balance, he fell into the rocky crevice for cover and slapped his hand over the stinging wound. The serape was torn where a bullet had cut through it, nicking his skin beneath. With no time to feel relief, he wiped the blood on his pants and retrieved the pistol he'd dropped when, out of the corner of his eye, he spied a man's head rising above the rock behind Manolo Benevides. Swinging his gun around, he fired and the assailant jerked and rolled down the embankment.

He grinned as the colonel spun about, but froze as the deadly Colt in his superior's right hand exploded. Before Tristan could react, he was knocked into the crevice again, this time by a body that fell limply on top of him. Shaking his head to clear it of the stars that burst and spun dizzily from the nasty crack of the rock that harshly cushioned his fall, he shoved the man aside and came up once again to fire.

353

One here, he counted, inventorying the assailants. Two below. "How many you got, Colonel?"

"Three!" Manolo Benevides shouted in what was now an eerie silence.

And there was the one that was dragged away. "We got one more somewhere around here." Tristan cocked his head sideways, listening for any telltale sign—a sliding rock, a snap of shrub. Leaning on the rock to his back, he reloaded his guns as Benevides cautiously stepped out to assess the damage.

Tristan saw the man leveling a rifle on a crag overhead before its barrel, glinting in the sunlight, betrayed him to the colonel. "Watch it!" He fired both guns simultaneously as the rifle went off. The uniformed man jerked twice as he stepped backward, his weapon falling to the other side of the rock, and then fell in its cover.

"You all right?" Turning back to the colonel, Tristan saw him staggering to his feet, his right hand clasped around his left arm.

"I am hit in the arm."

Tristan scrambled down the rocky incline, sending a shower of small debris before him before reaching the bottom. "Bad?"

Benevides shook his head. "Better check them over."

There were two wounded, Tristan discovered. The rest had gone to see their Maker—at least, he assumed the man who had been dragged off had not survived. At any rate, there was no time to chase him down.

The colonel had tied a bandanna around his arm while he listened to the younger Ranger's assessment of the situation. "Then we will take these two to the next rancho and ride on to the governor's."

Tristan frowned. "I'd hate to be caught with two wounded *soldados.*"

"I am very grateful that it was you up in those rocks

nd not some cutthroat," the colonel spoke up, chang-
ng the subject abruptly, "but I am anxious to hear why
ou were there. Even more so, I am eager to know why
ou are being hunted as an outlaw."

"I guess I killed Romero."

For a moment, Manolo Benevides waited expectantly
or further explanation. "You mean to say you risked a
ar with Mexico because you did not follow proce-
ure?" he demanded irritably. Heaven help him, the
oy was just like his father, no regard for authority and
rocedure!

One corner of Tristan's mouth turned up wryly. "I
oticed you didn't exactly identify yourself as a Texas
anger to those yahoos who were on your tail before
aking a shot at them. What if they had been real
oldados?"

"But there was no choice here . . ."

"Exactly," Tristan agreed, making his point most ef-
ectively. "What do you say we get moving?"

Chapter Twenty-one

Tristan. His handsome face with its ruggedly chiseled features haunted the images that drifted through Marianna's mind. Teasing blue eyes danced at her across a tiered candelabra of sterling and she felt her cheeks grow as hot as the flickering candles. Around them people conversed in French and laughter filled the air. Elena was there ... and her new husband. Presiding over the table was her grandmother, a queenly woman with silver hair crowned with a tiara glittering with gems.

But it was Tristan to whom Marianna returned her attention. Aside from that mischievous grin on his lips, he looked so ... so cultured—quite at home in the elegant setting. Catching her in her observation, he raised his glass to her and winked. Where on earth did he get that black evening suit, tailored to accent his broad shoulders and trim vested waist? Why, only a moment ago, he'd had on dusty hides with fringe, ragged from wear, and they were sequestered in a dark hole in the earth, not dining in the great hall of her grandmother's manor on the Seine.

He rose from his chair and walked around the table to help her up from her own. In disbelief, Marianna reached out and touched the black satin lapels of his cutaway jacket. "But where did you get this?" she whispered.

It was somber, no longer playful as it had been across the table from her. Alarm worked its way up her spine as she studied the changing face over her own. The eyes .. they were dark, dark as ebony, and fathomless. "Tristan?" she asked uncertainly.

He shook his head. Two long black braids secured by scarlet strips of cloth fell forward over naked shoulders ridged with muscle. The moment he spoke, Marianna's blood froze. It wasn't the easy drawl of the man in her dreams, but an abrasive run of syllables—something about a bird. Disconcerted, she glanced down to see that instead of a satin lapel, she held some sort of necklace in her fingers, leather adorned with beads and—she swallowed dryly—animal's teeth.

The arm beneath her tightened as she slowly pushed away, recoiling from the fierce vision. No, *this* was a dream. Tristan had been real. She had but to close her eyes, and when she opened them again, it would be the handsome young Ranger who held her, not this heathen savage. Struggling to fight the fog that closed in, threatening her consciousness, Marianna squeezed her eyes shut and then opened them warily.

"Eagle Wing."

Marianna shook her head. *"Non . . ."*

"Girl safe with Eagle Wing."

It couldn't be! she thought wildly, retreating mentally from the image. It was a dream, a nightmare! She would just close her eyes again, and when she awakened, Tristan would be there. Tristan, who could make her heart sing and her body dance to his pagan touch. Tristan, of sunlight and laughter, not this god of darkness. Tristan . . .

357

When Marianna awakened again, the figure was gone. She blinked in the dim light of the mine shaft, spying a hint of daylight streaking in in the distance. A glance around her told her that she was alone, aside from a spotted horse that stomped near the entrance. Had Tristan gotten another mount? she wondered. Carefully, she rolled over on her side and raised up on one elbow to look around. Where was he?

Her head seemed to float precariously atop her shoulders, as if it were hardly attached. Slowly she crawled to her knees. Perhaps he was just outside. Holding onto a support post, she pulled herself upright, grimacing at the pain that surged from the wound in her back. Perspiration broke out on her forehead from the exertion and her breath became shallow and rapid.

She ventured a step toward the entrance and her foot struck something. Glancing down, Marianna spied the satchel Liam had procured for her, when . . . weeks ago? A month? Time was a blur. She felt around the bag with her toes curiously. Something wasn't right. It had been thick and so heavy. Now it gave, as if stuffed with a pillow, not hard books. She struggled to employ her reasoning processes.

The answer came suddenly, striking her cold in the chest. The books! The books were gone! "Tristan!" Her voice echoed eerily in the emptiness behind her. He's here, she told herself unconvincingly. He promised he wouldn't leave her. He promised! Walking on legs that felt like rubber, she stumbled toward the pinto, causing it to dance sideways as she leaned on its hindquarters for support. It had a long shaggy coat, not like the short silken hairs of Tristan's bay. Maybe he'd gotten it for her. Yes! They were going home and the horse was hers!

She moved forward to pet the velvet nose of the animal when the light filtering in through the entrance was

ut off. Turning, Marianna had Tristan's name on the
p of her tongue, but it never emerged. Instead a
cream, generating from deep within her chest, filled the
arrow passage, reverberating in her ears. She took a
tep backward as the tall dark savage sprinted toward
er, but one step was all her weakened legs would per-
nit. Swaying dizzily, she pushed away from the arms
hat reached for her and suddenly she was falling, falling
nto a smoky blackness that was marked with stabbing
ain. From out of nowhere, steel bands caught her up in
he air and carried her effortlessly away.

Inanely, her first coherent thought was that the hea-
hen smelled of herbs, a woodsy scent mingled with that
f smoke. His dark vest was of soft hide, like the clothes
Tristan wore, and open to reveal a broad expanse of
hest, devoid of any body hair. Thongs and beads hung
round his neck in pagan adornment. As he leaned over
o put her down, Marianna had the sensation of falling
nce again and inadvertently clutched his banded fore-
rms. Afraid to look, yet more afraid not to, she forced
er gaze to his face as he effortlessly redeposited her on
he blankets that had been her bed. To her surprise, he
humped his chest. "Tristan . . . friend."

"Where's Tristan?" she managed in a squeak of a
oice. She had never seen an Indian and this one was
igger than life.

The Indian pointed to the entrance. "Gone long
vay."

Marianna felt her eyes fill with the dismay that welled
n her chest. He'd promised. Not only had he broken
hat promise, but left her with a savage who—she
linked her eyes to make certain—was wearing small
arrings made of shells and circles of silver. Unable to
ontain the raw emotion tearing at her, Marianna rolled
way, facing the wall to escape the impassive scrutiny of

her companion. How could Tristan have done this t
her? He ...

Her silent wailing was halted by the firm tugging o
the bandages encircling her waist. Startled, she rolled t
her back once again and stared with frightened eyes a
the Indian.

"Still, woman." His scowl encouraged her to mov
back to her side quicker than the hands that coaxed he
that way. Her heart beat so rapidly in her chest that sh
found it difficult to breathe as the man untied the ban
dages and began to press around the tender woun
firmly.

"*Non* ..." Marianna's voice caught as she met hi
warning glare and she stopped trying to pull away. Clos
ing her eyes, she withstood his ministrations in silence—
the warm fingers that examined her flesh familiarly, th
oddly cool poultice he used to replace that which ha
smelled so foul.

When he was finished, he reached into a pouch mad
of animal skin and withdrew what appeared to be som
sort of dark bread. Producing a large hunting knife, h
cut a piece off and handed it to her. "Eat."

Hand shaking, Marianna took the slice and studied i
suspiciously. It appeared to have nuts in it and chunks o
dried fruit perhaps. She sniffed it. Sweet, she mused i
astonishment. Tentatively, she took a small bite an
chewed it. It was amazingly good. She finished the Indi
an's treat and chased it with a drink of water from th
canteen he handed her—Tristan's canteen.

God, what if he'd killed Tristan? Her eyes shifted to where
the man hung a pouch over the nose of his horse, muc
like the one Tristan used to feed his. And the knife, tha
too looked like Tristan's. What if he was taking her bacl
to his tribe to be his woman? That was what Indians di
to women, wasn't it? She shuddered, refusing to let th

other horrid tales she'd heard into consideration. After all, if he meant her harm, he wouldn't feed her and seem so concerned over her injury.

Marianna forced the mouthful of pemmican down past the blade that wedged in her throat. She had to eat, to regain her strength. Wasn't that what Tristan had told her? A second bite, however, refused to be as cooperative, choking her. Sitting up abruptly, Marianna grasped her back, trying to put pressure there to assuage the injury in order to cough. Desperately, she tried to blow out the morsel, but the passage was blocked, letting air neither in nor out.

Through blurred vision, she saw the Indian loping toward her, as silent as a cat in his moccasins, but paid no heed. Starved for oxygen, she leaned over and beat on her chest, hoping to jar the food loose. Suddenly, she was grabbed from behind, her head drawn back to the point that she thought her neck would snap. Unable to fight the man, she watched in terror as he shoved the shaft of a half-made arrow, the head not yet attached, down her throat and forced the food past her windpipe. Just as quickly he withdrew it and, dropping to his knees, caught her in his arms and held her as she began to cough violently.

Her cheeks were streaked with tears when she finally was able to draw in a deep breath. Weak from the exertion, she continued to lay against the man, who lifted a canteen to her lips to encourage her to drink. The water was soothing to her raw throat and she let it lay in the back before swallowing it. A deep voice rumbled from within the chest supporting her and she raised her tearful gaze to the man who had just saved her life. His words meant nothing, but his voice was gentle and assuring.

Lost, she responded with a timid "Thank you."

Slowly, so as not to frighten her, he pointed to each of her eyes and toward the mine entrance where light filtered in. He then did the same to his own eyes and pointed to the back of the tunnel. Her expression was blank for a moment, for once again, she didn't understand his language. After he repeated the gestures a few more times, however, she began to understand. At least, she thought she did. He was referring to the contrasting color of their eyes.

"Tristan," he told her, touching her cheek just below her eyes again. "Yellow Wolf."

"Yes, Tristan and I have the same color of eyes," she replied, wondering if he understood her any better than she did him. The *Yellow Wolf* made no more sense than his presence there or anything else he had said to her.

He picked up the bread she had dropped and handed it to her. "Eat."

"*Non,* I . . ."

Slipping his hands under her arms, he sat her up against a thick post and shoved the satchel behind her to make her more comfortable. Again, he handed her the bread. "Eat."

This time Marianna took the food. Her throat was sore, but she nibbled at it a little at a time until it was gone. Leaving the canteen at her side, the Indian rose to return to whatever it was he had been doing with his horse before she began to choke. *Friend,* he had said. Perhaps he really was, she mused tiredly, tugging the blanket he'd laid across her lap up around her shoulders as she wriggled down into a reclining position.

As she beat a comfortable indentation into the makeshift pillow her satchel provided, she noticed something caught in the closure. Upon closer examination, icy reality swept over her. It was Tristan's hide clothing. Slowly, she pulled out the trousers that had clung so fetchingly to sturdy thighs, as if trying to disprove the suspicion forming in her mind. The sight of bloodstains confirmed it. Tristan hadn't left her. He'd stayed with her as promised and this savage had killed him, perhaps tossed his body in the darkness beyond.

Hastily, Marianna closed the bag and tucked it under her head as a shadow cut off the daylight, warning her of the Indian's approach. Numb with her discovery, she lay there, mind racing blindly through the fog of her exhaustion. If only she could think clearly, figure out a way to escape. *Heaven help her,* she prayed, closing her eyes and giving in for the moment to the undeniable demand for sleep.

She didn't know where the Indian had been, but her next meal consisted of hot corncakes spread with honey. Astonished at her appetite, for she hadn't realized that she was hungry, she actually finished two under the dark-eyed scrutiny of her keeper. Afterward, she lay back and closed her eyes, as if succumbing again to exhaustion. She would wait for him to leave and then try to make good an escape.

An eternity seemed to pass before she heard a light stirring to indicate the man was leaving her. Peering after his retreating figure through half-lidded eyes, she saw him busy himself with the grooming of his pony. The animal stood patiently, soothed by the Indian's low guttural tones. Once, Marianna actually saw the savage smile. His stony features seemed to melt with warmth directed at the small sturdy steed that affectionately nibbled a leftover corncake from his palm.

Perhaps that was her answer! she thought, an idea coming to mind for the perfect solution. He was so confident the pony would not wander that he hadn't bothered to tether it. If it bolted, he surely would go after it. She slipped a searching hand into the satchel he'd stuffed behind her as a pillow, delving deeply to the bottom until her fingers came in contact with the small tin box Liam Shay had given her. *A little drop o' that on a horse's nose'll set it crazy.*

Bless the man, wherever he was, Marianna thought, slipping the box into the pocket of her dress. Of course, it would be nice to have the horse to escape on, but it had no saddle and, small as it was, she didn't think she was strong enough to mount it without assistance, let alone stay on it. If she could make it to the first inhabited cottage, perhaps someone there would take her to Casa Valencia or the convent, whichever was closer. Doña Inez or the sisters would hide her until she could decide what to do, now that she was on her own.

Marianna swallowed the despair that threatened to overtake her and pulled herself upright, using the thick brace for support. Her legs were more wobbly than she'd thought, but once the room stopped moving and she reinforced them with resolve, she stepped toward the Indian. Her foot caught the saddlebag, sending it skittering across the hard floor and drawing the attention of her companion.

In less than two loping strides, he was at her side, his dark eyes questioning her. Afraid that he might force her back to her makeshift bed, she pointed toward the opening of the tunnel and inhaled deeply. "Air!"

The savage nodded curtly in acknowledgment and cupped her elbow with a strong hand. Relieved, Marianna leaned on his arm, astonished that she was so weak. Thinking the horse would need to bolt a long way away from them to give her time to find refuge, she popped the lid off the small box and dipped her finger deeply into the salve. If a little dab would set it crazy, maybe a big dab would send it all the way to the mountains.

To her dismay, however, the Indian placed himself between her and the pony as he walked her past it to the opening of the tunnel. She leaned against a timber near the opening and basked in the light of the sun filtering in through the thorny brush. Warm, she thought, momentarily indulging herself. Except for when Tristan had held her, she'd wondered if she'd ever be warm again. The tunnel seemed to breed a bone-chilling cold, especially without a fire to take out the dampness.

And the air. She inhaled, savoring the fresh air free of that musty smell that was tainted with the fumes from the burning lantern. Already her head seemed to be clearing from the dismal fog that had claimed her. Curious to know if she'd recognized their whereabouts, she tried to move some of the *huisache* carefully aside, but the same hand that had supported her, clenched around her wrist.

"No! Woman stay!"

Marianna shivered involuntarily under the dark scrutiny directed at her. The man was so ominous looking that it was hard to tell if he was angry or not.

"Enough." He pointed back to the bed, leaving no doubt as to his wishes.

Lips quivering in acquiescence, Marianna accepted his extended arm and started toward the inside of the tunnel. "Wait," she spoke up, upon coming abreast of the spotted pony. Her smile solidified as she reached toward the animal and gently stroked its silky thick coat. The Indian's eyes narrowed warily, making him appear more ferocious than ever. The fingers of her free hand dipped once again in the open tin. The further she sent the animal, the better.

"Nice boy," Marianna cooed, leaning over to nuzzle its coarser mane as she slipped her other hand from her pocket to reach for its nose. *A little drop o' that on a horse's nose ...*

The Indian pony recoiled from Marianna so quickly that she could not help the startled shriek that escaped her. Its own shrill protest blending with hers, the animal reared, striking its head with a loud thud against the brace overhead. Jerked out of the range of the pawing hoofs by her companion, Marianna clung to the rock wall as the Indian rushed forward to try to calm the excited steed.

Before he could lay a hand on the rope halter, however, the pony bolted forward, knocking him aside. It seemed as though he'd barely touched the ground when he was on his feet again, yelling something over his shoulder to her in a heathen tongue as he took up the chase. Fingers locked in the material of her skirt, working to wipe away the offending salve, Marianna drew away from the wall and started toward the opening, now cleared by the runaway horse. With luck, she would have hours, she thought, still in wonder that the salve had worked so well.

From the position of the sun, she judged that it was approaching noon. Squinting in all directions, she tried to ascertain her whereabouts. She and Tristan had ridden from the direction of the small creek shimmering at the base of the hill on which she stood. She recalled the splashing sound his horse had made before starting the climb that had nearly cost her her hold, although she didn't remember the small homestead further along it.

Not wishing to increase her risk of being caught, Marianna decided to take the opposite direction from Mirabeau. Perhaps there would be enough scattered thickets of brush and trees to afford her sufficient cover from the men who Tristan had said were looking for them. *If* they were still looking, she mused, wondering how many hours or days she'd slept.

It was Alexander Caine who first spied the bedraggled figure trying to climb out of a ragged trench cut by the overflow of an arroyo. His gun drawn and lean frame tense, lest it be a ruse to stop the fine coach carrying his wife and mother-in-law, he urged his roan over to the vehicle. "There's someone trying to get out of a ravine up the road to the right," he warned the coachman and passengers. "If you hear gunfire, do not stop for anything."

"Where?"

A blonde head popped through the coach window, blue eyes raking the landscape without regard to his warning.

Alex shoved his wife back inside the protection with an exasperated "Catalina, so help me, you promised!"

"But it they need help . . ."

"I'll bring them to you! Now stay with your mother!"

Alex took his frustration out on the stallion, digging his polished heels into its ribs. If anything happened to Catalina or her mother, he would never forgive himself—nor would Ross McCulloch forgive him. Handling Cat was difficult enough, but with her mother also pleading with him to take them to this Casa Valencia, he was at a loss as to how to dissuade them. So he followed his adopted mother's advice that he might as well give them their way, because they were going with or without his consent, and accompanied them. The only peace of mind he was left with was that the children were still at Silverado.

Neither one of the women was in her right mind. They had both been devastated by the news of Tristan

McCulloch's death, as had Alex. He knew that the young man, who had been like a brother to him, lived a dangerous life. He wasn't like Alex, who had been forced to arm himself and fight for what he believed in. Tristan seemed to have thrived on it, like his father before him. Alex simply figured that the young Ranger would eventually find some girl with whom to spend the rest of his life and settle down, also like his father. That his friend would not live long enough had not occurred to him.

As Alex rode closer, he drew his attention from the surrounding terrain where accomplices might be hiding to where a pained shriek seemed to drag the figure back into the cover of the ravine. *It was a girl!* Glancing about once again cautiously, he brought the roan to the edge of the steep incline and pulled it up shortly.

Lying on the parched and cracked bottom of the gully, a woman struggled to get up. Her hair, once black, was dulled a grayish yellow by the same dust that covered her tattered clothing. As Alex dismounted and climbed down into the arroyo, she lifted her arm over her eyes and squinted, her frantic unintelligible mumblings becoming silent. To his astonishment, not dark eyes, but wide frightened blue ones peered out at him.

"Cálmate, señor . . . ita," he finished, noting the streaked smooth flesh of a face not yet suffering from age. But she suffered, nonetheless, he thought, reaching for her as her knees buckled.

He had no sooner caught her when she gasped an agonized *"Non!"* and tried to pull away from the arm that had slipped about her waist while her own arms tightened contrarily around his shoulders. It was then that Alex felt the bulk of the bandages, now stiff with dried blood and covered with dirt.

"Madre de Dios, Catalina!" he shouted, startling his

368

trembling burden with his raised voice. "It's all right," he consoled, sweeping her up in his arms.

It was beyond him what the girl was saying—she spoke in French, he thought, but too fast for his limited study of the language to do him any good. At least she had stopped resisting him. He heard the coach approaching and looked for a way he might get her out of the narrow and deep ravine. A place a few yards away, where the dirt had caved in on the side, provided a gentler, although still considerable steep slope, which he attempted.

The coachman met him halfway and helped him up to where Catalina looked on anxiously. The moment she saw the bloodstained bandages, however, her professional reserve cloaked her fair features and the doctor in her took charge. "Bring her to the coach out of the sun. Thank heavens I brought my bag!"

Alex resisted a grin. His wife never left home without her medical bag, yet, the moment she had need of it, an occurrence that was more frequent than he sometimes cared for, those were the first words out of her mouth. And he wouldn't change her for anything. It was selfish to consider expecting a talented and competent doctor like his wife to give up her career to be solely a wife and mother. Thankfully, he'd come to realize that early in their marriage and given his blessing for her to follow her dream when she offered, out of love, to leave it for him.

Laura McCulloch picked up a blanket she'd used as a pillow to nap with on the long coach ride and unfolded it on the seat for Alex to place the dazed girl on, then retreated to the opposite side of the cab to give her daughter room to work. "Have you any idea what happened to her, Alex?"

Alex shook his head. "She'd fallen in the ravine and

couldn't find her way out. I don't think she's lucid," he whispered to his lovely mother-in-law. Black was not one of his favorite colors, but not even the mourning dress could daunt the woman's beauty—beauty of face as well as spirit, he thought upon seeing the compassion rise in her amber warm gaze.

Laura McCulloch had just lost her son, and yet it was she who offered Catalina comfort upon delivering the bad news and welcomed them into her home, as prepared as any hostess might be. Too prepared, Alex reflected, recalling how smoothly she had maneuvered Catalina's thinking along the same line as her own about visiting the home in which the twins had been born to find out what had happened to Tristan.

Alex was shaken from his reverie as the subject of his admiration stiffened, her complexion paling. At Catalina's astounded gasp, he turned to see his wife and mother-in-law exchanging looks of disbelief.

"Did you hear what I heard?"

Laura McCulloch nodded numbly in answer to her daughter's shocked question. "My God, it's *her* . . ." She glanced at a bewildered Alex. "Tristan's wife."

"Alex," Catalina whispered, her voice infected with a new urgency. "Tell the coachman to get us to Casa Valencia as soon as possible. I'll work on her on the way."

"Will you need help?"

"Mother can assist me." Catalina looked up from untying the filthy bandages wrapped around her and absolved him of responsibility with a knowing smile. "We speak fluent French and whoever did this to her might be following."

"Right."

Relieved, for he had not had to assist his wife since the birth of their niece and hoped he'd never be forced nto a situation like that again, Alex retreated to his horse. He'd rather face marauders any day.

"*Adelante, amigo!* The doctor says we must hurry."

The roan danced sideways as Alex swung its head about toward the direction they'd originally been headed when he spied the girl. Tristan's wife, he mused, his brow knitting. She had written in the letter notifying the McCullochs of her husband's death that she was returning to France. It seemed Ross McCulloch's instinct that she might be in danger was right. And now, so was the man's wife and daughter.

Although he kept a keen lookout on the hills rising on either side of the dirt road, he heard the approaching riders before he actually saw them. With no place to hide the vehicle, he warned the driver to have his rifle ready and to keep moving until the group showed themselves. To his relief, they were uniformed in the colors of the border patrol.

Alex waited until they were approaching the coach before pulling away to meet them. The commandant of the group moved forward, accompanied by a civilian garbed in the glittering garb of a *matador*. Biting the inside of his cheek to keep from showing his amusement at the ridiculous attire, he checked the question as to the whereabouts of the bullfight, greeting cordially instead.

"*Buenas tardes, señores.* Is there something wrong?"

The commandant, a thin man with sharp angular features which gave him a hawklike appearance, leaned forward on his saddle. "Might we inquire as to who you are and where you are going, *señor?*"

"But of course. I am Alejandro Reyes Caine of Los Angeles and am accompanying my wife, Doctor Catalina Caine, and her mother to Casa Valencia to visit the grave of her brother."

"Casa Valencia!"

371

Alex moved his hand to his thigh, within easy reach of the pearl-handled pistols the Arch angel had put away along with his outlaw life to let the authorities take over the protection of the Indians around Los Angeles. Something was definitely wrong from the grim exchange of looks between the gaudy *matador* and the commander.

"Do you refer to Don Tristan De Costa?"

"The same." There was no way he could take all of them. To try would be certain suicide and likely get the women hurt in the process. What the devil had he let them walk into?

"Then you have cause to rejoice, Señor Caine," the man in the suit of lights spoke up. "Allow me to introduce myself. I am Don Miguel Alvarado, acting mayor of the village of Valencia until another can be appointed."

"Did you say that my son is not dead?" Laura McCulloch climbed down from the stopped coach and marched straight up to the head of the column.

Like daughter, like mother, Alex groaned silently. "*Señora*, please remain in the coach."

"But, Alex, he said we have cause to rejoice."

"Only that he is not dead, *señora*," the *matador* explained patiently. "although, I must say, you look more his sister than his mother." Alvarado slipped off his mount and came to claim Laura's gloved hand. "Can it be that you are Doña Tessa De Costa?"

Laura stiffened warily. "I was, Señor Alvarado, but I am now Mrs. Ross McCulloch . . . and do not play games with me, sir. I was informed that Tristan was killed in a mining accident. I have come all this way to visit his gravesite and find my daughter-in-law wandering about in this wilderness with a gunshot wound in her back. *What* is amiss?"

Alvarado's gaze shifted to the coach. *"You* have her?" he exclaimed, starting for the open door of the vehicle.

However, Alex moved the roan to block his way. "I believe the lady has asked you a perfectly legitimate question."

The sudden snap of raised rifles brought a smug tilt to the acting *alcalde*'s lips. "Do not cross me, Señor Caine. Even now, I can have you and your family arrested for aiding a murderer."

"Murderer!" Laura gasped. She tugged on the man's sleeve. "She's a *murderer?"*

"Actually, it is your son who is the mayor's actual murderer. His wife helped him to rob some valuable papers and is wanted by the law as well." Alex blinked as the man turned to him, the reflection of the sun off the glittering spangles of the suit flashing in his eyes. "You will move aside, sir, and hand the girl over to me. She has many questions to ask."

"I'm afraid that's quite impossible." All heads pivoted to see Dr. Catalina Caine standing in the door of the coach, her small chin set in a familiar show of her stubbornness that only gave her husband further cause for concern. "This girl is half out of her mind. She has lost much blood, and if I do not get her to Casa Valencia, she will not be able to ever answer your questions."

"Then, you can tend her in the jail."

Catalina arched an imperious brow at the man. "Drive all the way back to Valencia? Don't be absurd! Surely the house is closer, and I doubt your men would object to our hospitality. She certainly can't go anywhere in her condition!" the young woman argued upon sensing Alvarado's hesitation.

Alvarado wavered, thoughtful in his appraisal of the haughty self-assured female version of Tristan De

Costa—the sister he heard about—the next in what was becoming a growing line of heirs to the De Costa estate.

"How can I refuse the prospective hospitality of such lovely ladies, Doctor? I have no choice but to yield to your expertise. You must make her well so that we might discover what really happened at Mirabeau. In the meantime"—the man spun on his silver spurred heels back to where Alex sat contemplating the hopelessness of their situation and extended his hand—"Your guns, *señor*."

Aware of the rifles poised and ready, Alex carefully unbuckled his gunbelt and handed it over.

"And the horse . . . in case you should decide to leave the ladies. You will dismount, *por favor*."

"I do not know of your upbringing, Señor Alvarado, but where I was raised, gentlemen do not abandon their women to the likes of you."

His upper lip curling, the other man afforded him a long assessing look. "Your ancestry is of the Spanish nobility, is it not, Caine?"

"So I am told."

"Well, that means little here to men who have had to fight for what they have. In fact, *this*—"

"Alex!"

Catalina's warning shriek prompted Alex to instinctively lift his arm, catching the full impact of one of the holstered pistols in the gunbelt whipped across his face. The second, however, lashed around it to crash against his temple. Alex felt the sting of the splitting flesh on his cheek, small in comparison to the explosion of pain that racked his brain. His head reeled as he struggled to focus.

". . . is what I think of your ancestry," Alvarado finished contemptuously. "This man is under arrest!"

"For what!" Catalina demanded, suddenly at Alex's side.

"For attempting to help a wanted criminal," Alvarado replied smoothly. "And how well he is treated depends on how well you and your mother behave."

"Why, you—"

"Cat!" Alex snapped, shaking the fog from his vision. "Get back to your patient."

"Come with me," she countered, taking his arm in hers.

"No, *señora. I* will join you in the coach." The prisoner will ride on top where my men can watch him. Commandant!"

"Sí, alcalde!"

Alex watched Catalina being escorted back to the coach on the forceful arm of the man in the suit of lights while two of the soldiers bound his hands behind his back. He couldn't do anything, he told himself sternly. He stepped up on the rungs to join the grim coachman, relying heavily on the two men who helped him to keep from falling. There was no point in fighting back . . . at least for the moment. Maybe later some of this would make some sense, he mused in reluctant resignation.

Chapter Twenty-two

There was little cause for celebration upon their arrival at the spacious stone hacienda built into the side of the hills riddled with the veins of silver that had paid for it. The poor woman who rushed out to meet them was as frightened by the presence of the armed soldiers as she was overjoyed to see Laura McCulloch and her daughter. To add to Doña Inez's dismay was the bloodied and tattered sight of the unconscious girl whom she stammeringly ordered to be carried to the master suite on the second floor.

"I do not know what to think, Doña Tessa! There are so many rumors!" she fretted breathlessly as Alex was permitted to carry Marianna to the room she'd shared with her husband. "How could I ever dream that such a joyous reunion could be tainted by such as *this!*" The old nurse cast a scathing look in the direction of the acting *alcalde*, who followed them with two armed guards. "My nephew at the governor's office shall hear of this, as well as Don Enrique!"

"Silence, old woman, lest I be tempted to cut out your tongue to guarantee that you not carry out your threats."

"All show and no substance!" the old nurse muttered

under her breath as Laura McCulloch grabbed her arm and hurried her along after Catalina and Alex.

Fearful that Doña Inez would refuse to be intimidated, Catalina halted at the door of the room where Alex had entered with her patient. "I will need linens for bandages and boiled water to start with. Also, have the cook put on some rich broth, in case she regains consciousness. She'll need nourishment."

Reminded of her duties as hostess, Doña Inez nodded eagerly, her ire at the glittering *matador* dismissed for more important matters. "As you all will, my little Catalina. I will see to the meals immediately."

"My soldiers can accompany you to the village for additional foods to supply them as well."

The woman stopped at the head of the steps with a disdainful sniff. "I do not need a bullfighter telling me how to run this house! Casa Valencia has never turned away the mangiest of beggars and will not start now."

Catalina waited until the woman had retreated before focusing her attention once more on her patient. "Alex, I will need you—"

"Your husband will be held in our custody in the courtyard, Doctor. If you require a man's assistance, I shall be at your service."

Alex straightened from the bedside and slipped an arm about his wife's waist. "I'll be fine. This isn't exactly my calling anyway."

"Indeed, if anyone is to help Catalina, decency demands it should be I," Laura McCulloch intervened primly. "We will call you when we've finished with the women's work, Señor Alvarado."

"You may place a guard outside the door, if you fear we are a threat to you, sir," Catalina added, a fine golden brow arched in utterly devastating challenge.

Miguel Alvarado bowed slightly to the fair creature

daring to defy him. "Once again, Doctor, I give in to your wishes. I am a great admirer of beauty and intelligence." He crooked a finger under her chin and lifted it, braving the icy blue contempt of her gaze. "And if you are as cooperative with mine, no one shall suffer."

Catalina maintained her cool demeanor, but something inside her twisted in revulsion and fear. She knew full well what the man meant, and worse, so did her husband. She avoided Alex's gaze guiltily, fearing the accusation she so richly deserved. But they'd had to do something. They just couldn't visit Silverado as if all were well, wondering what her father had found out about Tristan's death. *If* her brother was dead, she thought, turning away to concentrate on loosening the last of the bandages.

"If you will excuse us, sir, I have work to do."

She couldn't bear to watch Alex being escorted out, but felt his reassuring squeeze on her arm. At that moment, she could have cried, except that she had schooled herself to be above that. She was a doctor and duty called.

Paying no heed to the closing door behind her that pronounced her husband's departure, she cut away the last of the bandages, exposing the source of the lump she'd felt earlier. A prickly pear poultice! If she didn't know better, she'd think the Comanche had treated this girl. Beneath it were clumps of what? . . . cobwebs?

"Mama!" she whispered, removing them and staring in disbelief. "Tristan had to have done this! I think they're cobwebs."

Laura McCulloch took one of the blood-soaked clumps in her hand, finding it difficult to tell exactly what was its source. "They could be," she murmured, knowing full well what her daughter referred to. One of the ranch hands had nearly cut off a toe in a wood-cutting accident, and their foreman had packed the bleeding wound in cobwebs and wrapped it up. It had healed miraculously, impressing her son to no end. For months afterward, Tristan had insisted every little nick be packed with them, much to her chagrin. Tristan . . .

"We're going to get her talking, if it's the last thing she does," Catalina vowed soberly, digging into her bag for a more-conventional disinfectant.

"I can talk."

Both women stood agape as the girl on the bed opened her eyes to stare at them.

"Why didn't you say something before?"

Marianna swallowed dryly. "I was not certain who you were . . . but now I know. You can be no one but Tristan's sister."

"So you didn't really think you were in France," Laura McCulloch remarked wryly.

Lips trembling, the girl on the bed tried to laugh. "I did at first, when you began to speak to me in my native language. I . . . was confused."

"Where is my son?"

"This is going to sting."

Marianna buried her face in the pillow to keep from crying out as the liquid fire spilled into her raw flesh. It was too much to hope for and yet too horrible at the same time. Now they were all in the *matador*'s hands.

"He . . ." She raised her pained gaze to the lovely woman watching her anxiously. "I think that he is dead." A sob caught in her voice as tears glazed the eyes fixed on her. "He was caring for me and when I awakened he was gone. In his place was a dreadful Indian."

"Did the Indian dress your wound?"

Marianna's brow knitted in reflection. "I think so."

"Eagle Wing?" Cat suggested to her mother.

Laura shrugged, plainly bewildered and dismayed.

"I found Tristan's hide clothes ..."

"Buckskins?"

Nodding to the doctor's suggestion, the girl on the bed went on. "They were covered in blood and stuffed in a pouch. I think the Indian killed him."

"Did the Indian threaten you?"

"*Non,* but ..." Marianna hesitated awkwardly, trying to think. "He said he was Tristan's friend, but the blood ..."

"Could have been yours," Cat pointed out. "How on earth did you get away from him? It's a wonder you can even walk."

Beginning to feel foolish, as well as ill, Marianna looked away. "I was frightened. I have never seen such a savage and—" She broke off, biting her lip to keep from releasing the sobs building to insurmountable proportion.

"He's alive, Mama!" Catalina exclaimed in a hushed but nonetheless excited voice. "I'll bet he's gone for help and thought she would be safe with Eagle Wing! Oh, Mama!" She embraced the stunned woman beside her enthusiastically.

"Do ... do you really think so?"

"Can it be possible?" Marianna echoed in a voice strained to the point of breaking.

"I *know* so," the young doctor averred, turning back to her. "And we are going to get you well so that he'll have a healthy bride when he returns."

"And you, madame, are not angry at me?"

Laura's joyous smile widened with compassion. "Grant you, Marianna, there is a lot of explaining to be done about you and Tristan, but it's clear that you love him. Now let's get you bathed and in clean clothing. You need food and rest."

"But what of Alvarado and your husband?"

"As long as you stay out of your head, I think we can bide our time until the authorities come here. I'll bet Father is with Tristan right now."

"But these men are ruthless. Your husband—"

"Can handle himself," Catalina answered, unaware of the unconvincing manner with which she spoke. "You just buy us the time."

Marianna frowned. "Purchase time?"

Ready for a break in the tension, Catalina and her mother laughed at the literal translation. "Pretend to be delirious," the lady doctor explained. "So that Tristan and Father can come to our rescue."

"Oh." Marianna nodded in comprehension. Even if Tristan's sister was right and they all lived through this, she wondered if she would ever understand this strange English the Texans spoke.

Although she tried to help as best she could, Marianna was forced to let Tristan's mother and sister bathe her and wash her hair. She was exhausted when the effort was completed, but felt better, nonetheless. Clad in a fresh cotton nightdress with a high ruffled collar and billowing sleeves cuffed with the same, she drifted off to a dreamless slumber.

Once, she stirred as someone bussed her cheek. For one fleeting instant, she thought it was Tristan, but when she opened her eyes, she discovered the aged face of her old nurse hovering in concern over her. After hearing Doña Inez's explanation that Laura McCulloch and her daughter had gone downstairs to dine and to see to Alex, the girl closed her eyes again.

It seemed she had no sooner done so when the opening of the door preceded by impatient voices invaded the still retreat, jarring her into wakefulness in alarm.

"I tell you, Marianna is still not lucid!" Catalina

McCulloch Caine protested as Miguel Alvarado brushed past her.

"But she is awake, Doctor," Alvarado remarked sourly, stopping at the edge of the bed.

Marianna wished that she might close her eyes again and feign unconsciousness, but it was too late. The startling entrance had made that impossible. "Tío Enrique! What are you doing here?"

The smugness that had settled on the acting *alcalde*'s face faltered. "I am not your uncle, Marianna, and I believe you know that."

"Then get out of my room or I shall call *Granmaman!*" Marianna threatened, reverting to French. "Her servants will have you thrown into the Seine!"

"I tried to tell you that she thinks she's in France," Catalina whispered lowly at the *matador*'s side. "She expects her grandmother's servants to toss you into the Seine . . . a French river," she explained at the questioning rise of his brow.

"Granmanam!"

"I am sorry, dear niece," the *matador* spoke up quickly, moving to sit on the edge of the mattress. "I only meant to test your mental faculties. You have been quite ill, but are safe now, thanks to the doctor. Your aunt and cousin send their regards from Mexico City."

"But Elena was married, was she not? Has she received your blessing?"

Alvarado shrugged. "Alas, what can one do to change the course of true love?"

"Good." Marianna shifted uncomfortably, disconcerted by the game the man had chosen to play with her.

"And what of your true love, Marianna? Where is the this Texan I have heard so much of?"

"Dead."

"But that is not possible, niece. I heard that he murdered the *alcalde* of Valencia and is wanted by the law."

Marianna's voice remained flat. "An Indian killed him. I barely escaped with my own life."

"From where?"

"A cave, I think. It was dark and cold, I was hurting so badly . . ." Closing her eyes, the girl on the bed conjured an effective shudder.

"But of course you were. And what of the journals he had stolen?"

"The books?"

Alvarado nodded eagerly. "Yes, the books. Where are they?"

"The books," she echoed under her breath, as if searching her memory in a concentrated effort. At last, she shook her head. "I can not . . . perhaps the Indian got them." Covering her mouth with her hand, Marianna yawned. "I wish to sleep now. When I awaken, perhaps I'll remember then." She pecked her pointing finger and planted the kiss on Alvarado's cheek, startling him in the process. "And tomorrow, I shall write my congratulations to Elena. I am happy for her, if saddened by my own misfortune. Goodnight, Uncle." With a masterful trailing off of her voice, the girl turned her head away and snuggled against the pillow, ending the conversation.

Catalina caught the impatient hand that reached out to shake her. "Wait, *señor*. It is not unusual for rest to restore one's memory. As she improves, so will her mind. She's been through a dreadful ordeal. I think we all need a good night's rest."

"Then, you will join me downstairs for a glass of sherry, perhaps?"

Catalina was beginning to wish she hadn't insisted that Laura McCulloch retire in the next room, except that the very fact that her mother gave in so easily told her the long journey and distressing results were taking their toll. If her father knew his suspicions about her mother were true, he'd skin them both for the fix they were in. But if they hadn't come, Marianna would have fallen into the hands of this spangled wolf. And at least her mother had some hope now, that Tristan was alive.

Feeling the sacrificial lamb herself at the moment, Catalina shook her head. "That is impossible, *señor*. I will stay with my patient. Perhaps she'll awaken or talk in her sleep to reveal the whereabouts of these journals you're seeking."

"And why should I trust you to pass this information along to me, Doctor?" the man questioned suspiciously.

Catalina leveled a collected gaze at him in return. "Because, sir, you have my husband. I trust that when you have what you are seeking, you will let us return to Texas. Our only interest here was Tristan, and now that he is gone, there is little else for us to do but return."

"And leave a possible fortune in silver, Doctor?"

"From what I understand, sir, Casa Valencia belongs to Elena De Costa, or whatever her married name is now. My brother had no need of it, I have my practice in Los Angeles, and my mother has her eastern horse farm as well as Father's Silverado ranch. All Casa Valencia means to our family is unfortunate memories. As soon as Marianna—she is one of ours now," Cat pointed out purposefully, "As soon as she is well enough to travel . . ."

"She will go to prison."

Catalina's independent bravado faltered. "Even if she helps you find what you are looking for?" She flinched inadvertently as the man stroked her cheek with the back of his hand, his coal dark eyes taking on a glow

384

that made her stomach feel as though it were sinking into a quagmire of nausea.

"As I have said before, lovely lady of the sunshine, that all depends on you."

Cat knew he was going to kiss her and fought the urge to slam her balled fist into his face. Although he denied it, Alex's face had shown signs of additional beating when she slipped him the small knife she'd hidden in her sleeve during her tender examination of his cuts and bruises. He'd asked for time, sending his love silently with the warm ebony eyes she adored. Time he would have. "Then send the others back to Texas now, *señor*. I will stay with Marianna."

As if the suggestion were appealing, Alvarado stepped closer. "I do not think I have ever needed a doctor until now . . ."

Bracing for the inevitable assault, Catalina leaned against the edge of the mattress, when a moaned shriek behind her provided escape. Pivoting in the arms that were encircling her waist, she leaned over a tossing Marianna, who babbled incoherently in French.

"Wake up, Marianna! It's all right!" She pointed to her bag. "That bottle on the right, hand it to me."

Distracted, Alvarado obeyed hastily.

Catalina shook Marianna again and whispered soothingly in French while Alvarado uncorked the bottle. Batting her eyes open, Marianna gasped in relief to be freed of the feigned nightmare. The ruse was all she could think to do. Her reward was a vile taste of elixir that made her choke.

She swayed unsteadily. "I think I am going to be sick!"

"I'll get one of the women," Alvarado obliged, nearly stumbling in his eagerness to take his leave.

Although they dared not express their delight over

the success of her ploy, the door being left open, the two girls exchanged conspiratory grins as Marianna rested back against the pillow again.

"Such talent and timing should be on stage," Catalina remarked wryly, tucking her patient back in. "My brother has astounded me."

Apprehension returned to Marianna's face. "Why?"

"Because he had the good sense to marry a smart girl who seems as sweet as she is pretty, instead of one of those moon-eyed, ruffle-brained females always hanging onto him at the socials. I can't wait to hear how you all met."

Marianna gave a soft "Umm" in response, retreating once again into fatigue. She was tired, but that was not why she closed her eyes. She was afraid. If Tristan's family ever knew the whole truth, they might not think so highly of her—especially since she was not legally married to him.

From the thick post to which they'd tied him, Alex Caine watched the shadows on the balcony of the master bedroom. He'd seen a man's shadow moving toward Catalina's lithe form, his arms reaching out to encircle the tiny waist, unaffected by the birth of their three children. Incensed with a rage that made him feel as if he could rip the post from its supports, he concentrated on a less-conspicuous alternative with the knife his wife had slipped to him. Her resourcefulness never ceased to amaze him, even when she'd somehow managed to turn her attentions to the bed, sending Alvarado off in a rush and escaping the scoundrel's embrace.

The rope finally gave, so suddenly that Alex lost his grip on the knife, which clattered to the ground at his feet noiselessly. The breath that froze in his throat came

386

out in relief. The soldiers were busy finishing off a barrel of one of Casa Valencia's fine imported bouquets. It was an excellent example of what grapes, treated correctly, could become, the connoisseur in him had to admit when a glass had been slung in his face earlier. The man had found it too good for his taste, no doubt.

But good wine goes down easy and that is what Alex was counting on. It was an excellent sedative after a hearty meal that the woman called Doña Inez had rather ungraciously provided. The men had given her a hard time at first, but she'd held her own with amazing spunk. Alex could not help but wonder if the meal and the wine were a part of her own plan to help the ladies sequestered upstairs. Whatever the cause, he was grateful. Already some of the men were dozing off.

Keeping his hands behind him, as though still bound, he waited what seemed an interminable amount of time before others followed. When those who remained awake were too drunk to notice, he made his move. Stealing into the cover of the balcony and tall hedges, he made his way into the house, his knife clutched in hand. He could have taken any one of the men outside as a hostage, but knew instinctively that only one would ensure their safe escape—the one in the *traje de luces*. If instinct served him further, Alvarado would be found in the main salon, the combination of living room and dining room that Alex had seen from the foyer as he'd carried Tristan's unconscious wife up the steps.

The sound of voices located the room for him at the end of the unfamiliar corridor through which he entered the dark house. Alex counted four of them—Alvarado, the commandant, and two junior officers. All were boldly propositioning one of the servants who was apparently serving them. From the lack of response, their flirtations were not well received.

The sound of approaching footsteps forced him back against the wall, his knife ready. The girl they'd been talking to walked toward him, carrying empty goblets and dirty plates, which had been cleared from the main table, on a tray balanced delicately on her head.

Alex tensed, hoping that she would continue by, but, just as she came abreast of him, her gaze slanted his way. In spite of the warning finger Alex pressed to his lips, she started with a sharp gasp. The dishes precariously stacked on the tray slid sideways and crashed to the floor. Staring wide-eyed at Alex, the girl backed against the opposite wall.

"Please, *señorita*. I am trying to save the ladies!" he whispered urgently as the commandant appeared at the archway leading into the salon.

"What is it, woman?"

Alex couldn't breathe, but pleaded silently.

"A ... a mouse! I saw a mouse," the servant stammered nervously. "I am sorry, Commandant. I will clean this up right away."

"Perhaps you are better in the bedroom than you are in the kitchen, eh, *chiquita?*" Upon receiving no reply, he shrugged. "Bring us more wine when you are through."

Perspiration beaded on Alex's brow, yet when he tried to swallow the apprehension gathered in this throat, it was completely dry. Even after the officer returned to the table, it took a few moments for him to unlock the breath frozen in his chest. With a low *"Gracias"* he stepped over the rubble and squatted beside her. "I need to get Alvarado back here. Can you help?"

"If you escape, you will take me with you?"

The young man smiled and nodded in assurance. "I would leave you in no danger."

"And Doña Inez?"

"All may go who wish to," Alex promised, putting the

pieces of the glass he was picking up on the tray. Taking three women out of a place swarming with *soldados* was going to be difficult. Taking a household could well prove impossible. But if Alvarado valued his life, he would order the men to let them pass.

"You wouldn't know where my guns are, would you?" he asked, following her into the dimly lit kitchen where a cook, whose ample girth indicated that she enjoyed her fare as much as anyone else, cut up the last of a pile of loaves that had been baked for the uninvited guests.

"Quién es?" she snapped, eyeing Alex suspiciously. She raised her knife in front of her, as if daring Alex to even think the small one he held in his hand was a match.

"The husband of the *médico, tía*. He is going to help us."

Alex nodded again as the girl turned a questioning face up at him. "Yes, your aunt may go as well."

"And where might that be, Señor Caine?"

Although his hand tightened around the handle of the knife Catalina had given him, any further defensive or offensive measure he might have taken was checked by the prod of a pistol barrel at his back. Swearing silently that he'd been careless enough to let the cook distract him, Alex permitted Miguel Alvarado to take the knife from his hand.

"Soldados, aquí! Take him away! He will be shot at sunrise!"

"For what!" Alex demanded above the dismayed wail of his accomplice. "Trying to escape?"

"For attempted murder."

"Of whom?" Alex pulled away from the men who reached for him and glared at his accuser.

"Of me. The commandant is a witness."

"And these ladies?" he inquired boldly.

"Will hold their tongues or die with you."

389

Close enough to the table on which the servant girl had placed the tray, Alex closed his fingers around it. His adversary was mad, and playing the docile gentleman was no longer an option. Sensing the two soldiers closing in behind him, Alex swung the tray around, slinging the dishes, broken and whole, into their faces and driving them back. Continuing with his wide sweep before Alvarado could redraw the gun he had holstered, he plowed into the man, knocking him over.

"Hold, *señor*, or the girl dies!"

Glancing up, Alex spied the commandant holding his pistol to the head of the servant girl.

"Please, *señor*," she pleaded tearfully.

His hesitation cost him the time it took to fill the room with *soldados*. Breathing heavily, he straightened and tossed the heavy oak tray aside.

"You will regret this, Caine," Miguel Alvarado growled, brushing off the spilled leftover food he'd fallen in, vengefully from his shining suit. "I shall enjoy making your beautiful wife a widow."

"Do you always fight behind a woman's skirt, Alvarado?" Alex inquired cryptically, straining against the hands that checked his challenging step forward.

"My goal is to get what is under them."

Alex ignored the coarse snickers from the men around them, for there was no doubt in his mind as to whose skirts the man referred to. Recriminations of every manner rose to assault him, but before he suffered the attack, a more-physical one lashed out at him in the form of a slashing pistol butt. Thunder that burst in his ears, flashed, sending bolts of pain coursing through his senses until the bright lights glaring before him flickered and died, leaving him in total darkness where an anesthetic nothingness consumed him.

Chapter Twenty-three

The eastern horizon was beginning to brighten over the ragged landscape to the east of the mesquite thicket where Tristan McCulloch crouched lowly, watching the hacienda below. The frantic despair he'd known since Eagle Wing had ridden out to find him without Marianna gnawed at his insides still. The Indian had told him how his pony had run off for some unknown reason and that, when he'd returned, Marianna had left the tunnel. Her trail had been easy enough to follow, but it led straight to multiple tracks of horses and a coach, indicating she had walked into the hands of the *alcalde*'s men.

His Comanche friend was as contrite as he was embarrassed that he had failed to take care of the woman of Yellow Wolf's son and, even now, attempted approach to the hacienda from the north end. He, Tristan, and Ross McCulloch only had an hour to find Marianna, if she was in there, and get her to safety before combined forces of the Texas Rangers and the governor's select troops rode in to arrest the band that had been combing the hills for their leader's assassin.

Judging from the men that milled about in uniform and their less-than-savory comrades, Eagle Wing's the-

391

ory that they'd taken Marianna to Casa Valencia was very likely fact. A full-blown assault, however, could get the girl killed. At sunup, the joint forces would charge and surround the hacienda to take advantage of surprise. *And time was ticking by fast.* Tristan strained to hear the signal Ross McCulloch had promised to give as soon as he was in position.

Although he didn't exactly hear anything, instinct bade the young man glance over his shoulder in time to see a shadow stealthily approaching. As he stiffened in wary response, he heard his father's identifying voice.

"Trouble!"

"What is it?"

"Your mother's coach is in the barn."

"What?"

"That fancy coach I ordered from Philadelphia is in the barn . . . and the matching blacks."

Tristan was staggered by the unexpected news. *His mother* at Casa Valencia? "I thought you said—"

"I've sent Eagle Wing to tell Manolo we need more tine," Ross interrupted, scowling at the second-floor windows that had been lighted since their arrival.

The younger man exhaled heavily under the additional weight of this new development. "We'd best get inside, then. That Mexican general is a hard-mouthed horse, if there ever was one. Mano can only hold him back so long."

Ross McCulloch snorted derisively. "Don't know why the devil we didn't just bring along the Rangers and leave the Mexicans to polish their boots. Can't be more than thirty or so men inside, judging from the size of the remuda in the corral."

"We only have ten men," Tristan reminded him. He fell in behind the stealthy Ranger as they stalked across a clearing to another thicket of chaparral. To be discovered now would be disastrous for all concerned.

Ross McCulloch looked back somberly. "Ten *Rangers* is all we need."

In spite of his growing trepidation that, not only Marianna and his mother, but his sister and Alex might also be inside, the corners of Tristan's mouth tilted upward. His father had little respect for the army and less respect if they were Mexican, to boot. He'd learned to hunt and fight with the Indians, strike fast and retreat just as quickly. By the end of the war, he'd honed his Confederate command into a crack unit, known as McCulloch's Hellions, a force to be reckoned with by outlaws and renegades on both sides of the border. If crime knew no borders, it was beyond Ross McCulloch, much to his superiors' chagrin, why the law should.

Yet, of all the men to have on his side, Tristan would have chosen no other. The hard work on Silverado kept Ross in as good a shape as most of the younger men on the Ranger force. The man still moved like a mountain cat, quick, deadly, and silent, so much so that the guard he slipped up behind never heard him, nor had time to react to the hunting knife that flashed in the waning moonlight. The moment they were inside the barn, Ross pulled the striped serape off the man and over his head, donning it with a reckless shrug.

"Godawmighty! Smells like he's been sleeping with pigs!"

Instead of responding to Ross's disdainful comment, Tristan threw himself against the barn door as another man staggered inside, obviously suffering from the effects of too much sangria. He saw the whites of the man's eyes widen as he let fly a well-delivered punch, which silenced a startled shout that never emerged. Catching his victim to keep any one from hearing his fall, Tristan dragged him into the shadows and relieved him of a long woven *jerga* vest and a wide sombrero, complete with a bullet hole through the brim. In no time at all, he'd trussed him up like a spring calf and stuffed a gag in his mouth.

"Ready?"

Tristan tucked the spare pistols from the unconscious man's belt in his own and nodded.

Taking a hint from the reeking smell of alcohol that soaked his borrowed clothing, he staggered, leaning against Ross's arm. The double arched gate leading into the courtyard was open and the smell of brewing coffee wafted through the air. Men were lying about the courtyard, some snoring, and others showing less life than a corpse. Two broken kegs lying nearby evidenced what Tristan already knew. They were sleeping off a good drunk, and two more staggering about was not likely to arouse too much suspicion . . . hopefully.

A sudden sharp nudge in his ribs brought his attention to where Ross McCulloch motioned with his eyes. A woman was standing at the balcony door, the curtains parted just enough for her to look out. The light behind her outlined her graceful figure and upswept hair. Catalina? His mother? he wondered. No doubt Marianna was confined to bed.

"The only way I know up there is by the balcony steps."

Understanding the folly of that approach, Tristan bent his head toward the arched corridor that led to the central foyer ahead. "I need some coffee," he mumbled, aware that a uniformed *soldado* apparently on guard duty was watching them curiously. *"Donde está la cocina, amigo?"* He purposefully tripped over his own feet to be steadied by Ross's strong grip.

Cuidado, amigo."

"The kitchen is that way!" The man jerked his hand toward the arched doors and shook his head in what was either disgust or envy. Tristan was not sure. What intrigued him more was the man slumped over, the ropes binding him to a post that was the only thing holding him upright at all. Blood streaked the front of his fine linen shirt, having come from a swollen gash on his temple. As they passed by, Tristan heard his father curse under his breath, expressing the same feelings that had been generated within him as he recognized Alex Caine.

He kept on walking, waiting until they were in the tiled foyer by the fountain where he and Catalina used to play ... where he'd lost his head and his heart to Marianna Gallier. Distracted by memories that played havoc with his mind, his gaze had wandered to the top of the steps in speculation when Ross McCulloch shook him from his reverie and handed him the spare guns he'd taken from the man in the barn, increasing Tristan's armory to six.

"We'll not get out of here when those yahoos in the courtyard come alive. You take these and hole up in the room with the women. Hopefully, the attack will keep them too occupied to seek you all out. I'm going to try to free Alex. Your mother and Cat can help you out."

"Alex'll need a gun," Tristan pointed out, giving one of the pistols back.

Ross's teeth flashed white under the shadow of the wide-brimmed hat that covered his fair hair. "Keep it. There's plenty of guns to pick from out there. I doubt the ladies are as well armed."

Tristan acknowledged his father with a quick dip of his head and turned to climb the steps when he heard the echo of footsteps in the upper hallway and voices, women's voices. Withdrawing quickly, he dashed into the corridor leading to the kitchen.

"Señor Alvarado, I beg you, don't do this! Alex was only trying to help us. Wouldn't you do the same for your wife and family?"

Preceded by two armed soldiers, Catalina McCulloch Caine clung to the arm of Miguel Alvarado. Behind them, Laura McCulloch, looking on the verge of a faint, leaned heavily on the curved wrought-iron rail. Both women appeared to have been awake most of the night, and, from the red swelling under their eyes, they'd spent it crying.

"Ah, she is eager to be close to me now, *amigos*," Alvarado derided upon reaching the bottom of the steps to look down at the imploring face of his fair-haired companion. "It is a shame it was not so last night."

"I had a patient to care for!" Catalina stepped in front of him as he started ahead again. "I'll do anything . . ." She directed a fleeting look of apology at her mother and returned her gaze to the acting *alcalde* in desperation. "*Now,* if you wish."

"Catalina!" Laura gasped, her knuckles growing white as she watched her daughter throw herself into the arms of their captor.

Ignoring her mother's outcry, Catalina kissed the man who threatened to execute Alex with all her being, praying for a miracle. Her heart leapt with hope as the man accepted her bold ploy and returned the gesture enthusiastically, his hands running up and down her back, forcing her against him. When he finally lifted his head to peer down at her, her brief rise of hope was dashed by the mockery in his demon-dark gaze.

"Ah, Doctor," he sighed, catching a wisp of golden hair that had strayed from her once neatly pinned chi-

396

gnon and twisting it playfully around his finger. "We will continue this . . . *after* the execution."

Recoiling, Catalina wiped her lips with her sleeve in seething contempt. "Bastard!" Without warning, she was upon him, the scalpel she'd hidden in her skirts slicing through the thick padding of his jacket to draw blood.

"Seize her!"

Two of the soldiers grabbed the shrieking fury, forcing the weapon from her hand with a painful twist of her wrist. "I'll kill you! I'll cut your heart out!"

Miguel Alvarado cupped his hand over his shoulder as Catalina was dragged away and out into the courtyard. "You two, bring the woman!" he snapped, motioning Ross and Tristan to take Laura McCulloch under tow.

Ross reached his wife's side in two long strides, his arm going under hers as she swayed unsteadily. "I thought I told you to stay home," he rumbled lowly, for her ears only.

The pale woman snapped her eyes up at her captor and struggled to keep from betraying her joy to see him. Instead, tears sprang to the forefront, spilling down cheeks already raw from them. Almost as if afraid, she turned to peer up under Tristan's sombrero and a sob wedged in her throat. Tristan felt the brunt of his mother's weight as her legs failed her.

"Be still, woman! If you do not walk, we will drag you," Ross growled dispassionately.

Shaken from her shock by her husband's harsh tone, Laura regained her footing and straightened. "I do not need the likes of you to help me," she declared haughtily, a flash of indignation giving life to eyes that had, until that moment, been fearful and defeated. As she pulled away from them, Tristan felt a tug on his belt and looked down to see one of the extra guns his father had handed him earlier missing. Just in time, he spotted it disappearing into the folds of his mother's dress.

"That's my girl!" Ross murmured proudly to no one in particular.

At the sight of the drunken soldiers, most of whom were still asleep, Alvarado erupted into a string of curses that managed to bring color to Laura McCulloch's pale face and thin her lips in disapproval. Commanding the man who guarded Alex as well as the few who were sipping coffee at a wrought-iron table nearby, the acting *alcalde* assembled a firing squad for the execution.

Unaware that help was so near, Catalina tried once again to pull away from her captors to come to Alex's aid, but was as ineffective as the raging threats that fell on deaf ears. After shaking the commandant from the stupor to which he'd succumbed on a trellis-covered seat, Alvarado ordered everyone who was able to walk outside to witness the execution of the silent young man being dragged away from the post where he'd spent the night. While Alex was forced up against the outside wall of the hacienda, the motley collection of *bandidos* formed a group in front of him, fumbling with their guns.

Tristan glanced at the sun now peering above the edge of the horizon and wished that Eagle Wing had not stalled the attack. A diversion was what they needed. He looked around, seeking a place where he could get his mother and sister into cover when the gunfire broke out. With the element of surprise, it was possible that he and Ross could take the firing squad out, but not without risk to the women.

"Ready!" the commandant announced crisply, bringing the group into some semblance of order.

Tristan's hands closed on his guns as he exchanged a last look with his father. He'd start on one end and Ross on the other. The plan was made without a word being spoken.

"Aim!"

"*Tío Enrique, I remember!*"

Emerging from the massive arched frame of the back courtyard doors, Marianna Gallier walked toward them unsteadily, her ruffled robe and gown flowing around her as she innocently placed herself in the line of fire. Turning wide blue eyes toward the man who threw up his hand to halt the execution, she stopped as well, "But what is this?"

Tristan moved forward slowly to get a clear shot of the man rushing up to the dark-haired girl while Ross moved in on the opposite side.

"Are these not our friends, *Tío?*" she questioned in bewilderment.

"This man is a gringo spy, Marianna. Now, tell me what you remember."

Tristan was mesmerized by the sudden blue fire that leapt in what was no longer an innocent, but was now calculating, gaze. "I remember how to use this gun, *señor,*" the girl announced, producing one of Alex's pistols and jamming it into Alvarado's ribs. "And if you do not tell your men to drop their guns and cut Señor Caine free, I will show you what I know."

That's my girl! he reflected, chancing a smug glance at his father as he stepped forward and tossed off his sombrero to reveal himself to her. "Better listen to her, Alvarado! When *that* lady has a gun, you do not want to be on the other end."

Marianna's mouth dropped open in astonishment! *"Treestan!"*

"Marianna, look out!"

Tristan fired without thinking as Miguel Alvarado took advantage of her surprise and grabbed for the gun in the girl's hands. A second shot thundered in the deafening silence that followed, rendering time almost still. Alvarado jerked forward, taking Marianna down with him. Her scream seemed to weigh down Tristan's legs, until his steps were as labored as the breath that would not come. Oblivious to the strong warning to freeze, which Ross McCulloch delivered to the others from behind a deadly pair of pistols, he dragged the still man off the kicking girl, slinging him aside.

"Treestan!" Marianna cried, wrapping her arms about his neck as she was gathered up in his embrace. "Your sister was correct! You *are* alive!"

Tristan turned to permit Catalina access to the knife in his boot to cut Alex free when Ross McCulloch called out to him in Comanche sharply. Reminded of their precarious position, he set the girl down gently and drew his guns to help his parents cover the men laying down their arms in surrender.

"Well, we needed a distraction," he quipped lightly, his face coloring under Ross McCulloch's chastising gaze.

"The lady can distract you all she wishes *after* we've got all their weapons. There's a courtyard full to deal with."

Marianna stepped forward. "Oh, but *non, monsieur!* The servants have taken their guns. Even these guns have been tampered with, I believe, thanks to Catalina's sleeping powder. Doña Inez put it in the wine."

"That cranky old crow!" Ross exclaimed, more impressed with his daughter-in-law than ever. "She must be a hundred!"

"Ross McCulloch!"

The ex-Ranger grinned sheepishly at his wife. "You all right, Mother?"

Laura's admonition melted into a glowing look. "I couldn't be better, under the circumstances."

"Here comes the cavalry," Alex Caine chuckled wryly, his arms still wrapped around his fretting wife.

Ross looked over to where a cloud of dust and the thunder of hoofs betrayed the armed attack before the bugle call did. "Figures!" he snorted in disgust, ignoring the grinning exchange between his son and son-in-law. "Do you two think you can take care of the men inside while Mother and I hold these yahoos out here?"

Alex gingerly took up the pistol Marianna had dropped. "But of course, Colonel. I always wanted to be one of your hellions, especially since I married one."

Marianna, sobered by the sight of Catalina McCulloch leaning over the still figure of Miguel Alvarado, approached them slowly. "Did I kill him?"

Once again the doctor, Catalina answered without looking up. "No, he's still breathing. Two of you men carry him into the house," she ordered, rising to her feet and singling out two of the prisoners to help.

Lost in the confusion that ensued with the arrival of the governor's troops and Tristan's fellow Rangers, Marianna retreated to the secluded trellised enclosure where she could watch without getting in the way and drawing undue attention. Those men who could be roused were bound and forced to climb onto a hay wagon commandeered from the stableyard. The rest were likewise tied and tossed on the flat bed without regard to comfort. Meanwhile, Tristan, Manolo Benevides, and the general gathered at the wrought-iron table to divide the governor's men and Rangers into groups to begin searching the neighboring mines for any kidnap victims Victor Romero had passed off as prison labor.

"Even so, how will we know if we have everyone?"

the general exclaimed, throwing up his hands in frustration.

"We do not expect it to be easy, but we do have a list of Americans who were reported missing," Colonel Benevides informed him. "I would assume your freight companies had rosters of employees. They need to be gathered as well as any reports of men taken from the rancheros that were raided."

"Well, sí, but ... *Dios*, who could imagine an operation of this size right under our noses!"

"Texans have been trying to tell you Mexicans about this for the past two years!" Ross McCulloch spoke up indignantly. "Instead, you've been trying to lay the blame on us."

"That is because the raids have taken place in Mexico as well. It is only natural to assume that they were originated in Texas."

"Gentlemen!" Benevides intervened, giving Ross a warning look. "We are on the same side ... working toward the same goal, are we not? To argue among ourselves will only delay justice longer and there is much yet to be done."

Marianna watched the older version of Tristan McCulloch walk off to where some of the Rangers had gathered around a pot of steaming coffee. Now she knew where Tristan had inherited that savage nature of his that emerged when he was angry. If the son was intimidating, his father was more so. It was clear to her that he had little love for Mexicans, which did little to make her feel that she had a chance of being accepted. After all, although her mother was Mexican-American and her father was French, she was born a Mexican.

Yet she did not doubt the man's capacity to love. Never in her life had she seen such a feral gleam in one's eye as that which had lighted in Ross McCulloch's pale blue gaze as he held the firing squad at bay with his guns while his family was freed. Not a man tried his hand and Marianna could not blame any of them for it. The ex-Ranger was an enigma that both frightened and fascinated her at the same time. So caught up in her speculation was she that she didn't realize Tristan had left the table until she heard his voice at her side.

"Marianna, there's someone here I don't think has had a proper introduction, but you owe him your life."

Marianna nearly choked as she looked up to see the somber countenance of the Indian from the tunnel, the one she'd thought had murdered Tristan. Color burned a path up her neck, sweeping over her face to tingle at the top of her head as she extended a reluctant hand.

"I am pleased to meet you, *monsieur*."

Instead of taking her hand, the Indian merely stared at it and grunted. "Eagle Wing." Like he had in the tunnel, he thumped his chest with his arm and then rolled off a stream of unmelodic syllables at Tristan, his dark gaze never leaving Marianna's face.

"He wants to know what you did to his horse."

Mon Dieu, could she ever get used to Tristan's way of life, socializing with red savages? "I . . . nothing," she replied, forcing an innocently wide gaze. But at the dubious arch of Tristan's brow, she relented. "I put a hot drop which Liam Shay gave to me on his nose . . . but you must understand," she blurted out defensively at the incredulity forming on the young Ranger's face. "I thought that he had killed you. I found your skin clothes in the bag, covered in blood, and . . . and this savage grunting and poking at me . . . and, damn you, Treestan MacCoolach! Eet was not funny!" Marianna shoved the chuckling Ranger away from her angrily and rose from her seat.

"Where are you going?"

Aware that her raised voice had drawn the attention of most of those gathered in the courtyard, Marianna lifted her chin haughtily. "I am going to lie down! I am tired. *You,*" she ground out, tapping his chest emphatically, "can go play with your cowboys and Indian!"

She was tired, extremely so. So much had happened, so much that she wondered if things would ever right themselves. How could someone she loved so much make her so angry! Her ruffled hem swirled around her bare feet as she turned and ran for the foyer steps. Twice she had thought him dead. Twice she had grieved, and now, she wasn't sure that she could face a third time.

"Marianna, wait!"

"Take your hand off me, you big bool!" Marianna spun at the bottom of the steps and tried to pry away the fingers that closed on her arm. "I wish I had never left Paris!" she sobbed. "I wish——"

"What is the meaning of this?"

Marianna seized her bottom lip with her teeth and blinked away the glaze that formed in her eyes to see the elegantly dressed gentleman standing in the open front door, cane in hand. Of average height and stocky build, he exuded a possession of command that he was obviously accustomed to.

"Tío Enrique!" she gasped, hastily wiping away the tears that had spilled on her cheeks. So he had gotten Doña Inez's letter and come to her aid! Or had he received word of Elena's marriage? "I am so glad that you have come!" Tearing out of Tristan's loosened grasp, Marianna rushed up to her uncle and threw her arms around him in welcome.

The evident answer to the reason of her uncle's arrival came unexpectedly as a young Frenchman stepped around them, glaring in open hostility at Tristan. "And who is it that you think you are, *monsieur, assaulting* the lady in her own home. But for an explanation, I am tempted to call you to the field of honor!"

"Andre!" Marianna whispered, stepping back from her uncle in shock. "How . . . ?"

"Who the hell is *that?*" Tristan snorted behind her.

Clicking the heels of his polished slippers together, the Frenchman shot back. "*I* am the lady's fiancé. Who are *you?*"

Marianna's head reeled dizzily with alarm. This couldn't be happening. Andre was supposed to be with Elena and his brother in . . . where? she wondered frantically. Matamoros.

"I *was* her husband," Tristan's voice echoed cryptically, slashing through her shock like cold heartless steel. "Not that it was a *real* marriage anyway. Tear up a few papers and you're welcome to her, fancy pants."

"How dare you to insult my fiancée with such lies!" Andre reached for the elegant saber hanging at his side.

"*Non!* Stop this!" Marianna flung herself in front of him, her feet catching in her hem and costing her her balance. "This . . . this must not happen!" she pleaded, blinking furiously to stop the room from continuing to spin around her. "I can explain everything, Andre, if you will but take me to my roo—" A rise of nausea choked in the back of her throat, forcing her to give in to the arms that caught her. Her legs betrayed her and suddenly she was clinging, futilely clinging, to the consciousness that slipped through her fingers as easily as her newfound love had.

Chapter Twenty-four

All that helped the day pass quickly were the catnaps that spelled her between bouts of utter despair. For once, Marianna was thankful for the condition which required rest for recovery. That way she didn't have to face Tristan's family except for Catalina, who came in from time to time to check on her. Even then, Marianna pretended to be too sleepy to talk, unaware that her tear-swollen eyes betrayed that she'd done more crying than sleeping. Two trays had been removed from the room by the servants, untouched.

Below in the courtyard, which had come to serve as the main base for the joint operation between the two governments, groups of *soldados* and Rangers rode in and out, bringing news of found kidnap victims. Those who could write had taken brief testimonies in which the men identified those who had taken them hostage. Only once in her many trips to the window did Marianna see Tristan, and that was as he prepared to ride out with his men. Of course, he had his duty to perform. That always came first, she thought, overwhelmed by a bitter tide of self-pity.

She should be glad that Andre did come for her, she told herself sternly. If he had not, she would have made a horrid mistake and thrown herself at a man capable of freezing her blood with contempt one moment and melting her bones with passion the next. It was an emotional swing she could not bear. God forbid she stay in this land one moment more than it took her uncle to arrange their trip back to Mexico City. From there, she would return to Paris after visiting her aunt and cousin, perhaps as Andre's wife.

Her uncle had spoken with her briefly when she came to in her bed and assured her that Tristan's scandalous statement had not altered Andre's feelings for her. Tío Enrique had just arrived in Valencia when he overheard the young Frenchman asking the whereabouts of the De Costa estate. Upon questioning him, the man discovered Andre's intentions to find and marry Marianna and, astonishingly, gave his blessing.

Perhaps, since fate had so viciously placed her in this unsavory predicament, it was being kind enough to provide a way out. Nonetheless, Marianna felt guilty. Such a small deceit had grown into such a tangled web, more complex than she would ever have dreamed. Worse, she had all but forgotten the young man who had asked for her hand before she left Paris. True, she hadn't actually said that she would marry him, but she had not said no either.

Andre was a perfect gentleman, more than she could say for Tristan McCulloch. He loved to dance and attend parties. He always gave her her way. The fact that he still wished her hand was admirable, considering the circumstances Tristan had made so abundantly clear. So why did she feel so absolutely wretched?

Surely she only *thought* she was in love with Tristan. He had offered her comfort and safety from a common enemy. That the cost was her heart obviously meant nothing to him. After he had accomplished his mission with his precious Texas Rangers, abandoning her to the hands of a red savage, he had handed her off to Andre like a piece of used trash, something he no longer needed. *That* was how much she meant to him!

Pain welled in Marianna's chest, erupting in a tortured sob before she could bury her face in the tear-soaked pillow. She was so distraught that she failed to hear the gentle knock on the door or realize that anyone was there until a sympathetic hand came to rest on her shoulder. Instinctively, the girl stiffened, then quickly relaxed, but it was too late to feign sleep as she had in the past.

"You know, Marianna, you really disappoint me," Catalina remarked dispassionately, easing down on the edge of the mattress. "I thought you were a fighter."

"And more than that, no doubt." *A fighter*. The label struck a bitter note, so contemptible that Marianna was forced to laugh. "I am a coward, Doctor, not a fighter. And all I wish to do now is run. I can not bear this land of savages and ruffians who wear skins instead of cloth."

"Even if you are with the man you love?"

"If you have come to torture me, I do not need more!" Marianna retaliated, bolting upright in spite of the discomfort the sudden move cost. "Surely you can see that!" Instead, it was Marianna who saw, not vindictiveness, but compassion on the face of her companion.

"My profession is to heal, not inflict wounds, Marianna, and what I see is a young woman making a terrible mistake because she is weak and overwrought. Do you think a coward would have marched in front of the readied guns of a firing squad to save an innocent man?"

"I could not let them kill Señor Caine for his kindness to me . . . and yours," Marianna answered emphatically. "It was no matter of bravery, but what had to be done!"

Catalina shook her head in disbelief. "Well, I think it was one of the bravest acts I've ever seen and so does Father."

"Surely not!" Marianna was staggered that the rugged Ross McCulloch could find anything about her to be impressed with.

"He said he didn't think you had enough sense to stay out of your own way when he saw you walking into the line of fire, but when you pulled that gun on Alvarado, he saw guts few men possessed."

Marianna's brief and unexpected satisfaction faltered. *"Guts?"*

"Courage," Catalina explained with a patient smile.

"Is he still alive?" Marianna inquired, distracted momentarily by the mention of Alvarado.

"He's going to make it, I think. I got the bullet out of his back . . ."

"His back? But I thought . . ."

"That *you* shot him?" Cat filled in, a hint of amusement tugging at her lips. Upon seeing Marianna's disconcerted reaction, she quickly apologized. "I'm sorry, Marianna, it's just that Tristan said you couldn't hit the broad side of a barn, and when you missed at such close range . . ."

"But Alvarado had the gun too!"

For a moment, the two women locked gazes, one trying to check her humor and the other seeking reason for it. Catalina failed and Marianna succeeded, both falling into each other's arms giggling. It was a balm to the dark-haired girl, so much so that she hated to give it up when Catalina backed away. She liked Tristan's sister very much. In fact, she liked his entire family, even if she did feel intimidated by his parents.

"According to what Tristan said, you certainly led him on a merry goose chase."

"It was pigs, not geese, and he was not merry, I can tell you that!" Marianna differed staunchly, bewildered once more by the strange English the Americans spoke. "But," she added, face falling in sincerest contrition, "I meant no harm, ever, to Tristan. It was all misunderstandings, even . . . even Andre."

A golden brow arched curiously. "You're not engaged to the Frenchman?"

Marianna shook her head. "He asked me to marry him when I left Paris and I told him I would answer him when I saw him again. It was my uncle who has arranged this. Surely he thinks it the quickest way to be rid of me and all the trouble I have caused . . . but, since I met your brother, I have thought of no other man but him."

"Then tell him."

"For what? He has made it clear that he does not want me!" Her voice caught again, forcing her to clear her throat.

"What he made was a fool of himself," Catalina averred gently. "Men tend to do that when they're in love." She laughed suddenly. "Come to think of it, so do women."

Marianna wanted to believe what her companion was saying, but Tristan's manner had been so cold, so heartless.

"So, you are going to act the fool too, or shake some sense into his head."

"He will not listen to me, even if I could shake him."

"You mean to say that if he is so in love with you that he is insanely jealous of this Andre and too proud to admit it, you are going to let him walk away? After all, he thought this marriage was going to last and up shows a fiancé he has never heard of?"

"I only wish I could be as certain as you," Marianna sniffed, afraid to believe, yet not wanting to disbelieve.

"Then ask him. If you don't, then I'll agree with you. You are a coward." Catalina started for the door and stopped suddenly. "Now, I am going to send some food up here and I expect to see you try to eat it. Bravery needs sustenance."

"Doctor . . ."

"Call me Cat, Marianna."

"Cat," Marianna conceded timidly. "I . . . I am not certain what I will do, but I promise to consider what you have said."

Catalina beamed. "I know you will do the right thing. You're no coward, no matter what you think."

Marianna stared at the closed door after her new friend's departing footfalls had faded. What was it that she was afraid of? she reasoned, hoping to live up to the pretty doctor's kind assessment of her. Was she afraid that Tristan would ridicule her? If he did, she could hurt no more than she did already. She closed her eyes. Nothing could hurt more than that, not even the wound her new friend had pronounced healing nicely.

That evening Manolo Benevides returned to Casa Valencia with two other Rangers, but Tristan was not among them. From the conversation that drifted up from the courtyard, a group of Texans had ridden into Valencia to the tavern. Catalina came up to confirm what Marianna had overheard, declaring, somewhat perturbed, that Alex Caine had gone with them.

"He should be resting from that nasty blow on the head instead of rollicking about with Tristan!"

When the massive clock in the hall struck midnight and the household had grown silent, the ones who had gone into town had yet to return. Marianna, now restless beyond endurance, paced back and forth in front of

411

the window, straining to hear the sound of approaching horses. It had taken her all evening to build up her nerve to speak to Tristan and, if he did not come back, she might lose it.

At the strike of two, she tugged on her robe and walked toward the barn, a giant ghost of a shadow against a moonlit sky. Her eyelids were starting to grow heavy and she feared she'd miss him, if she remained in the comfortable room any longer. Besides, Catalina had said Alex sent word that he would be back. A light shining in the window next to her own indicated that more than one person was waiting up for the ne'er-do-wells.

The dry scent of fresh hay assaulted her nostrils as she stepped inside the barn. Surely here she would hear the men come in, and perhaps intercept Tristan before he made his way to the house. Thus resolved, Marianna patted a comfortable indentation in the giant pile of straw in the back and drew her feet up under her robe. The way she viewed it, there was little more to lose and everything to gain.

Although she didn't hear the horses when the men finally arrived, she couldn't miss their bellowing whispers as they turned the animals into the corral and carried saddles and blankets with them to bed down for what was left of the night next to the campfire their sleeping comrades had built. She tried to make out their identities from her hiding place behind the barn door, when two broke away from the group, ineffectively trying to keep their voices down to avoid waking the household.

"I think it best if you stay in here for the night, *amigo,*" Alex Caine, not necessarily the taller, but the decidedly straighter of the two, grunted as they stumbled into the shadows of the barn.

"To hell with women!"

"Shush! You'll spook the horses and . . ." Alex

grabbed Tristan by the belt as he stumbled forward. "*Dios,* you have an Indian's capacity for drink, not to mention an indiscriminate taste! How could you swill so much of that garbage?"

"Well, pardon . . . *hic* . . . me! I forgot I was drinking with a *conno . . . shure.*"

"No wonder your girl's thinking of going back to Paris, if you been assaulting her ears with your French!" Upon reaching the haystack Marianna had only moments ago abandoned, Alex let his intoxicated companion fall into it.

"Did I tell you about that night with the pigs?"

"At least a dozen times," Alex replied, feeling along the wall for a spare blanket. "And I've told you what I think you should do."

Marianna shrank into the shadows, curious to hear if Alex Caine's advice was like that of his wife. After all, she had saved the Californian's life.

"She . . . she don't make sense, Alex. I mean, she's not logical."

A deep chuckle rumbled from Alex's proximity as he found what he was looking for and tossed it over his friend. "Women are that way. Just think about what you would do in a situation and then expect the opposite from a female. Take now, for instance." He dropped to his haunches and squinted in the darkness. "See that light on the second floor? Cat's waiting up."

"Cat knows you wouldn't do anything wrong!" Tristan snorted skeptically.

"That's what you and *I* think, but what is she doing? Staying up worrying!"

"Least she gives a damn! You don't see a light in the master suite."

Marianna grasped a rough-hewn post, her heart quickening with hope. *Tristan did care.*

"I told you that she is probably up there waiting for you to come to her with a proper proposal and an apology."

"*I'm* not the one who married with a spare fiancé up my sleeve!"

Alex slapped his hand against his thigh and got up. "That is my point, *amigo!* Women have no logic in some matters and love is one of them."

"Then she can wait till hell freezes."

"And so will you. *Buenas noches!* I have an apology to make."

Tristan raised up on one elbow. "But you didn't do anything!"

"Precisely, *amigo*, and there is much to be said for making up! Sleep well."

In the dim light cast from the lantern hanging near the entrance of the barn, Marianna could see Alex's wistful smile as he approached her. Then, at the entrance, he stopped and looked directly to the shadows where she waited, heart frozen in her chest. To her astonishment, he winked and sauntered off toward the house, whistling a nondescript tune.

Uncertain as to how he knew she was there, let alone why he didn't betray her, she remained motionless until he disappeared inside the arched gates to the outer court. Catalina had been right, at least about one thing. If anyone was to make the first step toward a reconciliation, it would have to be her. Gathering her courage, she tiptoed toward the tall figure stretched out on the hay.

A streak of light filtering in through a crack in the wall of the stable cut a narrow path across the brim of the hat he'd pulled over his eyes and over the chest that rose and fell evenly. *Disheveled* was a kind word for the red calico shirt he wore. All but one of its buttons were

414

unfastened and the tail hung out of the waistband, which had dropped low to reveal the indentation of a lightly furred naval. His gunbelt lay within easy reach by the boots he'd evidently pulled off during his fascinating conversation with his brother-in-law. Under his head was tucked the blanket Alex had tossed him.

Until hell freezes, she thought solemnly. Such a long time to be without the warm embrace she treasured, the comfortable strength the arms flung over his head and across his chest promised.

"Treestan?"

The man on the bed of straw bolted upright, his hat falling aside as he blinked to focus his eyes on her. Suddenly he exhaled heavily. "How long have you been here?"

"I've been waiting for you."

He ran his fingers through his hair, sifting out the straw, and flung it away impatiently. "Any particular reason?"

Marianna dropped to her knees, searching his face for a sign that the coldness in his tone did not reflect his true feelings. "Because I can not wait until hell freezes before you hold me again."

"So you've added eavesdropping to your many talents."

She winced at the bitterness of the remark. "Tristan, do not do this. I . . ." She was a fighter, not a coward, Marianna told herself sternly. "I am going to give you one last chance to make a proper bride of me!"

A dry laugh echoed in the stillness surrounding them. "Proposals don't seem to mean much to you . . . or do you like to keep a string of men on hand?"

"I have had many proposals, if that is what you are saying," she blurted out, hurt by his cynicism, "from many admirers, but none from anyone whom I would accept. With you, you big bool, it is *I* who am forced to ask!"

Never in her life had she ever pictured herself on her knees before a man—she, Marianna Gallier, who had received her first proposal on her debut in Parisian society at sixteen. Worse, instead of the gallant gentleman a girl longs to sweep her off her feet, she was degraded to plead with an insensitive ruffian who reeked of bad liquor and sweaty horses. Love did make one the fool.

"Where do you think you're going?" Tristan demanded, catching her arms as she started to abandon her reckless mission altogether to go hide in shame. "Don't you want to hear my answer?"

Don't cry. God in heaven, don't give him that satisfaction! Marianna managed to summon a voice, devoid of all emotion. To let only one of the confusing feelings she suffered infiltrate it would be her undoing. "You already have, *monsieur.*"

"Oh no, I'm not *that* drunk."

Closing her eyes, Marianna gave into the firm grasp that pulled her so near, she could feel the heat of his flesh through her gown.

"Sit right here," he encouraged, easing her into his lap and securing her waist with one arm, as if to prevent her from escaping. His fingers moved through the silk of her hair, brushing it away from her face so that he could see it. "Can't say as I blame a man for wanting you, Frenchie."

Uncertain that he was not still toying with her, Marianna raised her gaze to his. *"Non?"*

His breath was warm against her lips. *"Non."*

As he dragged her down on the hay with him, Marianna twisted, not wanting their lips to part. She feared breaking the intoxicating spell binding them, compelling their limbs to intertwine until their bodies melded, raining to become one. The three-day growth of his beard assaulted the soft skin of her cheek, her neck, ddly inviting, until Marianna pushed herself upright so hat he could unfasten the chaste neckline of her gown) unveil her desire-swollen breasts to it as well.

She gasped in pleasure as he treated one and then the ther to a heady thrashing of his tongue, flooding her vith a molten need that bade her writhe her hips gainst him. "Tristan!" She uttered his name in a plain- ve moan as he moved her back and began to unfasten he buckle of his belt, his eyes never leaving hers.

"Hell'd never freeze if you were in it, Frenchie," he eased, lifting her with his hips in order to shove down he trousers restraining the throbbing desire that came ree.

Marianna leaned forward, coaxed by the hands that upped her breasts, until she was astride the hard evi- lence of his arousal.

"Fact is, I've been in hell ever since I left you, not nowing if you'd pull through." Tristan's breath was coming rapid as he maneuvered her with his hands. 'And now that I'm this close to heaven, I'm not letting rou slip by me again." With a sharp upward thrust, he aid his claim to her, branding her with his passion.

The very completeness of his possession scattered a housand shards of delight skittering to every part of her)ody from her innermost being, while his hands seemed o be everywhere at once, plundering and teasing, ca- ressing and kneading, until a whirlwind fever caught her up in its fury. While it was hot, bursting in a film of per- spiration on her gleaming white skin, it bore no other resemblance to hell. It was heaven in all its glory, with cloudbursts of light that filled her until she knew nothing but the explosive ecstasy of their wild and rampant union.

Later, drawn into arms that offered sweet retreat from the culmination of the savage lovestorm, Marianna lay breathless and exhausted atop her lover. She closed her eyes and reveled in the feel of him, within and without, flesh against flesh. And it was there that she later stirred, her bare skin assaulted by the prickly bed as she inadvertently rolled off Tristan and onto the straw.

Tugging her gown down belatedly, Marianna glanced around, bemused at first by her surroundings. Outside the sky was lightening as the moon left it to the sun to take over. Suddenly an arm snaked around her hips and tugged her closer, making her aware of her softly snoring companion. Her lover, she corrected, running her fingers along the beard-roughened taper of his jaw and across his lips. A sleepy moan generated behind them and he licked them, tasting something foul from the way he contorted his almost boyish features. Then they relaxed again, settling into slumber.

Much as she wanted to stay there and snuggle in the cradle he made for her next to him, Marianna realized that she had to get inside. It wouldn't do for them to be discovered in such a compromising situation . . . at least not until they were properly wed. A frown creased her brow as she sifted through her memory of the night before. He had said yes, hadn't he? The beginnings of a smile tugged at her lips as she considered his demonstrative response.

"Yes!" she whispered excitedly, easing away so as not to disturb the man at her side.

Thankfully, the night on the town to celebrate the capture of Romero's band of outlaws had done away with the risk of running into any early risers. Although she could smell breakfast being prepared in the kitchen, Marianna was able to tiptoe without detection through the courtyard and up the steps to the balcony door she'd

418

ft open the night before. After pulling the shutters to behind her to darken the room, she hurriedly worked at the ribbons she'd chastely retied on her robe to slip into bed when she caught a glimpse of someone rising from the highbacked chair near the tiled hearth.

"*Tío!*" Marianna clasped her hand to her chest and stared at the man in amazement. He must have spent a good portion of the night in her room, for the jacket he was never without was tossed carelessly over the chair back and his ruffled cuffs were rolled up to his elbows in uncharacteristic casualness.

"You spent the night with the Ranger."

"Yes." She neither acted smug nor tried to deny it. Naturally she would have to have her uncle's approval and an admission would certainly warrant it. "We are going to be married, sir, and I pray for your blessing." If he had approved of Andre, a schoolmistress's nephew, surely Tristan would be acceptable. "Then I will truly be Mrs. Tristan De Costa McCulloch."

"Pray what you will, Marianna, you will not have it. We will leave this morning for Chihuahua and proceed on to Mexico City with all haste."

Marianna blanched. "But why?"

"Because, my dear, you have caused enough trouble. The sooner you are wedded and shipped off to France, the better for us all."

"What is the difference whether I am wedded and shipped to Paris or Texas?" Marianna demanded obstinately. "I do not love Andre, I love Tristan!"

"Do not try my patience, Marianna."

"I will not go to with you!" She crossed her arms and turned away from the scowling countenance of her elder. "You, who tried to marry your own daughter off to a murderer! What judge can you be of a proper suitor?" Fuming with righteous indignation, she turned back to

419

further address him, when her eyes were drawn to a blue and yellow tattoo, all but hidden under the thick hair growing on his forearm—a bleeding heart, ensnared by a fanged snake.

Her indignation seeped away as she stood, transfixed by it. She was a little girl again, watching the tattooed arm drop the guns within her reach through the trellised fencing. It had been Victor Romero's arm then. *"You were with them?"* she asked in numb disbelief. As she recalled, Tío Enrique married her aunt two years later. So he, like Romero, had risen to find his place in society, leaving their murderous past behind. Except that Victor Romero had not left it behind. Had her uncle? She didn't like the instinctive answer that rose from her confusion.

"Now you understand why we must return with haste back to Mexico City."

"Before any of the men can identify you," Marianna murmured softly. Why hadn't she suspected it before, she wondered in self-recrimination. So much in life with the Corazons made sense now—the way he had insisted she and Elena be schooled in Paris and live with their grandmother, the distance he always kept between them when she had wanted a father figure so desperately, as if she'd made him feel uneasy, the alliance with Romero to be sealed by wedding Elena De Costa, and that he had taken so long to answer Doña Inez's plea for help.

"Only one man can do that and he lies at death's door, thanks to your lover's excellence with a gun. And then, of course," he hesitated, giving her a long and hard appraisal, "there is now *you*. Your resourcefulness has astounded me, Marianna, but it no longer does so. Unlike my colleagues, I do not intend to underestimate you. I have at my disposal the power to command this

420

place burned to the ground with your beloved's family in it."

"There are more men?" Marianna felt ill. A haunting vision of the shouting and shooting revolutionaries wreaking havoc in the courtyard and corridors of Mirabeau made the room blur. No one had survived.

"An army of them, supplied unwittingly, but most generously, by the *presidente*'s own government." The cold calculation brewing in the gaze fixed on her sent a shiver of dread racing along her spine. "And they will attack this evening if they do not hear from me in Chihuahua."

He would do it. He would unloose those hounds of hell on a innocent household, just as he had in the past. "But you are rich! Why do you pursue this hideous despicable life?"

"Such an innocent," Enrique Corazon tutted aloud to himself and held up his arm to display the tattoo. "You do not know what *this* means?"

Almost afraid to find out, Marianna shook her head in denial.

"We are members of a brotherhood dedicated to the independence of northern Mexico. The profits from the mines our foreign investors have so kindly opened for us are building us the army to do so."

"That is treasonous!" The man was surely crazy. Díaz would have him shot for even thinking of such a thing, let alone actually building an army of revolutionaries.

Corazon laughed, a devilish sound that seemed to rake the nap of her neck with icy fingers. "So it is, but it is very real, nonetheless ... and progressing successfully until one foolish girl decided to meddle where she did not belong. Now you must pay the consequences for your acts, or your new friends will pay as well."

Marianna looked up suddenly. "Andre is not a part of

this!" she exclaimed, her tone more of a question tha[n] a statement.

"Every man has his price ... even idealistic youn[g] fools. I have promised him the proceeds from the sale [of] Mirabeau and a handsome sum of silver as you[r] dowry."

Grasping the edge of the bed, Marianna took a dee[p] breath to fight the illness that washed over her. Bu[t] there was no fresh air to be had in a room with suc[h] vermin present.

"Ten times the number of men stationed here," he[r] companion reminded her sharply. "Shall I send a ser[-] vant up to help you pack or will you witness yet anothe[r] massacre in your young life?"

There was little doubt in Marianna's mind that he[r] uncle would carry out his threat. She knew his kind. Lif[e] held no value, only power and wealth. "I will start a[t] once ... alone, please," she added beseechingly. "I wil[l] need time to think of what to tell Tristan. He may no[t] be so easily convinced."

"According to the colonel, he is riding out early wit[h] the Rangers to continue to visit the mines in search o[f] those still on the list of the missing. We will be on ou[r] way by the time he returns." He motioned toward th[e] writing desk. "Go on, I will dictate it."

"I would rather—"

"I said, *I* will dictate it. Do you think I would leave[e] it to chance for you to somehow tell him what is hap[-] pening?"

Marianna found herself being shoved over to th[e] desk. Forced onto the chair, she took the pen resting i[n] the inkwell. Her hand was trembling as she began, caus[-] ing the ink to spatter across the white linen stationery.

Her uncle reached down and balled up the paper. "You must calm yourself, child," he instructed in a[n] sely placating manner. He placed a fresh sheet on the polished top. "I mean you no harm, Marianna, as long you do as I say. In time, you may even thank me."

Thank him? Marianna could not imagine such a thing. o take her from Tristan was to destroy her life. How ould one thank him for that? Death itself would be weeter, she thought bitterly as she scrawled the opening the missive in a shaky, but elegant hand.

My dear Tristan . . .

Chapter Twenty-five

My dear Tristan,

I am sorry to tell you that I can not go through with our plans to wed. So often plans made by moonlight go awry with the sobering light of day. Such is this case.

I see now that my uncle is right. Our feelings for each other are a result of the trials that we have come through together, not true love. My place is with Andre in the country in which I was mostly raised. I could never be happy for long in Texas with a man such as yourself. Our worlds are too different.

I wish you and your family a safe journey home and will always think of you fondly for making it so that I can return to my beloved Paris.

Sincerely,
Marianna

Tristan crumbled the letter his sister had given him to explain Marianna's absence in his hand and stared blindly out the window where he'd retreated to read it. He'd known something was wrong the moment Catalina met him at the back gate where he handed over his horse to one of the servants, but when he'd questioned her, she'd told him that Miguel Alvarado had died unexpectedly. While it was true that the general had hoped to question the man after the prospective recovery the lady doctor had predicted, Tristan didn't suppose it was critical. Surely someone else could identify the leader Ross McCulloch insisted was still at large.

But knowing how seriously Cat took her profession, even when dealing with scum such as Alvarado, Tristan accepted her explanation with a premature degree of relief. The anxious feeling that knotted his stomach, however, had no more than started to unravel when she produced a letter from her pocket and handed it to him with a reluctant "And Marianna left this for you this morning when she left with Andre and her uncle for Mexico City."

To think he'd come back to announce a big wedding at Silverado, he mused bitterly. With his head fairly throbbing at every step his horse took, and his mouth so dry that he'd filled his canteen twice, it was still all he'd been able to think about the entire day . . . the wedding and Marianna as Mrs. Tristan McCulloch.

Well, not quite, he admitted, smoothing out the note once more and scanning it quickly, as if the words might have changed. Memories of last night had managed to preoccupy his thoughts when future plans hadn't. Marianna was the last person he expected to see. In the barn was the last place he would have thought to encounter her. Yet, it was her proposal that astounded him the most. And that came *before* the moonlight madness that ensued, damn it, part of him swore in vehement rejection of her written excuse.

"Did I not tell you a woman always does the opposite of what one expects?" Alex Caine reminded him sympathetically. Tristan had given only a hint of his intentions to Alex when his brother-in-law rolled him out of the hay, his trousers half off, at sunup that morning. He'd asked Alex to stick around Texas long enough to stand up at the wedding.

"Yeah, well ..." Tristan slung the crumpled letter into the hearth across the room, aware that his family's eyes and hearts were with him. "A man can take a lesson from that book." His blue eyes burned with the intensity of the emotions he was feeling. "If she thinks I'm going to run off like a whipped pup with my tail between my legs, she's in for a surprise."

"Tristan, what are you going to do?" Laura McCulloch asked, alarmed at the determined set of her son's jaw. She'd seen it enough on her husband to know it meant trouble of some sort.

"I'm going to go get my bride, Mother," he announced, leaning down to buss Laura's cheek. "Or hear from her own lips that she wants to marry that air-slashing dandy in the tight britches."

"I'll ride with you."

Tristan held up his hand. "No, thanks. You've all done enough already. Any female that doesn't want to be part of this family's got to have her head examined."

Ross McCulloch put down his empty cup of coffee as the door slammed behind his departing son and walked over to where Laura watched the young man bound up onto his horse to ride away. "I told you there was a baby coming, Mother," he whispered smugly. "What about us packing up and heading back across the river? Might as well start getting the place ready."

"I am much of the same mind, myself," Alex chimed in, turning to catch Catalina exchanging a startled look with her mother. Misinterpreting her disconcerted expression, he laughed. "It's about time that brother of yours caught up with us."

"I only hope that's the right girl," Laura inserted

426

hastily, crossing her arms and casting a troubled glance back at the empty gate where Tristan had left.

"That pup thinks she is," her husband assured her, too possessed with his own troubled thoughts to notice his wife's smooth evasion. He took her under hand to usher her away from the window. "The rest is up to them."

The coach tracks were easy to make out in the dry trail, but when they deviated from the normal route south of Valencia and veered west, Tristan was puzzled. Not trusting his instinct completely, he rode back to the town and double-checked. There were several sets of tracks, indicating wagons, coaches, and drays of all sizes. It was, he supposed, possible that he had picked up the wrong one.

The coach that had left a single trail from Casa Valencia, however, had one wheel wider than the other. The right rear one evidently had been damaged and replaced, so the second time he tracked them, there was no mistake. For some reason, Corazon had turned due west into the eroding saffron hills, instead of taking the well-worn passage for Chihuahua.

Cursing himself for having wasted precious daylight, Tristan nudged his stallion into a trot. A new wash of adrenaline cleared his head and his gaze sharpened to follow the trail in the fading light until it mysteriously veered off into what appeared at first to be a pine thicket. A hundred questions came to mind, most unanswered, which only added to his growing suspicion. But when he found the coach with the mismatched wheels, abandoned, except for the body of the Frenchman he discovered nearby, he knew the sickening answer to at least one. Marianna was in grave danger.

As for the uncle, that remained to be seen. Aside from the Frenchman's wound, a single shot fired at close range into the chest, there were no bullet holes in the sides of the coach to indicate a shoot-out. The young Ranger couldn't help recalling Ross McCulloch's mention of the man he'd seen standing at the window of the *alcalde*'s office after the interview with Miguel Alvarado. Could it have been Corazon or was the man's timely arrival coincidental? If he hadn't been so wrung up over the Frenchman's claim to Marianna's hand, Tristan might have paid more attention when his father had remarked to him, "Something about that fish don't smell right."

But Doña Inez had sent for the man to come, the perplexed young man argued silently in his own defense. Just as it was possible that the coach, laden with Marianna's large trunks, had attracted the attention of some *bandidos*, although Tristan was hard-pressed to think the rogues possessed one ounce of good sense in attempting a robbery with the roads and hills swarming with the governor's troops and Rangers for the past twenty-four hours.

The hoofprints that led from the place where the coach had been stowed rose up a sharp escarpment and would have been impossible to follow, if not for the establishment of a narrow and rocky trail that seemed to wind its way deeper into the brush- and tree-covered slopes. Certain that the riders would likely keep to the existing path, rather than try to cut one that a string of packhorses bearing the booty from the coach could get through, Tristan continued the winding ascent.

In some places the road was practically grown over, precluding the passage of the large coach. Broken brush and limbs betrayed its recent use, however, and sometimes, when he'd light a match to look more closely, he could see evidence that at least one narrow wagon or cart, heavily loaded, had been through. Eventually it leveled off at a rocky and scantily forested plateau where, above the tops of the trees, Tristan could make out a few scattered rooflines of what he guessed were the remains of an old mining camp. Old, but not abandoned, he thought, catching the scent of woodsmoke drifting toward him with the breeze.

Leaving his horse behind, he moved closer in the cover of the mixed low-spreading oaks and mesquite toward the sound of men laughing and arguing half-heartedly in Spanish. Around a campfire, a group of roughly clad *bandidos* carried on a dice game. Some watched while the others took their turns. At the turn out of the roll, they'd break out in exuberant laughter and point over to a well where two other men appeared to be standing guard. With a cold dread twisting in his gut, Tristan circled around to get a better look, knowing from the lurid talk and speculation the nature of the prize the bandits gambled for.

Knees and feet drawn under her skirts, a pale-faced Marianna huddled against the stone base of the well, as if she wanted the ungiving rock to absorb her. Her hands were bound and a plate of untouched beans lay next to her. She closed her eyes, wincing as the men shouted at her, threatening that she should eat while she could and indicating that she would need her strength for the night ahead.

The reflection of the campfire flames in Tristan's gaze only hinted of the choking fury welling in his chest. Melting silently back into the trees before it drove him to do something foolhardy, he stealthily approached the dilapidated hoisting house, built over what had been the main shaft. Although it was leaning precariously away from the clapboard wall, the chimney was smoking and partially boarded windows were aglow with lamplight.

From what he had seen so far, the bandits were rather sure of themselves and their hideout, which was to his advantage. Aside from the guards with the girl, he'd seen no others. Upon peering through an opening in the boards, his mild surprise gave way in incredulity. Except for one small section where a half-dozen men were gathered around a table fashioned from an old door placed over a barrel, the room was stacked, ceiling to floor, with crates bearing the marks of gun and munitions manufacturers—a veritable arsenal.

"It is only a temporary setback, *amigos,*" Enrique Corazon was saying to the others. He waved at the crates surrounding them. "We have what is important! We have the guns! Men can be more easily replaced."

"But we were ready to begin taking the towns! Our people are in place, waiting for the word."

Tristan wiped the dust off a window so that he might identify the owner of the lisping voice that sounded so familiar. Hellfire and damnation, it *was* the spectacled clerk in the governor's office who had kept him waiting two hours with his urgent business with the governor and then announced that his superior was gone for the day. No wonder the little weasel had been squirming behind the desk, if he had an inkling of what Tristan had for the governor. Had Tristan not run around the back and intercepted the man, he'd have been put off until the morning and most likely not lived to deliver the journals.

"So we will wait another year. Is not the cause worth it? We can keep raiding and plundering on both sides of the border ... perhaps start a little war between the gringos and Díaz to weaken the government further with distraction. *El Presidente* will be too busy to worry about the northern provinces." The man rolled back his sleeve, showing his forearm to them. "And we will be our own nation and this will be on our new flag."

The others unrolled their cuffs and put their arms together in an unspoken toast, while drinking to the cause with the other.

Mouth thinning, Tristan backed away from the building. He had unwittingly walked into the midst of the planning of a revolution instead of a wedding proposal. But right now, all he cared about was getting Marianna to safety, which was going to be impossible without some sort of distraction. He studied the wall of the building, where some of the shorter lengths of siding had come off. Lord knew, there was enough ammo in there to do it . . . if he could get to it.

Wielding his hunting knife, he began to pry another section away carefully. With the moonlight at his back, he was able to make out the letters labeling a crate of ammunition. Powder would have been better, he thought, cutting into the side, but he'd have to make do. After clearing out a hollow with painstaking care to avoid detection, he gathered some sticks and pieces of the crate he'd split and put them inside along with some dry pine needles and leaves. All he needed now were some matches. Which were in his saddlebags, he thought impatiently. Unless . . .

Keeping low, he crept around to the side of the hoisting house. Through the crack where the fireplace had fallen away from the building, a space just wide enough for his hand, or a thin stick, to slip through, he could see a large chunk of meat, most likely rustled beef, roasting over a blazing fire. Fat spattered and flared from time to time, starting little blazes that lasted only a few seconds on and around the sides and skirt of the small hearth.

Tristan found a long dry stick and eased it toward the coals.

After what seemed an eternity, it caught up. Ever so carefully, he drew it out and started around to the other side of the building with it, his hand cupped around the flame to protect it. However, just as he reached the small indentation he'd made, the area around the campfire burst into a ear-piercing rattle of gunfire, haunted by a woman's screams.

Heart leaping to his throat, he shoved the burning stick into the pile of dried brush and, leaving the starting of the fire to Providence, scrambled around to where he saw a small cart being pulled around the campfire by a very nervous burro. In the back, one of the drunken bandits had assembled a gatling gun and was shooting at a tumbledown shack near the well, riddling the rotting timber with bullets on each pass. Although Tristen could not see her, he could hear Marianna's terrified cries from the other side of the stone wall where she'd sought refuge, while her two guards laughed heartlessly nearby, apparently accustomed to such shenanigans.

Thankful for the unexpected distraction, Tristan raced around the small cluster of buildings to the other side, guns drawn, but as he approached where the girl buried her face in her arms, sobbing hysterically, the back of the main building lit up like a Fourth of July picnic. Enrique Corazon stumbled out of the building with his colleagues, calling for water. Instantly, the well was surrounded by men, shoving Marianna away to follow orders.

Intent on watching the haphazard brigade forming, the single guard left with the girl failed to notice Tristan's silent approach. With a well-delivered blade between the ribs and a hand clasped over his mouth, Tristan dragged him around the corner of a shed, mo-

432

ioning with a jerk of his head for a startled Marianna
o follow. The moment he let the man fall, he cut away
he ropes that had rubbed her wrists raw and she was in
his arms, sobbing his name over and over, as if she
could not believe he was really there.

As much as he wanted to kiss away her tears and
hold her until her shuddering cries were assuaged, he
pushed her away. "Let's go, Frenchie!" he urged gently,
but as he started to lead her away and into the cover of
the trees, a massive explosion rocked the ground beneath them and the sky grew bright as day. The air
filled with fiery debris, as if the very core of the earth
had erupted, which fell all around them.

"La chica, allí!"

Glancing up from the prone position he'd taken to
protect his precious charge, Tristan drew his pistol and
fired, scattering the outlaws who collected to give them
chase. "Get behind the building!"

Half running, half crawling, Marianna followed his
orders, encouraged by the repeating gunfire behind her
that afforded her cover. She fell against the rough side
of the building, gasping for breath as Tristan dove down
beside her.

"Get under there!"

Marianna diverted her attention from the men that
seemed to be surrounding them in the cover of the trees
and peered into the dark underside of the structure. She
shuddered in hesitation. *"There?"* The crawl space was
little more than a foot off the ground and surely was the
home of all sorts of unimaginable horrors.

"They've cut us off from the trees, now go!" Grabbing her head with one hand, Tristan pushed her forward. "I'm right with you."

Not the least bit encouraged, Marianna forged ahead
on her stomach, trying not to think of anything but

reaching the other side where the burning building af
forded a light of promise. The ground was cold and
hard, with protrusions of rock that scraped her skin un
mercifully, but the man at her side kept pushing her on

"When I say go, I want you to make a break for tha
wagon."

Marianna turned a frightened gaze to her rescuer and
nodded. She had known when she said good-bye to the
McCulloch family that she was on her way to her death
that her uncle would never let her or her unsuspecting
fiancé live. There was never any chance for her to warn
Andre. Corazon saw to that. When the time came, she
found herself envying the single shot that took the young
man by surprise. It was at least swift and merciful.

It seemed her uncle had other plans for her. She had
been brought to the camp and forced to watch while the
men threw dice to determine their turns with her, to
imagine a fate that made her long for the same fate as
Andre. If she was going to die, at least now, it would be
at Tristan's side and not at the hands of the crude animals to whom her uncle had delivered her.

"Now!"

Ignoring the gunfire and explosions surrounding her,
Marianna pulled herself out from under the building
and raced blindly toward the wagon where the burro
dodged in a frantic path to avoid the debris spooking it
from one direction to another. Her lungs ached as she
threw herself into the back of it and gasped for air, her
body flattened against the rough plank bed.

"Get the reins!"

The wagon jarred with the fall of Tristan's body next
to hers. Scrambling to follow his instructions, she started
toward the shelf seat in the front where the reins had
been abandoned in the midst of the chaos. The bullets
that plowed into the wood surrounding her no longer

liciting startled squeals, she snapped the leather over he back of the burro and hauled it to the right to turn he cart toward the downhill trail that might yet lead o their survival.

To her horror, the sharpness of the turn, accelerated by the burro's fear, nearly overturned the wagon. A crash in the back caused her to look over her shoulder in time to see Tristan fall on the wagon bed, the deadly gatling gun on top of him, spitting a round of bullets into the air.

"I'm sorry!"

"Get us the hell out of here!"

In spite of the danger, Marianna could feel heat rushing to her cheeks as the man ignored her inane apology and righted the gun. With a determined set of her lips, she snapped the reins again and pulled the burro's head toward the downhill path. Ahead of her, two men leapt into the path, firing wildly. Behind, the machine gun began to rattle bullets almost as fast as her heart pounded, yet Marianna continued to urge the animal on. The men were no match for the frightened donkey, which sent one careening off to the side and dragged another for several yards before pulling the wagon over him.

His agonized scream seemed to echo in her ears above the gunfire—too close, an inner voice warned her, prompting her to look back. At that moment, she was jarred forward, struck by Tristan's shoulder as he sprawled to the side, dazed from the blow of his head on the railing that kept him from being thrown off.

"Tristan!"

Seizing him with her free arm, Marianna tried to help him up, when she saw his leg covered in blood. Her stomach shriveled sickeningly, but there was no time to be sick. There was no time to be cowardly. Leaving the donkey to find its way down the narrow path from which there was little room to deviate, she crawled toward the swinging gun at Tristan's feet, all too aware of the men on horseback who were rapidly catching up with them.

Pointing the barrels in their direction, she braced herself with her back against the seat and began to crank it as she'd seen the bandit do earlier in his drunken glee. At the first burst of fire, she lost her hold, but grasped the steel handle once again in desperation and held on with teeth-jarring will. The gun spat the bullets recklessly, which took their toll on the horses and men in pursuit, as well as richocheting off the rocky walls and trees sweeping past in the bouncing wake of the wagon.

Suddenly the wheel struck a *chinita* of rock and rose precariously over to its right side. Losing her hold on the gun, Marianna fell against Tristan. Certain that this was the finale to the blood-freezing terror at last, she clung to him, her face buried against his chest, when the wagon jarred roughly back in the other direction. To her amazement, a man, made giant by the shadows of the fire behind them, dropped out of nowhere to the wagon seat and grabbed up the reins, hauling back on them with all his strength.

At the very thought of being taken alive by the outlaws, Marianna pulled one of Tristan's guns from his holster and raised it to fire, when she recognized the expensively tailored clothing of Alex Caine. Before she knew what was happening, a heavy weight fell upon her, bearing her to the floor and knocking the gun from her hand. Her scream froze in her throat as Ross McCulloch rolled away and crouched low, a gun appearing like lightning from the holster at his side.

Bewildered, she crawled back to Tristan and held onto him, leaving their escape to the angels who literally seemed to drop out of the sky in answer to her prayers.

436

Eyes squeezed shut, she offered thanks and continued to plea that Tristan was going to be all right, unaware of the slowing of the cart or the fact that there were troops swarming past them to the sound of a bugle signaling to charge.

"He's going to be all right, girl. Just a little bump on the head."

Ross McCulloch's gruff announcement halted her fervent mumblings, interwoven with the plaintive kisses she planted on Tristan's face. "But his leg . . ."

"Just a scratch."

Whether from joy, relief, or both, Marianna didn't know, but she couldn't stop the sobs that kept coming, even when the man who intimidated her so took her in his arms and absorbed the brunt of them. "I am so sor . . . reee."

"Hush, girl, there's nothing to be sorry about. I'm sure you had your reasons for leaving."

"He . . . my uncle, he said . . . he said he had an army that would kill all of you if I did not go with him!"

She felt Ross McCulloch chuckle wryly. "I wouldn't call that bunch of yahoos an army."

Marianna pulled away, sniffing and wiping her face with her sleeve. "But I . . . I did not know . . . I . . ."

She broke off as the big Texan pointed to the man stirring at her side. "Better tell *him.*"

"Tristan!" In a rush of joy, Marianna pulled Tristan against her chest and kissed him long and tenderly, conveying all she was feeling in the only way she could at that moment.

"Watch that knot on the back of his head," Alex cautioned from his position on the seat.

Ross McCulloch climbed up alongside his son-in-law, grinning widely. "Right about now, son, I doubt the boy even knows what pain is."

If Tristan was in any discomfort, he didn't show it. Instead, he returned the kiss of the angel who had at first made him think he'd come to in heaven, and held her for the remainder of the ride down to the bottom of the escarpment while Ross and Alex told him how they *happened* along when they did.

While packing her medical bag, Catalina discovered a different bottle had been substituted for the one she'd left with the servant who had sat with Miguel Alvarado the night before—one containing a poison of local extract, rather than the laudanum Catalina had given her. When they questioned the servant, who was very defensive about having abandoned her duty for a short while to go to the kitchen, they were told that she'd found Don Enrique in the room on her return. According to him, he had come in to check on the man, and the girl thought nothing about it at the time.

Based on that and the strange silence of the girl who had left that morning with her uncle, Ross McCulloch had been able to convince Colonel Benevides and the general that Enrique Corazon was the man he'd insisted was still at large. After what seemed like an inordinate amount of time to the ex-Ranger, during which he paced like a caged cat, the general assembled his troops for the expedition. He and Alex were leading the way up the escarpment when the whole sky seemed to light up.

"We saw your wagon out of control and Marianna scattering the *bandidos* with the machine gun, and took to the trees to try to jump aboard."

"*Marianna?*" Tristan questioned skeptically, his embrace tightening before he laughed. "So you finally found a gun you could hit something with."

Marianna shifted in his arms to assemble an indignant look. "I shot the men *and* their horses."

"And the trees and the rocks," Alex teased.

"And the clouds," Ross chimed in. "Look, even the moon's taken cover."

The sky overhead had darkened from the smoke of the fire, yet not even the battle waging fiercely behind them could intimidate the embarrassed giggle that set off a round of general amusement for all as they cleared the path and pulled out onto the road where another group of riders awaited.

"Cat, come see to your brother's leg," Ross called out, hopping down from the wagon as it came to a halt.

"Tristan's been shot?" Laura McCulloch's voice rose in alarm as the women abandoned their horses to run to the wagon.

Ross intercepted his wife while Alex helped Catalina onto the wagon. "Just a scratch, Mother. He's had so much attention, I doubt he even knows it's there yet."

Reluctantly, Marianna moved away to let Catalina see to Tristan's leg, but only a short distance. She remained close enough to hold his hand as well as his gaze. With each, she expressed her love and concern. Although Catalina chatted brightly about how she knew something was amiss and that Marianna would never have left of her own will, Marianna hardly heard her. It was only when the doctor asked her to help cut off a strip of gauze bandage that she broke away from the tender spell that held both her and Tristan captive, and it was then that she became aware of the comforting arm Laura McCulloch had placed over her shoulder.

"Alex, you think you could ride over to Chihuahua and scrounge up a priest tonight?"

Marianna's head snapped back to the young man leaning against the side of the wagon. *"Tonight?"*

"Tonight?" his mother and sister chorused at the same time.

439

Tristan folded her hand in his and lifted a golde brow at her. "What's the matter, Frenchie? Don't t me you've changed your mind again!"

"Why, no, but . . ."

"Tristan, be reasonable," Laura implored, shoving her feet. "You've both been through so much, why—

"Mama!" Catalina and Alex both grabbed for Lau as she sank back to the bed of the wagon unsteadily.

Pulling himself over to her, Tristan took her han "Mama, are *you* all right?"

"Oh, for heaven's sake, Tristan," Catalina blurte out, laughing at the stricken look on her brother's fac "It's nothing another six months won't take care of."

From the patch of grass where he'd gone to fetch th women's horses, Ross McCulloch's explosive *"Six mont of what?"* drowned out all the other astonished response

"Six months of making Tristan's room a nurser Ross," Laura ventured timidly.

"But you said . . ."

"I was wrong," she answered, her cheeks regainin their lost color. "Catalina confirmed it."

The shock that had managed to glue the big Texan feet to the ground gave way to indignation as he left th horses on their own and marched up to where Catalin scrambled down off the wagon to intercept him.

"Now, Daddy . . ."

"You mean to say you women knew this and *st* risked coming here—"

"Ross—"

"In *spite,*" Ross raised his voice, cutting his wife's pr test off, "of my asking you to stay put?"

Jarred from his own astonishment by the accusin blue gaze that swung his way, Alex Caine threw up h hands. "I swear, I knew nothing. I would never hav agreed—"

"Now, you wait a minute, Ross McCulloch!" Forcing herself upright, Laura Mcculloch made her way purposefully to the end of the cart. "I will not have you putting the blame on anyone but . . . but me!"

Her voice broke, bringing Marianna up to return the comfort Tristan's mother had offered her earlier, only to have Tristan draw her back with a poorly disguised grin. "Bark's worse than his bite," he whispered against her ear.

"Besides," Laura went on, regaining her composure, "what harm has come of it?" She pointed back to Tristan and Marianna. "We have our son back . . . and new daughter and . . ." She sniffed loudly. "And soon we'll have a baby in the house."

Tristan's words were right. Before her very eyes, the raging bull turned into a lamb, reaching up to take his wife tenderly into his arms. Marianna couldn't hear what he was saying as he carried Laura over to the horses and gently placed her on one, but she could tell from the sparkling joy on the woman's face that it had been exactly what she wanted, no, needed, to hear.

Swinging up into the saddle behind her, Ross called over his shoulder, "You kids meet us back at the house. Mother and I'll be waiting at the hacienda when you get back with the preacher."

"Well . . ." Tristan smiled wistfully, watching the couple ride off slowly, "maybe we should wait, all things considered." He looked at Marianna in time to catch her wiping her eyes and sobered instantly. "Hey, what's wrong?" he asked, drawing her gently to him.

"It is nothing," she laughed in broken embarrassment. "It is just that your parents are so sweet to each other."

"I think Alex should go get the preacher," Catalina

observed, leading over the horse she'd ridden out, "and give Mama and Daddy some time alone."

"Why don't we *all* go, then?" Tristan embellished with renewed enthusiasm.

"You are loco!" Marianna accused in disbelief.

"I got my bride, my best man, and my doctor, what more could a man ask for? Besides," he added, stopping long enough to buss her on the lips. "Mama's not up to planning any big weddings, and Alex and Cat'll have to be getting back to California pretty soon."

"Sounds like a good prescription to me," Catalina quipped, looking up from where she tied the horse to the back of the wagon. "Mind if I ride up front with you, Señor Caine?"

Alex Caine met Marianna's startled expression with a shrug. "Might as well get used to it, Marianna. The whole family's this way."

Marianna was almost tempted to pinch herself to see if this was real. She was a filthy sight from her harrowing escape, hardly fit to be called a bride in her tattered traveling skirt and jacket. Tristan was no more presentable. Aside from his disreputable appearance, his leg was bloodied and surely sore, even if it was just a scratch. Instead of a fashionable carriage, they were riding in the back of a donkey cart driven by the groom's sister, who was a lady doctor, and his best friend. And furthermore, her future in-laws were unable to attend the ceremony because they were expecting their third child!

But if it was a dream, she didn't want to wake up. Instead, she snuggled into the cradle of her future husband's arms while Alex helped Catalina up to the seat beside him. Besides, it was too bizarre to be a figment of her imagination.

A blissful smile settled on her lips as Alex snapped the

reins over the burro's back and offered one last bit of friendly advice as one in-law to another.

"But I can promise you this, *chiquita*. Once you've married a McCulloch, you will never wish to go back to the sane world again."

This time there was no holding back the hysterical need to laugh that had been building gradually with each new development. Her amusement erupted against the lips that came down to underscore what her future brother-in-law had said. Sealed most convincingly by the man holding her captive in his warm embrace, the happiness welled inside of Marianna until her senses reeled.

Who would want to go back? she thought dizzily, bouncing along in her lover's arms. Who would want to go back when they could brave the sweeping currents of the wild and unpredictable Mexicali Lovestorm?

Epilogue

Teasing blue eyes danced at her across a tiered candelabra of sterling and Marianna felt her cheeks grow as hot as the flickering candle flames. Around them people conversed in French and laughter filled the air. Her cousin Elena was there with her new husband and recently widowed mother. Presiding over the table was their grandmother, the Marchioness of Bretagne, a queenly woman with silver hair crowned with a glittering tiara of gems handed down from her late husband's family.

Yet, it was the handsome gentleman seated across from Marianna on Granmaman's left that commanded the new bride's attention. Aside from the mischievous grin on his face, which he used to torment her into thinking he was about to start speaking that strange Texas English, he looked very cultured and quite at home in the elegant setting. At that moment, he winked suddenly and rose to his feet, making her aware that he had caught her in her less-than-discreet observation.

The movement stopped the various conversations going on, attracting the attention of those who were not already admiring the rugged physique fashionably attired, but not masked, in a black evening suit with a scarlet

444

cummerbunded waist. The soft drawl that infected his struggling French and captured the hearts of every female with whom he came in contact filled the great hall that had once hosted France's royalty in no-less-extravagant style.

"Ladies and gentlemen, Marchioness," Tristan said, pausing to nod to the grand dame on his left who had given the lavish farewell party for her niece and new husband from Texas, "I have to say that, while we take great pride in our shindigs . . . *socials,*" he corrected, noting the plea in his wife's gaze, a gaze that's glowing color put to shame the sapphires hanging in abundance around her grandmother's neck. "You people have given a whole new meaning to the word *hospitality.* My lovely wife and I offer our sincerest thanks to you all for making our visit such a pleasant one. To our family and friends in Paris," he finished, lifting the lead crystal glass in salute.

Dozens of compliments and expressions of regret echoed along the table amidst applause as Tristan resumed his seat with a smug little smirk that made it impossible for Marianna not to smile. The sharp tinkle of the silver bell in her grandmother's hand quieted the clamor as she cleared her throat to speak.

"And this," she began in heavily accented English, "is to all the *yahoos* and *hombres* in Texas! If they are half as charming as this young man, I shall have to consider a trip to this place." Her twinkling eyes catching the startled expression on her granddaughter's face, she laughed and nudged Tristan. "Well, *monsieur,* how did I do?"

"Finer than frog hair, Granny," Tristan quipped dryly.

In the time it took to explain this new expression to her grandmother, the group moved away from the tables to the center of the room for the beginning of the ball planned in their honor. As was custom, Tristan led Marianna out onto the polished parquet floor as the orchestra her grandmother had commissioned for the occasion struck up a beautiful Viennese waltz. With a gallant nod of his head, Tristan swept her off in a swirl of silk, his movements as graceful and well-timed as her own, in spite of the wound that had only just healed.

As she spun around under the brilliant glass chandeliers, she hardly noticed the other guests joining them. Who would have dreamed it, she thought, captured as much by the impassioned gaze only inches from her own as by the white-gloved hand at her sequined waist. She had been willing to never see Paris or her family again when she'd retaken her vows that night in Chihuahua. She was prepared to move into the hunting cabin her husband had told her about and do without servants.

It was Tristan's idea to take their honeymoon in France while his hunting cabin on the south range of Silverado was being built on to to accommodate a new wife and a housekeeper. It was within easy riding distance of the main house so that Marianna could help her mother-in-law when the time came, and close enough for the opposite to occur, her husband had pointed out one night after he'd carried her up to the bedroom soon to become a nursery to work toward that goal.

The masculine scent of his talc, mingled with that of the Madeira that had been served with the meal, pervaded her senses as the man in her reverie leaned forward suddenly and brushed her lips.

"Mmm, did you feel that, my little *Texican* fleur-de-lis?" he whispered mischievously. The moment he'd discovered her mother had been a Mexican-American, he had tormented her beyond measure about her being tainted with *gringo* blood.

Marianna glanced around self-consciously. "Feel that, you big fool?"

"I think a storm's brewing."

"But where?" she scoffed suspiciously, looking out the large arched doorways where a terrace led to a hundred-year-old garden that was her grandmother's pride and joy. "The sky is as clear as . . . as the glass."

"Down here," her husband growled, tugging her scandalously close and spinning her around as the dance came to an end. "Wouldn't surprise me if a little gringo doesn't crop up before the night's out." He nibbled at her ear, his action causing a titter of amusement nearby. "And you look good enough to eat."

"Tristan!" Marianna gasped breathlessly. "It is still too early!"

If she had not before, she could feel it now . . . the heat lightning that scorched her cheeks to a fiery hue and flashed with a weak hungry feeling in the pit of her stomach that had nothing to do with food. Her mind raced back to another storm, a raging storm in which she'd clung to him to escape a horrible dream, and she smiled at the irony. In his arms, storms, like dreams, were no longer threatening.

With a sigh, Marianna checked the massive gilded grandfather clock on the landing where steps rose to the right and left to carry on to the second floor. It would be at least two more hours before it was acceptable to retire for the evening. After all, the party was in their honor. Until then, she would have to be content to waltz on the arm of the most wonderful man in all the world and look forward to his tantalizing promise of a lovestorm.